KRAKEN'S
CLAW

BRUCE
FERGUSSON

Lucky Bat Books

A Lucky Bat Book

Kraken's Claw
A Novel of the Six Kingdoms
Copyright © 2019 Bruce Fergusson

Cover Design by Joe Calkin

ISBN 978-1-943588-85-5

LuckyBatBooks.com

10 9 8 7 6 5 4 3 2 1

To my mother, for *Ulysses*.

And to my father, for the 'what-ifs'.

BOOK ONE:

MILATUM

From *DAUGHTER OF THE LABRYS*

I HAD TROUBLE falling asleep before the events of that terrible midsummer night. The reason wasn't any lurking, shadowy awareness of what would happened later. The truth of it is, I lay awake thinking about the long voyage that would begin two days hence, taking me to a place to which I did not want to go, and marry a man I did not wish to wed.

It must have been close to midnight, when only a few starflies still winked about the room, that I parted the canopy drape of whisp and left my bed to go over to the settee under the open window. I pulled aside the curtains of spun glass, the moonglow becoming ribbons that ended where I'd just been, restless and wide-eyed. Usually the curtain music was softer—a tinkling—lulling me to sleep, but the breeze off the Queensmere was strong, though the night air was warm as it always is in Milatum except for a few months of winter. Regardless of the season, however, I could always hear the song of my city: the wind—gentle or fierce—playing our five bridges as if they were lyres of the gods.

I hadn't been sitting for long by the window when I heard someone coming into the room. My younger sister must have seen my silhouette as she paused only briefly by the bed, and joined me on the settee.

"I didn't think you'd be sleeping," she said. "I couldn't either."

I've been fortunate that Cymra and I are so close, because our temperaments and interests are different. Perhaps one reason is that the four-year difference in our ages is neither too close nor too far apart. I've been told she began talking much earlier than I; evidently I was well past three years old before I was speaking in sentences—which evidently caused concern for my mother and father. And then, as it happens, Cymra grew to be a shy girl, comfortable only in talking to her older sister; whereas I grew to be someone whom my parents must have often wished had remained mute or could be fitted with a muzzle otherwise suitable for a Demizell of the House of Keshkev.

If my mother and father—Epona and Rhakotis, queen and king—thought that something was wrong with me as a three-year-old, that opinion didn't change significantly. When I was sixteen, I overheard my mother saying to my father: "Cyalla will be a beauty, more so than her sister; but at least Cymra isn't disfigured by a difficult nature and inappropriate interests. Cyalla seems to have a new one with every book she reads."

I don't remember Cymra and I saying much immediately after she came in that night, though we did later, about Vaience Loquin. I was silent because the view from my chamber already seemed like a treasure lost. From my window you could see, almost on a straight line across the Queensmere, the dawnstone colossus of Pelagia that rose near the Cleave, the main and southern entrance to Milatum by ship. In two days' time, throngs of our citizens would be on Mago's Bridge that spanned the Cleave, throwing flowers cut from the royal gardens and distributed from wagons at either end of the bridge, to celebrate the coming union of Keshkevar's Labrys Throne with Myrcia's Cascade Throne.

That night, as always, the lights of the city reflected on the edges of the Queensmere, and from the height of my room in the Kelefion on the royal isle of Mereshaven, my home within a home, the street lamps of Colza's Way that linked the bridges and the hilly Linnises of Milatum, seemed like earthly constellations. Of those above, Kyria's Lyre was especially prominent for the summer.

By the time I was eight I could name most of our southern constellations. I asked my parents for a spyglass fixed to a tripod, so I could better see the fainter ones like the Hammer and Anvil, and also the fainter markings of the moons, Cassena and Suaila.

My father indulged me, grudgingly: "So it's not enough for you to simply know that they were named long ago for Roak's wives?" To which my mother added: "And should you discover that the heavenly fable is true—that they reside there in eternity—I'm sure you will inform Sulserra's thedrals; you're there often enough."

Indeed I was, always with an escort of Labryssons, our royal guard. Increasingly, my parents became alarmed that their eldest Demizell was growing up to be more of a thedral than a daughter they could marry off to advantage. They offered to have books brought to the Kelefion and returned to Sulserra's. But I was adamant: how would a messenger, literate or not, know what books might interest me; especially those I did not know existed until I saw them there myself?

The visits ended a few months after I met Vaience Loquin at Sulerra's.

But for years there were never enough for me to read. I began writing my own stories, though I was better at hiding them from my brother and parents than crafting them. I still have one of those early stories—a fable about how Milatum's five bridges were built. Given what the truth has turned out to be, the effort was not so childish, considering I was twelve when I wrote it. Still, I was lucky in my imaginings.

That night, Cymra broke the silence at the window settee. "You could always run away, you know; there's still time. We both could, together. I don't want to go to Myrcia either, because Mother and I will be coming back without you."

I took her hand in mine, squeezed it, glanced at the moons now high over the Orphic Gate in Linnisheer. Cassena and Suaila had been sisters, too. But the legends differed as to whether they missed each other after Cassena's famously unsolved disappearance.

Cymra went on: "Maybe we could disguise ourselves and find an edificia somewhere; aren't there other ones?"

"Small ones, in the north mostly. Semetros, Maraine."

And far away from the one in Girvan.

"Well then, we could go to one of *them*. You're almost a thedral, anyway. I'd find something to do besides be your sister. They wouldn't know who we were if we didn't tell. We'd be safe."

She was being so sweet I had to hug her.

"I mean it."

"Cym, never mind the getting there—do you really think we could keep our secret for long?"

"Vaience would, in Girvan."

"But the other thedrals there might not."

"You should try, anyway. Because…well…they say your husband-to-be… they say he can't mount a horse without help. You're eighteen and he's…how old is he again?"

"Forty-two."

"Oh Cyler, that's…*ancient*. Vaience is a *lot* younger than that."

"He's the same age as me."

"May I ask you a question?"

"Another one?"

"Do you love him?"

"Cym, we saw each other only six times; seven if you count the first time when we said only a few words to each other."

"Is that enough?—when do you know it's enough?"

Before I could give an answer I wasn't sure I had, she said: "I wanted you to, so I could see what it looks like. How else could I know?—I don't read nearly as many books as you."

I smiled. "You'll know someday, with or without books."

"I hope so. But I think you do. If you didn't you wouldn't have shut yourself in here for two days after they sent him to that Widow Yist's in Girvan."

"What happened was really my fault. I shouldn't have kept going back to Sulserra's. For a mazer thedral like him…to be forced to leave an edificia like Sulserra's and go to a pizzling one in Girvan…it's like being on a ship with only a mizzen sail."

"Pizzling is the same as a mizzen sail?"

"Yare; not the biggest."

"Well, you *do* love him; close enough, anyway. You sent him the mating pair of oikoes his mother gave you as a gift, that mother and father wouldn't let you keep—did he love *you*? I mean, even if someone doesn't say he does, that doesn't mean he doesn't, right?"

"Em…I think so." My sister's tongue sometimes got the better of her words. "I…liked him very much. I'm going to miss him and I think he'll miss me, too."

"I liked him, too, because he never seemed like I was in the way when I went to Sulserra's with you to make it seem like you were there just for the books. They say you can be in love and not *really* like someone, but I don't know if that's true. I think you can have one without the other, but not the other without the other one."

I hugged her again. Cymra's hair smelled of sweet tryony-scented soap. "What I know for sure is that I love you."

"Me too. I wish you were coming back after, but it doesn't work that way, does it?"

"No, Cym, it doesn't."

Father had arranged the marriage months ago, though he left it to mother to explain to me the reasons for linking the House of Keshkev with the

Cascade Throne of Myrcia. I'd heard our spies in the east—the city of Attallis in particular—had reported unsettling news about the activities of the Skarrian Priaptor, Vulsa Hork, the grandson of Gorta Hork who had led an army into the River Roan valley of Myrcia many years before, and besieged Castlecliff. Even in Milatum the story of what happened to that Skarrian army was well-known: if not for the heroism of a miner's son named Lukan Barra, and the intervention of an Erseiyr, one of the winged beasts revered as gods in Myrcia, Castlecliff would have fallen.

My father and his Council of Ephors could not ignore the intelligence about this Vulsa Hork, nor the benefit of closer ties between Keshkevar and Myrcia, should his ambition—or that of Skarria's High Priest, the Tholarsh—threaten either kingdom. I, too, would have seen the advantages of closer ties—had someone *else* been chosen for that purpose.

But there was no one else.

The Myrcian Sanctor, Urias, had no daughter for my older brother, Lerrist. And Urias had insisted upon me and not Cymra for his only unmarried son, Joffreck.

Our mother would be accompanying Cymra and I. Our father had to stay, of course; Lerrist as well. Otherwise, if anything should happen to the ship carrying us, Keshkevar would be without an heir to the throne.

"I do not expect you to be happy with this, Cyalla," my mother said. "But there is more to life than happiness, especially for a Demizell who should have been married off by now. As you recall, we've had three previous offers for your hand. And while two of the offers were middling enough, and would have seen you in Helveylyn or Lucidor, the third, to that Summer Prince of Trigel should have been acceptable to you and would have eased our concerns about nearby Gebroan.

"But you refused all. We have indulged you long enough and will not now allow you to spurn this offer from the Myrcian Sanctor himself; not with so much possibly at stake."

And those stakes rose considerably in the weeks after my mother spoke those words. There were reports of the Priaptor's army moving toward Phaistos, a provincial capital northeast of Milatum.

My father's legacy will forever be overshadowed by the events ushered in by that terrible night. He was an innately cautious king, yet he expanded our already renowned fleet and brought to heel most of the pirates infesting the

Shelter Isles. At mother's urging—to her credit and his—he had been about to make long-overdue improvements in the living conditions of the Skellig, the underground prison in Linnisheer. He opened the royal Chase twice a year for the general population to enjoy—something that had never been done before. He convinced the Council of Ephors of the necessity of bringing aqueduct water to Linnisheer and Linnismorn via underground channels. He refurbished Neskayuna, and replaced her corroded barrier chains which protect the entrance to the Cleave. He was a patron of half a dozen theaters and provided a royal subsidy for the Night of the Mistra festival enjoyed by all. Most recently he'd listened to grievances of Attalls laboring in Milatum's last quarry in Slagtown, and had been prepared to stop the abuses.

Some said he was weak and tardy in dealing with Myrcian encroachment in the Lakes, and in the depredations of the Wolf and Iron Lords of the Crumples who crossed the Girvan Awe into Keshkevar and came through the mountain passes of the Skysheaves, sometimes raiding far into the fertile vales of The Coombs. People certainly blamed him for what happened at Laggunsea, in Skarria.

Perhaps he was not the strongest king Keshkevar has ever had. Over the years I've come to realize that my father must have felt the burden of his own father's legacy. He wanted people to say about him what the venerable Ephor, Thanage the Elder, had once famously said about King Shimsinnion: *Give him a shovel and he'll find a way to make a mirror of it; give him a mirror and he'll find a way to move a mountain with it.*

All too often a yearning for greatness is commensurate with the fear of losing it; one may become reluctant to act, and so is acted upon.

Still, my father acted on his chance with a mirror: marrying off his eldest daughter to the advantage of his kingdom.

There were days of sulks when I hated him for that, as well as days of guilt and shame for thinking only of my fate and not what might be best for so many others....

Cymra squeaks when she yawns and and after more of those she left my room that night. And when I finally fell asleep on the settee, I was not the only one on Mereshaven or in the surrounding Linnises; in the towns of Bannery and Humber at the far ends of the causeways east and west; or in the countryside close to Milatum, who was concerned about Vulsa Hork...but not overly worried.

Protected by the Kingsmere water surrounding the Linnises, a fleet unmatched by any other kingdom, and the outer bluffs of the Linnises themselves, Milatum had been successfully besieged only once before—by Hestimion, a renegade scion of the House of Keshkev who sought to begin his own House in the name of the long-dead prophet Attallis. And this was before Milatum's city wall was built atop the outer bluffs.

To be sure, there undoubtedly were Skarrian spies among us, easily hidden in such a large and diverse city like ours. I am sure father had in mind those spies during the course of planning the events for the scheduled leave-taking of the royal mother and daughters.

Those Skarrian spies might well have been among the thousands of spectators expected to witness the grand departure of three ships of the fleet from its base at Snarlshome, in Linnismorn. They would have seen, if they hadn't already, the might of that fleet. They would have seen our renowned kite-artists scrying the skies over the Queensmere as the ships passed through the Cleave and into the Kingsmere.

Father knew the spies would report back to their masters about the coming union between Keshkevar and Myrcia. Myrcian garrisons in Riian in the far east could be sent south into Skarria, to punish an aggressive Priaptor and those whose hooves he polished, the zealot Tholosians—should he be so foolish as to leave his homeland unguarded. And unguarded as well from the sea, and the reach of Keshkevar's fleet....

I woke that night to a distant roar. Smoke drifted into the room through the window, enough to make me cough and lift the hem of my nightgown to use as a mask. The wind, brisk that night, seemed to carry the heat of the inferno across the Queensmere, or maybe I felt it through my eyes as I stared at the fires at Snarlshome. Much later, I learned that of the hundred ships berthed there, Keshkevar's pride, only five remained intact.

I am ashamed to admit that my first thought at witnessing the horror of this conflagration that took so many lives was that I would not have to make the voyage to Castlecliff.

I was wrong, of course.

That night I gave farewell keepsakes to all my handmaids, and desired to give to Teshria, my favorite, a sunstone brooch that she had especially admired; and made a point to tell Jesso, the Kelefion's fifth-floor chamberlain that I had personally given it to her, lest he assume she'd stolen it—such was my state of mind that night.

Teshria's family originally had come from Attallis in eastern Keshkevar, and while that territory was prone to…difficult loyalties, her family had served the House of Keshkev for many years; a reward, if one can call it that, for some service rendered by her grandfather to one of mine.

I could not find her—until I heard a muffled weeping in the larger linen closet adjacent to the fifth-floor servants' quarters. I thought she was crying about my departure, as some of the other handmaids had done. But there was another reason. I drew her out, as Cymra appeared down the corridor, then Jesso, telling me it was time to go. I embraced her and pressed the sunstone brooch into her hands. She didn't thank me; it was as if I'd given her a tissue to toss away. She wept, saying: "They will blame us, Demizell. Forgive me, but they will."

She was right, beginning with my mother who forbade me from taking Teshria with me.

I learned much later what had happened in Slagtown, where most Attalls lived. The Meresguard hadn't done much about the rampaging mobs. Some Attalls had been apprehended, a dozen supposedly confessing to being paid by Skarrian agents to assist in setting the fires that had destroyed the fleet. I know now that torture is not a guarantee of discovering the truth. Perhaps a very few had been complicit. But if that was the case, the Skarrians never boasted about it later, only the cleverness, heroism and sacrifice of their own agents who had well-timed their deed—the hour, the brisk wind that had quickly spread the flames, and a drier than usual summer.

That night no one could be certain more fires would not be set in Milatum, that the inferno might not be a signal to a Skarrian vanguard to commence an attack; or that further treachery might not reach the royal isle of Mereshaven. Though father threatened to bundle up mother and personally stuff her into a carriage of the quickly assembled baggage train, she refused to go, as did my brother, Lerrist. There was no thought of taking Cymra and I to safety in a mere galliot or bawley requisitioned from the commercial docks of the Lazza, and thence out the Cleave to safety. No one knew if the Skarrians weren't waiting in ships somewhere out in the darkness of the Kingsmere beyond the pharos.

So it was decided that we would leave the city with an escort of fifty Labryssons, via the Orphic Gate, and quickly journey to Girvan where there were two suitable royal ships on station for use in dealing with corsairs of the Shelter Isles.

Jesso and four Labryssons hurried Cymra and I down to where Mother, Father and Lerrist awaited us by the silver phaeton that would take us through the Orphic Gate, over the causeway through Humber and then by the coast road to Girvan. Two lesser wagons had already been filled with only a portion of what I had expected to take for the journey to Castlecliff and my wedding to Joffreck, whose few princely moments never did include mounting a royal Keshkan mare without help—or a horse for that matter.

Jesso gave my sister and I masks of the finest whisp, scented with elixith—smoke was drifting thickly over the Queensmere, obscuring most of Colza's Bridge that linked Mereshaven to Linnisvale.

Cymra and I never saw our mother and father and brother again.

Teshria survived, and upon our meeting years later, it was my turn to weep when she told me how the sunstone brooch—just one of my many pieces of jewelry—had saved her life.

CHAPTER ONE:

SLAGS

FALCA BREKS HAD to step over the butcher's corpse to get into the shop—where better to hide from a mob than the wake of its rampage?

Maybe the man had tried to defend himself, but Falca didn't see a cleaver or carver on the sawdust-strewn floor or in the block. The murdering looters must have taken all the knives he had in the shop. Blood smeared his trews and leather apron that hung by one strap from his neck. The other strap had obviously been severed with the same sword-strike that killed him. He couldn't have been dead for long. The stench of voided bowels fouled the air. Flies pestered him, the only meat left in the place. Blood pooled around his bare feet.

They'd hacked off his plaits, stuffed them into his mouth, smashed his left eye to pulp; the right stared at the shattered shop window where Falca knelt, slingsack at his side, relieved to be away from the street…and disgusted. They'd killed the man for what?—the crime of selling meats and sausages in this neighborhood of Attall immigrants?

Falca had heard enough talk at the Slagtown hostelry where he stayed the night before, and the fear that came with it: that Skarrian agents who surely must have set the Snarlshome fires in Linnismorn would be the death of loyal Attalls here.

It wasn't likely the Attall butcher was a Skarrian agent, a spy. So he'd died because he went barefoot, as was the Attall custom; for wearing his hair in plaits like any other Slagtown man, most of whom evidently worked in the nearby quarry.

For being a...*slag.*

Falca didn't hear the oikoe deeper in the shop—the shouting outside was too loud. But he glimpsed movement out of the corner of his eye. The animal was standing on its hind legs, watching him with black eyes, its teeth bared, claws of one paw at the edge of the counter. A red mange splotched the brown fur, exposing scabbed skin.

This oikoe wasn't as large as others he'd seen—about as big as a small dog. Ossa said that Rohaise often kept a few oikoes at her cottage, that many were used as messengers. But evidently oikoes were used for other things, too. Day before, he hadn't been an hour off Milatum's eastern causeway and through Ozold's Gate—late afternoon it was—when he'd gotten a swallow's wink and finger-hook on the main thoroughfare, Colza's Way. She'd cooed her price; he shook his head, moved on. Excited though he was to come to the end of a long journey, he was duffed, tired to the bone; had been walking on the road south from Carrick since early that morning and only wanted to find a place to sleep for the night. She yelled after him: "I'll throw in an oik-tail for free." *Ah'll thrawn'n oiks-tail fer fray.* Later, upon Falca's asking, the innkeeper only hinted at what the swallow had suggested: something to do with an oikoe's long, gorgeously furred tail.

The end of this oikoe's tail was now wrapped around a thin, curved flensing knife.

Falca was ready with his falcata, should the feral oikoe attack. But it dropped to all fours again, and though it still held the flensing knife, the oikoe sidled off to the right, revealing the outstretched arm of a woman. It had been gnawing on the dead woman's hand, working around the ring on one of her fingers, and now went back to its meat, keeping an eye on Falca. Oikoes could talk and what he heard now was halfway between a growl and words Falca couldn't understand but he knew what the oikoe was saying: *It's my meat, not yours.*

Which was more or less what was going on outside.

There was no point in risking a peek over the windowsill. They were out there, another procession like the other he'd seen and managed to avoid: younger Milat men mostly, armed with make-shift clubs, crude flouts, swords and strutters. Hidden, but only three spits away from the mob, Falca could hear repeated chants of a number—*866,* whatever that meant—and the rumbling of a cart or wagon and the smacks of a club or flout against it. The wagon's rumbling on the paving bricks changed momentarily, its wheels passing over the shop's hanging sign that earlier had been knocked to the street. A woman shouted shrilly: *"Get up, slag! Get up!"*

Falca knew he'd been lucky. He'd gotten looks before he'd darted into this street corner shop. He might have been in trouble if not for the distraction of looters emerging with a few Attall prisoners from one of the tenements down the street, not too far from the hostelry on Bentbacks Lane, the Quarry's Lift, where he had only a few hours sleep the night before—given what had happened.

He didn't talk like any Attall—who spoke with less of a burr than Milats. But the ones out there weren't in a mood for such distinctions. What he'd seen, most Attalls were physically bigger than Milats and so was Falca. They wore trews and so did Falca, though his weren't side-cut. He didn't have plaits but his hair was long, could have loosened them. Just as he could have put a pair of chasers on his feet to try and fool the mob looking for Attall scapegoats to blame for what had happened.

He'd put them on, all right, weeks before—at the Barras' handsome stead—to replace the chasers worn out by the trek from Scaldasaig in the Rough Bounds, through the Rivals Mountains and into the valley of the River Roan in northern Myrcia. A heroic fit, this extra pair of low-cut boots of Lukan Barra's, the famous Myrcian and grandfather of Raleva who'd been at Scaldasaig with Falca, and almost died there during the battle for the fortress.

All this way…to crouch below a windowsill while a feral oikoe gnawed at the flesh of the Attall woman behind the counter…and the festers outside not yet finished, either. Would they see the dead butcher, reckon the shop had already been picked clean of anything to loot, kill or take captive?

The mob had more captives out there, jeering at them, shouting that *"866!"*, over and over; screaming, *"Skarrie-lover!…Cut his fecking plaits!"* Hitting them with strutters or flouts—Falca could hear the thuds and smacks, the cries of the prisoners, one of them sobbing.

Whoever threw the paver had poor aim if he was trying to hit an Attall: the brick crashed through the window, narrowly missing Falca but showering him with shards of glass, and causing the oikoe to back away, out of sight. He brushed off the broken glass.

And right now his reasons for coming all this way, a month's journey—Scaldasaig to Milatum—to find a woman he'd never met before, seemed just that: litter of broken glass.

Maybe it always had been. Ever other day coming south, he'd wondered if Rohaise Loquin was still *alive* after twenty years…if she'd even want to know what had happened to the man she knew as Mott Demoul and the reasons why he took the name of Ossa Vere and never returned to the woman he still loved up to the moment he died at Scaldasaig.

Yahh well, she'd never know now, and neither would Falca because he was not gonna be trapped here, caught in a coming war in which he had no stake.

Within an hour, maybe by noon, the mobs would have dispersed enough for him to safely make his way to the Orphic Gate he'd been told about, that led to the western causeway and the mainland. And if that gate was blocked, he had more than enough shine in his safekeep to pay for passage by ship to Gebroan…and then? Whatever happened *then*, he might never be able to return here to try and find Rohaise Loquin.

All this way….

The journey for nothing.

But he was here now and he had to do something about the oikoe; the woman deserved a better fate.

The oikoe bared its teeth, gave a low-pitched hiss this time, pawed at the tip of the falcata as Falca moved around her. She was female; that was obvious enough as he kept circling her, hoping that the wonder of an animal standing on two legs and holding a knife with its tail didn't also include an ability to throw the fucking thing at him.

He got behind the oikoe, and kept thrusting with the falcata, backing her up, slowly forced her away from the dead woman, got her past the counter. The animal dropped to all fours, dropped the knife, leaped over the butcher's body and into the street.

In the back of the shop Falca found a spare apron and a shirt hanging on pegs. He covered the faces of the Attalls—best he could do for them—and went back to the window to wait a little longer before he left his refuge. All he wanted to do now was escape from the place he'd spent half his life dreaming about seeing, long before he met Ossa Vere.

THE DAY AFTER his arrival he crossed two of Milatum's fabled bridges; the first was Phodry's that linked Milatum's northeastern district of Linnishill to the southeastern, Linnishill. Ossa had told him about the bridges, the only surviving structures of a ruined city Roak's son Colza claimed for his own and gave it a name for what it would be, not what it was: Milatum. And named the four hilly islands after his daughter Linnis who died very young. Over time, the Milats leveled the crests of their city's hills, and used the rubble to fill in the channels that had separated the eastern and western Linnises, and planted gardens around and below the bridges linking them, leaving only two open channels north and south.

Ossa said that Rohaise—and her father before her—had the municipal contract to maintain the vast gardens below Delmarrion's Bridge, the westernmost. And as Falca crossed the easternmost—Phodry's—that day, he wondered if Rohaise Loquin still had the contract; if that's where he'd find her, in those gardens if not the cottage somewhere on the heights above the Lazza where her husband, then the mast-lord of a Myrcian windwhipper, berthed his ship and hurried up the steps to see her after too long an absence.

Which would you have chosen, Falca, had you been able to escape your captors after you survived that storm and the wreck that claimed all but you and and one other? Which direction? Toward which home, Milatum or Castlecliff? It was my own fault I had wives in both places, neither of whom knew the other existed. If it had been a matter of choosing between them, I wouldn't have thought twice: Milatum. But I had a daughter in Castlecliff. Before I finally did escape, the weeks and months had turned to years. I told you what happened in Castlecliff…but yes, there was still a choice to go back to Roh. But a woman like her, she would have found someone else by then. And even if she hadn't, I would've had to tell her what I should have long before; what I'd never had the courage to tell her. She had a laugh of a carillon's noon bells, and I wanted to keep hearing them in my mind instead of silence or the whisper of a final goodbye….

Perhaps it was Falca's imagination, but as he'd walked over the bustling Phodry's Bridge, he thought he caught the scent of the garden below. There were no gardens under Mago's Bridge that linked Linnismorn to Linnisheer; only the Cleave, the main passage from the Kingsmere to the inner Queensmere water of Milatum.

He kept his hand on his bulging safekeep—not that he looked like a mark to any thief working Colza's Way that led to Mago's Bridge. Everyone seemed to be walking faster than he was. Jostled on the right, he'd step to the left— and be told there to get out of the way. In the space between two particular lampposts, from which hung cresset lamps to illuminate the thoroughfare by night, he was almost run down by a wagon, and then by a two-horse phaeton with a canopy roof.

Still on the Linnismorn side of Mago's Bridge, he left Colza's Way and took the steps up to the top of the city wall by the Cleave. From the allure there he could see the channel itself, how the wall continued on to the entrance and then around and above the outer bluffs of the city; how the Milats seemed to use the wall's wide, less crowded allure as a quicker way to get around.

An oared pilot ship was towing a merchant galliot past the pharos, approaching Neskayuna—what Ossa called the half-colossus that guarded the entrance to the Cleave. She rose from her waist, her outstretched fists clenching chains that could be winched tautly from the base of the Cleave's cliffs in times of peril.

Another arrival, a windwhipper, was farther along the channel, its masts passing easily under Mago's Bridge. The square towers might have been constructed of the same bluestone from which most of Milatum's buildings were built, but these towers were far older. There were two at each end of the bridge. From their tapering height, thick cables—gleaming yellow-white in the early afternoon sun—curved down, with lesser cables supporting the long span of the bridge itself. The ends of the main cables stretched tautly, buried in gigantic slabs surrounded by gardens.

He wondered if the legends were true, that these cables extended far below, reaching down into the bowels of the earth.

I doubt they're true, Falca, these legends about the cables being earthly vines. But the fact remains that nowhere else in the Six Kingdoms are there bridges like these…the woven cables and surfaces that cannot be cut, burned or corroded and weakened by time….

He left the allure, walked through the gardens and crossed Mago's Bridge—which took him longer than he'd thought, given the narrowing of Colza's Way that congested the bridge, and preparations for some coming celebration. He passed a wagon filled with rolls of blue, green and white streamers—the colors of the Keshkan flag. More bunting had been tied to the bridge's rails and the lower reaches of vertical cables.

One worker dropped a streaamer and before it reached the bridge road the wind swirled it away. Falca snatched it from the air, the Milat looking at him as if he'd performed a magic trick. Returning the streamer to him, Falca stayed for a while at the rail, watching the windwhipper he'd seen earlier. Towed by another oared pilot boat, the ship had turned to the west—as Ossa, then Mott Demoul, had once turned with his—passing the open dawnstone arms of Pelagia.

Falca smiled: only in Milatum would they build a colossus probably as tall as that of Roak in Draica's Manger Bay—without any clothes. Over the tresses that draped over her right shoulder to cover one of her breasts, the royal isle of Mereshaven rose in the distance from the Queensmere.

Pelagia's many things to these Milats, but she's a sailor's goddess in particular, because she's always there to bless his departure for blue water, and to welcome him home....

An hour later he was buying a small round of bread and a trencher of six fish—sprats—each the size of his middle finger, from a lisping vendor on Colza's Way who hadn't a problem with Falca's Myrcian shine. The fish came with a sauce—sloritsa—that Milats evidently slathered on everything. He was surprised it tasted much better than it smelled. He paid extra for a cup of blige, a Keshkan wine that the vendor spiced with sinnot to cut the sweetness.

The vendor had a pair of oikoes working for him. Standing on their hind legs, they took coins in a little cup held in their paws, and put the food on a trencher. Falca had to ask the vendor what the bigger of the two oikoes said after Falca's coin clinked in the cup.

"Annu anks?"

"He knowth more'n a hundred wordth, doth Tuppie. But not all of 'em are ath polite ath 'many thankth'."

Farther along Colza's Way he stopped at a flower cart, this vendor nodding at Falca's grin, maybe thinking that he was appreciating the display—which he was but only because it reminded him of a lesser one in Draica: Poash's. That one-eyed flower and fruit monger might have given what little hair and the few good teeth he still had, to sell such exotic beauties as tormentear and fourflame besides his usual sunsbreath, meadowbride and harlequin roses. Old Poashie had once been a sailor, claimed to have been to Milatum. That probably wasn't true, but a young Falca—after he stopped nicking the occasional piece of fruit from Poashie's cart, anyway—listened to his Milatum tales as if they were.

T'ain't no other city in the Six Kingdoms, boy, whurra man can make a fortune an' lose it in the same year....

The Milat floriste still had most of his teeth and hair and correctly judged that this disheveled northron—Falca hadn't shaved or cut his hair since he was at the Barras' stead—had no intention of buying anything. He ticked his head for Falca to move aside for the two couples behind him. Falca did, glancing over at the couples.

What he'd seen so far, it sure seemed that the more affluent the Milat, the less clothing you wore. Measure out the cloth for *both* these men—side-split kilt and trews and armless tunics—and it would be just right for Falca on a summer's day in Draica. The two women wore the sheerest whisp—pale yellow and rose, that left nothing to the imagination in front or behind. The men carried bronze-tipped strutters of some reddish wood, with knobs of gold. The women's dark hair was styled in curls and ringlets and each wore a nimbus—one of pearls, the other of amber and red jewels.

"Flowers for the ladies?" the floriste said to the nearer and seemingly more interested woman, Nimbus-of-Pearls. "The mare's-tail and sunsbreath are especially fresh."

"Yare, it's tempting, but not today," she said, brushing a hand over the tormentear. "A fine display though."

"Some other time, perhaps," the floriste said, and handed her a single mare's-tail.

As they passed Falca, he heard the man next to her say: "Suli, it will only wilt while we're all in the baths."

"Speak for yourself, Taggmul," the other man said, prompting the butt of his joke to roll his eyes, the women giggle, and Falca to smile at yet another wonder of Milatum: men *and* women going together into the same baths?

He followed the four until they turned off Colza's Way and into a side street and presumably the bathhouse, remembering again what Poash had once told him, and chiding himself for the thought. He hadn't come to Milatum to work the streets as he had in Draica. But still—shide!—without a doubt, he could work this Colza's Way from only one bridge to the next, and probably make in a single afternoon what took him months of reiving in his old territory of Slidetown— *and* Tidesback and Catchall, the bricks he'd taken over from Lambrey Tallon.

That evening he paid for a pallet near the roof cistern of The Quarry's Lift, the only place that still had any room given the arrival that day of Keshkans from the mainland and Girvan, mostly. The dour Attall innkeeper took Falca's Myrcian coin with a shrug—shine is shine—saying that a lot of people had come into the city for the celebration of the imminent departure of the queen mother and daughters for Castlecliff, and the older Demizell's wedding to a son of the Myrcian Sanctor; a barrel-belly was the word, and twice her age.

Falca didn't care about the thinness of the pallet—he'd slept on much worse in the past months. Sure, depending on how long it took to find Rohaise Loquin, he'd try for better elsewhere than Slagtown. But he was…close, assuming she *was* still living at the cottage.

There were once bluestone quarries all over the Linnises; four—no, five if you count the Skellig. Built the city from what they took out. Now there's only one left that's not a lake, big or small, and that's in Linnisheer, Slagtown. You'd think, where Roh's cottage is, tucked into that steep hill above the Lazza, that it would be quiet. But it never was. We were close enough to the windmill to the west to hear the rumbling during the day; and close enough to the Slagtown quarry to hear the mining going on. Sometimes, a breezy day, you could hear the tink and chunking; the shouts, the squeaks of hoistings, as if the quarriers were working just outside the door to that cottage. And at night there was always what came up from the Lazza—faintly, mind you—but you could guess what they were doing down there, what I used to do in Castlecliff, the Carcass there; and what you must have done when you were my age in your Slidetown, depending on your thirst and company and what you had in your pocket to pay for both. Still, when I was with Roh—and it never was enough time—I never wanted to be anywhere else....

He was awakened later that night by voices, many of them. His first thought was that the innkeeper had neglected to mention that Falca might be disturbed by some local Attall custom of greeting the dawn.

But the glow to the east wasn't the dawn.

FALCA SHOULDERED HIS slingsack, ready to leave. Things seemed to have quieted out there, but he peered over the sill to make sure—and was glad he did.

They were coming down the narrower street that intersected with the bigger one that fronted the corner shop. At first he couldn't see how many, but the ones in front carried cudgels, strutters. The oldest of them—shaved head—had a short sword. Directly across from Falca, a man emerged cautiously from the doorway of a tenement, holding a bulging sack. After a moment, a woman behind him followed, holding the hand of a boy and her own sack. The boy carried a much smaller one. All wore plain, drab clothing. The man's plaits reached almost to his waist, a glass teardrop earring and delicate chain dangled almost to his shoulder. The woman's hair was cut short. No shoes on any of the three.

They probably had the same idea as Falca: waiting out the worst of it until the mob was gone and only a few stragglers on the street. Maybe they, too, were for the Orphic Gate, getting out while they could. Maybe a lot of Attalls had already done that earlier, before the mobs stormed into Slagtown.

Falca thought of shouting a warning—*get back inside!*—but it was too late for that. A few of the gangers had already passed the corner, looked like they were going on through the intersection. But then they saw the Attall family.

The father had time only to push his wife and child back toward the door, yelling at her to bolt it. He dropped his sack, drew a long-shank dagger, kept his back to the door, saying nothing as the gang came on, taunting and jeering.

He kept them at bay for a few moments, stabbing at one, then another, trying to parry the thrusts of cudgels and stutters. He was burlier than most of them, but had no chance against eight, nor would Falca if he left his refuge to help the Attall. It was sickening to watch but he'd seen much worse and this wasn't any of his business.

The Attall broke through the cordon, taking blows to his back and arms, trying to both shield his face and stab at his assailants at the same time, as he tried to run down the street. Maybe he was just trying to escape but Falca reckoned he wanted the men to keep after him, and in their frenzy they'd forget who was huddling behind that bolted door.

He didn't get far. The gangers with cudgels had the better length to strike. Blows to the legs took him down; another to his right forearm and he lost the long-shank which was quickly picked up by the lead-dog of this pack, Shaved-head.

The door to the tenement swung open and the woman charged into the street. Neither screaming nor cursing, she ran to the nearest street-buster, tried to wrench his cudgel away. She wouldn't let go and tumbled away as he did. She got the cudgel but before she could swing it he punched her in the stomach so hard she seemed to lose her breath.

Seeing this from the doorway, the boy ran toward her, and attacked the man who'd hurt his mother, his plaits swinging as wildly as his little fists.

Falca left the window of the shop, went to the doorway, stepped over the butcher. Three of the scuts were hauling the Attall to his feet. He slumped but they jerked him back up by his plaits. One of the gangers gripped a fistful of the boy's, a dagger at his throat. Another had the woman's arm behind her back. Shaved-head held his sword at her throat, gesturing at the others with the long-shank, saying. "Make sure the slag gets to the castlet. You kill him, he can't tip what he knows to the nobs."

"What about you and—"

"Quicker you get him there, Stoffie, sooner you're back for your turn," Shaved-head said, grinning, ticking up the woman's chin with the point of his sword.

Five of the gangers went off with the Attall, the other three with the woman and the boy. One of them said something to Shaved-head that Falca couldn't hear.

"Don't fash yourself, Bekrie—she's only a slag, but she'll spread her legs wide for you too, oyah, knowing there's a blade at her cutling's throat."

Falca watched them disappear into the tenement.

They didn't close the red door.

He slid out his falcata.

Just this, then I'm gone....

CHAPTER TWO:

THE RAPPAREE

T HE BOY'S CRYING led Falca to the room on the first floor.
He peered around the edge of the half-opened door.

Closest to him, on the left side of a table in the middle of the room, one of the festers had an arm around the boy's neck, a dagger in his other hand. He was looking away, as was the second man, this Bekrie, who waited his turn halfway between the table and the pulled-back curtains of a sleeping area.

The other men blocked most of Falca's view of the woman and Shaved-head on the pallet.

They'd put the cudgel, short sword, and the Attall's long-shank dagger on the table, within easy reach.

Falca ducked his head back, heard Shaved-head telling the woman, "Off with the sark. Let's see if it's true slags mark their quivs."

"Dant look," she said to her son. "Keep your eyes closed."

Shaved-head laughed. "He'll hear enough. Come on, get your rags off."

Falca wiped the sweat from his hand, gripped the falcata.

The boy was still crying.

First him, then the weapons....

Falca slipped through the doorway, then heartbeats to cover the distance to the nearest man. He struck at the back of the right knee, a slicing half-swing that severed the tendons. The man shrieked, dropped the dagger. Falca grabbed his wrist as the boy broke loose, and spun the scut around, slamming his head to the table so hard the cudgel bounced off to the floor. Falca kicked the dagger away, grabbed the sword with his left hand.

Weaponless, the second man had backed away. Falca kept his eye on him as he skimmed the long-shank from the table with his falcata, sending it skittering to a far corner of the room, the boy's pallet, where no one could get it, least of all the first ganger who was crawling away toward the door.

Nor could this Bekrie get the boy; he'd crawled under the table with the cudgel. Bekrie fled, giving Falca a wide berth and ignoring the others' pleas for help. Shaved-head's shouts were muffled—the woman had flung the sark over his head, her eyes wide, lips tight with her effort to twist it, keep him blinded.

He broke free, lunged forward, pulling off the sark—and Falca kicked his jaw, snapping his head back, momentarily stunning him. The boy rushed to his mother, giving her the cudgel. She took a few steps away from the pallet and swung the staff straight down on the ganger's head. Whether from that blow or Falca's kick, Shaved-head's mouth seeped blood; he'd probably bitten his tongue.

The woman threw the cudgel away—a clatter—and for a moment all was quiet except for ragged breathing and the groans of the first ganger as he hopped on one leg toward the door and then was gone.

By the time Falca had recovered the dagger and the long-shank, the woman had put her gray sark back on, was tying the belt sash, telling her son they couldn't stay here, the others might be coming back.

"You may need these," Falca said, and she took them, sliding her husband's long-shank under the belt sash, giving the dagger to her son.

"And this," she said, hefting the short-sword. "Yours is heavier and the edge seems keener, and there's good, but I must do it with his."

She walked over to Shaved-head, looked back at her son. "*Now* you watch."

As did Falca, standing by the table with the boy.

The ganger's right arm was curled. She put a bare foot on the wrist to flatten his right hand. Bending low, she raised the sword high over her head and swung the blade down with a loud grunt, slicing off half his thumb and most of the nearest two fingers.

OUTSIDE, FALCA COULD still hear Shaved-head's wails and shrieks. A few passersby heard too, glanced at the tenement and went on; nothing unusual for this particular day in Slagtown.

The boy had his sack, the woman hers—and her husband's. She had the same long teardrop earring as her husband's, but wore it at her left earlobe.

"My son and I thank you," she said. The boy began walking in the direction the five gangers had taken his father. "No," she said to him. "They might see us. We need help to get your father and that's the other way."

To Falca again: "May Rusavarr be with you always."

Whoever that was—but a blessing was still a blessing. He nodded.

Falca watched them heading toward the intersection and then crossed the street to get the slingsack of belongings he'd left at the window of the butcher's shop. The hour couldn't have been much past noon but he could feel the heat rising up from the street bricks. He'd had nothing to drink or eat since he got to the Quarry's Lift the day before. Well, he'd get both soon enough before he got to the Orphic Gate. Smoke tainted the air; probably the last of the smoke drifting west from the Snarlshome fires. Or maybe the mobs weren't done yet with Slagtown.

Inside the butcher's shop, he paused at the window, slingsack over his shoulder. Shaved-head was leaving the tenement. His right hand, swaddled with a bloody cloth, tight against his belly. Blood smeared his chin.

Now you watch....

The boy was four or five years younger than Falca was when he took to the streets a week after his mother fell to her death from Rushes Bridge, two years after his father never returned one night to their own tenement by the Corry Roads in Draica. Falca hadn't been with her on the bridge, but he knew her death wasn't an accident, as he'd been told. He'd watched his mother spitting blood the week before, and blamed himself for not being with her on the bridge, maybe stopping her from doing it, pleading with her not to. But he couldn't blame her for taking her life, wanting a quick end instead of a painful, lingering one—and sparing her two sons the sight of it, day after day....

Shaved-head was no longer a threat to the woman and boy. Still, Falca waited to see which way he'd go, and felt better when the fester didn't turn right at the corner—the direction the woman and her son had taken.

Flies scattered as Falca stepped over the butcher's body—then stopped, frowning. *Shide!* If he'd looked the other way at the window he would have seen what was coming down the street, four of them.

He'd noticed a few on Colza's Way—skimmer caps, blue and white-checked tunics, the long-shaft maces with an iron bulb at the gripping end and a bigger one at the other.

Milatum constabulary. Meresguard. Nobs they were called. And one of them was now pointing to the red door of the tenement where it happened.

To bolt would only get their quick attention, set him apart from the others on the street. In Draica he would have run, knowing the twists of alleys, the best places to hide, leastways in Catchall and Slidetown. Not here. And Draica's Red Feather constables didn't have the likes of an oikoe to chase him down, this one white with black paws, tail and muzzle.

There was one place—the butcher's shop not far behind him—but that was no longer a hiding place. Soon enough, if they hadn't already, the nobs would see the body in the doorway, find the woman's in the back of the shop. And *him*.

Falca kept walking, his back to them now, thinking maybe he'd do it again here, like he always had in Draica or anywhere else: escape.

"*You there! The falcata!*"

TERROS VANNION SAID she could spare only one man to take the Draican to the Skellig, so Loyasa was it, seeing as how he'd have the oikoe, Vlix.

"And after you bring him there, Optos, tell them to dispatch a wagon to pick up the Attals in the shop. Then meet us at the quarry. We'll be needing you and Vlix there; this day isn't done done yet." She took off her blue skimmer cap, wiped her brow, put the cap back on. "Yare then, he's all yours, bound and bagged."

She strode over to the Draican who stood taller than both Tofer and Flerric who'd been guarding him during the questioning. She thumped him on the chest with the heavy end of her mace. "If ever I meet that woman—" She looked back at Loyasa. "What did he he say the name was?"

"Rohaise Loquin, Terros."

And back to the Draican: "So you came all this way to find this Rohaise Loquin even though you'd never met her. Well, if ever I see her, whoever she is, I'll be sure to tell her she's damn lucky that a rappareee the likes of you never found her."

Terros Vannion slid the mace back into its baldric loop and left, flanked by Tofer and Flerrik.

Loyasa didn't have to tell Vlix where they were going. The white-coat oikoe was only three years-old but he knew there was only one place where he had to lead someone kipped, bound-and-bagged, and having worked only in Linnisheer Vlix knew how to get there. The oikoe rose to wrap his long tail around the end of the lead rope knotted to another tightened around the Draican's chest and arms. Vlix dropped to his fours and set off, keeping the rope taut, keeping the Draican moving toward a fate Loyasa felt he probably didn't deserve, all in all. But orders were orders.

Loyasa walked behind, holding the Draican's falcata and scabbard, occasionally glancing at the wrists, all too aware of the man's size, but there was a lot more going on with this one than brawn. Every merser carried a hood, was supposed to blind a prisoner—keep'm docile—but usually the hoods were used only for those deemed threatening. This one hadn't resisted, been violent, but there'd been no question about bagging him—not today. And you never knew…which was why Loyasa reminded him about Vlix: "A word from me, the oikoe will spray. You don't want that."

More Attalls were coming out of the Cricklow Street tenements, mostly women; a few staring, maybe wondering why the strappy-jack had boots on, where he got them, because who else but an Attall would be bagged on a day like today, never to be seen again.

But in his ten years with the Meresguard—five of them in Linnisheer as an oikoe handler—Optos Staffa Loyasa had in fact never taken an Attall to the Skellig. Whatever else you could say about them and their loonzie customs— like the little square box of grassy earth they kept in their homes to remember their prophet what's-his-name's Throne of Turf—Attalls weren't usually where the trouble was. Until today.

And in those same ten years, Loyasa couldn't remember encountering a rapparee as…*smooth* as this one ahead of him. Fact that he wasn't from Milatum had nothing to do with it. When you're caught, you're caught. Loyasa had seen them sullen, guilt in their eyes, oyah; seen them shaking with fear; heard the pleas and whiny protestations of innocence, the curses, threats, whimpers.

He could usually tell right off if someone was innocent or guilty, regardless of what a magistrate later decided. But he wasn't sure about this northron, giving his answers like *he* was the one doing the questioning, not Terros Vannion; calmly explaining everything and nothing at the same time, seemed like. Starting with what sent them down Cricklow Street to begin with: Bekrie Bellew coming up to them as they and five other mersers were breaking up the mob, Bellew shouting about an Attall with a falcata just killed two of his friends in a tenement near the corner of Cricklow and Wither.

Maybe Terros Vannion, who'd just gotten transferred to Linnisheer, didn't know as Loyasa did, that Bellew was a sculchy yape who was doing very well selling flush and some skid to a few deadfall dens in the Lazza. But she knew like they all did that Bellew was the son of the Orphic Gate castellan, a royal appointment.

So they had to go.

There was blood in the room where this Falca Breks—from Draica he said—went to stop three men from raping an Attall woman. But no bodies, which there should have been; and no woman and her son to confirm the story. Why would he want to get involved? someone from fecking *Lucidor*.

What does it matter where I'm from? I saw 'em dragging a woman where she didn't want to go...then saying he was here looking for a woman named Rohaise Loquin, that's all. Was hiding in the butcher's shop over there, waiting for the mob to pass.

There's another in the back of the shop, both of 'em dead when I got there, the place already looted. You think I'd have covered them up if I killed them?

And the money Terros Vannion confiscated from him? *Cor!* maybe a year's wages in gold and silver in that safekeep; shine he shouldn't have, looking like he did: a dock-heave hadn't worked in a month.

He must have stolen it, never mind none of the shine was Keshkan. Stolen the Gebroanan falcata, too. Even a Labrysson didn't carry steel as fine as that. Had to be a rapparee, coshed a wealthy Gebroanan merchant here; there were enough of 'em around, doing business. Terros Vannion, too, thought that was the only explanation, saying, *You expect me to believe a scapegrace like you just walked into the city a rich man?*

To which the Draican shrugged: *You wouldn't believe the truth of it any more than a lie about winning the money at a game of three-star at the Quarry's Lift where I was last night, seeing as how it's all Lucidorian and Myrcian shine.*

Maybe the Draican got lucky with that last. Loyasa knew the Lift's proprietor. An Attal, oyah, but a decent man. Didn't allow gambling in his hostelry, Attals in general not tempted by such-like.

Terros Vannion had persisted about the money. The Draican turned his head at the sound of Vlix snapping his jaws at a fly. Spit it out, get another, spit that one out. A game. Vlix bored. The Draican sort of looking like he was, too. Or was he just resigned to something he couldn't do anything about?—yet.

Vannion turned her head back, a tap to the jaw with her mace. He looked her squarely in the eyes, saying, *So you're thinking maybe it's what they paid me, the*

Skarrians, for helping them out last night? Whoever did, I wasn't one of 'em. Why would they hire someone like me, doesn't know Linnismorn from the morning after? And they wouldn't have paid me in Lucidorian and Myrcian shine, now would they?

The Draican smiled and Loyasa thought Vannion might crack his skull for that, but she only said she'd wasted enough time with him—meaning that it didn't really matter where he got the shine and his vaunty blade, so long as they were going one way, and he the other. She had her orders, to supersede the usual routine: all suspicious persons to be taken directly to the Meresguard's Linnisheer castlet—no exceptions—for either immediate incarceration in the Skellig below, or interrogation. Optos Loyasa had his orders, along with the gut feeling that while this Falca Breks probably wasn't guilty of anything here, he surely was somewhere else.

THE QUICKEST WAY was through the Glass Gardens; and coming up on the fountain there, past a Rainbow Trellis, Vlix looked back at him, put a paw to his muzzle, saying he was thirsty. Loyasa was too. So they stopped, the oikoe taking his lapping slurps first; then Loyasa, a few cupping handfuls.

He motioned for Vlix to stand, slid free the falcata. "Hold," he said, and gave the oikoe the scabbard, which Vlix took with his tail. Loyasa removed the Draican's hood, stepped back. A stout woman at the fountain quickly grabbed the handles of the buckets she'd been filling. Water sloshed over the rims as she hurried away from what she probably thought would be an execution.

"Go ahead," Loyasa said to the Draican, gesturing with the falcata.

Breks knelt at the fountain, dunked his entire head in once, then again, and stood back up.

"So where *did* you get it, all that shine?" Loyasa said.

"That why you let me drink?" Water dripped from the northron's straggly black hair, glistened in his beard.

"And this?" Loyasa sighted along the flat of the falcata. "Jeweled hilt but it's no carpet-knight's blade. Crucible steel to hold the edge you've kept very keen. Heavy but nicely balanced. Fish skin grip like they do in Gebroan. I'd say gorefin."

"It was a gift."

"And the money, too, I s'pose."

"Some of it. Friends in Myrcia."

"The rest?"

"From an island fortress probably bigger than the one on your Mereshaven, except this Scaldasaig was built in the wilderness of the Rough Bounds by the Allarch of Lucidor's Wardens. Traitors, all 4,000 of 'em, not that I much cared about that at the time."

"Right, and I'm tall enough to suck Pelagia's tits—but garn, tell me how you skimmed the shine and *somehow* managed to escape from 4,000 Wardens."

"Not so hard to do—they were all dead."

"Ah, so you were a soldier with the army that took this…Scaldasaig."

The Draican shook his head. "Just a few of us, and a lot of Timberlimbs and—you know what they are?"

"Oikoes without tails, I've heard. Live in trees."

"You didn't hear the half of what they are."

"Who else?"

"A kraken."

Loyasa laughed. "This is getting better and better."

"A lake kraken," Breks said, as if a *lake* kraken made his story more believable.

"And the rest of the money, the gift part?"

"From a graylock named Lukan Barra, the Myrcian who lifted the Skarrian siege of Castlecliff with the help of an Erseiyr. Long time ago, that. I wasn't going to accept the money but he and his wife—she's Skarrian-born, by the way—they insisted. Said it was the least they could do for bringing their granddaughter safely home from Scaldasaig; and that you couldn't have too plump a purse to enjoy a city like Milatum, so they heard."

Loyasa walked around behind Breks to make sure the man hadn't been working those big hands and wrists all the while. The leather straps were still tight, where they should be.

"A rouncy tale, Breks. And maybe even more believable than your other one, about coming all this way to find a woman you've never seen. Or…let's see…maybe this Lukan Barra told you about the courtesans here. Highly skilled and beautiful, these heteras—and very expensive. But if a plunger's got the money—"

"She's had a very profitable day with mine, that officer—Terros Vannion was it? You gonna get any of it? what she took."

"Confiscated. You're a rapparee."

"Not here."

"Somewhere else then."

"Which is where I was going when you nobs came along. Let's say I had second thoughts about staying to do what I came here for. I'm done with Milatum. You know I'm no Skarrian lickspigot, didn't kill anyone; or steal the money here, even if you don't believe me about where I got it. So why don't you and the oikoe walk away. Your Terros will never know. You'll never see me again."

"But I would."

Breks nodded at the falcata. "Then sell it well and sell it quick, before someone takes it from you."

Which is what Loyasa intended to do. Get what he could for it at the Skellig, the money to his younger sister, five months along, married to that whoreson glave serving on the *Kinnion*, what was left of it at Snarlshome. Whether Clevket was dead or not, Loyasa had to get her out of the city quick—no telling what might happen now, the rumors about the Skarrians following up what they did last night. Shulia and a friend would need money to get to Syarra where she'd be safe, where her friend knew people who'd take her in. She'd want him to go with her, but he couldn't...no more than he could let the Draican go.

Loyasa made sure Breks felt the point of the falcata at his back, bagged him from behind. He'd done it one-handed before. Vlix took the lead again with her tail. They'd be at the Meresguard castlet very soon.

The northron clearly wasn't any kind of Skarrian agent, and wherever he got the shine probably didn't deserve to wind up a cruppie in the Skellig down under the castlet. But that's what had to happen now. Because if not, within the hour a man like this one would have the leathers off his wrists; within six he'd have found out where two mersers named Loyasa and Vannion had gone; and within a day he'd have his money and his falcata back, and another tale to tell somewhere else, and this one would be true.

Chapter Three:

ABOVE AND BELOW

WHAT ELSE COULD you do but laugh and shake your head; that and a finger up the arses of the Fates at their Loom Eternal: all the years in Draica doing the things that *should* have led, sooner or later, to a River Rhys prison hulk—but didn't. Now, only two days in Milatum, you do what *shouldn't* have dunned you and you're on your way to some prison, escorted by an animal with a leash for a tail.

And maybe Falca would have laughed about it had his bagged head not made him feel like he was being poached in his own dripping sweat—at least until the heat stopped coming off the paving bricks, the rumbling and clatter of wagons and carriages fading now, replaced by a much closer creaking. The opening of a gate? Were those trees he smelled? Something, anyway, was between him and the sun: the scrim of light had diminished at the bottom of the hood. It faded still more after more creaking of a doorway or gate—and this one closing with an unmistakable thud.

And on: maybe twenty paces before he felt a hand on the back of his shoulder, the nob Loyasa stopping him, someone else to Falca's left, saying, "This one a slag, too?"

"No, says he's from Draica," Loyasa said, and pulled off the hood.

Cool air bathed Falca's face. The light was dim, coming from narrow windows high in the surrounding walls. Ahead and to his right, a nob held a mace. Another nob stood by a thick wooden door, ready to close it. Loyasa stood a few paces away, tucking the hood into his belt, the sheathed falcata in his other hand, the oikoe on its fours, at his side.

"Don't sell it cheap," Falca said.

"I'm not selling it for what you think, Breks."

For some reason Falca believed him, maybe because the nob didn't have to say that; nor did he have to let him drink from the fountain on the way. The nob pushed him ahead, toward another by the door of a room farther in. As soon as Falca was through, the door quickly closed, and yet another merser opened his. This room was about twice Falca's height. Steps led up to its roof. He felt the prod of a mace at his back, stepped into the large cell, the nob following him in.

The door slammed shut. Directly ahead, two more mersers grabbed the handles of an iron-strapped hatch, lifted it. Beyond another, larger hatch there was a closed door on the far side of this cell. Falca heard movement above: someone on a walkway set across the iron bars of the room's ceiling.

A merser pulled on a lanyard, and through the maw of the hatchway came three rings of a bell. The other nob shoved him toward the hatch, saying, "You got ten steps down to a landing. Stop at the third, facing away, you want your hands free."

As soon as Falca did it, hands free now, the hatch closed so quickly that he had to duck to avoid getting his head cracked. The steps, hewn out of rock, were so slippery he skidded down the rest of them. If he'd completely lost his balance, tumbled to his left, he would have fallen off the landing, plummeted to his death—it was a long way down: three tiers of switchback steps, sheer rock on one side, nothing on the other. He could feel the sweat drying off him as he looked out over this cavern, an underworld of amber light, the heavy air stinking worse than a Draican canal at low tide. The myriad spots of brightness weren't torches or fires though the dank air was smoky. He felt disoriented, as if—impossibly—he was beyond the constellations looking down at the vault of heaven.

Falca coughed, rubbed his watering eyes.

They'd built a lid over it instead of letting it fill with winter rains, what Ossa said they'd done with Milatum's other quarries. Pillars rose in serried ranks to the arches of the roof, the lid of this place. He'd been walking over it above.

The amber light came from dawnstone rubble.

Only shadowy movement below.

All right, only place to go is down....

He felt his pocket for the chunk of krael that Vannion's men had overlooked. Or thought it was nothing more than a chunk of dark ginger—let him keep it—not knowing that it was worth far more than the shine they'd taken from him. The krael would keep him alive if he got sick down here, was hurt in some ruck, but he had to make it count. Once it was gone....

He took the steps carefully, and after the second switchback he noticed a pipe angling down, probably from a cistern on the roof of the Meresguard castlet above. The pipe extended down to a circular pool and two cauldrons? nearby. The water in the pool had to be as bad as the air, the stinking weight of it something you could almost chew on and spit out. Already he was coughing. Maybe he'd get used to it. Wasn't any choice in that, was there? People were moving about, but many weren't.

One prisoner—a child?—seemed to be squatting on a level shelving of rock near the end of the steps, eating something. But as Falca kept going down, getting closer, he saw it was no child but a tiny man who rose from his haunches, to stand not much higher than an oikoe on splayed back legs. He dropped the end of his beard. Eating his fucking beard?

"Long time comin' down, cruppie" he said, a squeaky voice. *Lang tame coomin dune.* "Tinkin' about jumpin' were you? Some do, first ting; some later."

He sidled up to Falca. "But 'ey never hit the water there, never do."

Falca stood his ground, the little man not having anything in his hands except his beard again. He bobbed his nose, close enough now for Falca to see that one of the flecks of debris in the beard was moving.

"Yer taint's diff'rent, oyah. An' I know what yer tinkin, fresh-smell strappy-jack like you, no Milat thass fer sure. Swat ole Sniff aside?—you doan wanna be doin' that to the gatekeeper, what I am here, to pick you a boney, which I'm tinkin' that'll be Rekkie's house." A toothless grin. "Come on then, cruppie, an' I'll tell you a lotta what's what."

Falca followed, thinking that if this abandoned quarry had a lot of something it was rocks...to wrap his fists around when the time came to let a...boney? know right off...what was what with the new cruppie. And if he managed to survive the first few nights, maybe for the rest of them he wouldn't have to sleep with a rock in both hands.

HE PICKED UP two as he followed Sniff along the twisting, undulating path. "Over there, that's Heifok's house and Hortwull's," Sniff said, pointing off to his left, as if the "houses" were something more than merely a hundred prisoners—mostly men but a few women—lying on clusterings of pallets, shadows in the pale of dawnstone cairns.

"Rekkie's begins here," the little squit said, making a turn where the path intersected with another. Two cruppies were scratching something on one of the pillars supporting the vaults of the lid. "Him being the Mitoll's First Bone," Sniff went on, "he's closest to the Mount, soeeze got more half-bones doin' his bid; half-bones bein' more'n a cruppie and less'n a boney. W'out cruppies, a boney hant a house, and w'out boneys cruppies hant nane. An' w'out boneys and cruppies the Mitoll hant got much, dooey?"

Sniff turned around like it was a question Falca was supposed to answer—and went on, pointing his beard this way and that, like he held a strutter. "I know what's what so I getta drink from the pool when I want. What the nobs send down to eat, the Mitoll gets *his* first to cook on his own brazer, th'only one 'cept Rekkie and the other boneys what have their own. The halfsies cook the food fer cruppies in the big pots, and out water. But I get mine 'fore the cruppies Same ting with quivs, few we get worth a slide, but I got no use for 'em anyhow."

Two more turns and Falca followed him to the entrance of an enclosure bordered by a low rubble wall, a chest-high cairn of dawnstone in the middle of it.

"Here's yer byre. Rekkie's got his own, a lot bigger'n this. But we're in his house, like I said, seeing as how he's First Bone. Now I gotta go find'm, which the bell's just rung twice, and Rekkie don't hear so well, but that's all he ain't got. The nobs ring a twain means they want something an' Rekkie's the one allays goes up to find out what."

Before he left, Sniff flicked away something he'd pinched from his beard. "Sose y'know, you'll be here with Stitch. He's a fawky loonzie, but he's the best we got, what he does, fixin' Rekkie's jaw strap, an' the Mitoll's clothes an' sewin' up his special gloves, an' what not."

There were four pallets in the byre, one of them occupied by a man Falca at first thought was sleeping—until he saw the blood, a stab wound at the side of his belly. A rat was looking too, not far away on the rubble wall.

Falca put down the rocks he'd palmed and tossed a smaller one at the rat. It scurried away, chittering, disappearing through an open box on the wall near one of the pillars that held up the fucking heaven down here. He went over to take a look at the strange thing: a six-sided box made of some kind of animal hide and bone ribbing; all of it handsomely sewn together.

Another box—this one half-finished—lay near the pallet closest to the pillar. Next to the dawnstone cairn: a stack of hide scraps, a bucket that reeked of piss. Another pallet—a mattress?—was rolled up nearby. Scissors, bone needle and a skein of coarse thread lay on top of the patchwork hide. A busy cruppie, this Stitch. It was obvious what was going to be stuffed inside the mattress—that large pile of hair, some of it plaits, next to one of the two other buckets in the byre.

Falca picked up the scissors, turned over one of the buckets and began cutting his hair and beard close to the skin. What he tossed into the pile wasn't much, but the less there was for things to crawl around in, the better.

He put the scissors back on the rolled-up mattress, was looking back at the dead man on his thin, unstuffed pallet, wondering why the cruppie's hair wasn't yet in the pile, when he heard a voice behind him: "Works better you shit over the open end."

Falca swiveled on the bucket.

He was tall for a Milat, sticks for wrists, maybe a few years older than Falca—hard to tell. He blinked sunken, reddened eyes. Whatever his talent with needle and thread, he hadn't used it to repair the rips in his trews; the frayed, uneven sleeves of his raggy tunic. Had to be Stitch but Falca asked anyway, not getting up, hands over his knees like he was using the bucket.

"Yare, been Stitch for a while now. You?"

Falca gave it.

"Myrcian, is it?"

"Draica, by way of Myrcia."

"Sniff must have liked that. The wee yape doesn't get to bring down many northrons, though we got a lot of Attalls today."

Falca pointed up. "They tell you, while you were skimming their plaits?"

"Enough. Got mixed up in it, did you?"

Falca kept it short, never getting close to what was so much cut hair: that he never should have gone south, should have gone to Castlecliff instead with Tolo, Lannid and Raleva—like they wanted him to; fucking *should-haves* always having a stench all their own, stinking worse than this place, and that included Stitch still standing where he came in, telling him now that he had his pick of pallets.

"But not the one over there; that's mine, by the kite. But if I—"

"A *kite?*"

"What, you never saw a box-kite before?"

"Aren't they s'pposed to be made out of something besides leather?"

"Doesn't matter *what* you make them of down here, does it."

Which Falca had to admit made sense, but he decided not to ask him why you'd make the stiting thing in the first place: for all he knew the dead cruppie had made the mistake of rolling his eyes and asking the same question.

He's a fawky loonzie....

"Like I was saying," Stitch said, "take any pallet you want, even Hosi's over there, maybe a better fit for your long shanks. Soon enough he won't be needing it."

"He's dead."

"He was alive when I left to bury Shevso."

"Yahh well, he's not now."

Stitch went over to look, muttering about how the cruppie must have been worse off than he thought.

"You do it?" Falca said.

"Shevso took my scissors. He and Beveen had a squabble about a cruppie over in Blassop's house. Hosi got caught in the middle of it before the other two dunned each other. Unless you're a fighter, which I'm not, you stay out of the way, which is what I did."

"The other one?"

"Haven't buried him yet, Beveen. He's just beyond the byre. So I'll drag him and you take Hosi—you might as well see where you'll be dragging me before someone else does the same for you."

"Bury as in piling on rocks on 'em?"

"Rocks don't figure in."

"It's an old quarry, what else is there?"

"The Chute. Which you also have to know about since it's where we empty buckets like the one you're sitting on. But first we have to strip the clothes off Hosi and Beveen."

WHEREVER THAT BLESSING was, Falca thought, sure as Roak's arse hairs the Attall woman's Rusavarr wasn't with him now; only the cold ankles of the corpse Falca was dragging, the head chuttering along the well-worn but uneven path to the Chute; and in front dragging his, the Skellig's tailor who made box-kites out of leather. At least Falca hoped it was leather and not like what he'd seen in Bastia, the vendors there selling parasols and hats made out of the skin of Timberlimbs.

The path wasn't the only one leading to the Chute. An older woman came down from another, her long curling fingernails like claws around the handle of a bucket, and crossed in front of Stitch. At the Chute they waited for her to empty the bucket—*slissh*—into the knee-high opening. She stopped near Falca, the fingernail she pointed at him as long as a dirk. "You're a big 'un—don't you be making it worse for the rest of us, getting stuck in 'ere."

Falca ticked his head back when she tried to pat his cheek. She grinned. "But maybe you won't be when it's time, slide down easy." She picked up the bucket, fingernails clicking on the rim, and left.

"Don't mind her, she's having it on with you," Stitch said. "Getting stuck doesn't happen *that* often."

"When it does?"

"They lower Sniff on a rope to unblock it.

"Gatekeeper for the other end, too."

"Yare, coming and going."

Stitch went first, hauling Beveen over, lifting him over the edge of the maw, then his legs…and letting go. "It angles down very steeply," he said. "Your turn."

Falca got it done, breathing through the mouth, which didn't help much. Bent over, hands on his knees by the nearer of the two dawnstone cairns flanking the Chute, he was sure he'd puke but the moment passed.

He glanced over at Stitch who was taking something out of a pocket. Whatever it was he threw it into the maw, then something else.

"Where does it all go?" Falca said.

"Reef of Bones. Above or down here, that's where you wind up. From where *we* are, there's only maybe forty feet of rock to the outside, the bluff of Linnisheer, and then the final drop to the Kingsmere. Maybe you got room in Draica to get tucked in, but we don't in Milatum. Unless your family can afford to bury you somewhere outside the city, or cremate you and pay the tax comes with that—or unless you have a certain dispensation like I once had.

"But for us cruppies down here, hant committed the worst crimes, it's the Chute. Otherwise it's the Eight Steps tower on the wall. Take the eighth, the step that isn't, the nobs behind you pushing you off, and you wind up Reef-meat for the gulls and spanners to pick at while the tide's out. When it's in, the gorefins and snapteeth take over.

"Never mind you've lived a worthwhile life—if your family can't afford cremation you still take the Eighth. All you can hope for is maybe having someone toss flowers after you, after they give you to the air."

Listening to Stitch, Falca felt like he was already halfway the Chute. "You mind telling me what you tossed in there?"

Stitch shrugged, the cairns' illumination enough for Falca to see the faint smile. "Nothing so big as a kite. I'm saving that for my time, assuming someone will toss the pieces in after me. Hosi and Beveen weren't much, but maybe at one time they were."

FOR A LONG time after the Mitoll—one of his boney guards at the Mount, anyway—had ordered night to fall in the Skellig, Falca sat on Shevso's pallet, his rocks within easy reach, trying to ignore the snoring and moaning and coughing and rutting of cruppies in the byres of Rekkie's house and Hortwull's and Heifok's farther away.

He was cold almost to the point of shivering, but he couldn't bring himself to drape some of the dead men's rags over his own clothing. The pile of it was right over there—what they'd stripped from the corpses at the Chute—by the newly-stuffed and rolled-up mattress he'd helped Stitch finish. That's what you did to keep warmer, and when you were dragged to the Chute, someone else would take yours.

He was tired enough to have gone to sleep quickly if he'd lain down on Shevso's pallet, the largest of the empties. But he couldn't bring himself to do that either. So be it if—at least for tonight—he'd fall asleep sitting up, rocks in his hands.

Stitch lay on his side, a scrawny left arm over the mattress by the pallet. Maybe in his dreams the mattress was a wife, a lover, a child—whoever he'd left Above.

The mattress wasn't for him. Rekkie would come in the morning and deliver it to the Mitoll. Stitch had been visibly relieved when it was finished—there would have been consequences if it hadn't been done when the First

Bone wanted. "He's a gleggy half-brick, Rekkie is," Stitch had whispered, "but I've seen him lift a cruppie off the ground by the neck. With one hand."

And he wanted no lumps in the Mitoll's new mattress. So while Stitch worked needle and thread, Falca loosened and smoothed out the tight plaits of the Attalls' hair. Then they stuffed the pile into the mattress. Stitch sewed it up, worrying that his handiwork wasn't good enough, Rekkie having told him that the Mitoll must have tighter stitching this time.

The both of them need tight stitches, all right—ten across the mouth for a start, Falca thought, catching himself before he said it. While the tailor was clearly fearful of the fester, he didn't seem like he was a lickspigot who curried favor with Rekkie, whom Falca hadn't seen yet. Stitch *seemed* all right—that blessing, whatever you wanted to call it, at the Chute. But he also could have been lying about what happened to the men. And he was clearly a favorite when the half-bone trusty doled out the food and water for the day, Stitch getting extra, or so it seemed to Falca. So far there'd been only vetch, but sometimes the mersers sent down sacks of moldy bread and crates of rotting fruit.

Falca draped a leather coverlet over him now for the chill, the stitching as tightly done as the mattress. Augor hide it was, nothing worse. Stitch said every so often the mersers sent down on the supply lift the heads and quarters of augors killed by the augeron dancers in some arena called the Palestra. The meat was tough and gristly but good enough for cruppies, though Stitch said he'd rather have rat meat in his vetch, grubs in the bread, worms in what little fruit they got.

The hides were used as shrouds for dawnstone cairns, Stitch having made the one for the Mitoll's cairn, biggest in the Skellig. If a cruppie disobeyed a boney, he'd get coshed with a flout from the thick end of an augor tail, though Rekkie carried an augor leg bone big enough to crush a skull. Stitch had seen him do it three days ago, when one of the boney guards at the bottom of the steps leading up to the Mitoll's Mount had told Rekkie that a cruppie had wandered too close to the steps.

Boneys…houses…cruppies…Mitoll….

Different names here for the same thing Above.

Different names in Draica.

Back then, Timberlimbs were only…mottles to him; what a cruppie was to Rekkie. And what else had Falca been to a Limb except a boney? when he took from them half of what they made selling scrape along the canals of Slidetown. That was part of his territory—his bricks. His house.

He'd thought he left that all behind, getting out of Draica with Gurrus and Amala, before her father's...boneys killed him. But here it was again, only he was on the other side of it now.

And this Mitoll, somewhere sleeping now on his Mount, where no one but Rekkie was allowed to go? He might be king of only an underworld prison, but not even the king of Keshkevar had the power to tell his subjects when it was time to sleep and when to awake.

It was believed, Stitch said, that hidden in the caves of his residence behind the Mount's terrace, there was another chute that led to Above, but much smaller than the one that led to the Reef of Bones.

How big? Falca had asked Stitch, stuffing hair into the mattress.

Big enough for people Above to drop things they wanted prisoner relatives to have. Gifts never received. How else to explain why the boneys and the Mitoll in particular were not as scrawny as cruppies? Or from where the linsey blankets came, that Rekkie gave Stitch for the mattress? Or the Mitoll's red and gold mantle?

And a private chute big enough for things that people Above didn't want—such as infants.

Stitch hadn't been in the Skellig when it happened, but he'd heard the story, whether it was true or not, about the baby who survived the descent in the hidden chute—only to die shortly after. The Mitoll at the time ordered a young, six-fingered cruppie named Prastagi to dispose of the infant in the other Chute. Which he did, and then claimed that the Mitoll—jealous and fearful of the miracle—had murdered the baby himself. And with a few followers, Prastagi killed the Mitoll's guards and then the Mitoll himself, and became the latest king of the Skellig.

Not many cruppies had lived long enough to know what previous Mitolls had called the hidden chute, with its opening that could only be an oculus that brightened and darkened as days turned to night Above. But the Mitoll Prastagi called it his Eye.

Not long after Stitch finished the mattress, one of the Mitoll's boney guards shrouded the Mount's dawnstone cairn, shouting: *The Eye has closed!*

And all over the Skellig, beginning with Rekkie's byre closest to the Mount, cruppies shrouded their smaller cairns, and night began.

Such as it was. Falca could still see the marking on the backs of Stitch's hands, both of them; tattoos that looked very much like box-kites.

There would never truly be a night or day down here, always something in between—like that time in Draica when he was a dock-heave on the Catchall wharves, and lifted the topmost sack of grain from a pile, and found a nest of newly-born rats squirming in the sack below.

CHAPTER FOUR:

STITCH

FALCA WOKE UP that night to screams and shouts not far away, and men running along the path closest to the byre—Stitch, too, on an elbow: "That's Heifok's house."

The scuffling and yelling, the thud and crashing of rocks got worse before the ruck ended. Stitch lay back down, and Falca—who'd fallen asleep sitting up—finished the Mitoll's night stretched out on the pallet, back against the rubble of the byre's low wall.

When he awoke, Stitch was working on the other kite, the dawnstone cairns unshrouded, the mattress gone. Falca sat on the wall, blearily watching Stitch push holes into a scrap of augor hide with a bone awl not much bigger than the needle he had in his mouth, and grunting with the effort. Falca pointed at the scissors on his lap.

"Where'd you get them?"

"Rekkie wanted some things done—him and the Mitoll—and I said I needed scissors to do it right. This was a while ago. Dunt know how he got them, maybe trading one of his women—sometimes we get younger ones, gretels—to one of the nobs for a few days in exchange for the scissors. He has wits enough to know I wouldn't be a threat with them to anyone but myself."

"Cruppies being one thing and boneys another," Falca said, thinking that if he needed the scissors, he'd know where they were. But he might not have even the few moments to get them. He needed a weapon of his own, hidden but on him at all times. A crude blade to go along with a fist weighted by a rock.

He'd have to make it himself—maybe from the iron straps of the bucket over there, the one he sat on; use a rock to pound the straps flat into one length, grind and edge. Work on it best he could without Rekkie or another passing boney seeing him. But nothing he could do about Stitch knowing.

"That happen much, the ruck last night?"

Stitch plucked the needle from his mouth, Falca a little surprised his teeth weren't worse than they showed. "Not like that—a score of cruppies and six or seven Attalls."

"How'd you know?"

"Two of Rekkie's halfies told me when they were taking the mattress."

"So he doesn't come to get it after all the shitspit about the Mitoll's gotta have it today."

"He *would* have if it wasn't ready, oyah."

A mattress today, something else tomorrow, Falca thought. *Above or Below, all the same. What the festers want is for someone else to empty their bucket....*

"Anyway," Stitch said, "he's probably snoring away. He was busy last night, they said. Went over to help out Heifok. Down here, doesn't matter either who starts what; there's only the finish. But my guess is the cruppies went after the Attalls first."

"That's no guess, no more than the needle in your hand, and the Mitoll and his First Bone are stooly scuts."

"*Shhh...*You keep that up and some cruppie's bound to hear, and he'll sell you out to Rekkie for an extra ladle of vetch."

"Maybe you'd better tell me more about the Mitoll's licklog."

"Rekkie? What's to tell? You don't want to cross him is all."

"What got him sent down, you know?"

"Word is, he was an augor-drover, bringing them south to Milatum for the Palestra, working the teams. There was some family trouble in Carrick, but not his: a father, and what happened to his two sons and daughter. Seems Rekkie killed the sons—something to do with their sister—and the father followed him to Milatum to settle the score, which he didn't."

"So why wasn't he shoved off the Eight Steps? Meat for the gorefins, more bones for the Reef."

"Should have been," Stitch whispered. "But *his* father owns a share of the Palestra, made the bribes, got him sent down here instead of executed, which is also why we began getting augor meat."

"Now he's coshing heads over in Heifok's house."

"More than that. Killed three Attalls but not with his club."

"What, then? Fists, rocks?"

"Something new—a sword."

"They say where he got it?"

Stitch shook his head. "No one's going to be asking him, either, except the Mitoll."

"But where *d'you* think?"

"Who knows? Maybe his father brings it to the nobs with a bribe they get only when he sees Rekkie go back down with it. Nobs don't care he's got a falcata. He could kill half the cruppies—what? that surprises you?"

Falca swallowed hard, pulled a hand over his mouth.

"No, the nobs don't care," Stitch went on, "just so he doesn't kill the younger cruppie gretels which the nobs want every now and then...which Rekkie wouldn't do that anyway, at least the ones he gets after the Mitoll's done with 'em."

Stitch resumed punching holes in the augor hide with his awl. "What does it matter anyway, what he's got?—club or sword—as long as you don't cross him."

Falca nodded slowly, as if he understood now. There was no point in asking Stitch more questions he couldn't answer, maybe get him wondering why his new byre-mate seemed to be so interested in the fact that the Skellig's First Bone now carried a falcata instead of an augor-bone club. If Stitch knew or guessed that the falcata was *his*....

Falca didn't think Stitch would tell Rekkie. But still, he hadn't the full measure of the man yet. And if Rekkie found out....

Could it be a different falcata? No, *had* to be his. Too much of a coincidence: one day the club, the next a falcata. The merser nob, Loyasa, was going to sell it.

There was no question about getting his falcata back—only *how* he was going to *do* that, dun the Mitoll's fucking First Bone before he killed any more cruppies with it.

THAT NIGHT, AFTER the Eye closed, Stitch said: "It was yours, wasn't it? What the mersers took when they kipped you—what *he* has now."

Falca almost didn't hear the whispering; in the byre closest to theirs, someone was calling a name—*Josulla*—and saying over and over, *Wasn't my fault.*

"Roak's balls, Stitch, I'm sleeping."

"It's all right; last thing I'd do is what you're probably thinking I might. See, I'd have to drag you to the Chute somehow and you're twice Shevsull's meat, and then I'd wind up with someone else who whimpers all night like Prexses over there."

"Let it go."

"I'd like to know if I'm right, is all."

Falca sat up, couldn't sleep anyway, all the scratching he was doing, whatever was causing it. Stitch had all he needed now—a guess, suspicion—if he was going to tell Rekkie.

"You're right."

On his pallet, Stitch rolled to his side, facing Falca. "I figured. A man doesn't get to Slagtown from Draica by way of Myrcia without a blade."

"That all that tipped you?"

"Well, you weren't around for most of the day—doesn't take that long to empty your bucket. And not a word when you were. So—"

"Maybe I was taking your advice, keeping my mouth shut."

"So I'm thinking you were looking for it—looking for him—seeing what you'd be up against getting it back, where best to try."

Falca said nothing for a while, wondering what Stitch had been Above. Whatever else he'd left up there, it wasn't his wits. "I kept my distance when he was going back to his byre, but I saw enough."

"But not enough to think twice about it," Stitch said softly.

"What I saw was his augor-skull helmet that's vaunty enough—but it's gotta shrink his eyes to what's only in front. Maybe good for rocks to bounce off, someone throws at his head, but that wouldn't be me. Those meat arms might be strong enough to lift a man off his feet, like you said before, but one's a hand's breadth shorter than the other. The halfsies with him, yahh, they're a problem—there were three—but they can't be with him all the time. I didn't see the stupid on him but you say he is."

"There you go again—keep your voice down."

"Any lower, why bother."

"Cruppies have tried. He'll kill you with your own blade."

"Anything's possible."

"There's nothing after that."

"It's been taken from me before and I got it back."

"You mind telling me?"

Why not....

It took him a while.

He still felt sweet heat at the deaths of Maldan Hoster and Lambrey Tallon at Scaldasaig—Hoster's for certain because he'd seen it. Remembering the Warden's gruesome final moments was like a cup of the best scorchbelly going down. He hadn't actually killed *either* Warden, but he'd put their heads on block. But here, the augor-skull helmet that masked the First Bone's face made it so easy to imagine the face of the man who killed Amala with the falcata... and the one who made it possible.

Stitch was silent for a while, then: "Well, maybe you've had practice getting back what's yours—and taking what isn't, but Falca—"

"Naah, there's enough of me—what about you? your scissors, needle and thread? Seems like you've had the practice of *making* something yourself; maybe the sort of fine clothes I saw up there on Colza's Way, before I got kipped for doing what I used to do in Draica."

"I wasn't making clothes."

"Didn't think so. You mind telling me what they were calling you if it wasn't Stitch?"

HIS NAME WAS Cofor Solenz, and he hadn't been a member of the Kiters' Guild for long when it happened on Queen Epona's birthday.

She wanted kites for the celebration and that's what she got. Cofor had just been accepted into the guild after serving his apprenticeship, which included kite-making as well as scrybing—the coordinated display of kites in the air. Everyone said he was very talented, possibly better than some of the senior kiters. Still, he hadn't expected to scrybe for this event, the biggest—and for the guild the most lucrative—of the year, the commission calling for 100 different kites to be scrybed over a period of four hours. No, Cofor expected his involvement to be limited to preparing the kites for lofting. Even so, that was a big honor for him, and a crucial responsibility given the duration and complexity of the display.

But the day before the event, two of the senior kiters were seriously injured in a carriage accident not far from the guild hall. Cofor was asked to be one of the replacements on Kite Hill.

They were confident he *could* do it. He was relatively young but he had superlative dexterity, stamina, timing, and a sufficient knowledge of the Queensmere's often tricky wind currents. And he'd shown a gift for a special quality that couldn't be taught, that experience couldn't provide: artistic flair.

But *would* he do it?

Oh...well, yes—he'd be honored to perform for the Queen.

He left the guild hall thinking that timing is all, whether with kite strings in your hands—or in a carriage that bore the brunt of a heavily-laden wagon that had careened down a steep hill in Linnisheer, someone having forgotten to adequately chock the rear wheels.

Of course, the timing *could* have been better if Hullion and Respeen had been injured much later in the day. Or even better, that he'd been asked to perform the morning *of* the event, so he wouldn't have the *time* to think about the thousands of people all over Milatum who would be watching the display, as well as the Queen and King Rhakotis...and their children...and prominent ephors...not to mention the guild-master himself.

What began at his favorite tavern that night, to toast his good fortune—if not Hullion's and Respeen's—had ended with Cofor getting so drunk he passed out on his way back to his home near Shimsinnion's Square in Linnisvale.

He never showed up at Kite Hill.

The hundred-kite scrybing for the Queen's birthday wasn't a disaster, though the royals were said to be disappointed in a rather mundane display, considering the winds over the Queensmere were brisk as usual.

The guild-master and elders were furious.

Cofor was demoted to glue-making and the cutting of the skensy and whisp used to make kites.

His drinking got worse, which led to an easier embrace of excuses, which festered into resentment and anger and saying things he shouldn't have.

Had it really been *his* fault? *They* should have known he wasn't ready to be a lead-kiter for such an important event. It wasn't *his* fault that Hullion and Respeen got hurt the day before. The elders *should* have chosen old Nossos and never mind his hands had been stiffening up since he was one of the leads for the Night of the Mistra celebration the year before.

The woman he'd been living with left him two days after he was expelled from the guild. She said she'd wanted to marry him not his ale tankard. He promised he'd quit; they made love; he woke up to an empty bed. Maybe she didn't think he'd keep his promise but there was also the likelihood that all along she'd wanted the status of a kiter guildsman more than the man himself.

But he did stop the drinking, if only because he didn't have much money left. He got a job as a cooper's helper in a cramped, stifling shop in the Lazza. And he was doing all right, after a month given the responsibility of making deliveries by wagon around Linnisheer. That went on for another month, but not long enough for guild elders to forget certain intemperate remarks he'd made.

Someone had robbed the guild hall.

He didn't do it but he would have if he'd known he'd wind up in the Skellig anyway....

Cofor trailed off and Falca thought he'd fallen asleep. But then, one last whisper: "He'll kill you, Falca, if you try. It's enough, isn't it? to keep telling yourself you'll try, and leave it there. Isn't it enough to have only that pizzling thing down here to keep you alive for a day more, then another?"

Falca lay on his pallet, staring up into the ever-twilight of the Skellig, unable to cross over like Cofor and the sair cruppie who'd ceased calling out the name; and wondering what it was he heard above.

Bats. Sounded like hundreds of them up there, a sudden hurry of wings.

However they got in—could they leave, too?—they were here now.

You work with what you have, inside or out, Above or Below.

He had to figure out a way to do that down here. And it occurred to him that Cofor already had.

What, after all, was that box kite he made himself if not a kind of wing?

CHAPTER FIVE:

BUCKETS AND SCISSORS

H E FINALLY FIGURED out how he was going to do it, but he was running out of time—they all were.

Shortly before the Eye closed on his seventh day Below, Falca went over toward Rekkie's byre for the third time, got as close as he dared to the circular enclosure without arousing the suspicion of the guard at the entrance and the other halfies—six of them—around the pool and the nearby supply landing now empty of grain sacks. He guessed about twenty paces from the nearest half-bone to the byre's entrance.

Shide, he was tired, the mild dizziness that had begun in the morning hadn't left and wouldn't unless he got more food in his belly. Whatever Rekkie had in there, the last thing Falca would have time for is food. They'd be coming at him straight-on at the entrance and soon enough over the shoulder-high wall—which seemed a little higher than he remembered on his first foray.

He couldn't be everywhere at once, but he'd have to be…for as long as he could.

Still only the one guard, no change from before—that was something in his favor, anyway.

From where he was kneeling, looking around a pillar at the byre, he couldn't tell if Rekkie was in his byre. He *should* be—where else would he be now?

It had to be tonight, after the Eye closed. Couldn't wait any longer, grow weaker. If Rekkie wasn't there, he would be later. But if for whatever reason the wankspit didn't show, then everything else didn't matter. And there'd be another head on the Mitoll's wall—his own.

Falca was about to leave when he saw a halfie coming down another path, pushing a woman ahead of him, her wrists bound in front, hair cropped short. At the byre's entrance he shoved her inside. Falca heard him laugh but not what he muttered to the guard.

Go on, back where you came....

The half-bone stayed.

So two now—again—what he planned for, but one would have been a lot better.

At least he knew now for certain the scut would be in there. Even after he'd finished with the woman, he'd be there. With any luck, it would be the last time she got shoved in there, for Rekkie anyway.

On his way back to his own byre, Falca picked up two buckets from another. Three of the cruppies were asleep; another who wasn't stared lethargically at him, not caring. Nor did Cofor immediately notice the extra buckets Falca placed by his own. He lay on his pallet, back to Falca, lifted his head slightly. "There's another on the Mount."

"I know, I saw it."

"Six now," Cofor murmured, and dropped his head back to the crook of his arm.

Heads atop the wall—the stacked rubble ramparts of the Mitoll's Mount.

He hadn't seen Rekkie behead any of the cruppies but he had the falcata that Falca had always been obsessive about keening; what else in the Skellig but his falcata could do that? Not a boney's usual bone dagger or a halfie's smaller one.

The day it happened he *had* seen Rekkie coming back from the Mount with his escort of lickspigots. And later the fester headed *back* toward the Mount, carrying a bucket, went right past the byre with it, one-eyed, red-bearded Heifok with him carrying another—boneys carrying buckets?

Things had changed.

After the mersers stopped sending down food—and prisoners—the boneys halved rations. If Falca and Cofor were wondering what was going on Above, many other cruppies had to be also, especially Attalls and others who, like Falca, had recently been sent down. Were the Skarrians approaching the city? Besieging it? Had already taken it?

The only thing that seemed certain was that the Skellig was the least of the mersers' concerns now. And that the cruppies would probably starve to death by the time it was over Above, one way or the other.

But not the Mitoll, his First Bone and the other boneys.

They were hoarding food.

The day Falca finally saw the Mitoll began with Rekkie and Heifok passing by the byre with buckets. The Mitoll had the means to do his own cooking up there on the Mount, behind the wall, the food usually brought in a sack but maybe the halfies had cleaned the buckets.

But Falca didn't think Rekkie and Heifok were carrying food to the Mitoll, and neither did Cofor.

Falca wanted to see what a thumb and five fingers on a man's hand looked like, so he worked his way around the two byres closest to the Mount, pushing past listless cruppies—and there he was, the right hand gripping the weapon Cofor said he always carried: a Keshkan marine's short-shaft glave. No one knew how he'd gotten it, though everyone knew who'd stitched the gloves he always wore: Cofor had made them himself from linsey scraps marked with the size of the Mitoll's hands.

The Mitoll Prastagi stood on his Mount behind the waist-high wall, his black hair spilling over the red mantle. No crown on this king who never left the Mount. The short-shaft glave didn't impress Falca. Steel was useless unless you knew how to use it and he doubted Prastagi did. The pus-heart was younger than Falca, had been here longer than Cofor, so where and when could he have acquired skill with a glave? And why was he up there, anyway? Just because he had size and those hands? That legend about him that probably wasn't true?

Falca found out soon enough.

Only the First Bone was ever allowed to walk up the long steps that flanked the Mount, and never with a weapon. So Rekkie put down the falcata, took Heifok's bucket. At the top of the nearer set of steps, he left the buckets on the Mount's terrace, touching the horn of his augor-skull deferentially. As soon as he left the Mount, Prastagi carried both buckets over to where he'd left the glave on top of the wall. Then, with the glave in hand again, he jabbed into one of the buckets and withdrew a head he'd impaled at the neck and, with the help of a dirk, slid the head onto the wall, like he was serving meat at a table. He swiveled the close-cropped head as if arranging a centerpiece for Falca and

Cofor and the hundred other cruppies who were close enough to see what he was doing and spread the word throughout the Skellig.

He did it again with the second head, except he lifted it out by a glass teardrop and chain. Falca heard the faint clink when the Mitoll tossed it in one of the buckets.

There must have been a bowl of vetch below the wall because he reached down, came up with a handful of it.

"*You want more to eat? This is how you will get it!*" he shouted, and stuffed the open mouths of both heads.

Then he took his glave and vanished into his chambers beyond the terrace.

The next day, the vetch that was in the mouths was gone: feed for the rats.

FALCA SAT ON his pallet, a mantle of rags—Cofor had made it for Shevsull—draped around his shoulders. He still hadn't gotten used to the chill down here.

"Cofor?"

The kiter cleared his throat, or was it a sigh?—and whispered: "What?"

"It's tonight."

"You'll never get close enough to his byre, past the halfies around the pool and food-drop. Even if you don't wake any of 'em up, there's what he has guarding the byre."

"Which is why I need your help. There's a better chance with the two of us."

Cofor rose to an elbow on his pallet. "It's yours, not mine."

"Yes, it is. But he's also got what's *ours* in that byre, and we're starving—*all* of us."

"What does it matter? It makes no difference in the end."

"Maybe you're right, but that doesn't matter *now*.

"You still don't get it, Falca. You *still* think you're Above. But even if you somehow *do* it, you and I and everyone else will *still* be cruppies when they come down to kill us all."

Cofor slumped to his back, Falca stood up. Not far away, Prexes was whispering the name again—*Josulla*. At the Mount, one of the Mitoll's guards called out the closing of the Eye.

"All right then," Falca said. "But your scissors…I'll need them."

Cofor always kept them close at night. There they were, the finger loops sticking out from under his pallet. He rolled over, drew out the scissors. "No."

Falca held out his hand. "Cofor...I need them."

"No! I'll use 'em myself. Shroud the fecking cairn and tell me how we're supposed to do it over there."

○

We both will *use them, but I'll be leaving before you, so I take the scissors first. Make sure you stay about fifteen paces behind me; we don't want the guards to think we're together when they first see us on the path. I'll be stopping, but you keep going. When you're about five paces behind me, I'll move on. They'll be on our left; the one farthest away'll be mine....*

Falca blew on his fingers to warm them, taking his time, telling himself again: what could more more normal than two cruppies carrying buckets and heading back to one of the byres beyond the pool and the now-empty food drop?

He picked up the bucket he'd been carrying by its strap in his left hand, turning a little—a glance was all—to see Cofor trudging ahead.

Falca had a meal-cup in his right hand so the halfie ahead couldn't see it as he approached. Leaving the byre he'd stuck the scissors in the belt, after considering whether to hide them better. But he decided he couldn't risk fumbling for the scissors when the moment came. Wasn't likely the guards would see any glint of metal, not in the deeper twilight of after-Eye.

Still, he hid the scissors' finger loops best he could with an elbow as he shuffled on, feigning weariness—easy to do—feeling the scissor blades in his groin.

So far so good—for him if not the woman Rekkie surely still had in his byre, one of the halfie guards turning now, to sneak a peek inside. The other one—Falca's mark—stepped away from the entrance: "You! what're you doing here?" *Wharr ya doon 'ere?* He drew his dagger, a flash of white bone, took another two steps.

That's it, come to me, Falca thought, and gestured toward the cruppie byre beyond the pool and the snoring half-bones.

"Move on quick, then, ya stoolin' crupp."

Falca nodded, fighting off the urge to look back—Cofor would either be where he should...or he wouldn't. He drew abreast of the guard.

It took only a moment to draw the bucket closer, dunk the cup—and half his hand—in the foul contents.

Now....

He turned quickly, the brimming cup in his right hand—taking aim within heartbeats—and splashed the shit and piss into the halfie's eyes. That was the signal for Cofor to do the same to the other guard. Bucket down, Falca stabbed his in the belly with the scissors as the shrieking half-bone pawed at his eyes, and shoved him toward Cofor's. He slapped the bloody scissors into Cofor's outstretched hand, and darted into the byre with the sloshing bucket, hearing the grunts as Cofor stabbed the yowling second guard with the scissors.

The woman scuttled off the pallet one way, Rekkie another, the fester reaching for the falcata leaning on his augor-skull, had it in his hand...

Falca hurled the bucket's swill into his face. Rekkie grunted, swiping at his eyes. Falca closed on him—a quick side-step around the falcata—and swung the bucket down on Rekkie's wrist so hard that the strap broke...the *crack* a breaking bone? He howled, dropping the falcata. Falca grabbed it before Rekkie could with his other hand—and struck, a vicious back-hand stroke to Rekkie's right upper arm. The First Bone stumbled back, turning to get his club propped against a sack of grain. Falca swung the falcata, cut his tendons at the back of a knee, a *pop*.

Rekkie fell, yet still reached for the club, had his hand on it as Falca struck the side of his neck, the falcata biting so deeply to bone that Falca had to lever out the falcata.

He stepped back, chest heaving, turned from Rekkie's last shudders on the floor of the byre, blood seeping from his neck. Cofor was shouting his name at the byre's entrance, the kiter supposed to have kept the roused halfies at bay while Falca was inside. He was—the bucket gone—swiping the scissors at three of them, more behind. Falca pulled him back, took his place. Seeing the falcata, two half-bones retreated but the third came on.

The halfie's hand that Falca sheared off still gripped the bone dagger as it fell to the path. He grabbed the dagger, tossed it back into the byre, yelling at Cofor to block the entrance with Rekkie and the vetch sacks. Maybe it was the hand he flung over the head of the fleeing, screaming halfie to whom it had been attached; maybe it was the longer length of the falcata...but none of the closer half-bones dared rush him. Others jabbed at the gathering cruppies.

Behind him came the huffing of Cofor and the woman helping him drag out Rekkie's corpse, each with an arm. Falca stepped aside. They swiveled Rekkie around lengthwise by the feet, to better block the entrance. Cofor yanked out the scissors he'd stuck in Rekkie's belly, went back in, followed by the woman, to get the sacks of vetch.

Falca stood over the corpse, saw Sniff at the end of the cordon of halfies, screaming at the cruppies: "*Go back, alla you! We'll kill the Draican, what he's done. Back to yer byres!*"

But only a few of them were going.

Nor were the half-bones coming on, none of them wanting to be the first to die so the others could overwhelm the man who'd somehow killed the First Bone.

Falca dodged the first of the rocks they began to throw, trying to force him back into the byre. He ducked his head to avoid another. He couldn't back in. Do that and they'd move around the byre, climb over the wall. He couldn't be everywhere, nor could Cofor and the woman. Scissors, a bone dagger and Rekkie's club couldn't stop them all, and they'd soon be reinforced by boneys from the houses farther away; the Mitoll, too, with his glave—no, not yet. There he was, still on the Mount, maybe six others on the steps, protecting him.

"*Falca!* Get inside!"

Another rock smashed against the byre's wall near the entrance where Cofor crouched, the woman behind him, by a heavy sack of vetch they'd been too exhausted—or fearful—to bring out outside.

"Slife, man! *get in!*"

But Falca wasn't going to do that. The byre was a cage...*like the one Lop had put him in; he and Gurrus, Styada and Ossa...at the krannog in the fens of the Rough Bounds. But then the young woman came out of...another byre on another Mount—Lop's Rise—and stood where the steps led down, just like here. Raleva Barra, they found out later. And she began to throw handfuls of gold and jewels from Lop's hoard-sack at his fenners below, shouting at them to take what was theirs, getting his dogs fighting amongst themselves for the gleaming scraps; giving him and the others time to escape from the cage...saving their lives though she didn't know then who she was saving....*

Cofor was pulling at his arm now, pleading with him to get inside the byre before he got hit, one rock all it would take to—

"Take this," Falca said, giving him the falcata. "Keep them away. Give me time."

"What? Falca!—" Cofor ducked a near miss to his head that cracked against the wall behind him.

Inside now, Falca said to the woman holding the dagger: "Follow me back out with with the augor skull. Will you do that?"

She nodded.

He lifted a sack of the hoarded vetch over his shoulder, and outside slumped the sack off onto Rekkie's corpse. The woman knelt at Falca's side, two fingers through an eye socket of the augor-skull helmet. Falca took the falcata from Cofor, then the skull from the woman. He flung it toward the halfies, scattering the nearest of them. A cruppie picked up the skull, and threw it down, the skull rolling away. Another cruppie got it, did the same, then turned and heaved it toward the Mount, over all the cruppies, hundreds of them now watching Falca slice open the sack with the falcata, and stuff a fistful of vetch into Rekkie's mouth.

He began flinging out more handfuls—in sweeping arcs for all to see; sowing the stony field of the Skellig. And he would have kept on, emptying the sack of vetch—and maybe himself of rage—if he hadn't seen the flare out of the corner of his eye, to his left and above: something that shouldn't have been there; something fiery dropping down the steps—a skidding torch that stopped, still burning, at the mid-steps landing for all below to see.

CHAPTER SIX:

THE LAST CRUPPIE

THEY MET IN the Glass Gardens one day in the spring.

She was fifteen, forbidden to go there, but she went anyway because Mehetha, an older girl and her best friend in the fhold, was getting married and pleaded with Simi to accompany her and help her pick out a virra—the traditional glass teardrop earring that she would give her husband-to-be, as he would give one to her.

Simi would have agreed without the pleading. She had long been curious about the affluent neighborhood, whose Rainbow Trellises she could see from a window of the third-storey room of the fhold, that she shared with a younger sister and three brothers. The neighborhood's frivolous and unnecessary glass sculptures were the usual reason given for the bans, but Simi knew the real one: there were several heterias in the district. And Simi wanted to go into one—not because she was tempted to become one of their highly-paid courtesans—far from it. The heteras were also exceptionally skilled in weaving, their 'spanner's-wing' looms a marvel of beauty and utility, so she'd heard. She wanted to see one. She wanted to become a weaver and not just a seamstress of common cloth like her mother, a repairer of rips and tears the males of the fhold brought home from the quarry.

The Glass Gardens, though, had many more glassmakers' shops than heterias. And it was in one of these shops that she met seventeen-year-old Ghoshen, already in the second year of his apprenticeship. She liked his smile, the way he met her eyes, seemed sure of himself, let her finish what she was saying before he spoke. He was handsome enough and tall for a Milat. And she had to admit to herself that the fact he would never work in the Slagtown quarry was…well, she'd seen enough of the calloused, crabbed, and gnarled hands of the older men in the fhold; hands her brothers would one day have.

After that first time, they never met in the Glass Garden again, always somewhere in the South Gets, Linnisheer's sprawling open-air market off Colza's Way. They'd both come to Milatum at about the same young age, it turned out.

His mother and father were farmers in the west and there had been trouble—the worst yet—with brigands coming across the Girvan Awe from Gebroan and then through the passes of the Skyshanks, to raid villages and farms of the fertile valleys of the Coombs. Ghoshen was sent to Milatum with his pregnant mother, to stay with her sister and brother-in-law who owned a small bakery in Linnisheer. As he was a member of the local militia which was to track down the brigands, Ghoshen's father had to stay in the Coombs.

Ghoshen never went back. His father was killed in the fighting; his mother died in childbirth and so did the baby. The sister, Solula, who had been at her side, said it was probably the cord wrapped around the baby's neck.

By their fourth meeting Simi knew she wanted to marry Ghoshen, and was certain he felt the same way. In a single day she twice heard the words, *I love you*, for the first time in her life. He was the one who said it first.

When she met Solula—who was in charge of the bakery's stall in the Gets—she was immediately drawn to the woman, and not just because Solula seemed to think that her nephew marrying an Attall girl was no more unusual than selling day-old bread for half the price of fresh. "We were hoping Ghoshie would take over the bakery," Solula said. "Yare well, there are ovens and then ovens, and it seems he'd rather sweat in front of a glassmaker's."

Simi's mother and father—and many others in the fhold—weren't happy about the match, especially her mother and brothers who thought Ghoshen soft as a sponge. Her father was worried about that too, but he gave his reluctant blessing. After all, marrying someone who wasn't an Attall was not strictly forbidden, though the person had to become one. Which Ghoshen did, saying it didn't matter what he wore or didn't, how he looked, what customs he had to adopt, what he believed in when he was working his trade. Showing a practical side that reassured Simi, he said becoming an Attall could only help his prospects since many of his customers would be Attals—glassmaking being one of the things they couldn't do themselves.

Ghoshen made both of their earrings, infusing the color of her choosing—sky-blue—into the teardrop glass.

The first issue of their union was the decision to eventually sell what they both would make in the same shop, Ghoshen's tongue plumping out his cheek when he said he was confident she'd find a weaver's appenticeship somewhere else than a Glass Gardens heteria.

The second was Gevret, when Simi was seventeen, delivered into the hands of Solula, and named after Ghoshen's father.

They were living on Cricklow Street at the time, apart from the fhold, which did not sit well with her family there. She told them there were practical reasons for that: proximity to Ghoshen's work in the Glass Gardens and he at a crucial point in his apprenticeship; and the fact that the fhold was overcrowded, with thirty families crammed into the three floors of the tenement.

She didn't—couldn't—tell even her father the other reason: she felt her dream of becoming a weaver would be safer apart from the fhold. It had been her home, but it was a place where dreams were considered a weakness. For a long time she thought something was wrong with her, to be so dissatisfied and questioning. But she finally decided it wasn't...her. How could dreams be considered a weakness, and faith a strength? They were too similar, weren't they? to be judged so differently.

There were other consequences of Cricklow Street, where Solula was visiting when Simi's water broke. So Gevret's first breaths were not those of an Attall. Had the first hands he'd felt been those of an Attall midwife, he would have had the Attall birthright—such was the law, the twelfth of Rusavarr's Thirty-two.

And if she, Ghoshen and Gevret had been living at the fhold and not on Cricklow Street that terrible day after the burning of the fleet at Snarlsome, they would not have had to risk getting to the refuge of the fhold. Afterwards, when she and Gevret got there she sent him inside, and still with her long-shank dagger took her place among all the rest guarding the fhold, over fifty of them; the young women and wives with knives and long-shanks; the men and husbands with heavy quarry tools—mauls, crush-hammers, pick-axes and pry-bars.

Few talked to her. That night, when her mother asked why she had come back, she said only that Ghoshen was gone. Her mother said nothing; the look she gave Simi was enough: *Of course he is. What did you expect? He's not really one of us....*

Her mother asked no more questions, as if Ghoshen wasn't worth the answers. Simi knew then it would be useless to tell her what really happened on Cricklow Street—and the only thing she could think of to do something about it.

She would have told her father; she would have asked him for money to bribe Meresguard constables and free Ghoshen from the Skellig, for she was sure that's where he'd been taken. She had some money, but not enough for bribes. But her father had been killed months earlier in an accident at the quarry.

Two days passed. Bullies picked on Gevret until he bloodied the nose of the worst tormentor. Most of the women in the fhold shunned Simi, and she in turn ignored their smug smiles. They didn't know what had happened to Ghoshen and to her, but they took pleasure nonetheless because *something* had: he wasn't with his wife and son.

She had to ask her mother for money, and never mind the feeling that she hadn't the right to do so. The longer she waited, the worse it would be for Ghoshen.

When she finally told her mother about Cricklow Street and asked her for help, she refused. "You're twice foolish, Simi—then and now. You made your choices and now you must live with the consequences. You insult me with your request. Money for a bribe? The mersers would only take it from you, laugh at you; at best defile you *only* with words, calling you a stupid *slag*, a bare-foot, short-hair *quiv...a slash*."

And then: "For you and the boy—and for us—it is best you leave the fhold and go back to Cricklow Street where you belong. You are wayward, your faith merely convenient, though you claim otherwise. Still, you are my daughter, so take with you what food you need as well as my promise to pray to Rusavarr on your behalf that the Skarrians—if they come—will pass you by."

ALL THIS WAY now and Simi could still feel her son's little fist at her waist, gripping the back of her belt.

When they'd left Cricklow Street she said: "Hold tight, no matter what you see or hear along the way, unless I tell you to let go, is it? I wish I could hold your hand, but I need both of mine for the torch and the long-shank."

Earlier that night, the fifth since they'd left the fhold, he'd stared at her, wide-eyed, as she broke off a leg of the table, scoring the end with the long-shank to prepare a torch, using ripped bedsheet cloth, soaking it with lamp oil. She'd lit the torch outside.

"But where will we eat when we come back with father?"

"Same place as always except that I'll hold up the corner while you two eat, then you take your turn—you're a strong boy."

She couldn't run with Gevret behind her and the slingsack of food and waterskin at her side, but they had to hurry nonetheless. He never complained about the pace, or the stink of the extra oily rags she'd stuffed in her belt. He never let go when they had to cross Colza's Way to get to the Glass Gardens; she thought that was the quickest way to the Meresguard castlet.

The lamps along the thoroughfare were not lit, probably hadn't been for days, so all was dark except for the bitten moons and the torch, one of the few in the seething mass of panic-stricken people surging from the west—had the Skarrians taken Delmarrion's Bridge?

She and Gevret were jostled, pushed aside, but they'd gotten across and he never let go, not even when they had to veer away from a fight: men pummeling and kicking someone who'd been ranting about...*getting what we deserve...punishment for the wicked....*

From the Glass Gardens it wasn't far—two streets south, maybe three. The night was warm and she felt the heat of the torch. She was sweating now, wanting to wipe it from her face, but she couldn't. They hurried through a Trellis, past the lagoon, the glass foliage of glass trees overhanging the winding pathways glinting in the moonlight, and Gevret asking her now what that sound was, that distant *eeeyisss...eeeyisss....*

She'd heard it too—seemed to be coming from the west—and she knew what it was because she'd heard it long ago when she and her family fled their village by the River Laggun in eastern Keshkevar:

Skarrian vairgs.

She was going to tell Gevret it was the wind playing through the Glass Gardens; instead she whispered that she didn't know.

This time there would be no fleeing the Skarrians and their Tholosian priests who had judged the Attalls of the river villages impure because they refused to submit to belief in Tholos. But whatever happened, she wanted to face it with Ghoshen at her side; all of them together again.

She couldn't yet see the guard tower of the castlet but it had to be close now. She told herself again that it was almost a certainty the mersers would have left to defend the walls, or gone to Mago's Bridge where the Skarrians would be trying to cross over the Cleave from Linnismorn and Linnishill—she'd heard the attack had begun in those districts.

So…the mersers wouldn't have locked the gate after they'd left—why do that?

And there it was, the guard tower. No one shouted at her from an embrasure.

Her torch illuminated only one half of the bronze scrolling of the royal triskell that would have been whole had the gate been closed.

Simi nudged Gevret; he'd come around to her side as she hurried through the opening in the gate. There was a chance that people might have sought refuge here, and there was no telling what frightened people might do. But her greater fear was that the mersers had freed the prisoners in the Skellig below the castlet, forced them to the walls or the Linnisheer side of Mago's Bridge to serve as a sacrificial buffer.

And if they had….

Mother and son kept on; Simi pleading wordlessly for the torch to stay lit until she found the way down, deeper within the castlet.

They passed through one gate, then another. Then: a large cage, a walkway above. She waved the torch low, in front of her…and saw it; where they brought prisoners: two hatches, the bigger one flanked by winches.

The smaller hatch had to be the one where the mersers shoved Ghosen—all prisoners—down. It was still shut, a short iron bar thick as Gevret's wrist through the big clasp.

They left them here…still a chance he's alive….

Simi belted the long-shank, took off the slingsack, set the torch in a bracket fixed to the surrounding cage, and knelt. The bar was heavy but loose enough to rattle. She wrapped two hands around the raised chock and pushed hard.

Thock.

"Mother, you did it!"

"Now the hatch, Gevrie."

She lifted the clasp, got up, gripped the wide handle bolted at the edge of the wooden, iron-strapped hatch.

Seeing her straining to lift it high enough, Gevret sank to his knees to push up. "Get back now," she said, wary herself of losing her balance and falling in.

Grunting, she pushed with all her strength. The hatch fell back with a loud thud to the stone floor of the cage.

"It smells bad," Gevret said.

"Breathe through your mouth when we go down, is it?"

She got the torch, and on her knees again peered over the edge of the maw. She couldn't see much else besides steps and a landing. But this prison was once a quarry she'd heard; there had to be many more steps down.

Suddenly she realized that a long flight of steps could be a serious problem.

Going down there with Gevret, one hand holding the torch, the other keeping him close wasn't the problem, dangerous as the descent might be. It was the prisoners below, maybe hundreds of them. They'd see the torch; they'd see her before she and Gevret got all the way down. And they'd rush to the steps, desperate to get out. They'd block her way down. She'd have to go back up.

And there was a risk that the prisoners, euphoric with imminent freedom, might overtake her and Gevret before they could get back up. Even if the steps had a railing....

Leave Gevret up here, go down by herself? No, she would not do that.

But there was another way.

"Gevrie, we have to stay up here. But I'm going to drop the torch down there. They will see it; they will know what it means. You and I will call for your father, and we'll wait for him to come up with all the others. We'll wait for him back at the gate, the second one."

"Where we left the moonlight?"

"Yes. He'll see us. Now, after I drop the torch, you shout as loud as you can, is it? and so will I."

Simi let fall the torch, and this time she held on to her son's belt so he would not fall through the hatchway as they leaned over.

"*GHOSHEN!*"

"*FATHER!*"

THE TORCH FLICKERED out on the landing where the steps switch-backed halfway down, and by then Cofor was caught in the midst of hundreds of cruppies surging toward the bottom of the steps, his initial exultation replaced by fear of the very ascent to freedom.

After the shock of seeing the torch that could only mean a merser had opened the hatch—for whatever the reason—he'd bolted like everyone else, and was already in the thick of the press when he heard Falca's shout above all the others': "*Cofor, wait! Wait!*"

He couldn't have stopped then even if he wanted to, would have been shoved aside, trampled. And he didn't *want* to wait. For *what?* For the merser above to change his mind, or have it changed for him by another, the hatch slammed shut again. Falca wanted to *wait?*—what was *wrong* with him?

Someone next to Cofor tripped on the first of the steps, stumbled and fell. Cofor tried to help him up, was pushed hard from behind, a lucky shove that smacked him against the sheer rock face, the inside of the steps. There was nothing on the outer side, why the cruppies—crowding two, three abreast on steps made for only a single file—were pressing in, fearing a fall. And cruppies on the inside were pushing back.

A man ahead of Cofor and to his right—cradling a bowl of vetch—was jostled, dropped the bowl; another cruppie slipped on it, lost his balance, and tumbled off the edge of the steps. Two others fell, shrieking, and then another. The line was slowing down, the man behind Cofor shouting, "*Keep moving! Keep moving!*" He pushed Cofor, got too close, cuffed his ankle, and for a panicky moment Cofor thought he would lose his balance, knock the man to his right off the steps.

After this he flattened himself against the rock face, side-stepping up, facing out...so tired...had to rest, but he couldn't, not now. He heard more screams; one below, one above.

Falca was right...how did he know?

The bottleneck near the top of the steps was bad—so close to freedom and almost at a standstill—but it was even worse after the final steps up to the hatchway and then through: the dark, the cage Cofor remembered, the cage so tightly packed he couldn't raise his arm; the stench worse than below. Someone's elbow hit him in the jaw, a foot stepped on his. The cries: *Is it open?...We're trapped...No, it is!...It's open!...Get out of my way!*

Cofor's release came with a shove that sent him sprawling. He got up, was knocked down again, scuttled away; got up again and collided with someone who yelped. "*What? you stabbed me, you fecking yape.*" He punched Cofor—a weak, glancing blow from an exhausted cruppie—and stumbled away

Cofor had forgotten he still had the scissors in his hand.

Enough moonlight shone through windows high in the walls to see scores of cruppies passing him by, some running, most moving slowly—the lame, the sick, the weary—but all of them reeking shadows moving toward the block of brighter moonlight ahead: the entrance gate of the castlet.

The way out.

Not far away, some men were talking:

"Where're the fecking nobs? They open us up and leave?"

"Who cares? We're out."

"They must have left some food up here."

"Yare, the nobs won't be eating on the walls, if it's the churgs what's coming over."

"There's enough below, what the boneys—"

"*I ain't* goin' back down."

"Don't have to, gotta be food up here I tell ya."

A hundred must have passed Cofor before he went on too, telling himself he'd wait at the gate for Falca.

They streamed toward the gateway, three and four at a time, momentarily silhouetted by the moonlight and then gone into the warmth of the night. But there were two who weren't moving at the edge of the gate, and as Cofor came closer he saw them: an Attall woman—the short hair, bare feet, a long earring and a dagger glinting in the moonlight; a sling-sack at her feet, a boy clinging to her side. She was calling that name he'd faintly heard below—*Ghoshen*—calling the name over and over as cruppies passed her by.

One of them stopped—it was Ribble from Hortwull's house, the sideways nose and drooping eyelid—and tried to grab the sling-sack.

The woman swiped at his hand with the long-shank. Ribble glanced at his wrist, fingered a smear of blood on his grin, showing a bone dagger now in his other hand. "You'll pay for that, you Attall slash."

Cofor stepped behind Ribble, lashed out with the scissors, scoring him in the back. Ribble yelped, spun around, and would have come at Cofor if the woman hadn't sliced his back again.

That was it for the cruppie—two against one. "You always were a fecking loonzie," he snarled at Cofor, and then shambled away.

Cofor returned the woman's nod of thanks. No doubt she expected him to move on, too, like all the others pouring out of the castlet into the tree-lined bailey, toward the outer gate and guard tower. When he didn't, she moved away a little.

"I won't bother you," Cofor said. "I'm waiting for someone, too."

"Soon as father comes up," the boy blurted out, "we're going home and hide from the Skarries—why do you have scissors?"

The mother *shushed* him.

"It's all right," Cofor said, "I used them to make things down there."

The cruppies were still coming out of the entrance gate, and the Attall woman kept calling out her husband's name.

And still no Falca.

Cofor was getting worried: no way he could have missed seeing him, the falcata. He should have been up by now, the steps crowded no longer. Falca was as hungry as everyone else...but how long did it take to heat some of the hoarded vetch? or eat what Rekkie had left already cooked up in his byre?

Or...*no*, he wouldn't have been fool enough to go after the Mitoll, storm the Mount. Then again, Falca had been in a fury at the end, throwing the skull, flinging out handfuls of vetch from the sack.

Something had happened.

Cofor swallowed hard. *Come on Falca, get up here...Cor, don't make me...please don't make me go back down to get you....*

Fewer cruppies were passing by, and Cofor was feeling desperate now to see a glint of the falcata, what he'd see first in the moonlight. After all Falca had done to get it...if he was capable of crawling up the steps and out, he'd have it with him.

Two older cruppies approached, the one propping up the other asking the Attall woman, "Is't churgs out 'ere then?"

"Yare. They're into Linnisheer, Delmarrion's Bridge. I dunt know about Mago's."

"What'd she say, Quilp? She talks soft."

"Said the whoresons're close."

The cruppie wheezed a laugh: "Sure they are. Tole you it was them's what it was."

"Looks like we ain't got nowhere to go, Snerri, but we gotta get there. C'mon with you."

Cofor felt like bolting past the two...find some place to hide...but here was the woman, asking another cruppie carrying a box if there were any more coming up. He ignored her, and full in the moonlight dropped the box, smashed open the lid with his fist, ripped away wood, and scooped out a handful of the contents—which he threw down in disgust. He seemed only now to notice Cofor, raising his hands. "Fecking nobs; up their arses with the lot. I'm s'posed to eat *candles?*"

The cruppie kicked the box and stalked off.

Cofor picked up a candle that had skidded to his feet, remembering now: *"That's what they were going to do with them."*

He didn't realize he'd said it—and loudly—until the boy whispered, "Mother, why is Scissorman talking to himself? he's not going to eat it, is he?"

She bent low and whispered something to her son as Cofor he walked over to the box and dropped the candle. Of course he wasn't going to eat the candle....

He wasn't even supposed to be the drover that day, two weeks into his work as the cooper's helper, but the man had taken sick so he had to do it: deliver a wagon-load of lidded boxes with rope handles—a special order—to Sulserra's edificia, the black-jest at the cooperage being that the thedrals there were doing more than what everyone assumed, since the boxes looked very much like the coffins the shop occasionally made for those who could afford a burial rather than cremation for a very young son or daughter.

He'd grumbled as much to an older thedral named Fetlar, who was accepting the last of the boxes because the day had been hotter than usual and there'd been twenty boxes, not counting two smaller ones of candles he'd been told to pick up at a chandler's shop on the way, and he'd carried every last one from the wagon and into the edificia—sweating up the steps—and then once inside, through the oculus atrium and along a central corridor, down more steps, into the bowels of the place and a storage room. None of the thedrals, start to finish, had offered to help him except a young one with spectacles. He waved him off, saying thanks anyway but this is the last of the lot.

Surprisingly, this Fetlar took no offense at the grutchy jest about coffins for wee wains, the graylock thedral saying somberly: "We must prepare as best we can for the inevitable."

He left the edificia thinking not about the thedral's strange comment, but about having an ale, telling himself he deserved one, just one, but fighting the temptation because he knew he'd want more than one, so he couldn't have the first—unless he wanted to go back to being a galloon who poured his life down his throat....

Cofor had no doubt at all now of what Sulserra's thedrals would be putting in those coffin-like boxes—and why; maybe doing it right now, making the hard choices of which to save, which to leave; then waterproofing the seams of the boxes with melted candle wax. Had they already made the other choices of who would go? Because surely most of them would have to stay above; only a few of them could go...below with the sealed boxes.

The way out.

Below.

Yare, that's where they were, or would be soon. Even if he left now, there probably wouldn't be time. And if there was, they wouldn't let him go with them. Who was *he*, after all?—a failed kiter, a hauler of boxes and corpses, a cruppie tailor who'd stitched mattresses and gloves for the king of the Skellig.

Still, it came as a shock to him…that even if he *could* go with them, he didn't *want* to. Not alone. This was almost as much of a shock as seeing the torch flaring high above on the steps in the perpetual twilight of the Skellig.

He heard the Attall woman telling her son they had to go down now because his father might be too weak to come up by himself or could be hurt.

"I'll go with you, if you want," Cofor said. "We'll find them both." *Though they're likely dead, your husband, and my friend.* "It's dark, but there's enough light from the dawnstone down there to find them."

Then he saw the falcata sliding into the moonlight.

THE BIG NORTHRON was thinner, his hair cropped, the reek and grime as bad as the other's, Scissorman. Bad as all the prisoners that had passed by.

He was shocked to see her, and so was she. However he'd come to be a prisoner in the Skellig, he shouldn't have had that crooked sword. She wanted to ask him if any more prisoners were coming up, but she knew the answer, had known it for a while now, that Ghoshen would never again embrace her and Gevret.

Scissorman was asking the northron what took him so long and he said that he waited until everyone who could leave had done so.

It was all she could do to obey Rusavarr's Twenty-second: *Weep Within.*

"The Mitoll's dead, then?" Scissorman said.

"Didn't see him killed but he won't be getting out. I'm the last. I barred the hatch," the northron said, glancing over at her and Gevret, as if he knew who they'd been waiting for. "If the scut isn't dead, the Skarries will see to that—it's them isn't it? what we thought."

"They're in the city; maybe Linnisheer."

Simi turned away, knelt by Gevret, taking his hand, whispering that they had to go down and find Ghoshen, and get his virra. Gevret nodded. He knew what it was, the boys at the fhold taunting him that his father wasn't really an Attall, had taken off his virra and abandoned him and his mother.

Gevret was facing away from the moonlight, and Simi grazed his face, his tears moistening her fingers. She wanted to hold him but she couldn't, not now. Time enough for that when they came back up, and waited here for whatever would come because there was no going back to Cricklow Street tonight. By now the Skarrians and their vairgs probably controlled most if not all of Colza's Way.

She had found and opened the hatch before, and she would do it again in the dark. And once they were below, Scissorman had said there'd be enough illumination. She stood, took Gevret's hand and said again—to the two men— what she'd said before to the northron: "May Rusavarr be with you." Then she and her son left the moonlight and passed into the darkness of the castlet.

Before they got far, the northron called after her—that deep voice— asking her not to go down, and the Scissorman adding something she didn't hear because Gevret had twisted around, saying, "We have to get father's virra. He wears it from his ear."

Of all the things to remember now, Simi thought of the last argument she'd had with Ghoshen: about their son's boldness in speaking, which Ghoshen encouraged. To her, raised an Attall, such boldness was unseemly for one so young. But she was proud of him now.

They went on, the northron calling louder now: "He doesn't have it anymore."

She stopped, turned. For a moment he was a tall shadow in the moonlit gateway, and then coming closer he was a shadow blocking it entirely. "Your husband's...virra was thrown away."

"How do you know?"

"That day...I saw him from across the street...what he wore. I didn't see him killed down there but I know why and who did it. That man is dead. Your husband was killed because some men were hoarding food and he didn't think that was right."

Simi's throat clotted. *Ghoshen...oh, my love....*

She'd known all along there was a good chance he might be killed simply because he was an Attall. But she felt a fierce pride that he hadn't been cowering when he was killed, that he hadn't begged for his life to be spared because he wasn't *really* a *slag*; and that his son now had heard his father had died well.

"But if you gotta go down to look for it," the northron said, "I'll go with you."

"So will I," Scissorman said.

"Thank you both, but no," she said. "There's another way."

It was not often taken, yet it meant the same thing, the mirror of the vows she and Ghoshen had pledged on their wedding day: if one of them died, the other would wear his or her virra also. If that was not possible, then neither would be worn.

She let go of Gevret's hand and took off her virra, feeling a deep welling in her heart for her husband, knowing that he would have done the same had she died first, her virra unrecoverable.

When they all were back at the gateway she put it in the slingsack. And she knew, too, that Ghoshen would want her and Gevret to go with these two men—strangers but good men—when the northron spoke about a place where they all might take refuge: the home of a woman named Rohaise Loquin who had a cottage on the steep hill above the Lazza. He was confident she would shelter them—though he couldn't promise she'd be there. But if she was not, he felt sure she would want them to have the refuge.

Then the Scissorman said there could be another way, possibly a way *out* of the city: Sulserra's edificia. Taking not Colza's Way to get there but the allure on top of the city wall. Both would be dangerous but the wall-walk was by far the quickest way to get from here to Sulserra's.

"That's where Father took us once to show me what books are," Gevret said. "Please Mother, I don't want to go back home without him. I want to go where the Scissorman says we can if we hurry."

"I think the boy's decided for us," the northron said, and smiled.

Simi squeezed her son's hand. "If we're all going together we should know names."

Gevret said his before she could say it for him.

CHAPTER SEVEN:

ON THE ALLURE

MERESGUARD OPTOS STAFFA Loyasa stood at the allure's chest-high outer parapet. His pike, resting at a slant on his shoulder, had two flanges to push against for better thrusting—one near the butt, the other a third of the way down. He wiped his sweaty hands on his bloody trews, thinking that if somehow he survived this night and all that followed, one thing was certain: never again would he hear just the crashing of the Kingsmere surf far below because it sounded like a stalker; louder, but the same.

Yare, and for that matter, so did the rustling of the wind through the terraces of trees in Phelonia's Forest behind him. Little chance then, that he— or any of the others with him on the allure—would hear a stalker coming up, with churgs on its trailing silk line.

Which was likely.

Gelcacus had thought so, whispering the order, eyes half-shut as Stoba twisted a crimp around his forearm so he wouldn't lose any more blood from the hand he'd lost to a Skarrian's axe: *Take three men...all I can spare...leave the oikoe, need him here...go down the wall, no farther than the Terraces. They've failed twice here at the Cleave—barely—and may attempt to breach the wall over there...now that the pharos has gone dark. Do what you can, Optos, but if they...one of you must get back here to warn us so we're ready for them on our flank....*

Loyasa couldn't take a firehoop; none were left. Nor arrows for bows. One pike. Tofer had the bucket of oil and a torch for *one* stalker—but if more crawled up the wall...you couldn't set a stalker on fire with only a torch; had to have oil to splash on the bristles. Otherwise, it was like trying to light a fire without kindling. Everything that could be soaked in oil, set afire and flung at the stalkers to snag on the bristles—caps and tunics and trews from the dead and some from the living—had already been used.

It was even darker now that the pharos was gone. Its beacon had illuminated the churgs' last assault across the Cleave at Neskayuna that had been repulsed with heavy losses—no one had reckoned the Skarrians would also use the chains to get across, like rats using a fecking mooring line.

Either the churgs had doused the pharos or the soft coal had run out. But even with the pharos and the fires on Mago's Bridge where the Skarrians were—for now—stopped, it had been hard to see the black stalkers coming up the steep rocky slope below the wall. And if you looked over the parapet as Terros Vannion had….

Loyasa had been three men down, separated from Vlix, when Vannion looked, taking a torch from Kezlis. Such was the fighting down the line she didn't hear the *eeeyisss*. Loyasa didn't see the stalker's serrated mandibles take off her arm at the shoulder, but he saw the falling arm and the hand still gripping the torch.

He had a different pike now than the one he'd thrust into the eyes of the stalker which fell away—but not before its mandibles snipped the pike in half.

The night air was warm, carrying the smell of the tide-wrack below and not enough of the sweet scent of Phelonia's Forest and its Terraces behind him. Between the inner and outer parapets, the allure was wide enough for six men to walk abreast, and certainly wide and dark enough now for one man and an oikoe to keep on walking while they still could.

Except for the smoke in the air, the pike and the guttering hope he'd last till dawn, the night could have been any in his first year in the Meresguard when he'd been assigned the patrol of the Linnisheer wall—Orphic Gate to the Cleave and back again; this before he became an oikoe handler.

In all that time since, the branches of trees hanging over the inner parapet hadn't been cut back, and he heard the same faint *whick-whick* of the windmill at the bottom of the Terraces, the vanes no doubt disengaged but still turning.

Helega….

For two nights that one week he'd passed her at the same place farther up the wall, close to the Eight Steps. She was older than he was, though how much was hard to tell, the night having something to do with that. On the third they got to talking, leaning against the parapet, the Kingsmere surf far below filling in the pauses. She said nothing about why she was alone on the allure. The fourth night they wound up on one of the terraces. A midnight slide. He was young, the lost time for the patrol easily made up. He heard her laugh only once, when he told her about how the windmill-powered screw brought water up to the top terrace from the pool below. She was at the same place on the allure the next night, and this time there were no words, nor the next; she just took his hand. After that night he never saw her again....

The wind had picked up, making Loyasa turn to check the archway behind him, where he and Helega had gone through that last night, holding hands. The rustling of the tree branches hanging over the inner parapet was also like the *eeeyisss* of a stalker, that sliding of one mandible over another. What they did sensing a threat? Like he'd trained Vlix to do, curling the tail over the body, and keeping it straight out, rigid, the tip pointing at the source of danger.

While the allure was dark toward the west, there was a glow of a fire. The Orphic Gate, probably. To the east, darkness instead of the pharos beacon. Phelonia's Forest on the Terraces hid the view to the north. Word was, the churgs had taken Mereshaven, had been halted at the inferno of the South Gets along Colza's Way, Linnisheer holding on—for now. Probably the churgs had taken all the Linneses and bridges, except Mago's. Which was why they would ferry more men and stalkers across the Cleave on those flatboats they'd use to cross the Kingsmere south of the east causeway on the first day.

Or bring some farther west.

Here.

Vlix returned from his third patrol so far, ranging to Eogan, the farthest away from Loyasa along the parapet. Loyasa didn't have to tell the oikoe to do it again. He watched Vlix padding away, his white coat gray in the moonlight. Loyasa felt better when he was close, but that wasn't possible. A stalker could be coming up anywhere. The oikoe could sense one of the fecking things before anyone heard it—smell the churgs too, on the silk line.

Loyasa had taken Vlix anyway. What was Gelgacus going to do? Dun him a rank? Send him to the Skellig for insubordination?

The four of them were well apart from each other on the allure, Tofer the closest to Loyasa but back in the archway leading to the Terraces. Loyasa had told him to keep the torch hidden. No point in letting the churgs know anyone was on the allure here. Vlix would know if a stalker was coming up while it was still crawling up the steep slope of the escarpment below the wall. And Tofer would need only moments to get to the outer parapet, dump the oil from the bucket, drop the torch and…one less stalker. And the churgs on the trailing silk line—it was usually ten of them, depending on the size of the stalker—would plummet to the rocks below.

Loyasa still didn't know the name of the royal marine. The glave had come up to the wall from Mago's Bridge, his dented helmet missing a sidepiece, the bronze discs of his corselet smeared with blood. Asked him his name but the marine just shook his head.

Loyasa couldn't see Eogan beyond the marine. He was a bandy-legged merser from the Linnisheer castlet that had been abandoned the day before, the only guard there not killed or wounded in the two Skarrian assaults across the Cleave from Linnismorn.

Vlix was probably past Eogan now, would be coming back soon, and when he did, Loyasa decided to send the oikoe down the allure past where he was now, make sure there'd be no surprises coming over the wall in that direction. Which—he hoped—maybe wasn't likely as the slope was higher and steeper rising up to the Eight Steps tower, the rocks a formidable obstacle— nothing like the Cleave. While a stalker could crawl over the rocks, the churgs themselves would have a more difficult time.

And when Vlix did come back, maybe….

Maybe they'd go together. Skelter while their luck still held.

He'd done more than his share, hadn't he? It was only a matter of time before the churgs had all of Linnisheer, too. So, find some place to hide and maybe later, *somehow*, get out, cross the Narrows at the royal Chase in Linnisvale; yare, find a piece of driftwood big enough for him and Vlix and get to the mainland. Get to Syarra….

There he was now, Vlix, on his back this way, almost behind the marine.

No…we have to stay, Vlixie, you and I….

He couldn't skave the others…live the rest of his life knowing he'd abandoned them; every night closing his eyes and seeing Flerrik stepping in front of him and taking the spike of the Skarrian war- axe that—

Vlix was motionless, the long tail stiffened out over his body, pointing past the marine at the parapet. Loyasa thrice tapped the butt of the pike, the signal for Tofer. The marine who stepped back from the parapet, did the same with his cut-shaft glave for Eogan down the line.

Loyasa moved toward Vlix, and if he hadn't paused to dry his sweaty hands again he would have been splashed with oil. Tofer was halfway across the allure with the heavy bucket of oil when the handle broke, the bucket thumping on the stone, oil gushing out toward the wall.

Vlix leaped—a four-legged hop—away from the stream, the oil all but useless now. Tofer's torch revealed his indecision about what to do with it. "Optos, should I—"

"*Yes...now!*"

The whoosh of flame and heat forced Loyasa back a step. The fire blocked him from the others—and the stalker coming over the parapet now. Bristly forelegs, thick as wharf pilings, rose and then fell at the bulbous joints, the pads smearing the stone with the secretion that gave the thing its purchase. The pointed, serrated mandibles appeared, sliding over each other, the *eeeyisss* so piercing it pressured Loyasa's ears.

The marine was backing away—on the verge of skeltering? No, the stalker was avoiding the fire and the marine was giving the beast a wide berth—and now he rushed back to the parapet, hacking with his glave at the lengthening line of hawser-thick silk.

Loyasa retreated from the fire, moved to where Tofer had been, couldn't see him, the stalker filling the allure. A leg kicked aside the burning bucket. Vlix darted past it, turned with a snarl by Loyasa, his tail whipping around, slapping against the pike, Loyasa feeling the tremor in the shaft. The stalker's carapace glistened in the firelight, the scissoring mandibles half as long as the pike.

They'd done it before: he going low, Vlix high. He crept closer, trying not to gag at the stench—a barrel of sour wine—and thrust with the pike at the high meat of the forelegs, then under the carapace over the abdomen. Vlix leaped high over the mandibles, his teeth and claws ripping at the hideous constellation of eyes. He screeched, furiously digging at the stalker's eyes... and then he was a blur hurtling past Loyasa, skidding on the allure, half of him gone, back legs and tail.

Enraged, Loyasa stabbed harder, thrusting the pike under the carapace, wrenching it out, stabbing again and again. Close now...too close. He didn't care. The writhing, severed end of the silk line was too long—some churgs surely had gained the parapet.

Blinded, gushing blood made yellow by the firelight, the stalker moved toward the Terrace archway, two of its legs dragging, the mandibles no longer scissoring, the beast dying. Another leg scored the side of Loyasa's face before he could duck away, the bristles pulping his left eye, crushing a shoulder, snapping the pike in half. He staggered back, dropping it as the stalker collapsed in the archway.

The churg was coming toward him through the smoky fire, a head impaled on the spike of his war-axe that had a blade opposite the frowning spike. He stopped to put a boot on Tofer's head, yanked it off the spike, flung it by the hair. What was left of Vlix stopped the head from rolling farther.

"Now *you*, slorrie." The churg's head seemed to be on fire, but it was only the yellow plaits of his hair woven through the stalker carapace mesh of his helmet, black like his breastplate.

Loyasa had his mace out, left hand, couldn't raise his right arm...his shoulder. The Skarrian saw his ruined eye, was trying to herd him toward the wall where he'd have no room for the mace. Loyasa wouldn't let him, swung the mace—a sweeping strike to the knee, his only hope to shatter it, cripple him—but too slowly. The churg easily side-stepped the left-hand effort, whirling in the same motion to deliver a vicious blow that Loyasa managed to block with his mace. But the shaft of the war-axe struck his head, stunning him, his back colliding against the parapet.

He tried to deflect the next strike but was too late to stop the burst of searing heat in his belly.

He screamed, didn't hear it, only the grunt of the churg and the dull clang of the mace dropping on the allure. The Skarrian stood in front of him, hands on the shaft of his war-axe, head down, his eyes bulging, as if wondering why he couldn't rip out the spike...why the front of his breastplate was—

Loyasa was falling away...and so was the churg who collapsed on the shaft, levering it out, falling on top of it, his right arm hitting Loyasa in the eyes.

The arm didn't move. Loyasa feebly pushed it away, and for a moment he thought the man kneeling beside him was the marine, or Eogan, but they had to be either dead or gone.

Loyasa couldn't see much, only the hilt of the falcata...the big hands, one over his knee.

The rapparee.

"You...you got it back."

The Draican couldn't hear him, lowered his head. Loyasa whispered it again.

"Only because you sold it where I could," the rapparee said.

"I...it's...not what you think...she's safe now."

The Draican nodded as if he understood. Loyasa wanted to tell him but there was no time—he heard the faint *eeeyisss* of another stalker coming up somewhere down the allure, and so did the Draican, a glance to his right. Then another voice, a woman's, not far away, calling to him, telling him to hurry. Loyasa thought the voice was his sister's, but that wasn't possible. He'd watched Shulia leaving through the Orphic Gate, took her there himself...by now in Syarra.

"I have to go," the Draican said.

What was his name?—Loyasa couldn't remember. "What you said then... was it all true? the kraken?"

He nodded.

Loyasa felt a hand on his shoulder and then the Draican was gone.

The Sisters were blurry high over the rustling trees of the terraces.

Loyasa was sure he was already dead, somehow managed to kill the churg himself.

The Draican had never been here. No more here than that woman's voice...a woman on the allure?

Maybe that was what it was like...nothing more than a dream in which you say things...see things that make no sense, aren't possible, never happened... like the Draican getting out of the Skellig with that beauty of a falcata that paid for Shulia's escape.

But he had to know before the stalker got him, the *eeeyisss* louder; neither the sound of the surf crashing against the rocks far below the allure nor the wind through the terraces of trees.

Reaching over took all the strength he had left. He felt the blood seeping out of his belly as he ran a shaking hand over the back of the Skarrian...looting the body...a rapparee now, too, looking for something to take with him.

He found it, the blood-soaked tunic leather, the rip where the falcata had entered, then thrust through the heart, all the way through, pushing out the breastplate the churgs made of stalker carapace.

Neither he nor anyone else on the allure had a blade like that, nothing that could have done what the Draican had.

And before the Sister moons vanished forever, Optos Staffa Loyasa wondered why it had taken him this long to realize why Helega had been alone on the allure the night he met her...but at least for a week, anyway, he'd delayed her from ending her life by jumping off the parapet.

CHAPTER EIGHT:

SULSERRA'S

F ALCA CRAWLED ON his belly through a pool of stalker blood, dead meat the size of two horses over him, the stench of it as bad as the Chute. Twice now he'd had to shave the underside of the stalker's collapsed legs with the falcata—short, *careful* backhand strokes—so he could get through without the bristles snagging at his head and clothing.

Mandible teeth tore at his trews. He pushed away a pendulous gobbet of... *something* hanging from an eye bigger than a dinner plate. That oikoe must have clawed the eye—the mutilated oikoe he'd seen as he and the others huddled in the dark near the archway, where branches draped over the allure's inner parapet.

He'd had to kill the Skarrian before the churg saw them; had to do it quick—he was in no condition for anything more. But he was too late to save the merser, and only realized after who it was. What was his name? If only they'd gotten here sooner....

Loyasa...his oikoe was Vlix...

If Falca had been the Skarrian crawling out from under, he would have been dead before he got to his knees: Simi to his right with the long-shank; Cofor on the left with the scissors, tucking them away now as Falca stood, the boy saying, "We were worried you wouldn't be able to get through. You're bigger than we are." Sounding like he was much older than he was.

"This way; we have to hurry," Cofor said, for probably the tenth time since they left the merser castlet. He took the lead again, Falca thinking once more, as he had when Gevret as much as made the choice for them, that if there was scant hope either way they went—Rohaise Loquin's cottage or this edificia—at least Cofor knew how to get to what little chance they might have.

Or so he said.

Once after he participated in a scrybing on the city wall where it widened at the entrance to the Cleave, he'd gone down the Terrace steps—a quicker way home—and saw the pedestrian bridge that linked the terraces of Phelonia's Forest to the western entrance of Sulserra's. But he'd only been *inside* the edificia the one time he'd delivered those coffin-like boxes.

Cofor was a shadow up ahead in the Sisters' moonlight that shone through breaks in the tree canopy. Still, it was enough for Falca to see the glimmer of Simi's long-shank in one hand, her son's hand in the other.

They walked quickly along the low wall that ran the length of this narrow promenade of bricks that seemed about as wide as the allure on the other side of the parapet. Wind moaned through the trees that must have been planted a hundred years ago below this, the topmost of these terraces; a forest of them, the serried rows separated by walkways. Cofor said he had to stop on the steps that day to let thedrals pass by. "Maybe ten of them, and only two looking where they were going; the others were eating or had books in their faces."

Falca paused twice to make sure Skarrians weren't following them, the ones coming over when he'd left Loyasa. No telling if they'd seen him crawling under the dead stalker at the archway. But he saw no Skarrians now, heard only the creaking of branches, and the *whick-whick* of a windmill's turning vanes somewhere below.

Up ahead, Cofor called out: "Here they are. Careful! they're steep."

The steps were mottled gray where moonlight wasn't blocked by the adjacent trees of Phelonia's Forest. The low wall on the right matched the descending angle of the terraces. Beyond the wall seemed to be a wide gap, what was probably an alley below. Falca couldn't see the footbridge yet, that Cofor had said was about halfway down and linked one of the terraces to the western entrance of Sulserra's. Dark windows spotted the upper facade of the white-washed edificia.

If the postern entrance was locked....

Falca didn't think it would be. Sulserra's was close to the Cleave, Cofor said. The thedrals would have fled, wouldn't have locked all the entrances, prepared to defend their edificia.

Defend with what? Books and scrolls? Thedrals weren't soldiers or mersers. Sure, they would have skeltered—and why bother locking up after you had?

But maybe not all of them had gone.

Maybe some had stayed—the lucky or chosen—preparing to escape with the boxes Cofor had once delivered to the edificia.

Boxes filled with books, not candles.

Maybe....

Falca glimpsed the glow off to his right, over the near wall of the footbridge. Cofor ran ahead. When Falca made the turn after Simi and Gevret, there he was at the base of one of the sculptures of caryatids flanking the sides of the bridge, picking up a luneling. By the time Falca reached the others, Cofor had already wrapped it around his wrist: what some thedral had discarded when he got outside; what they would need inside Sulserra's.

But from the middling brightness of the lune's greenish-yellow light, it had been dead for a while, the illumination scarcely reaching the stone book the caryatid was holding.

They would have to hurry before the luneling's light faded.

TULLZIE MAGRUNE SAT on the edge of Sulserra's six-sided plinth, facing the main entrance to the edificia, waiting for the Skarrians to come.

Everyone was gone—edificiates, thedrals, refectory cooks, annex custodians, luners—everyone except him and Sulserra. She wasn't saying much about it, sculpted of whinstone as she was; a rare kind of blushed marble, so he'd been told once. But Tullzie had a good idea of what she would be saying if she could, seeing as how he knew her top to bottom better than any of the women he'd had when he was younger, even the few he hadn't paid for. How could he not? dusting her off like he did—which maybe wasn't always necessary but no one had ever told him not to, probably because they could see he was careful with the padded ladders.

She sat behind him, on a stone settee so big it would have filled his room in the annex, reading a book bigger than his door. She, too, was facing the entrance of her namesake edificia, her tresses higher than the grand staircase behind her that led up to the second floor.

And higher still, the oculus shaped the formless moonlight outside into a circular silvery pool on the tessellated floor of the atrium, the plinth an island, with Tullzie and Sulserra its only inhabitants.

He'd sat here before, those nights over the years he couldn't get to sleep, sometimes seeing a thedral who couldn't either—had a lot on their minds, oyah—looking for this book or that scroll among all the thousands in the niches of the shelves on the second-floor gallery that curled above and around the atrium; or searching for one in particular among all those below in the reading rooms beyond the pillars. The thedrals—sometimes a younger edificiate eager for advancement—were shadows, their presence revealed only by a luneling or two they'd draped over a shoulder. No candles or lamps—the Big Rule: any open flame was strictly forbidden, except in the annex.

No lunes now, maybe never again. Everyone was gone, everything dark. Mostly.

Still, he was pleased at the amount of moonlight coming through the oculus and the high windows; as if he, Tullzie Magrune, was somehow responsible for the Sisters' chaste offering. Yare, a foolish thought...but maybe not so much. After all, he'd cleaned the oculus only two weeks ago, as he had every month for twenty years. All the window glass, too.

Before that he'd been living for a while on a mid-level terrace in Phelonia's Forest, which was probably the reason why the thedrals took him in: they got tired of having to step over him on their morning walks there. In those days he slept late—what was there to get up for? Though why they just didn't get a nob to roust him like he'd expected to happen eventually, was still a wonder after all these years. All he knew for sure was that a senior thedral, Dattic Metagnion, asked him if they gave him a bed inside, would he work for his keep? Tullzie said he'd try, but doing what? He had no skills other than a dock-heave's and he wasn't going back to that. Dattic said well, perhaps you can give us better light inside. Tullzie had no idea what he was talking about but he found out soon.

Even after Dattic died five years later, Tullzie stayed on because there was always grime and dust inside, and smoke silt and the droppings of gulls and spanners to clean off the oculus from the outside, the high windows, too. Full-time work it was, because once he'd gone through one course of cleaning it was time to begin the next.

Maybe he wasn't afraid of heights because he didn't know any better. Maybe about anything. *Sair simple*, they'd say when he was young, shaking their heads. *He's gleggy, that one.*

No one here had ever called him that, but he probably was. Nah, not maybe; he was. In all the time here, surrounded by thousands of books and scrolls, he'd never learned to read. For a while the thedrals tried to teach him; Vaience Loquin, one of the younger thedrals when he came here, tried hardest.

But he wasn't interested. It was enough for him if someone *told* him what was in a book; what the words meant on the inscriptions carved all around the sides of the plinth he was sitting on now; or any of the banners of words carved on the walls, on the pillars that held up the roof. Words everywhere and he couldn't read a one. Didn't bother him nane because he was strong, oyah; always had been. And still fit, doing what he'd done for twenty years. And when you thought about it, how many words did you need to know if you know you have a home, right?

Had his own room in the annex, too. Had to keep all his ropes and buckets in there, the small ladder too. And his long-handled scrub brushes, the cloths, the soaps and vinegar—but for all that still his own room. Even the edificiates and some of the thedrals didn't have theirs, slept in dormitories. But he had his, oyah, and took his meals with them in the refectory like he was one of them, called him by his first name, they did....

Tullzie thought he heard someone on the second floor, beyond the grand staircase, and got up, walked around the plinth. Was it Eban and Melusine, come back to try again? The sounds faded and Tullzie sat back down where the edificiates had pleaded with him to go with them. *Please, Tullzie! They'll be coming soon. As bad as it is out there, it will be worse for you in here....*

They were eddies so they were probably right. He'd heard stories about the Skarries, what they did to people like him, just as he'd heard the thedrals talking about what they would do to the edificia. But he wouldn't leave Sulserra. Besides, where else could he do what he'd been doing here for so long?

He thought that when they did come, he'd hear them them on the broad steps outside, and then see the torches, but it was the other way around: the moonlit high windows along the northern side of the atrium brightening to yellow and then a red-orange glow. Then came the shouts, the first of them indistinct but then louder:

"For Tholos!"

"Burn the impure!"

"There are no others books but *The Vate*!"

Tullzie Magrune stood, the carving knife he'd taken from the refectory in his left hand; in his right the sharp wall hook used to spit lunelings for light in the corridors. The hook had been coming loose anyway, and now he intended to spit a Skarrian with it before the rest of them killed him.

FALCA MOVED SLOWLY, sliding his hand along the wall to his right, his scabbard scraping along this corridor wall of the cellar—as far as they'd got before the lune faded out completely by the doorway of a storeroom.

He cursed, but not because it was so dark he stepped on the useless luneling Cofor had dropped.

He smelled smoke.

So did the others.

For there to be smoke down here, the edificia had to burning above—all those books and scrolls in the shadowy rows of high, niched cases, the fading luneling illuminating only the closest of what had to be thousands of books and scrolls.

Darkness could hide fear and despair, but not in voices.

What now?

To go back they'd have to go all the way up to the second floor where they'd come in through the western postern, because surely the Skarrians must have come in the front. And even if the fire wasn't raging yet, that only meant there'd be Skarrians up there—everywhere—tipping over the cases, adding to the pyre, probably more than one, the flames providing all the light for them to see and kill two men and a boy, and drag the woman outside.

Still, Falca would have made the attempt—and Cofor said he would also—but Simi refused, saying they'd come this far together and one way or the other would finish it together. "Gevret has seen enough; I won't have him see more. Either he sees this darkness for an end, or his freedom."

They began crawling now to something that couldn't be seen, but *had* to be there: a doorway, and steps leading down.

Falca felt a hand graze his leg—Gevret behind him, then Simi. All of them on hands and knees, brushing along the corridor wall. Cofor coughed somewhere on the other side of the corridor. Simi had asked him earlier if he remembered seeing another staircase at the end of the corridor. He hadn't, only the thedral by the storeroom. All he'd wanted to do then was deliver the last of the coffin-like boxes and be done with it.

What had that thedral said to Cofor? *We must prepare as best we can for the inevitable....*

He'd predicted the inevitable all right: the edificia a furnace above, and the smoke down here getting worse.

But the rest of it?

Falca sensed the opening of a doorway on his right. A storeroom? He crawled in, feeling for the edge of steps. Finding none he backed out into the corridor, Simi's and Gevret's coughing his beacons in the blackness. He crawled on, wondering if he'd just sealed their fates by not searching the room more thoroughly...if he'd just missed sweeping his hand over the first step of a staircase.

No, the thedrals wouldn't have built a way out in a storeroom accessible to all.

We must prepare as best we can for the inevitable....

We? Falca thought.

That couldn't mean *all* of the thedrals. Because however they'd prepared for the inevitable, it didn't seem likely that all of them could go. But all of them would *want* to—who wants to be left behind?

Which meant...what?

Had to mean that either Sulserra's residents had the discipline of Wardens or...the way out had been kept a secret from all but a few, who told the others to...*Leave...go! Take a luneling and may Roak deliver you from the Skarrians out there...* and then the select few would...what would they do?

You could see anything in the darkness, like Gurrus had with his visions, his...kesslakors. And Falca had one too, or thought he did, deep beneath the keep of Scaldasaig; someone else behind him too—Shar Stakeen.

And what he was seeing now in the blackness, his eyes stinging from the smoke...*was a door that one of the thedrals unlocked, tossing aside the lock that would never be needed again, as Cofor tossed the luneling. But some of the thedrals carried lunes that hadn't faded out...and more carried boxes heavy enough to require two thedrals to bring each one down....*

Falca crawled on, the smoke getting worse, feeling it in his throat. Behind him, Gevret and Simi were coughing more now.

He felt the boy's hand leave his trews.

"Here, Mother, I found something."

"What?—Oh Gevrie!"

"My hand found it."

It took a few moments for Simi to move up, find Falca's hand and put the key in his palm.

"May I keep it?"

"Yare, and whispers now, is it?—and stay close; we'll have steps. Give me your blessed hand."

They were on a landing; ahead in the blackness—a stride, two?—was the first step down. Falca felt for the door he'd opened, and closed it, the hinges creaking, sealing out the smoke. Somewhere on the corridor they'd left was the lock a thedral had tossed away along with the key.

He thanked Roak...Rusavarr...the Fates at their Loom Eternal...and Cofor for making his deliveries then and now...and Gevret—the boy calmer than any of them in the darkness—for finding the key, though they all would have reached the door at the end of the corridor. Only another few crawls ahead it was.

And he thanked the last thedral who'd gone through here for not barring the door, because there *was* a bar on this side; he felt it. But why bother barring the door?—the Skarrians wouldn't be coming down, nor any other thedrals.

He thanked them all in the time it took Simi and Cofor to find and grip his belt from the back, so he wouldn't fall as he tapped his foot to find the first step. He stretched his arms, leaning carefully to the left, and found it: the cold, roughly hewn side of this passage. One side would do to help him keep his balance though he sensed these steps were narrower than those in the Skellig.

Then the next step...and another...a third—feeling for the edge of each before taking it, and telling himself...*don't think of anything else but the next*....But he couldn't help it, not when there soon came the faintest tang of salt in the chilly, moist air. A chute is what it was—though not to the Reef of Bones. This one had steps that were gradually spiraling down to the sea, the Kingsmere. But if the thedrals had left, a Chute it would be. The food and water in Simi's slingsack wouldn't last long.

Falca kept going down…down; the blackness giving way to shadows: he could see the steps curling away to to his right, moisture brightening the passage walls with a dull sheen of luneling light.

They're down there…they're still here….

The smell of the sea, tide-wrack, was stronger now. That rotten-fruit smell of lunelings. And something burning. Then: thumps, grunting….

Falca stopped when he heard the voices. He turned, gesturing silence to the others, but Simi was already doing that, a finger to her lips, Gevret nodding. If smiles had sounds, Cofor's would have been a roar.

Falca slowly drew out his falcata, took a few more steps, stopped again just shy of the misshapen portal, falcata tight against his leg, back pressing against the cold-sweat stone.

And peeked.

Four of them were scooping melted wax from a pot set atop a smoky brazier, using flat-end utensils to smear the wax into the seams of one of the four lidded boxes nearby. Spreading wax dripping down down the sides of the box, a luneling coiled on the lid. More lunes on the other three boxes provided additional light.

Falca was close enough to see the gobs of wax they'd spattered here and there on their light-blue tunics, the darker waist-length mantles, even the longer hair of two female thedrals.

"We'll not have enough to finish this one," said the nearest of the thedrals who had their backs to Falca.

"It's my fault," said another. "I should have told you to bring more candles from the annex when we got the food and water. All we can do now is finish up with what we have—and hope the Kingsmere is calm for the boats."

"And sweep the oars like we've done it before."

There was no movement in Falca's smile that these thedrals could notice, nor his eyes as he looked around the chamber, which was scarcely more than a wide rocky ledge carved out of the Linnisheer escarpment. Enlarged from what had been a sea cave? A discoloration marked the high-tide level on the walls. Shells and seaweed littered the ledge.

To his left, a ramp led down to a small jetty and four boats tied by long mooring lines to stone bollards. Two of the boats seemed to be already loaded with boxes, and on each of these boats two thedrals sat on oar benches, a luneling atop the box nearest the bow. Thedrals who looked younger than the others were loading the third boat.

Falca made a quick count: eight thedrals down there, including the ones on the boats. Four on the ledge. Out of the twelve, three—no, four—women.

He slowly leaned back, then turned to Cofor who had his scissors out, and Simi her long-shank. Falca held up his hands to indicate the numbers—which weren't good but could have been worse. Some of the younger thedrals had knives tucked in their belts. Only bread-cutters, these thedrals but still, no telling how they'd react to him reiving that last, empty boat. Falca didn't want to hurt anyone but he *was* going to take that boat, and if he had to put his falcata to the throat of one of the thedrals up on the ledge, so be it—that seemed the only way to get those thedrals down at the jetty there out of the way.

Unless....

He peeked again. *Wait for 'em to do it....*

The thedral nearest to Falca peered into the pot, shook his head, muttering something about putting mantles on the other boxes to keep the water off. Tossed the flat scoop in the pot. *Clang.* The other thedrals did the same, one summoning those below to come up and get the rest of the boxes.

Falca drew back, cupped his hand to whisper into Cofor's ear. "There's a ramp down to the water, one empty boat. You three run for it. Make sure the thedrals in the other boats stay there; I'll handle the rest. Tell Simi, softly now."

While Cofor did—more whispers the busy, grunting thedrals couldn't possibly hear—Falca took one last look: eight of them now clustered by the four boxes near the brazier.

He glanced back at Cofor and Simi—tight lips, deep, silent breaths—and grinned, to let them know he was sure they could do this. But there was no time to whisper that the boat down there wouldn't be the first he'd stolen—from Wardens no less.

He nodded—*Ready?*—and walked quickly into the chamber.

The startled thedrals gasped, shouted, dropped the boxes; the closest of the eight backing away from the intruder with a sword. Falca was halfway to the top of the ramp before two of the thedrals drew knives.

"Stay where you are, all of you!" Falca yelled as Cofor, Simi and Gevret passed behind him. "No one's getting hurt, but we're taking that empty boat."

"What?—no!"

"You must not do that!"

Falca paused at the top of the ramp to give Cofor, Simi and Gevret time to reach it. More thanks to Roak, this time for giving Falca thedrals, not Wardens;

for their not having the wits to spread out so they could close on him; and for none of them wanting to be the first to do so.

A sputtering from one of the boats: "You threaten with…scissors?"

Cofor: "Yare—now sit down."

Simi: "And this." The long-shank.

Falca backed away, side-stepping, the falcata ready to discourage any thedral from acting on his outrage. Were those cleats on the ramp? All the better for footing if they charged down.

A thedral—one of the women—stepped ahead of the others. "Please… if you take a boat there will not be enough room for—"

"There's room, but not for all boxes."

"You don't understand! The books are priceless. Out of all we had, *these* are the ones that *must* be saved. Cyro's last volume of verse…the only surviving biography of Orphias…Hoshellion's *King and Cauldron*—it's 900 years-old."

"Yahh, and the boy down there is seven"—Falca saying this on the landing, the thedrals at the top of the ramp, yelling at him:

"Scapegrace!"

"Rapparee!"

"Toe-rag!"

The thedral who'd pleaded with Falca flung out her arms, as if to prevent the others from attacking, though she couldn't see what Falca could: that for all their cursing, attacking him wasn't in their eyes. "*Quiet!*" she shouted. "Insults will not stop him."

Falca cut the mooring ropes of the two boats laden with boxes and thedrals, prompting one of the thedrals to stand up, protesting: "What are you doing!"

"A little distance is all, to make sure you don't do something foolish." He shoved the boat, spinning the bow enough for a drift, and toppling the thedral back to his oarbench.

"Let's go," Falca said.

Simi and Gevret were first in, then Cofor, who brushed a fading luneling from a bench. Falca unwrapped a brighter one from a bollard, tossed it to Cofor, asked Simi: "Do we have food and water?"

"Ehhh…yes. One big jug and a leather…yare, there's food."

Falca was about to cut the mooring rope, and get in the boat, when he heard the sound of something not much louder than lapping water, the knocking of the two remaining boats against the landing.

She wasn't weeping, the thedral who'd told him he didn't understand; the one next to her was. She took his hand.

Shide...Roak's balls...all right, maybe one....

"The books," Falca said, "where are you going with them?"

"The Widow Yist's."

"What's that?"

"A provincial edificia...in Girvan."

"Where's that?"

"On the mainland to the southwest. Down the coast."

"All right, since you seem to think that's far enough away from the Skarrians, we'll take *one* box there, then. But you try to dun us—now or later—the box gets dumped. Agreed?"

"Two."

"One."

A sigh, a nod: "Very well."

Falca handed the falcata to Cofor. "Cut the line if there's a problem—Simi I'll need your help."

Together they managed to transfer to their boat one of the four boxes from the third, and put it between the oar benches. Cofor cut the mooring rope, put the falcata on top of the box, next to the luneling. "Stern or bow bench?" he said to Falca.

THEY FOUGHT THROUGH the worst of the breakers.

The wind had died down from what Falca remembered on the wall, but still the boat rocked and dipped on the moon-ribboned Kingsmere.

He hung over his shipped oars, exhausted, wet, and the gash on his head stung with salt. He'd hit it near the passage out, a swell lifting the boat a moment after he glanced behind to see the moonlight silhouetting not only the entrance but also the dangling arm of a Skarrian or Milat fallen off the parapet far above.

Gevet was saying that he could do it, take his turn; that he was eight years-old, not seven like Falca said; could sit by his mother and use both hands to pull one of the oars while she had the other. But Simi told him that the pulling was only part of it; you had to pull together, or the boat wouldn't move well, so "best you be our lookout at the bow, is it? and keep sharp for a rock sticking out of the water after we rest."

Which wouldn't be for long, or they'd drift back toward the escarpment.

Cofor and Falca took turns drinking from the jug, Simi spreading her knees on the box for balance in the lively boat, holding the jug for them; and a good thing that: Falca's hands were oar-tired, already starting to chafe, and Cofor's had to be too. The last thing they needed now was to drop the jug and break it.

They ate—golos, bread and dried, fingerling sprats—and decided their best course was to follow the escarpment of Linnisheer, staying beyond the surf yet not so far out in the open water of the Kingsmere, keeping in sight of the causeway linking the Orphic Gate to the mainland. Then continue along the shore until their hands were too blistered to grip the stiting oars. They'd probably never be able to reach Girvan by boat. Unlike the thedrals, there were only three of them for the oars. But there was the coast road; Cofor said he'd taken it once.

The boat was drifting in, the surf louder now, a silvery, roiling band against the darker escarpment and the gray Reef of Bones. Simi offered to row but Cofor said he'd be all right for a while and so did Falca, running out the oars through the rattling locks.

"We don't need these anymore," Simi said, and flung the lunelings overboard—the one that had faded out completely in the passage and the second that brightened the fretted water until it, too, was gone.

Falca's first stroke was more skim than pull, but not the second and he dug even harder after that, all too aware that they could lighten their load and dump the box of books.

He was surprised neither Simi nor Cofor had said anything about taking it. He didn't know why he had. Maybe it was the thedral's weeping, or the sound of what Falca couldn't hear—the roaring of the inferno above that was Sulserra's. He couldn't hear that either now but he could see it in the distance, off to his left and slowly diminishing to a mere beacon that marked their escape, and his escape from a fight that wasn't...well, in a way it *would* be his until they brought the books to—what was it?—the Widow Yist's.

But he said he'd do it, and he would.

One way or the other the box would get to Girvan, even if they had to cut two saplings, slide 'em through the rope handles, shoulder the swinging load along the coast road, he and Cofor and Simi taking her turn. It was the least he could do for their luck in escaping Milatum.

There'd been other places where he'd tasted the sweetness that came from dunning the Fates, skeltering with no regrets.

But here...no—because his friends had left so much behind, especially Simi and Gevret.

And because he *was* leaving Milatum with regrets: it hadn't worked out finding Rohaise Loquin; and he hadn't killed the Skarrian soon enough to save the merser's life.

Falca pulled, recovered, pulled again, the oarlocks creaking.

And with each stroke his left arm rubbed against the lump in his pocket; he'd forgotten he still had the krael.

There was no sign of the thedrals in their three boats, no dots of luneling light, but maybe, as Simi had done, they'd tossed the lunes overboard.

Toe-rag? Falca thought. *Rapparee...scapegrace, sure. But toe-rag?*

CHAPTER NINE:

PRAYERS OF PURITY

VULSA HORK SHARPENED another vairg bristle with his recently acquired dagger. The edge was keen enough, but otherwise the blade was of poor balance, the hilt overly encrusted with sunstone and blueveil gems. A showpiece. King Rhakotis probably had never used it—except, of course, on himself, after the Labryrssons with him in Labrys Hall had been overwhelmed and killed.

The Skarrian Priaptor stood by the south-facing window of what likely had been the bedchamber of one of the House of Keshkev Demizells. These quarters would be temporary; preparations for his own—what had been Rhakotis' and Queen Epona's—were not yet complete.

The warm breeze coming in the open window tinkled the curtains of spun glass, wafting in a charred smell, no doubt from the ruins of the edificia on Linnisheer, across the Queensmere—and also the even fainter fragrance of the extensive and now mostly trampled gardens far below. That the Keshkev royals would surround much of their citadel, the Kelefion, with gardens instead of a wide ditch or moat still amused him since obviously even the Queensmere hadn't been enough of a moat to protect them here on Mereshaven.

*Mereshaven…Kelefion…Queensmere…*whatever the new names would be for this royal isle, citadel and Milatum's sparkling inner water, one thing was certain: the city would henceforth be called *Tholosia*.

To the west, Vulsa could see the Red Cape purisees salvaging dead vairgs for eyes, carapaces, bristles and blood. Zyarees, the prick, was fond of calling his elite warrior priests the 'Hammers of Tholos', but they'd proven less than that during the battle. Nearby, some of Vulsa's Ghosts were feeding more prisoners to surviving vairgs, what the Milats called stalkers.

It was just as well the screams of the first captives had woken him when they did: he had the convocation at noon with his karls and purisees attached to their 1000-man skirranx. But if he was late, so be it. *Let them wait....*

He'd had to write his report to the Tholarsh and while it was brief, he chose his words carefully; they were, after all, for the Seven-eye himself...Slevaig's Shepherd...Bane of Threads...Keeper of the Nimbus and The Vate...Aurach of Tholos...Most Pure...First Select....

So many names for the Tholarsh who held the short leash affixed to the King of Skarria's collar.

And then there'd been preparation for the requisite gift to the Tholarsh.

It had taken a surprisingly long time to find a vessel large and suitable enough to accommodate the head of Rhakotis and his heavy eyebrows. The blue-and-white glazed stirrup pot was filled with a mixture of Queensmere saltwater, more salt from the citadel's kitchens, and vairg blood—what kept the army's churgassa rations from spoiling.

The Tholarsh's gift was waiting below in Labrys Hall along with Vulsa's report, ready to be escorted by Red Capes back to Zakros. And the dagger, too, of course; a gift for King Harxis who would doubtless wear it proudly, surely missing Vulsa's point in giving to him the King of Keshkevar's personal dagger: that death was preferable to emasculation.

The Priaptor finished sharpening a second bristle, sat down at the escribore by the ledge below the window, and pushed aside a bauble one of the Demizells—Cyalla or Cymra—had left: two tiny porcelain oikoes with entwined tails and stardonyx eyes. On second thought he tossed it out the open window, perfectly gauging a space between the curtains. His men had encountered these oikoes everywhere—in the streets, on the walls. The Milats kept them as pets, used them to carry messages and otherwise trained them as helpmates for this or that. Vulsa's spies had cautioned him that oikoes might prove more than a nuisance, and so they had.

He dipped a bristle into the jar of vairg-blood ink. As usual, when he was done, he would coat the pages with a special wash that would hide what he'd written. Vulsa had concocted it himself long ago, for a particular reason. The same wash, when heated, would reveal the writing again, should he choose.

All of it was a necessary precaution: if any purisee ever read his journal, Vulsa would be deemed impure, a criminal, and subject to the Eighth and last Purge as decreed by the sacred *Book of Vate*: self-inflicted death.

He was about to begin when one of his Ghost guards knocked on the door and entered upon Vulsa's curt response, gave the Rising Fist salute—fist to chest then forehead.

"Priaptor, I've been given word that Zyarees wishes an audience before the—"

"Tell him I am presently with Tholos—my Prayers, Rullo—and that I will see him at the convocation."

Rullo nodded, saluted again, and closed the door.

Prayers, indeed, Vulsa thought, and began writing.

MILATUM IS MINE.

To be sure, as the Tholarsh decreed prior to the campaign, should we be victorious, the so-called Navel of the World—that "seeping pustule that must be cleansed", as he put it—will be renamed Tholosia.

So at the convocation today, I shall announce my intention to strictly enforce the conversion: if any Milat is heard saying the old name, he or she shall be summarily executed. I mentioned this edict in my report to the Tholarsh. Zyarees, his eyes and ears for this campaign, his spiritual factotum and prized hoof-polisher, will no doubt mention this in his own report.

By now I'm sure the Tholarsh has forgotten I was the one who first proposed the name change, knowing the suggestion would please him—though in Milatum's case that's like putting fresh clothes on a man who hasn't bathed in a year. I could not care less what the city is called, of course—unless the Tholarsh, grateful for my services to Skarria—might choose to bless it with mine after all.

Which he should. I took it.

I have done in a week what took Hestimion—that outlawed scion of the House of Keshkev—eight months to accomplish almost 300 years ago, and he with an army twice the size of mine. Moreover, Hestimion did not have at the time the complication of a wall encircling the city atop the bluff that rises from the Kingsmere on all sides. The escarpment varies in steepness, to be sure, but in places it was formidable indeed.

My task would have been even more difficult if not for my own initiative in destroying the Keshkan fleet at its Snarlshome base in the lee of Linnismorn. The galleys would have come out of the Cleave, infesting the Kingsmere, preventing the ferrying of my soldiers and vairgs. The work of my agents who set fire to the fleet and otherwise provided intelligence about the city and the disposition of the Meresguard within and without, was crucial. The agents' dyed, unplaited hair and superficial disfigurement—which I insisted upon—helped them blend in with the populace. So far, it appears none of the eighteen has survived. Their sacrifice shall be recognized with a suitable memorial, perhaps in Linnisvale's Scunder Square, directly across from Mereshaven.

Cavilers might say that Hestimion did not then have the benefit of the assets I did, such as vairgs, especially those we've bred to a more useful and intimidating size. True enough, perhaps. But in my study of Hestimion's campaign, I learned that he made the mistake of besieging cities to the east—Terenure and Anaktora in particular—sustaining casualties, weakening his forces and giving the Milats more time to prepare defenses. In any conquest, speed is all.

Apart from the necessary confrontation with the Keshkan army of mostly levies, southwest of Phaistos, I conserved our men and vairgs for Milatum. Now that I've potted Rhakotis' head, these demoralized cities should fall easily in the coming months.

As in the rout of the Keshkan army, I used vairgs at night here to maximize their terror on the enemy, and minimize their vulnerability to fire. We lost many of the males, but since I kept the egg-laden females in reserve, we shall replace the losses soon enough.

Also, I used the very size of the city to our advantage, drawing the Milats—my soldiers call them slorries—to one salient and then landing men and vairgs elsewhere, ferrying them across the Kingsmere under cover of night. This was done most effectively along the northern bluff of Linnisvale, and from there it was not far to Scunder Square, Colza's Bridge and Mereshaven.

Given their reputation, I expected fierce resistance from the Labryssons defending this area, and that was indeed the case. But I'd chosen my three skirranx of Ghosts to lead this assault, commanded by my best karls; Hevket was especially effective. The Ghosts took Mereshaven as well as most of Linnisvale and Linnishill while the Red Capes and the skirranx of the karls Ullbor and Lomilar were still bogged down in the western and eastern parts of Linnisheer, especially around the Cleave.

How to explain the difference in performance? One factor might be the parls that accompanied the skirranx of Ghosts, and no others, into battle—if only because there were not enough parls for all the skirranx.

The parls were my earlier innovation for the Ghosts, tasked with composing verse in the midst of battle and not after the fact. I emphasized to the parls yet again the need to include the names of not only ferocious Ghosts, but the laggards as well. After all, it is obviously a soldier's wish to be immediately lauded as courageous rather than cowardly. Foremost among the purisees, Zyarees had objected to the parls, protesting that the morale of all the soldiers in the army were the responsibility of the priests. After such a victory, I doubt he will make these objections in the future.

But a more important factor surely rests with the fact that the Ghosts had something to prove, as if they hadn't displayed their worth already. After all, they were once scorned, exiled to the Cazcus Wilds, punished by the Tholarsh for their humiliating defeat at Laggunsea by the Keshkan marines, along with my predecessor who was forced to take the Eighth Purge for his failure. Had I been there, I doubt if the Tholarsh would have allowed me the chance to rehabilitate these men; certainly if we'd failed again at Laggunsea I would not be here.

Of course, that almost happened anyway. Victory purifies all, yet still I remain wary of the reasons why the Tholarsh was so reluctant to give his blessing to my suggestion that we march on Keshkevar and the prize of purifying Milatum.

There are tactics for a military campaign…and elsewhere. I impressed the Tholarsh with my recitations by heart from The Book of Vate. *Thank you, Mother! for impressing on me the fact that when a family has lost one kind of wealth—as ours did after my father proved as much a failure in his own way as did his—it must be replaced with another for advancement. And insisted on the…tactic of devotion to Tholos, giving me The Book to memorize. I used the same tactic to successfully woo Lucetra. I do still think of her, my exceptionally beautiful and devout Lucetra…and the last look she gave me at the Stone Manger.*

Still, the Tholarsh was initially underwhelmed with my suggestion for the Keshkevar campaign. It strikes me that unless you are the original, priests have a fear of audacity. Slevaig, that original, had no position to lose, whereas the Tholarsh must never forget that the Council of Six-eye Selects who elevated him from their midst can also choose another to replace him, though I believe that has never happened—yet. Was that it? Or a reluctance to name as Priaptor another Hork?—giving me command of an army, the Ghosts included, and taking it out of Skarria. Surely there were whispers in his ear about the prudence of having it stay in Skarria. What else would he fear? Not the Myrcians in Riian; they pose no current threat in the north.

The Tholarsh kept telling me we've punished (we? I did!) the Keshkans for Laggunsea, and Attallissia is under our control (thanks to my efforts there!). But I persevered, promising that I would spread the word of Tholos across Keshkevar and to its capital.

Of course, spreading the word of Tholos is as important to me as eating a bag of roasted locusts—though I am fond of them. But I do care greatly about someday succeeding where my grandfather Gorta failed: Castlecliff. Now that Milatum is mine, Myrcia's capital is that much closer. Perhaps when the Tholarsh visits Tholosia to consecrate the victory, I will find the opportunity to broach the subject—but enough of that now.

There is much to be done presently.

Zyarees and the lesser-Eye purisees will be responsible for the spiritual domestication of the populace here. He will be eager to boast to the Tholarsh upon his arrival—my guess is in three months—of the number of conversions to Tholos and the effective imposition of Skarrian law, the Breedlaws in particular. I assume Zyarees will also wish to remove as many of the city's statues as quickly as possible, and in this matter I agree.

Whether monumental or not, they are invariably strange and otherwise offensive, and they will have to be broken up and dumped in the depths of the Queensmere or Kingsmere, whichever happens to be the more convenient latrine. A few of the statues on Mereshaven have evidently stood for ages, woven like the city's fabled bridges and, I assume, similarly impervious to fire or demolition. But however we do it, the monuments on the royal isle will nevermore be seen as they can be now from any point in the city. Hestimion obviously chose not to topple them; then again he was Keshkan by birth.

My purview remains the military, securing the surrounding territory and cities: strategic Girvan to the west, Terenure to the south, and Carrick to the north; and seeing which provincial nobles—kennards they are called in Keshkevar—will kneel and accept the customary tithes to Tholos, and which will have to be executed.

I also intend to immediately begin the re-blooding of selected Milat youths who will eventually be the troops for new skirranx. Others will follow, drawn from the provinces. These will not be mere levies; they will be trained at length at a location outside the city by certain of my best korredidors, first-blades and hammerons. Zyarees doesn't know it yet but they will all be officers from the Ghosts, not Red Capes. The Five-eye priest will not be happy about that, but so be it. Still, he is smiling now, possibly because he ignored my request regarding the edifica. By all means, I told him, loose the Red Capes to kill the impure within; and burn some of the books for the time being. But not the structure. The turd knows that since he is the Tholarsh's proxy here, there is little I can do about what he did.

It would have taken but half a day for the Capes to bring out all of the books and destroy them. I told him as much after the fact, but he was unapologetic, his attitude such that he believed I wanted to save them. He fingered his necklace of five vairg eyes and said: "If the library included such that was already in The Book of Vate, then such books were not needed. If the library had such that was not in what Slevaig wrote by the will of Tholos, then such books were an abomination and had to be destroyed without delay."

To which I responded that I only wanted to save the fucking building. Re-purpose it as a formidable military castlet to anchor our presence in the southern Linnises and the Cleave.

Now, we'll have to devote time, resources and men to oversee the forced labor of Milats to break down what's left, clear the rubble and build the castlet there from the ground up. Not surprisingly, though the building was of stone, the roof of tiles, there were vast amounts of tinder within—books, scrolls, furniture, timbering for the roof—all of which provided sufficient heat to collapse the roof and fracture much of the walls. All of the thedrals had fled save for one, evidently. But I am confident that in the coming weeks we will find enough of them for a suitable public execution.

Faugh!—what can I say about Zyarees here that I haven't already?

I've yet to see the purisee's fingers fetch smells from his ass-crack but he still sniffs his fingers under that nose of his that's shaped like the snout of a war-trumpet. He remains an ever-present affliction, a canker I thought would have healed by now, after this last and most glorious victory of the campaign. Hezruval too, in a different way.

Both were with me and and five Ghosts when I first inspected the royal chamber. Zyarees and Hezruval had their usual escort of Capes. If anything, the Five-eye priest has stayed closer to Hezruval as success leavened the campaign. It's as if the closer we came to Milatum, the more intent Zyarees was on shielding the Tholarsh's eldest son from the corrupting vapors of the city.

I couldn't resist the temptation to add a post-script in my report to the Tholarsh, informing him that Hezruval was indeed making progress; that he remained in good hands, mine and Zyarees, though confessing my lack of the purisee's natural instinct, his personal touch for grooming such a well-formed young man.

I felt like puking that time I saw Zyarees tenderly brushing Hezruval's golden, unplaited hair—and the youth with his eyes closed, enjoying it.

The royal chamber: Hezruval happened to discover two householders hiding in a massive, gilt wardrobe and under the vast canopy bed. The servants were hardly more than girls, not a threat. Hezruval had turned seventeen the day we sighted Milatum's eastern wall, the drum towers of Ozold's Gate, so I told him to consider his discoveries a birthday present and enjoy himself.

By our standards the girls were nothing much but still, either one could have coaxed a quick bolt from the youth, no doubt his first. But Zyarees intervened, trilling that they were impure, not fit for the Tholarsh's eldest, and better he kill them now, a mercy to relieve them of their burden of ugliness.

The executions would have been either sloppy or unnecessarily prolonged: Hezruval has remained more devoted to his daily Prayers of Purity and Purges than to the martial training I had assumed was the seasoning the Tholarsh had in mind when he said his son would accompany the army.

"Ugly they may be," I told Zyarees, "but perhaps still useful to interrogate."

I was thinking that these householders might have heard useful gossip—such as the whereabouts of Epona; if she'd stayed in Milatum or had gone with her daughters to Girvan to take ship for Castlecliff, the elder Demizell evidently to marry a son of the Myrcian Sanctor. That much I knew from the agents I'd placed in Milatum many weeks before.

I prefer to handle interrogations myself, whenever possible. And I am not one to waste opportunity. These girls were not that ugly.

I cleared the chamber, leaving only two Ghosts outside the door, and the girls bound at the wrists.

As it turned out, they knew nothing of Epona's whereabouts, and while I would have preferred to give them to the Ghosts whom my parls had particularly celebrated, I had to dispose of them.

I may have aroused suspicion in purisees from One-eye to Four, by never marrying again after Lucetra, and certainly offended them by siring Skarrian bastards over the years. But siring slorrie bastards would be something else entirely.

The other reason why I had to kill them—it was quick for them both, the necks—was because of a single question that had nothing to with Epona, or seeding them. I am not sure why I asked it. Milatum is a large city, second only to Castlecliff, and the odds against their having seen Koll were as great as those of him still being alive after all these years. But I asked the question anyway, perhaps because I was here now, in the place to which I sent him as an infant; where, far from Skarria, he would be safe in a city of mongrels and in the care of the midwife who'd delivered him. I paid them well, Yola Prastagi and her husband Cashol, for their exile and the care of my son—and to keep my crime a secret.

Which remains a secret.

All are dead, even Hellyarx, who was the one—not my father—who taught me how to ride a vairg. He was the only one I could trust to journey to Milatum every two years, discreetly meet with only Yola and her husband, and report back about Koll. Hellyarx died not long after his last trip in which he found out the family was no longer living in the Linnisheer tenement.

Evidently there had been an attempted robbery, the speculation being that when the rapparees found out that Prastagi was but a lowly gullyman with little to steal, they killed him and took his wife and son to sell. At that time Koll would have been thirteen or fourteen.

Still, I asked the Milat girls if they'd ever seen a six-fingered young man—who would be about four or five years older than the golden-haired youth who'd found them hiding—walking along Colza's Way or Scunder Square.

Of course, even when I asked them I knew it didn't matter whether they had or hadn't seen him; and the question alone sealed their fates. They were householders, and if I let them *live to gossip about such a strange question from the Skarrian Priaptor himself, there is no telling how far such gossip might spread. And if by chance or the mischief of a Thread, some purisee heard it, and passed it along to Zyarees....*

So my crime, my violation of the Breed Laws—punishable by the Eighth Purge— remains hidden, though I wonder what I would do if, in the months ahead, I ever saw an impure, six-fingered young man foolish enough to be walking the streets of Tholosia. I would have to pass him by, pretend I hadn't noticed him. And let someone else apprehend him, take him to a purisee for a summary execution; or worse, an Iron Wicket.

Perhaps it is better that my son's fate was likely decided years ago and thus absolves me of a direct hand in his death, now that I have taken the city in the name of Tholos—and my own ambition.

Only this remains: the hope that Koll escaped his fate and is living elsewhere than Keshkevar.

Even when this campaign began, I knew that should I be successful in claiming Milatum, I'd never be able to reclaim my son.

THE PRIAPTOR'S GRANDFATHER, Gorta, supposedly had made the small but beautifully crafted campaign chest, all that was brought back of his from the disaster at Castlecliff. The russet hanthwood inlay of a snarling flenx-head seemed to dare anyone to open the lid, but that wasn't the reason Vulsa had hesitated doing so as boy. He'd wondered if the bones of his beloved grandfather were in there, or maybe his ashes.

But now, among other personal items such as ink, vairg bristles, a rarely used flesh-whisk and the seemingly blank pages of his campaign journal, there *were* ashes in the chest: a large vial of Slevaig's Ashes and another of his Tears. Common ashes and water they might be, but having been blessed by the Tholarsh they were thus sanctified for proper observance of the rituals of Prayers and Purges.

The second vial, however, contained not the prophet's sacred Tears but Vulsa's wash—or should have.

At some point since he'd last written after the victory near Phaistos, the vial had cracked, and the wash had seeped out, dampening the thin red gloves the Tholarsh had worn to bless the Priaptor's Gavilor. Had one of his men dropped the chest? Possibly. But if so, why hadn't the other vial broken, too, as the chest's contents tumbled about? And while scratches and gouges marred the old chest, none of the scars looked new.

Vulsa scratched his forehead, even as he knew there could be only one resolution for the mystery—and that was not the divine interpretation that a purisee—especially Zyarees—would make, had any been present.

There was still a scrim of oil in the Demizell's standing cresset lamp, and below on a petal of bronze the means to light it.

Vulsa watched them burn, the pages of what he had just written. Of course, the Milats had their own gods, useless as they'd shown themselves to be. But perhaps one of their gods *was* responsible; a petty reprisal indeed for the burning of the edificia.

After Vulsa made sure all the pages were completely charred he left the chamber, taking his Gavilor, its blunt hammer and frowning spike wiped of Milat blood and newly polished. He ordered Kassux to remain at the door—doubtless to ponder what the Priaptor had burned within.

Halfway down the corridor, accompanied by Rullo, Vulsa turned his thoughts to what Zyarees might have wanted. Well, he'd find out soon enough at the convocation. No doubt the waiting karls and purisees—maybe even Hezruval—had been passing the time by trying to cut the cords of the Labrys in the Hall, as Vulsa had failed to do, first with Rhakotis' blood-smeared dagger, then a dead Labrysson's sword, and lastly Rullo's axe.

CHAPTER TEN:

THE ROAD TO GIRVAN

THEY'D SWITCHED SHOULDERS twice since resting in the shade of a swing-back tree off the road, Simi doling out careful measures of water from the almost-empty jug; and now they switched again, right aching shoulder to left and trudged on, linked by the cut sapling from which the box of books was suspended by its rope handles.

Simi and Gevret were not too far ahead up the rise in the road, the boy at her side, holding the two books she'd given him to carry, lighten the load a bit for the men. Much earlier, the lid of the box had cracked open when they'd dropped the box, taking it from the boat.

How did she do it—the bare feet? By this time of the day, the worn cobbles might as well have been oven bricks. You could step over a pothole here and there—amazingly few of them for a road as old as this one, built by the Orphics, Cofor said—but you couldn't avoid the rising heat. Rivulets of sweat dripped down Falca's armpits. He skimmed away sweat from his face with the back of his hand

Simi stopped, Gevret turning to shout: "Falca! Cofor! There's a carriage up yon!"

"Maybe we're in luck," Cofor muttered.

Falca said nothing. There'd be little chance in persuading the carriagers to take four strangers and a box of books to Girvan—surely that's where they were going. They *might* take Simi and Gevret, which would be luck enough— *meet you in Girvan at the Widow Yist's....*Of course, there was harder persuasion... but Falca wasn't going to do that.

Soon enough he saw it: a maroon phaeton, something only a wealthy patroon would own. Maybe the benchman had stopped the carriage to let someone out to do his business in the nearby woods, but wouldn't he have opened the door opposite the road?

And then he saw why the phaeton, which must have come from Milatum and left before the siege began, and should have been in Girvan by now, would never get there.

"Maybe they broke an axle, took the horses," Cofor said.

"You see a cant to it?"

"No."

"Neither do I," Falca said.

By the time they drew abreast of the carriage, Simi and Gevret were walking beyond. As the boy looked back he dropped one of the books. After he picked it up his mother put her arm around him, shielding him from the bodies.

Falca and Cofor lowered the box near the carriage's open door. They walked past the limber, its stiff, drooping tongue angling away from the road.

Two corpses lay beyond the raised border of the road—or what was left of them after gulls, spanners and scavengers from the nearby woods had their feast.

"Oikoes, too," Cofor said softly.

"Why cut the tails off?"

"Black market for the fur, musk glands."

And another corpse, also a man's, beyond the others.

"Brigands," Cofor said. "The Skarrians wouldn't have gotten this far yet. Took the horses."

Falca looked away to Simi and Gevret up the road, her arm still around her boy, waiting for them. *And the mother and daughter....*

There was a girl's doll under the carriage.

"They also took the outriders' horses," Falca said. "Whoever could afford a carriage like this would have hired escorts. The whoresons were probably hiding over there, the lee of this rise. Coming up, the outriders wouldn't have seen 'em until it was too late. Let's get on, Cofor; we've nothing to bury them with."

Cofor toed the box. "What do you think, we leave it here, be done with it?"

"Maybe if we knew the thedrals would be along to pick it up, but they probably won't be."

On the water the night before, they'd seen what they guessed was a signal fire along the shore, to the north: a beacon for the thedrals coming along behind them in the other boats. Made sense that they would have earlier sent out a few across the Kingsmere in a fifth boat, to the mainland. Find a wagon or cart to take the culled books to Girvan. Falca had thought of rowing to that signal fire and giving the thedrals there the box, and continuing on.

But by the time he and the others might have gotten there, the wagon likely would have been gone. Even if it hadn't been, the thedrals' mood wouldn't be…welcoming. And there would have been more thedrals there.

"I reckon they've already passed by here with the wagon," Falca said.

"Yare, probably when we were still blistering our hands at the oars—right shoulder or left?"

As soon as the weight settled on his left shoulder, Falca thought, and not for the first time: *Roak's balls and a dog to lick'em…a box of books? what was I thinking?*

Still, a deal was a deal. And blisters on his fucking shoulders, too, were a small price to pay for still being alive to sweat all the way to Girvan.

Simi pointed at the box when Falca and Cofor approached, saying to Gevret, "Another book for you, is it?"

"*Two* more won't be too much, Mother."

"There's good, but one is enough." She took off the lid, handed a book to him, and refitted the lid. "Falca, Cofor…when one of you needs to rest, I'll bear."

Gevret's carrying two books hadn't made much of a difference to this point, nor would three from here on out. Nor would it make a difference to all those who'd been murdered and abducted here when Simi walked back to the phaeton to close the door.

Then again, as they all set out on the road, Falca supposed that wasn't the point of either of Simi's gestures.

VIROCO LEFARRION HADN'T ridden far beyond the western outskirts of the town before his legs began to ache from gripping the horse's flanks, his left hand and arm too, from pressing down on the dead boy draped over the horse where a saddle's pommel should have been. His right hand held the makeshift reins.

The boy's name was Tig. Viroco didn't know what his proper name had been. As a mere footman who'd been employed for less than a month by the Gullion family, he'd just heard *Tig* this, *Tig* that. But he knew the boy's age.

There had been many places to hide in the abandoned town, but none where you could properly bury a four-year-old. As the Gullions left the manse in Linnisvale the morning after the fleet was destroyed, Viroco had heard Tig complaining about not being able to celebrate his upcoming birthday now on a Queensmere boat-cruise like he'd been promised. It took both parents to shut him up with another another: celebrating his fifth birthday on a much bigger boat once they reached Girvan.

If Viroco had ever dared to whine and grutch when he was a boy, his father would have cuffed him.

He had only Kerquin's knife to use to scrape out a shallow grave for Tig. No doubt there were steads farther up the road where he might find a spade— probably the last thing a farmer would have taken as he fled west like everyone else in the area, frightened by the rumors of Skarrians on the march from Milatum. But searching for a spade would take time, and the boy…well, he was becoming *very* dead now. So Kerquin's knife would have to do for a shallow grave by the shoulder of the road, where there was a patch of grassy earth that could be worked.

THE KNIFE WASN'T bloody; Kerquin never got a chance to use it when the brigands ambushed the phaeton. Viroco had been at his station on the footboard at the rear of the carriage, wondering what he was going to do when they reached Girvan.

A month ago, Viroco was standing by the Gullions' phaeton—his first day on the job—as the houseman was lecturing him on Master Simicus' preferred method of polishing its burlbright wheel spokes; Viroco all the while nodding but listening to the squabble in the manse's portico, Gullion trying to placate the Lady Panni, who was clearly annoyed at her husband for not consulting her about the new hire. "Now dearest, we've already been *weeks* without a footman, and this one comes sufficiently recommended. And never mind his complexion—you must remember, honey-lick, that most of the time he'll be where we can't see his face."

Honey-lick? If his father had ever said that to his mother, she would have cuffed *him*.

And his complexion wasn't *that* bad, a few pox scars is all.

The wattle-throated Gullion was a member of the Council of Ephors in Milatum—and a prominent one, evidently. He also had to be the most cowardly for fleeing when he did, assuming the worst after the Snarlshome disaster. No one told Viroco where they were going, but where else but the *end* of the road? Which meant Girvan. And if you're skeltering, want to make sure you and your reputation are safe, why stop in a place where they'd know you for what you are? Which meant that Simacus Gullion and family were for Gebroan, across the awe.

But what about the footman?

The Gullions would certainly take their oikoe pets. They would take Huitt, Gullion's' bodyguard; and Borry, the houseman who luckily also knew how to sit a horse. They would take the Lady Panni's handmaiden, Kinewin. They'd probably take Kerquin who, like Borry, had been with the family for years.

But they weren't likely to take a mere footman, only recently hired, whose usefulness would expire once the phaeton was probably was left on the Girvan quay, no room for it on the ferry.

A moment before it happened, Viroco told himself that at least he'd gotten out of Milatum. But what then? Whatever severance Gullion gave him—if anything—wouldn't cover the price of paying for his own passage across the water. And if Gullion was right about the Skarrian threat, if the worst happened, it was only a matter of time before the barbarians came south and west to Girvan.

At the back of the carriage, Viroco didn't see Kerquin slump over and fall from the board in front, but he saw him on the road, an arrow sticking out of his chest. The horses skeered, the carriage kept going. The oikoes that had been scampering alongside the phaeton were screeching something Viroco couldn't hear over the rumbling of the out-of-control carriage and the screams within.

Viroco jumped off the footboard, tumbled to the ground—lucky he didn't hurt himself other than scrapes and a banged elbow—and scrambled to his feet. He bolted into the nearby field, plowed through the waist-high vetch, expecting any moment to hear them coming after. They'd surely seen him skeltering; how could they miss his red-and-gold livery or the path he was making through the vetch?

But he *couldn't* be worth the bother of pursuing into the woods ahead, not when they had much better prizes much closer. He almost stopped to scream it out—*I've got nothing you want! I'm only the fecking footman!*—but he kept running and even when he gained the woods he didn't stop...until he couldn't run anymore and collapsed behind a split-bole hackhard, chuffing like a bellows.

He listened for...*them* but heard only the trills of birds, the burbling of a stream.

His shaking, the drumming of his heart, gradually subsided, replaced by something else.

There was nothing he could have done...right? Didn't have so much as a dagger. Hired to fetch and carry baggage, open and close the carriage doors, feed the oikoes—*not* get himself killed defending a family that wasn't his.

Which is what would have happened if he hadn't fled; what surely had happened to Huit and Borry.

Gullion was going to skave him in Girvan, anyway.

Which was where he had to go now, on foot; the brigands wouldn't leave any horses.

They hadn't.

But they'd taken the Lady Panni, the daughter Mima, and Kinewin. And everything else. Taken the oikoes' tails to sell, too. The oiks—bloody claws and teeth—had died defending the boy and his father. Tig lay underneath the female of the pair and the fat thighs of Simacus Gullion. The boy groaned. Nasty wound in his leg; no wonder the whoresons left him to die.

Whatever else Viroco had done—or hadn't—he couldn't leave the boy here to die. He got him out from under, picked him up, took to the road. That town—Argell, was it?—couldn't be far away. At least that's what Simacus had muttered an hour before the attack, when the phaeton stopped to accommodate a necessary for his wife, who must have complained that she couldn't wait till they got to Argell because she was still grutching when Viroco opened the door for her.

Farther along the road he saw the bodies of Huit and Borry and a dead horse, arrows in them all.

Darkness had fallen when he got to the town, exhausted from carrying the boy.

Approaching the roofed well in the center of the square, he heard muted but distinctively drunken shouts: the brigands. Who else would be celebrating in this deserted town? At first, Viroco was dismayed. The sounds were coming from somewhere close to the square. He'd have to go around, take side streets, and return to the main road farther west. But likely the scuts would only be staying here for the night before also heading on to Girvan—and sooner or later they'd overtake him. Carrying the boy he might not be able to flee in time. Without him he might have a chance.

But he hadn't carried Tig all the way here, only to abandon him now.

Then Viroco remembered the horses.

The handle of the well-draw creaked, and thirsty though he was, the boy even worse, Viroco forced himself to turn it slowly—that was better—until he cursed himself for a fool. They wouldn't hear the sound over their carousing. He first gave the boy water from the bucket, and then took his fill. Cleaned his hands and washed the sword cut on Tig's leg, best he could.

He was surprised they hadn't left someone to guard the horses. A moonlight count put them at ten; he had to leave the well, skulk over a ways to get it, because a close count was important. With the three horses they'd taken, that could mean there were at least seven of the whoresons inside the tavern, whatever it was, on the far side of the square. No doubt they'd done their looting for the night, so none of them—made sense—would want to stay outside guarding horses in this abandoned town while the rest were dividing up the booty and getting drunk on what the tavern-keep had left.

As Viroco moved away to do it, the boy reached out, caught his ankle, whispered that he didn't want him to go.

"I'll be back, promise you."

He unhobbled the horse farthest away from the flickering candlelight in the tavern. It was one of the phaeton's mares, make-shift reins. Viroco led it away as quietly as he could, but there was nothing he could do about the slow *clip-clop* of the horse's hooves on the bricks of the square, or his shakes. By the time he got back to Tig at the well, the fear that had clotted his throat was back in his belly.

Viroco lifted the boy on the horse, told him to hang on tight to the mane, and walked the mare back in the direction from which they'd come. If he was hungry the boy surely had to be, but searching for food now, at night? No. He'd be heard by one of the brigands coming out to piss, the man maybe seeing the missing horse.

As a plan it wasn't much, but all he could think of: get away, come back into the town, hope the bastards had left. Tend to the boy until he was better, then on to Girvan, leaving the horse in the outskirts. After that? All he knew was that he couldn't carry the boy to Girvan, and even if the boy's leg was better, he'd still have a hard time walking.

But for now…it all depended on what the reivers would do. Whether they discovered the missing horse in an hour or not until the morning, it seeming likely to Viroco that they would assume the thief had ridden it on toward Girvan where everyone else had fled, or maybe north. But not east, toward Milatum, the Skarrians—he hoped.

Viroco and the boy spent the rest of the night in woods just east of the town. For a while Tig whispered questions Viroco could answer but didn't: *Where's Maima? Where's Mima?* Kept whispering his leg hurt, that he was hungry. All Viroco could do was tell him it would be better when they got back to the town.

And cautiously done, that—it was past noon when they returned, the brigands gone.

Viroco found a bakery on a side-street around the corner from the tavern, hobbled the horse in an alley behind the shop. The proprietor had left a cracked bowl which Viroco used to carry water from the well in the square since he'd found a drowned rat in the bakery's water barrel. And rats had eaten through a half-empty sack of flour, but it was enough for him to make some crude flat bread, finding what he needed to light the oven; though later, to keep it going after the bakery's wood supply ran out, he had to break up a bed, footstool and a cradle. Viroco's third attempt at baking the bread wasn't much better than his first, but at least he and Tig wouldn't starve. He found a crock of butter, which helped, though the butter was almost rancid.

For days Viroco repeatedly cleaned the boy's wound with heated water, but he had to stop doing that after the leg swelled up even more, becoming too painful to the touch. The streaky redness moved up the leg with each passing day, and Viroco knew it was only a matter of time…unless he cut the leg off above. He'd looked for what he'd need—but an axe, a sword, a saw were also what was needed by those fleeing this place. Kerquin's knife? Even if he tied off the boy's leg to lessen the bleeding, Tig would die from the shock of a slower butchering.

Viroco had found an apothecary's shop fronting the square, but what little the proprietor might have left had been looted: the shelves were bare.

Besides getting water from the well, the only other time Viroco left the boy was when he was roused from sleep by sounds on the road through town.

At first he feared the reivers had returned. But the noise seemed more like the rumbling of a wagon, and by the time he'd walked to the road, the one-horse wagon was moving away to the west. All he glimpsed was some men on it, and more walking alongside and behind. It was hard to tell in the moonlight, but they didn't look to be farmers or soldiers. Maybe he should have run after them, but Tig was too far gone now. Whoever the travelers were, whatever was in the wagon…wouldn't be enough to save a dying boy.

VIROCO KNEELED, USING both hands to grip Kerquin's knife and cut away squares of the weedy turf beyond the road's shoulder. There were stones about but not nearly enough to mound over the boy; and while he saw more in the fallow field adjacent to a ripening one of vetch, he figured if the farmer hadn't already dug them out they'd be too big to bring over. A shallow grave and then the turf over the boy should keep off the birds and discourage less persistent predators.

Viroco had just begun scraping away at the grave when he noticed a woman and boy approaching from the direction of the town. Either they'd lost their shoes or they were Attalls. Then, two men appeared, carrying a chest that bobbed and swung slightly from a pole resting on their left shoulders. Viroco would have noticed the men earlier but the hobbled horse was in the way.

He stood, knife in hand, as the men put down the chest, and he realized he was probably going to have to walk to Girvan instead of ride: the big man had a falcata in the curved scabbard; the woman a long-shank at her belt—and she was now closer to the horse than Viroco. The only consolation was that the brigands would think these three had stolen it from them.

The tall one—a northron, blue eyes, beard as black and scroungy as his hair—came forward, then the other man, to stand by the woman and the boy. She had her hand on the hilt of the long-shank, the strappy-jack on the falcata's. "Toss the knife," he said. It came out almost a sigh. The man was obviously weary. So were they all; even the boy who put down the books—*books?*—he'd been carrying.

But the northron, tired as he was, still had the look of someone you didn't want to challenge.

Viroco tossed the knife at the pile of turf.

The man seemed to be thinking about something—or was it fatigue, carrying that box? Didn't matter, Viroco just wanted them to leave so he could get back to digging Tig's grave.

"Go on then, take it, and leave," Viroco said.

"We will but not the way you think. Maybe we can *all* ride, but first—"

"What're you talking about?"

"Your son over there, he needs a coffin."

"He's not my son."

"Yahh well, he should have one anyway."

THEY'D BEEN ASLEEP for a while now, Gevret and Cofor. Her son's head lay on her lap, his feet across Cofor's, whose hands rested on Gevret's ankles, his chin bobbing a little with the phaeton's movement. She'd let Gevret spend some time walking with the men—"but no pestering them with too many questions"—which of course he had. And in the carriage, Gevrie had asked Cofor about the kites he once flew, and if you needed magic to fly more than one kite at a time; and Cofor said no: no magic, only practice, especially if you scrybed kites at night, because you had to use smaller, quartered lunelings for the tails; and Gevret asked him if cut them with his scissors.

Simi stroked her boy's head, not caring about smearing butter on his unruly hair which she'd have to cut with those scissors at some point. Ask Falca to sharpen them.

Like everyone else's, Gevret's hands were dirty, and with the exception of Falca's, greasy with butter. While they'd been scraping out the grave with falcata, knife, long-shank, and Cofor using his scissors, Gevret had helped scoop away the earth, occasionally glancing at Tig's body which was covered with Viroco's maroon and gold tunic.

The phaeton wasn't moving very fast—not with only one horse to pull it along an unfamiliar road at night, and an inexperienced man on the board. After they'd buried the boy, they decided Viroco should have the reins, such as they were, but really there'd been no other choice in the matter. He'd ridden the horse back to the carriage, got it back

Falca was up on the board, too. He'd declined butter for his oar-chafed hands, didn't want them slippery, because Girvan was still about forty miles down the road and there could still be trouble ahead, though likely not from the brigands. Simi couldn't hear the rasping of Falca keening the falcata, but he'd had the small scabbard whetstone in his hands after he climbed on the board with Viroco.

The carriage's rocking wasn't enough to tumble the books stacked on the wide, velvet seat opposite Simi; or the crock of butter, the refilled jug of water and a little sack of the unleavened bread Viroco had baked. But the swaying of the phaeton had been enough to first lull Cofor, then Gevrie to sleep.

Or so she'd thought. She had been falling asleep too, but then she felt, more than heard, his crying. She knew what it was, and whispered to Gevrie that she missed him, too. But Gevret was angry—all this way and he'd kept it in but he was angry now that the worst was hopefully over—whispering fiercely that his father never should have been taken to that prison. Cofor and Falca, too, Gevrie saying he heard them talking about that with Viroco. Cofor said some people thought he was a thief but he was only a fool, that's all; and Falca said he'd been both those things in Draica—*where's that, Mother?*—doing things that should have gotten him in prison there but that it was only until he got to Milatum that he was finally thrown in one.

"Yare well, maybe we don't know that much about them *before*," she said, "but there's good to have them as friends *now*; Viroco, too." Then, something else occurred to her—what was it?—something Ghoshen had said once. He was always better than she in saying what was on his mind.

But by the time she remembered, she realized Gevrie had fallen asleep.

The rocking of the carriage and the rhythmic *clip-clop* of the horse began to lull Simi, too, now. And before she crossed over, she thought she'd probably never have to remind her son of what his father had once said that time when Gevrie admitted to some mischief. Their son was well on his way to understanding that while yesterday was important, it wasn't as important as what you did today.

CHAPTER ELEVEN:

THE WIDOW YIST'S

THE SIGN—*Heefer's Roost*—dangled from a brace hanging over a street so narrow you could lean out from a second-storey window and shake hands with your neighbor on the opposite balcony. The swagbelly stood on a wobbly ladder, talking to himself as he fumbled with the sign. Nearby, two young men loitered by trundle carts piled high with casks, crates and leather trunks, watching not the fat man on the ladder but a cluster of people down the street.

Falca asked Viroco to stop up ahead. "Maybe we'll have better luck with one of them than we've had so far."

He wasn't sure if the carriage could get past the carts, but Viroco guided the weary mare past the first of the carts and pulled up alongside the second with a hand's-breadth to spare. Falca realized that the swagbelly on the ladder hadn't been talking to himself but arguing with a tiny woman who'd been hidden behind the two young men. And they were still going at it:

"...Then leave it *be*, it won't come off! You fall you'll break your neck *and* squash me."

"I *won't* leave it for them to steal; they'll take everything else inside once we're gone—damn this crapped hinge."

"Heef, they don't *care* about the sign; can't eat it or drink it. And the Skarries won't give a cudgie's lick—"

"Watch your tongue, woman!"

"—Or a swallow's dew about it either once they get here."

"Essie, I made it and it's damn well coming with—*there*, it's off."

One of the young men—a son?—whispered something to her. Still gripping the ladder, she peeked around him.

Falca seized his chance, leaned over, and asked the woman for directions to the Widow Yist's.

"What'd he say?" the husband said, coming down the ladder, cradling the sign.

"Wants to know where the Widow's is," she said, and smiled at Falca.

Her husband wheezed a sigh, gave Falca a disgusted look, as if he'd fouled the top edge of the sign instead of gulls. "Tell him—" The fat tavern-keep missed the last step, tumbled to the street bricks; might have hit his head on the phaeton's near front wheel if his son hadn't caught him.

The wife rolled her eyes, shook her head, said to Falca: "Yare then, here's your way: keep on as you are, up the Bowl and—"

"The Bowl?"

"What we're in, the bottom of the Bowl, what we call it—so up you go, toward the castle until you come to a crossroads where you'll see our wee statue of Pelagia, but here she's got her clothes on, which for my money she should be bare-arsed like the big one, but we're in Girvan, not Milatum where you must be from, fine carriage like that though the horse looks sair…where was I—oyah, the left turn. You'll be wanting one of those at the crossroads, for the High Street, mind. Then keep on and you'll see the Widow's; there's a fountain in front. Careful you don't go past the campanile sea-side of the gardens there or you've gone too far, and if you do you'll have to go almost to the snarls for a turn-around and—"

"I think I've got it. Thanks." *Snarls?*

She winked. "Always a pleasure to tell a handsome young man where to find it. Like I said, it's not far."

"Wharr you for then, that fancy high-wheeler?" one of the sons asked.

"Books for the Widow's, what else, Lunty?" the woman said before Falca answer him. "See the cutling in there? I do believe he's got one in the window."

Viroco shook the reins. The phaeton lurched ahead, but Falca caught the last of the couple's squabbling.

"Time like this, half the town gone, and he's taking useless books to that place."

"Which you're a fine one to talk useless, that sign."

"*My* sign is going in the cart—and no thanks to you, woman, we'll have to hurry now to get quay-side for the last ferry over."

"Without *your* fussing with it we'd already be there."

"*My* fussing? We could have *built* our own boat for the crossing in the time it took you to…."

SET BACK FROM the mostly-deserted High Street, the Widow Yist's was a manse that rivaled the best of what Falca had seen in Hearthill in Draica, and bigger even than the Damarr manse there though without the gables: two storeys of whinstone with the third being a square tower rising from the middle, the tiles of the roof red instead of the blue that predominated elsewhere in Girvan. Sunset glazed the windows.

Viroco's turn into the circular gravel drive wasn't easy, the near entrance in the low wall fronting the High Street scarcely wider than the carriage. Between the edificia and the campanile farther down the slope of the street, there was a large garden whose winding paths extended far to the rear of the Widow's and converged at a pergola on the edge of woods. The tops of the trees glowed brightly in the gloaming.

Viroco pulled up the reins close enough to a round pool opposite the recessed archway of the Widow's front door. A bird flew off the upraised tail of one of four alabaster dogs facing each other within the pool, play-bowing at the spurting fountain in the middle. Falca couldn't help thinking that in Draica the beautifully carved dogs would've been stolen a day after they were put in.

They drank their fill from the pool—the mare, too—and Falca and Viroco splashed the dust from their faces. Cofor, wiping his mouth with the back of his hand, nodded toward the door.

"Are they all deaf in there?—you'd think someone in there would have heard us."

"Yahh, leastways peek through windows," Falca said.

Simi shrugged: "Maybe they're out back in that garden—Gevrie, get out of the pool. I know it feels good but there's a better bath elsewhere tonight."

"I'm hungry, Mother; I'd rather have that."

Simi smiled. "Food too, is it?"

"You said everything looked closed."

"We'll find a place that isn't."

"Yare," Viroco said, "not everyone hereabouts has skited, they've got to eat, too."

"Let's get to it, then," Cofor said. "Books first, then bellies."

"I'll let 'em know we're here," Falca said, and walked over to the Widow's door, was about to clap the bronze door-dog, then noticed the door cracked open.

He paused—a quick recollection of Lambrey Tallon's toast one drizzly night in Draica at the Glass Anchor, when they'd decided to expand their bricks to the more affluent districts of Heart Hill, Beckon and Falconwrist: *Here's to unlocked women and willing doors....*

Falca pushed the door open all the way, stepped inside.

No wonder they didn't hear us....

Cofor was right behind him. "Why're you laughing?"

"Take a look," Falca said, stepping aside, sweeping an arm from the room to his left, past the corridors flanking a central stairway, to the larger room on his right.

The others came in, put their armloads of books down near the door.

"Where are they all, Mother?"

"I dunt know, Gevrie; maybe we have the wrong place."

"No, it's the right place," Falca said. "Plenty of tables, escribores and chairs and cases and scroll niches...just no books."

"Or eddies," Viroco said, but a moment later came a voice from somewhere at the top of the stairs:

"Go on with you; there's nothing to steal here."

"Looks like someone already has," Cofor shouted. "We're—"

"What do you want?"

"Don't *want* anything," Falca yelled back. "We've *brought* you books."

Two men came slowly down the stairs, the younger assisting a graylock with spectacles. At the bottom, the elder handed him the book he was carrying, touched his companion's sleeve with ink-stained fingers and approached Falca, a hitch in his step. Was that blood spotting the thedrals' light blue tunics? The others had to have seen it too, Cofor glancing at Falca: *What were they doing up there?*

"So you're the ones," the graylock said. He wasn't the one who'd spoken first; his voice was deeper—surprisingly so given his frailness. He wasn't smiling, but neither was he frowning like the younger thedral.

Falca glanced up the stairs. "Just you two here?" He said it to the graylock, but the younger thedral replied.

"You missed Ucletia and the others by a day." Saying it as if he wished that wasn't the case.

"Tisht, Iolus," the graylock said. "We must think of what we have now, which is more than before."

"But not what it might have been."

"Oh now, what's done is done," the old thedral said, looking Falca squarely in the eyes. "Of course, I would prefer to put *names* to the deed in my journal—my daughter mentioned none, understandably so as it was scarcely the time for introductions with Sulserra's burning above."

Cofor glanced at Falca, who shrugged: *What does it matter now if we give them our names....*

The graylock smiled when Gevret was first to say his.

"And I am Lenarrion. Iolus here has, ah, introduced himself. My daughter Ucletia and the others would have done so even more...emphatically, I'm sure. But as Iolus said, they are gone, as are all the other resident thedrals here, and with them—what was it, Iolus? eight wagon-loads or nine?"

"Eight—and the three trundle carts."

"Oh yes, the carts," Lenarrion said. "Ours was a small edificica but perhaps that made us all the more determined to prevent here what happened in Milatum."

"You picked up a third man," Iolus said, staring at Viroco. "He's limping—surely that wasn't caused by carrying books."

"Bringing them would have been much harder without the phaeton he jumped from on the Girvan road," Falca said. "But you have them now, so we'll be—"

"You brought them in a...*phaeton?* Where did you steal a phaeton and from whom?"

"Indeed!" Lenarrion said, his white eyebrows lofting. "While the conveyance hardly matters, I assumed that you arrived here in the same boat you...requisitioned from my daughter."

"We rowed as far as we could, then took to the road," Falca said. "We happened upon the carriage which...yahh, you're right, Iolus; we *did* steal it—from its dead occupants."

"Killed by brigands," Cofor said.

"Viroco was the only survivor," Simi said.

"And you—what?—you *yoked* yourselves to the phaeton and pulled it here?" Iolus said.

"It may please you as well," Falca said, "to know that we also stole the horse to bring the books here." *Wankspit*....

"We appreciate your efforts, of course," Iolus said, without enthusiasm.

"Even more so considering," Lenarrion said, "that you, ah, exceeded my daughter's...expectations, shall we say. As you would have mine if I'd been there. You could have dumped the books anywhere between the Kingsmere and Girvan."

"Which crossed my mind—before the horse," Falca said.

"There's the day's conundrum—an honest thief." He smiled and hobbled over to the nearest stack of books. He picked up the top book, brushed a hand over the clamshell cover. "Oh my! *Heaven's Lyre*—you must copy it up north, Iolus." Lenarrion caressed another. "And certainly *this* one; it's the only copy in existence of Joshar's *Ripples from the Shelter Isles*. And here's Fassevion's *Anticipations*—you chose well, Breks!"

"What I did was choose the nearest box of books to take."

Lenarrion murmured something Falca couldn't quite hear since the thedral had turned to see Gevret wandering into one of the rooms, carrying one of the books he'd brought in.

"Come back, Gevrie," Simi said. "It's time for us to go—and put that back with the others." To Lenarrion she added: "I'm sorry; that's one of those my son carried for a while on the road. He thinks it's his now but he can't even read yet."

"All the more reason for him to keep it, so he can begin," Lenarrion said. "Let's see, what does he have?"

"Gevrie, show him the book, is it?"

"Ah, Bekla's fables—that will do fine for him! I read *Mists on the River* to my daughter when she was young. The margin engravings entranced her as much as the stories."

"Oh but we couldn't take it. She must have saved it for her own—"

"Her daughter died many years ago. I know she'd like the boy to have the book."

"Well...thank you."

"Thank you," Gevret said.

"We'll be on our way now," Falca said.

"But have you accommodations for the night?" Lenarrion said.

"Not yet."

"I'm afraid you won't find much available, and what there is will be crowded and dear. You're welcome to stay here if you'd like, the upstairs rooms. We have food and drink as well. Of course, it would only be for the night since Iolus and I expect we'll be leaving tomorrow."

There were nods all around, and it was Falca's turn to thank Lenarrion. "The night it is. And then we're for Gebroan."

"I hope you've brought a tidy sum for the passage across the awe," Iolus said. "The fare has risen obscenely high; I've heard it's almost ten times what it was."

"We're hoping to sell the phaeton and the horse for—"

"Doubtless you'll find a buyer for the horse; not so the phaeton. But even if you did, I daresay the price it fetches wouldn't cover the fare for all of you."

"So much for Gebroan," Cofor muttered.

"Yare, seems I'll be back on the board, then, for somewhere else," Viroco said.

"We were prepared for high but not that high," Falca said.

Lenarrion shook his head. "And all the more outrageous since the ferryman, Chez Boaig, is from Girvan."

"A few people *are* paying the scoundrel," Iolus said. "But most can't. Of course, I'm sure Boaig's evidently saying he has to cover increased expenses, such as an added traff to the harbormaster at Tuleen across the awe, for all Keshkan refugees. Beyond that, there are reports of Gebroanan slavers taking those who had just enough money to get across, and couldn't afford to hire protection in Tuleen."

"So where is everyone going then, who can't afford this fester's slap?" Falca said.

"Where Iolus and I will be going," Lenarrion said. "Where my daughter and all the other thedrals have gone with the books—north up the awe to Averdenn."

FALCA WAS THE last to take a bath, by lamplight, in the annex near the well by the garden path. Normally, Iolus had said, the edificia used lunelings at night for the usual reason, but since there were no books left, they were using lamps instead.

Viroco had pulled a wheel pin from the phaeton's front axle—just in case. He'd tethered the mare to a trellis not far from the well, brushed her down. The thedrals had taken oats and vetch for the other horses when the wagons left for Averdenn, but Lenarrion said that the mare could graze in the garden.

Falca had never taken a bath in a bronze tub, or any tub that, unlike this one, didn't leak. Even the Barras' leaked. Seemed like years since he'd been at their stead north of the River Roan, but it had only been a couple of months if you included his stay.

And no filling this thing with buckets. A spigot—another first for him—released water from the cistern atop the annex, and another emptied it to a pipe that led out to a basin in the garden. He took his time soaking and relaxing in water that still had warmth from the day, thinking that maybe it had been worth it, the books. The lamplight wasn't enough for the polished bronze to reflect his face very well, but he shaved himself anyway with his falcata.

Afterwards, he joined the others at the trestle table in the refectory, whose size gave him an idea of how many thedrals had resided here; looked to be ten, including Iolus and Lenarrion. Upon his trencher he heaped sprats and picarels; a meat and grain dish called pirlo; and bread and butter, slices of hard-rind cheese and fruit—from the orchards north along the awe, Lenarrion said.

Falca hadn't had a meal like this since, well, since the Barras'. Even the blige—the sweet Keshkan wine—tasted better than it had before.

It was soon apparent that his companions had already decided they should go with the two thedrals up the awe to this Averdenn; evidently Lenarrion had suggested as much. "When the time comes," the graylock added now. "Probably tomorrow, but certainly the next day."

That seemed a little odd to Falca—why wait to go, if going they were?

And would he go with them all? Yahh, he would, sure.

On the road they'd decided to stay together, for a while anyway, in Gebroan. And what other choice was there for anyone at the table? You couldn't cross the awe with what you didn't have; couldn't stay here, the Skarrians coming to Girvan sooner or later.

Falca pushed away his trencher and filled his cup again with blige from the flagon, asked Lenarrion about the edificia…and where *was* this Widow Yist? On the road to Averdenn with the others?

"Would that Shuvelia Yist was still with us."

A hundred years ago, Lennarrion said, she inherited from her wealthy father the manse, gardens and adjacent woodlands. And in her will she stipulated that the manse would be used as an edificia, to permanently keep the books and codices her father, husband and she herself had collected over the years, from every kingdom—including the *Book of Vate*, from Skarria.

Simi scowled.

"I know," Lenarrion said. "I had the same reaction when I read it years ago."

"My father insisted I read it."

"He was wise."

"My mother didn't think so."

"Well, even the *Book of Vate*—that smear of excrement—is on its way to Averdenn, because...hmmm...think of it this way, my friends: knowing that darkness exists is the first line of defense against it. One can no more hide from darkness than an artist can paint sunlight on a canvas without shadows—where was I? Oh yes, Shuvelia."

She had been born in Girvan, yet evidently never once traveled to Milatum to visit Sulserra's. Lenarrion said he always thought that so puzzling he'd decided the story was probably not true. At any rate, she wanted an edificia in Girvan.

"We've used it also as a retreat for Sulserra's thedrals," Lenarrion said. "For studying, copying manuscripts and reflection in a setting less hectic than Milatum or even Thetis—occasionally we've hosted thedrals from there."

He added that the collection of books here was, of course, far smaller than Sulserra's, but unique in its own way, having books of a sort not found anywhere else. "The Widow Yist had interests not shared by others...or were forgotten about."

Gevret had fallen asleep, his head on the table. "I'd best get him to bed," Simi said.

Viroco yawned, and patted his full belly. "A good idea."

Iolus said he'd show them to their rooms upstairs, and put some cheese and picarels on his trencher. Before he left with Viroco and Simi—Gevret in her arms—and one of the three lamps to light the way, he bent low to whisper in Lenarrion's ear. The graylock nodded slightly—and somberly it seemed to Falca.

"Iolus has a big appetite," Cofor said.

"The food's not for him," Lenarrion said. "We...keep a pair of oikoes upstairs and neither has eaten all day."

"Remarkable creatures, oikoes," Falca said. "It wouldn't have surprised me if yours had come down and gotten their own food—which was wonderful; thank you."

"You're welcome."

"So you'll be taking them up north, the oikoes?" Cofor said.

"We'd like to, but with these—they're a mated pair—it's up to them."

Falca took a sip of the blige. "I'm curious, Lenarrion, why you and Iolus didn't go with the others, your daughter."

"You missed that part, Falca," Cofor said.

"Just so," Lenarrion said. "As I told your friends earlier, it's a personal and unfortunate matter that requires our staying here a bit longer."

Falca took another sip, and over the rim of cup he exchanged a glance with Cofor, who gave an eye-shrug: *Maybe none of our business...and they didn't have to be so hospitable....*

"As it happened," Lenarrion continued, "Iolus' brother has been delayed in his leaving as well, and will be taking us. Ucletia wanted to wait for us, but I had to insist otherwise. There's a wagon—Birrus is a wine-merchant here. But what with a case or two of his best, the books you've brought us, his wife and youngest child and all our supplies—and a gimpy old man...well, some of us will have to walk, I'm afraid."

"Em, I think not," Falca said. "You're forgetting about our horse and phaeton."

"Oh, my, that's...of course!...would you?"

"Sure we would," Falca said, smiling. *Yahh, and so what if maybe you didn't forget about it after all....* "So how far will we be going up the awe to this Averdenn?"

"About six days as the coast road goes. Iolus and I went up there once— we could have done it in half the time but for all the twists and turns. Still, it's beautiful country thereabouts, orchards and vineyards tucked away here and there. And it can be dangerous too, especially to the north of Averdenn."

"Brigands?"

Lenarrion nodded. "The so-called Wolves of the southern Crumples occasionally cross the awe, coming over from Gebroan, and sometimes raid as far as the vales of the Coombs. Their Keshkan ilk in the Skysheaves on this side of the awe were almost as predatory until the garrison at Averdenn was increased. As it will be again very soon."

"From where?" Cofor said. "Not Milatum, that's for damn sure."

"From *here*, the castle's garrison," Lenarrion said. "Many in Girvan—including Ucletia and our thedrals—left with the troops."

"I hope the garrison commander kept a few soldiers behind," Falca said, "to keep watch for the Skarrians when they come, and hurry north to report the news."

"I should hope so, too," Lenarrion said. "But only fools—and there are as many here as elsewhere—believe he and the entire garrison should have remained to defend Girvan, when Milatum itself fell so quickly. The castle is not very formidable—the fate of Keshkevar has always been in the hands of the navy. I doubt he received orders from Milatum to defend the castle."

Falca smiled. "Here's one: heat the skillet *before* the Skarrians get to Averdenn."

"Which they probably will. Perhaps not for a while but eventually."

"What are you tipping, Falca?" Cofor said.

He picked up the table knife and tapped his trencher. "A difficult road that has twists and turns means that fewer men can defend against many more. Places for an ambush or three—front and rear."

"You have the instincts of a soldier," Lenarrion said.

"Now and again people confuse me for one, but my only instinct now is for some sleep."

LENARRION STOPPED HALFWAY up the stairs, the lamp swinging as he turned to Falca behind him.

"I'll miss much here but not these stairs."

He continued on, as if talking to himself. "There was a time when I—there is for all of us, isn't there?—when I thought it a lark to ride down the High Street late at night, on my father's mare, drunk and without a stitch of clothing—and this in winter, such as it is here. The horse threw me by by the campanile. Lucky I wasn't killed. Still, that night changed my life. I couldn't run well anymore, but I later went to places here that I never would have even if I could. My father was a blacksmith, his hands big enough to span a trencher, and he was always ashamed of my small ones, the skinny arms; always looked at me as if he wondered where I came from. He never spoke to me after I came to the Widow's six months after my almost-fatal foolishness; but then he never much spoke to me before, either, except by way of reprimands—here we are, your rooms. Which of you wants the lamp?"

"It's yours, Falca," Cofor said. "I'm so tired the darkness can't keep me from finding the bed."

Falca took the lamp from the graylock, but had to ask him one more question as Cofor closed the door to his room: "Lenarrion, if the Skarrians get to Averdenn, what then—for you and your daughter?"

"And the books. If Averdenn is threatened we shall all move on to the north, to Syarra in the western Lakes; there's an edificia there."

"Keeping ahead of the gutterwipes, is that it?"

Lenarrion smiled. "Just so, my friend. It's what we've always done, whatever their names; what my daughter has done—what you all have done even if you didn't realize it: moving as needed with the lamp from one room to the next. Goodnight, Falca."

"And you, Lenarrion."

He nodded and limped down the hallway. Falca was about to go into his room when he saw Iolus emerge from another several doors down, holding his own lamp, the light silhouetting the approaching Lenarrion.

Falca went into his room, put the lamp on the bedside table, thinking how much he liked the Lenarrion—but also about the...*personal* matter he hinted was close to...what? Some kind of resolution? Was this...*unfortunate* matter in the room Iolus had just left? He heard the thedrals talking now, but instead of closing the door, he listened.

The hallway carried the whispers well.

CHAPTER TWELVE:

LAST OF THE KRAEL

L ENARRION, A SIGH: "How is he?"

"I gave him another draught of feverfew to ease the pain and help him sleep, but I doubt he'll last through the night. The festering of the wound has spread within. There's nothing else I can do for him."

"Iolus, you mustn't feel as if you've failed him. It was your ministry and skill that's kept him alive for this long."

"Skill? Ach, whatever skill I had was remembering that oikoe tongue can be beneficial, letting Bej and Avla lick his wound for hours on end. It's almost as if they knew why Cyalla sent them to Vaience here. But they've stopped. They know he's beyond help. It's such a *waste*. I still wonder if the—I'm sorry, this is not the time for suspicions."

"No, it's a time for everything *else* but not that, nor anger at the Labryssons. They were only doing what they were supposed to do—protect Cyalla. Of course it was an outrage in their eyes, a garden tryst of a *Demizell* and our youngest thedral. Swearing us to secrecy could only follow: what if word reached Fallskeep in Castlecliff? The marriage would be annulled, the House of Keshkev disgraced, not that it matters now. But Cyalla—"

"I know...you've already told me you don't think she might have been using Vaience toward that end."

"But I don't remember telling you that I initially had my own suspicions, too; especially since she was the one who had come here from the castle supposedly to get books for the voyage. What young woman—never mind a Demizell with a well-known reputation for…difficulty—would want to be forced to marry stranger old enough to be her father?

"I changed my mind when I saw her fling herself upon our Vaience, pleading with the Labryssons not to kill him. Iolus, had you been out there…she was crying…she was so distraught—it took two of them to pull her away from him."

Silence. Another sigh. "Well, it's an end regardless. Whatever skill I had now turns to the spade tomorrow."

"Vaience should be elsewhere than the graveyard."

"But that's where all thedrals—"

"I doubt we'll be put to rest there, either, when our time comes; mine anyway. No, Vaience's grave should be where he fell, by the pergola."

"Then that's where I'll dig it. But there will be no marker for him."

"Nor would there be one in the graveyard proper—who is there left in Girvan to carve a headstone?"

Falca had heard enough, the mystery of those bloodstains on their tunics solved: Iolus carrying this Vaience up to the room, Lenarrion helping as much as he could. And there to attend a dying friend and fellow thedral foolish enough to believe he might plow a royal furrow without consequences.

He was about to close the door when Lenarrion said something about leaving on the grave a Myrcian spurrose pendant. "…Because he always wore it. I remarked once on how handsome it was, and he said his mother gave it to him to remember the father he never knew."

"A mastlord, wasn't he?" Iolus said.

"Yes. Vaience said his ship foundered off the Flaggy Shore, all hands lost."

"You realize of course the pendant will be stolen."

"Undoubtedly. But what else to mark the grave? His spectacles? Would that I could inform his mother—Rohaise is her name, if I remember correctly—but that is hardly possible now."

"No, I'm afraid not."

Falca turned away, staring at the door, then the light of the lamp, the door again. They were still talking quietly, but he wasn't listening anymore. He heard them pass by his room and soon all was quiet except for Cofor's snoring in the adjacent room.

He had to sit down.

A moment later, he realized he was sitting on the edge of the bed, the lamp at his feet.

A mastlord, wasn't he?...his ship foundered off the Flaggy Shore...inform his mother...Rohaise is her name....

What were the chances of escaping Milatum, never to meet the woman he'd come so far to find...but winding up here with her *son*—and Ossa's—dying in a room just down the corridor...only Ossa Vere never told him he *had* a son; only the daughter, Flury, in Castlecliff.

*Chances? Roak's balls—the chances were better with the street-seer on the Skull's Roll in Slideown that time....*He'd been with Lambrey Tallon, who first gave the old man a coin for his fortune told. Tallon laughed, showing mostly white teeth; he hadn't the blue gums yet: "I'd say *that's* worth a coin, Falca! Your turn—I doubt you'll better'n that!" Falca plunked a coin into the cup—for the beggar, not a prediction that could only be what the ragsman figured any ditchlicker would like to hear....

On the other hand...what were the chances that in Milatum there was *another* woman named Rohaise who had been married to a *Myrcian* mastlord who supposedly died not just *anywhere* at sea but in a wreck off the *Flaggy Shore* of Gebroan?

What were the chances he'd misheard Lenarrion and Iolus?

None.

I heard what I heard, Ossa. You have a son. When you said goodbye to Rohaise Loquin for what turned out to be the last time, she didn't know she'd be heavy by the time you got back, or she would've told you....

Falca got up, took the lamp, paused at the door, feeling for the chunk of krael he'd kept in his pocket ever since Scaldasaig, figuring there might well come a time when he'd have to use it to save his own life.

The krael was the last of what he once had: to save Ossa's life all too briefly; save Styada, make Tolo whole again. And the reason why Shar Stakeen—Flury as a girl—had followed Falca through the Rough Bounds wilderness to Scaldasaig, where she would have tried to get the secret of where more of the krael could be found. And kill him after she got what she wanted. She'd been looking at just that place when Ossa made sure she never would.

Krael could not bring back the dead—but it could heal the diseased, the maimed, and the dying.

AS HE ENTERED the room one of the oikoes—the female—loosed her tail entwined with the other's and rose to her hind legs. Her mate, lying on the floor by the bed-side table, raised his head, showing his teeth, too. "S'all right," Falca whispered. "I've come to help him."

The oikoes chittered something, moved away as Falca came closer, and plopped down a few feet beyond the table, their tails whisking over the empty trencher on the floor. But they watched him intently, their eyes glistening in the lamp light. Falca could feel the touch of the gentle breeze coming through the window, but it wasn't enough to waft away the smell of the young man's festering wounds.

Falca put the lamp on the table cluttered with vials of unguents and the feverfew; also, a small ewer of water, a cup, a book whose cover depicted a rearing horse—and spectacles. He'd still need those; for all the wonder of krael, it couldn't heal the eyes. Falca didn't know why, and neither had a sightless girl of the Banishlands and her equally remarkable and blind mother: Sovay and Laineth.

A handcloth was draped over the edge of a wash basin on the floor.

Vaience lay on his back, tall like his Myrcian father, his feet touching the bed's footboard upon which clothes were draped. He wore only a cloth wrapped around his loins. An insect buzzed away from the biggest of the bandage swathes on his belly and right arm, and settled on his scruffy beard, crawling toward the open mouth. Falca shooed it away, and again from the cup. Leaning over Ossa's son to check on his breathing—shallow, slow, labored—Falca could feel the heat rising off him.

Over the cup he rubbed out the krael to a fine powder, as Gurrus had done for Ossa; as he himself had done for Styada and Tolo. He added more water to the cup, cleaned a finger with the moistened handcloth, and then stirred the russet liquid as the oikoes moved closer to him. Both were standing now, the male pointing a paw—and the tip of a claw—at the cup.

"It must be stirred," Falca whispered, "until there are no more flakes." He didn't know why he'd spoken to them. Oikoes might understand more than the most intelligent of dogs, but he doubted this pair—Avla and Bej was it?—understood what he'd said. Still, they were obviously curious about what he was doing, knew this stranger offered mercy. Maybe they'd be able to tell Iolus and Lenarrion in the morning what had happened during the night; maybe not. But they *could* point a paw at who was responsible.

Falca didn't want that. Better the thedrals—and Vaience—believed a miracle had happened; better they didn't know the miracle had a name. They weren't shaddens like Shar Stakeen but still, apart from Timberlimbs, Falca trusted no one when it came to krael; and for a while at Scaldasaig he hadn't trusted himself, either.

He kept stirring the krael, wondering if he should tell Vaience that his older half-sister was Shar Stakeen. Who she was, what she'd done. But he had to, didn't he? If he was going to tell the young thedral about his father, what happened to him, then he'd also have to include his sister…and the names both father and daughter had to take, for different reasons, to replace those they once had: Mott and Flury Demoul. One thing Falca wouldn't tell Vaience was about those hours of slaking his sister—before he found out what she *really* wanted from him.

Falca turned at a poke on his shoulder. The female oikoe squeaked some words he didn't understand; then again he didn't have to, the meaning clear: *Is it done? What are you waiting for?*

He put the cup on the table, shook Vaience's shoulder to rouse him— gently at first, then harder—enough to be concerned that the feverfew draught Iolus had given him had been too potent.

But Vaience stirred, moaned, his eyes flickered open, then shut.

Falca kept shaking him until the eyes remained open, then showed him the cup. "You must drink this; it'll make you better."

The young thedral nodded slightly and groaned more loudly when Falca put an arm around the back of his shoulders, raising him up enough so that he could swallow the precious liquid. Falca poured carefully, slowly, so Vaience wouldn't choke on on the potion of krael, spit it back up.

Done.

He lay Vaience back down, and immediately the eyes closed again.

"We have much to talk about tomorrow," Falca whispered.

He paused by the door, lamp in hand. The oikoes stood by the bed, the female looking at Vaience, the male at Falca, their tails entwined again.

He put a finger to his lips and left the room wondering which of them, Avla or Bej, had nodded back at him.

FALCA'S DREAM THAT night began at Lake Meleke, in the same kind of boat he, Amala and Gurrus had taken from the Wardens who'd stolen the Shofet's hoard. He knew exactly where he'd dumped the provincial governor's sacks of treasure because there it was: the outcrop of rock Gurrus had likened to the shape of a flenx' head.

In the dream he could swim, and he was alone in the small boat. All the others were on the shore—Lannid, Raleva and Tolo; Cofor, Simi, Gevret and Viroco—and they had to be wondering what he was doing with the empty flour sacks he'd gotten in nearby Bastia.

He had to swim down again and again to fill the sacks with the treasure, the sacks tied to a long length of flessok, that very strong rope without which the Timberlimbs—Kelvoi like Gurrus and Styada—could not have built their villages and roads in the Rough Bounds forest canopy.

He used the rope to pull up the sacks when they were only half-full—he was strong but not *that* strong, and he had plenty of sacks to get all of the treasure. He could see everything clearly in the murky waters because he still had the golden-eyes from the time Gurrus had given the krael to him, saving his life at the waterfall in the Rough Bounds. In the dream that made a difference. In the dream the golden-eyes lasted forever.

All his friends on the shore didn't know it yet, but there would be enough treasure for each of them to live well for a lifetime, as would he.

Falca thought he'd collected all of the treasure, but he went down one last time to make sure…and that's when he was surprised to see he wasn't alone down there. Where had they come from? Why hadn't he noticed them before?

They drifted by him, parting the lake-bottom reeds, their arms and legs listless in death: Amala and Gurrus and Ossa, and Shar Stakeen. How had they gotten here? They'd all come to their ends in water, but not here; not Lake Meleke.

Someone else drifted by him, a young man whose eyes were closed, unlike the others'. Did that mean he might still be alive? Surely not, but Falca reached out to touch him—and the eyes opened, blinked.

Golden-eyes.

Falca brought him to the surface, hauled him into the boat, revived him. And after the last sputtering gasp, the young man asked: "Who was he…the man down there?"

"Your father, Mott Demoul. But he died as Ossa Vere and he never knew he had a son; leastways he never said he did. There's sadness enough for all of us, because in the short time we were friends, he became like a father to me."

CHEZ BOAIG WAS dreaming, too—at the point where he was reaching up to cup the breasts of the speckled hetera as she pulled off a golden band and released the ringlets of her black hair—when he was awakened by a shout somewhere above him on deck.

Sounded like Tetrik or Kelpie, amid-ship, just two of the four men he posted for the deep-night watch to keep the shammocky Girvan yapes away from the *Lysidia*, his 100-foot galliot that made the Girvan-Tuleen run across the awe. There had been an incident just the night before, three of the flats trying to take his ship, making it aboard after swimming all this way from the quays. They were fought off, and he personally dumped the last one over the side. The man was Flasso Ketarrion, a fishmonger from whom Boaig bought sprats and picarels when he was ashore.

Cor, better see if more of the scungey yankers are at it again....

He swung out of his berth, the little tent his cudgie had made in his nightshirt collapsing all too quickly. He slid the cord and key from around his shoulder; always happened, that, when he was sleeping. But there was no better place to keep the key to his strongbox than around his neck.

Halfway to the cabin's door he was still grutching about it. Wasn't *his* fault they had nothing themselves...not *his* fault what was coming from Milatum. And when something happened that made what *you* had suddenly in great demand, you raised your prices is what you did. *They* would do it too, if they had what was wanted. Didn't *he* pay extra for what he wanted? when he took the *Lysidia* up to Thetis for repairs she didn't need, but never mind that. Didn't *he* pay a lot more'n he should have for the new hetera at the Spindle, which maybe wasn't the best hetaria in Thetis—that was the Honeycomb—but she was still worth the money, oyah.

Same with what he was charging the yapes now to get across the awe.

Yare well, that demand was slackening, and soon he'd be taking the *Lysidia* elsewhere, maybe carving out some business as a packet for the Thetis-Karsor's Bay run. Maybe change the ship's name. His wife's family, who fronted him the money to buy the galliot, made him name it after their daughter—which he was more than willing to do, since at the time she didn't have a beam as wide as her namesake. She was still in the High Street town house, still nagging him about when he would take *her* across, too; worried about the Skarrians.

Of course the last thing *he* was worried about was the Skarrians marching down the High Street before he could take her to safety in Gebroan. Such an excuse for a tragic—and hopefully permanent—marital separation didn't come along very often.

Chez Boaig unbarred the door, had his hand on the latch when he heard more shouts—and scuffling now. The door burst open as he was cursing himself for not taking his hangar with him.

He stumbled back, colliding with the table where he made his daily counts, overturning the chair, and fell. Light swung crazily behind him, a swaying lantern. Scrabbling on his hands and knees toward the hangar he always kept near his berth, he heard someone laugh, a woman.

Which didn't make sense: Lysidia should've been snoring away in the High Street townhouse. A moment before they were on him—a boot to his arse—he wondered how much she'd paid for the quay-stompers to take over his ship.

CHAPTER THIRTEEN:

THE CORSAIR

THE TOLLING OF the campanile's bell came to Vaience from afar, as distantly as the awareness that his darkness had been interrupted by someone at his side…a man whispering words he couldn't remember. In that place between awakening and dreaming—or was it imminent death?—he waited for the incessant, urgent ringing to end.

He opened his eyes to a room whose darkness was softened by dawn or twilight—and heard voices beyond the partially opened door.

"…Should have told you, Falca, but—"

"Iolus, it won't take me long. I'll carry him myself."

"There's no time! There's nothing here for them to take, least of all a dying man. But we still must hide in the garden until they go."

Them? The garden? Falca?

Iolus he remembered. Who was the other one?

What were they talking about? What was happening?

He was still groggy, his eyes oddly weighted, and soon he fell away to a place where he didn't feel confused, the bell no longer tolling.

HOW BOLD SHE was, walking into the Widow's, leaving her Labrysson escort outside, risking the chance the other thedrals had been fully informed of the reason why he had been forced to leave Sulserra's; and asking him for the same book she'd already read, knowing it

would be here, that he'd have taken it with him; and inquiring about where in the garden was the most comfortable place to read. She said nothing else, she didn't have to, the whisper was in her eyes: Wait, but not too long, and meet me by the pergola.

And off she went with the same book he had taken a risk recommending to her when she first came to Sulserra's, saw her for the first time. Zoshia had been dead for over a hundred years, but people still thought his folk tale not suitable for proper young women, least of all a Demizell, but she had an air of mischief about her and he sensed she'd like the book. He didn't expect her to return it to him at Sulserra's but she did. He was right: she was delighted with it, not offended, and they'd talked about it while her Labrysson escorts waited impatiently in the atrium.

At the pergola she said the book would be their pretext if they were discovered before… or after. *Earning him no doubt a stern rebuke for being alone with the Demizell Cyalla, but nothing more since these Labryssons surely didn't know the full particulars of the situation. "Why, he was only reading to me, as I requested," she planned to say.*

But the Labyrisson officer did know.

He'd taken off his spectacles, put them on the pergola railing next to the book—The Enchanted Mare. There had been time enough only for an embrace and the one kiss….

HE AWAKENED AGAIN to pressure on his arm.

Avla's white paw.

"Vaience must go! Go!" *Vence mosgee! Gee!*

Bej was at the door, pawing it wide open.

His eyes no longer felt as heavy. Was it dawn or dusk? Enough light, anyway, to see his torn and bloody clothes draped on the footboard; the vials, cup, his spectacles on the bedside table, a book.

He put on his spectacles.

The Enchanted Mare.

Which could only mean that she'd been reading to him…that she was still here. *No…she couldn't be….*

She wouldn't still be here after what happened. How long had it been since? She was on the ship, maybe still off the Flaggy Shore, not even to Sandsend. Weeks more until she and Cymra reached Roak's Awe and Myrcia. But long enough for his wounds to completely heal? There was no trace of any wounds, the skin unbroken, not even puckered scars.

He was so thirsty he drank from the ewer after draining the cup.

Avla was at the door with Bej, the both of them standing, Avla telling him again they had to go, *go!*

Vaience had always understood her better than Bej from the day they'd arrived, with no note—and no explanation from the two men who delivered them and promptly left to return to Milatum. But Vaience had known without a doubt that Cyalla had sent the oikoes to him.

He dressed quickly, though not as quickly as Avla wanted: she kept raising one hind paw, then the other—what she did when she was nervous or impatient. The cuts in his blood-stained trousers and thedral's smock marked where his wounds should have been but no longer were.

He felt no pain, anywhere, nothing except a slight pressure in his eyes. A mystifying wonder slowed him down: he was able to walk toward the oikoes without collapsing!

The edificia was quiet—nothing unusual about that; everyone was sleeping. Then again, he should have heard Lenarrion's snoring. And he remembered Iolus and the other man talking in the hallway…the quick tolling of the campanile's bell. Was that why Avla and Bej were eager for him to leave? He heard nothing now, only distant shouts. The ones within seemed closer: *Cyalla's pleas, then louder commands to the Labryssons to…spare him!…no more!…it's my fault, not his….*

He followed the oikoes down the hallway, past Lenarrion's and Iolus' rooms, the doors open. Bokeen's and Hemellion's closed. He pushed both open. The rooms were empty.

Where *were* they all?

More shouts…outside.

Suddenly he didn't want to keep going. Something was wrong and it was… outside. But he couldn't stay here and…and *what?*—pick a bed and hide under it? He had to know what was happening.

The clamp of fear at his throat tightened more downstairs.

Avla and Bej scampered around the stairs as Vaience gaped at the rooms, right and left, whose cases had been crammed with books, scrolls and codices. All were empty, only a few piles of books by the door.

What's happened?

His own escribore was as clean as the others. He had been copying Auriau's *Across the Chasm* from the only copy here—his precious other one was still at home, the Linnisheer cottage and—

And turned when he heard his name called softly...and there she was with her sister Cymra, everyone gaping at the Demizells of the House of Keshkev come to the Widow Yist's...and he spilled ink on the page, smearing it, so shocked he was....

And still with the splotch of ink on his left hand, the only evidence that he was not in the grip of the strangest of dreams.

Avla called to him again—"Vaience must go!"—from beyond the balustrade of the stairs, in the corridor leading to the refectory and the rear of the edificia. "Garden! Garden! *Kehar-tun! Kehar-tun.*"

The front door crashed open.

One of the two men wore a leather skullcap, the second a hawk's-bill as brown as his teeth. Both carried short, nicked hangars—seamen's blades. "Told you we'd find an easy skim here; look at'm," Skullcap said to the other.

Vaience backed away, nothing else he could do, couldn't get past the men—corsairs?—to where Avla and Bej were by the door, hissing.

"I'm lookin' but I'm not likin'; he's poxy eyes—*sheer!* there's oiks!—*watch it.*"

Avla and Bej racing by Skullcap, tripping him with their tightly linked tails, taking him off his feet. The oikoes quickly separated, Avla snapping her tail, spraying Skullcap's face with musk. Bej leaped at the other man, teeth bared, claws out. But Hawk's-bill was quick, and batted Bej away, a back-hand fist.

"*Avla! Bej! With me! Leave them!*" Vaience bolted toward the corridor beyond the stairs, the back entrance. But he turned at Avla's screeching at Skullcap who was furiously scratching his reddening face and neck with one hand, keeping her at bay with hangar in the other. Then the corsair fled out the doorway.

Bej had gotten up, shaking his head, still stunned. Vaience shouted again for them to leave off—"*Come with me!*"—but Bej, blood showing on his bared teeth, ignored him and leaped at the corsair, who slashed at him. Vaience charged Hawk's-bill, knocking him to the floor before he could strike again with the hangar. The corsair punched him in the face, and again—breaking a stem of his spectacles where it met the glass. Vaience flung them away. He flailed away with his fists, Avla with him now, snapping at the corsair in such a fury her front claws stuttered on the floor.

Vaience chopped the corsair's wrist. He dropped the hangar. Avla snatched the blade with her tail, flung it away. But Hawk's-bill wrapped his arm around Vaience's neck, and began pulling him toward the doorway, using Vaience as a shield. "*No more, Av—*" he screamed, the corsair choking him off.

The last Vaience saw of Avla, she was at Bej's side, in the pool of her mate's blood.

Outside, Hawk's-bill punched him hard in the stomach. As Vaience gasped for air, the corsair slammed shut the door, then grabbed him by the hair, shoved him down on the portal bricks, took a collar and attached rope from his belt and slipped it over Vaience's head.

"Some help you were," he said to Skullcap, who was two spits away on his hand and knees, retching. "An easy skim you said, ya shammy yape, face swole up like a melon."

Skullcap got up, wiping the puke from his face, and then clawed again at his face, neck, chest. "Fecking oiks, the fawk-eyes—"

"Yare, well, whutever's goin' on with'm, he can still sit 'n pull. We came for benchbait, and we ain't goin' back to Duna palms up."

HE CROUCHED, FALCATA in hand, behind a gap in the hedge separating the garden from the High Street, watching four of the scuts running out from a lane that led to the High Street, pushing along two captives—one in his nightshirt—secured by neck ropes. One of the men stumbled, and his captor shouted a curse, yanked him to his feet again, and thwacked him on the back with the flat of his hangar. Somewhere farther down the lane a woman wailed.

Nothing he could do: four of the whoresons were too many for him to handle.

Corsairs from the Shelter Isles, Lennarion had said. Even if they didn't know the castle garrison had left, they'd seen the gate to Girvan was wide open: the usual two ships of the Keshkan navy—and their complement of royal marines—were gone.

Cofor, Simi, Gevret and the two thedrals were well behind Falca, hiding near the pergola at the far edge of the garden, where Falca had been until he said he'd keep watch closer to the street. They'd thought that an unnecessary risk—he might be seen, Iolus saying it wasn't likely the corsairs would be searching flower beds for loot and captives. Falca said he'd be careful as he smeared garden earth over his face. But what he didn't say was that he was keeping watch for the young thedral he never should have left in the room.

There were no other corsairs close by, but he waited a little while longer, cursing himself for not having gotten Vaience Loquin before—and by now done with explaining why the young thedral hiding with them in the pergola wasn't dying anymore, his eyes gleaming golden like a flenx' in the dark.

What the fuck did it matter if they all knew about the krael *down here*, when the source of it was *up there* on the islets of Lake Shallan?

Why didn't he ignore Iolus, grab Vaience anyway? What was it? the habit of secrecy about krael? the legacy of Shar Stakeen?

Falca stood, and headed off with his falcata in hand, expending the last of the anger at himself by slicing off stems of harlequin roses bordering the gravel path that led toward the back of the manse.

⬡

HE KNEW HE was too late when he saw the oikoes by the stairs. The female keened as she licked her mate, her tail entwined with his. The male's eyes were vacant. The blood-pool spread almost to the stacks of books. She stopped keening, looked at him and Falca knew—as surely as if she'd spoken words he could understand—that she was wondering if what he'd given Vaience could help her mate.

He shook his head. "It won't. I'm sorry."

She released her tail, pointing it at the doorway. Then she curled her tail tightly around her mate's again.

"I'm sorry," he said, and was out the door.

And down the High Street at a run, passing alleys and lanes where the darkness had not yet lifted with the brightening dawn. He could see the single-masted ship berthed at a wharf, the ends of the drawn sweeps twigs in the distance, and also a smaller ship—Boaig's?

If people hiding in houses or rooms above the darkened shops along the street were peeking out, hoping the raid would soon be over, they'd see him not as a corsair but as a fool hurrying toward a futile attempt to save a brother or father.

Still, at this point Falca was more concerned with Girvaners than corsairs. If he met a group of townsmen who'd finally gathered their courage to do the same, there was nothing he could say to convince them he wasn't one of the scuts, other than point to the fact he had no loot or captives, just the falcata.

Maybe that would be enough…but they wouldn't recognize him. He was a stranger to Girvan, and talked like one.

But he encountered no one. There was little courage to be had in a town half-emptied by a worse fear than corsairs from the Shelter Isles.

Two long stone structures—marble and dawnstone—rose from the quayside bricks, forming a wide gateway at the end of the High Street. Falca veered toward a corner of the odd monument, and knelt to catch his breath. Then he crept forward, past the first of three massive, fluted bronze rams—snarls—that fit into sockets in the marble and jutted out ten feet or more, their bottom edges resting on the paving bricks. Above the marble a layer of dawnstone was carved with inscriptions that probably boasted of some long-ago Keshkan victory, the rams no doubt from the ships of the vanquished enemy.

Peering over a snarl, Falca saw two corsairs leading a man by a neck-rope toward other captives being herded toward the end of the biggest wharf, where the two ships were docked. The man stumbled, fell, and one of the pressgangers yanked on the lead. "*Get up*! and shut yer poxy eyes—you don't needa see where yer going."

Vaience's golden-eyes were about thirty feet away but it might as well have been three hundred.

I'm too late…again….

Farther back on High Street he could have easily taken on these two, one of whom was scratching, pawing at himself. But not here—there were too many of the corsairs on the quay, never mind all those on the bigger ship.

Falca stood up, stepped away from the monument wall, not caring if they saw him now. Having gotten what they came for, they wouldn't delay their departure to kip just one more. Some of the corsairs were hefting small casks, chests; some with swag-sacks over their shoulders, carrying them up the gangplank of the bigger ship; a few of them securing the aft lines from that ship to the bow of the smaller one, a galliot.

Soon Vaience and the captives would be at the sweeps, towing the galliot to open water, replacing those corsairs at the benches who would be the prize crew for the galliot. Vaience was looking back now—the golden eyes—maybe seeing the man standing by a snarl of the monument. Or maybe he'd just been jostled by another captive shoved ahead toward the gangplank.

We have much to talk about tomorrow….

Was it so terrible that would never happen now?

Maybe not...but that wasn't good enough, was it?—*always knowing for the rest of your life that you might as well have kept the krael in your pocket, let him die. That you as much as condemned Ossa's son to a shortened life, chained to an oar bench....*

Falca walked to the last snarl, telling himself he'd done what he could. He'd tried. Vaience would never know now, and maybe it was better that way. The father was dead—the man who did something unthinkable at Scaldasaig to save the lives of two people who had become like his own son and daughter in so short a time. Ossa would never know about what had happened so far away in Girvan—and neither would his son about Scaldaisaig, and everything else.

But Falca would.

I can't do it...can't skave him...but there's nothing I can do to help him....

There was, though.

But what about the others—Cofor, Simi and Gevret. Viroco? They'd think he was dead, or had abandoned *them*.

So be it.

They had each other. They had protection up north, in Averdenn. They had hope.

Vaience had nothing.

Falca didn't know how much a difference he could make. But maybe... *maybe* he could make things easier somehow for him. The corsairs wouldn't be on the water all the time. Had to have a home base. *Maybe* there might come a chance to skelter, the both of them. The other captives too.

If he was good at anything, it was escaping.

And until then...would he be so much different than what he'd been in Draica?

Falca slid the falcata off the bronze snarl—*skeen*—and sheathed it, the better to run.

DOMO STRUKE SHOULD have already been aboard the *Sea-Flame*. But Rasher, the swale, had twisted him a little more, telling him to check the towlines to the galliot *again*, even though he'd just tied them off. "Duna wouldn't like it, would she now? anything happens 'fore we don't need 'em anymore."

Struke stood off from him, waiting for Keers and Thumzy to push the last and biggest casks up the gangplank, Rasher bellowing at them, "C'mon, c'mon you flats; we're late for the tide as it is."

Struke was in a foul mood. As the *Sea-Flame's* second swale he should've brought something back, roped or in his hands, but he hadn't. Maybe he should have taken the quiv's father, but he would have been laughed at, kipping a graylock who'd pull his last halfway to Angessa. Still, his own fault, the time he took with the quiv, her pleading with him that she was three months heavy. Wherever the husband had been, Rasher had him—maybe a brother—when he saw Struke grunting his finish with the quiv.

So now Rasher had *that* over him with Duna; Duna saying when they were coming up on the galliot in the gig, that there would be no wasting time with women, not what they were here for tonight. If Rasher said anything to her—*sheer!*—good-bye to playing hide-the-cudgie in her breasts, her hair a copper sunburst on the pillow. She'd pick someone else. She was up there now, amidships, Kellusa at her side like always. Well, whoever the Lady Vane did pick, give the Glove to—*if* she could find anyone who could get a spar like he could with Kellusa watching him slake her—wouldn't be Rasher, the swale ugly enough to wither Duna's pots of sunsbreath.

Struke turned, saw the man coming at a run and stop. As he kept on at a walk, Struke thought that maybe here was some luck, this Girvie fool. He was big but so was Struke, who figured he could dun him. More bench-bait, this one—Duna wasn't pleased with the haul of cullies. If not, there was that falcata the man had out: a beauty, the looks of it.

Seemed like he wouldn't be leaving empty-handed after all.

As he complained later, how was he to know the man had the left hand, too; defted both ways? Could change hands so fecking quick?

Which, for all to see now, extended his reach for the parry…which snapped Struke's hangar in two, the bitter half clanging on the quay bricks.

How could he have known the falcata was crucible steel?

He wasn't Keshkan either—a northron's burr: "Go tell your captain I'm not here to plead for kin—"

Rasher came blowing hard behind Struke, shoving him aside, Duna shouting, "*No!*" But maybe Rasher didn't hear her—his bad left ear. Struke was hoping Falcata would kill him—*see, not even Rasher could dun him*—so that Duna would never know about the quiv. But not a chance, not with Rasher; Rasher gristle, all those ears he'd taken, some of the vanes scared of him worse than Kellusa, having seen what he could do with that baling hook. Hook or slice— he'd filed down the outer curve sharp enough to cut limp rope, so he could kill a man both ways.

Rasher was grunting with frustration, trying to do that—but he was quick, Falcata. It was *him* doing the slicing—through Rasher's short trews, above the knees. Rasher bellowed with rage, swung overhand, Falcata there when he swung, but side-stepped. The baling hook cracked on the paving bricks.

The northron stepped back, telling him to *leave off!*; shouting he only wanted to join *"you corsairs."* But Rasher, heaving his breaths, had his blood up. Maybe he heard Falcata, maybe not; didn't matter. Struke wasn't going to tell him to quit like he should, his legs dunned bloody.

Rasher pulled his long-shank but it was over a moment later.

Falcata sheathed his blade. Struke made for the gangplank. On board, he pushed through the men who'd come to the rail to watch; could tell they were waiting for Duna's command to make good for Rasher. Some had quick-bet on the outcome, were scowling now as they shined Blear's palm with coin, the old man smiling.

Duna glared at Struke, could have boiled water with the look. Kellusa leaned close to her, whispering something in her ear, and for a moment Struke thought that had something to do with him, and he was ready to bolt down the gangplank, take his chances ashore. But Duna walked to the gangplank, the men moving aside for her, and said to Falcata. "If you want what we are, take his ear."

"The man's dead and didn't have to be. That's more than enough. He's one of yours, so why—"

"Not now he isn't. We're away. Do it or go back to what you were."

Chapter Fourteen:

ROHAISE

S HE ENTERED VAIENCE'S room and put the lamp on his escribore, next to the extra pair of spectacles he always kept here. There was another lamp on the writing desk but she didn't light it. She was less concerned with conserving precious oil than with keeping the cottage as dark as possible at night. All she needed was enough illumination for writing the letter. Beyond the nimbus of lamplight, the Sister moons and the distant glow of torchlight and campfires on Mereshaven softened the room's darkness by the single window. Banch had estimated at least two thousand troops were bivouacked there.

She had been born in the cottage, as had Vaience; in turn they'd grown into their years here. Should he ever return, he'd find the letter on the escribore at which her mother taught her to read and write, and where she had taught her son. Of course, she'd used quills, and Vaience the pen Mott had given her long ago. She'd often wondered if the eagerness with which her young son took to his lessons had something to do with that.

The silver-nibbed Myrcian pen still worked fine, and she would use it now, with the small bottle of ink bought the day before the fleet's destruction.

She had intended to write Vaience in Girvan about Banch Redallion, and the improbably delightful circumstances of how they met on Mereshaven—this was after Vaience had been sent away to the Widow Yist's.

But she couldn't do that now.

He'd never met Banch—Ikonos Banch Redallion, a Labrysson officer.

There had been other men, suitors, over the years since she lost Mott, but none she ever seriously thought of marrying. She had with Banch, and still wanted to. So did he. But not now; not here, certainly. Maybe in Averdenn.

Assuming they could get there....

They'd have to get to the Chase, which normally would take less than an hour by way of Delmarrion's Bridge that linked Linnisheer to southern Linnisvale, where the densely wooded Chase overlooked the Narrows. But now they'd have to go at night, carefully avoiding curfew patrols. She knew a way to bypass the bridge—through the adjacent Roishan's Gardens below—but there would be more Skarrian patrols before they got to the Chase. And once there, they'd have to swim across the Narrows, as Banch had ordered the other Labrysson survivors to do, assuming they hadn't run afoul of patrols in getting to the Chase in small groups.

Well, Banch would be swimming anyway; all Labryssons could, part of their training. She couldn't. All she could do was hold onto a cut tree, keeping the sack of Epona's jewels atop the middling log, while he swam and pushed them both across. He was strong, he could do it, but after that…it was a long way to Averdenn to meet up with the other Labryssons…and begin what could be the most difficult task of all: fulfilling Queen Epona's dying command.

She picked up the pen, dipped it in the ink, reminding herself again that she couldn't mention anything about Banch—and what he'd brought here. The letter had to be worthless to anyone else who might find it—Skarrian or otherwise—except for the mother who wrote it, and the son who might never read it.

◯

DEAREST VAIENCE,

My hope with this is that long after our city is free again, all that's on these pages you would have already heard from me, and some of it told again to your children.

I suppose the only place to begin this is telling you how fortunate I was to be here, at home, during the worst of it.

As the King's Own Gardener my duty was, of course, to help with the festivities surrounding a royal departure to Castlecliff and Cyalla's wedding to the Sanctor's son. I was responsible for the vast amounts of flowers to be provided to the anticipated thousands of people gathered on both sides of the Cleave: flowers to fall like the snow neither you nor

I have ever seen, upon the royal ships passing below. What I'd taken from the parterres on Mereshaven would not be enough. More was needed from the various municipal gardens, especially Roishan's and others in Linnisheer and Linnismorn.

So for these preparations I was elsewhere than Mereshaven. I stayed here at home at night, preferring convenience over the Gardener's cottage on the royal isle.

The burning of the fleet changed everything.

There had been rumors that only the Demizells fled the city shortly after that, escorted by Labryssons; and rumors of the defeat of our army somewhere near Phaistos. As you can imagine, there was no need for the royal floriste especially after her workers were shunted to auxiliaries of the Meresguard; their spades, trowels and wheelbarrows replaced by swords and pikes.

So I was at home, then, when the siege began, but I didn't stay. I helped tend to the wounded in the defense of Delmarrion's Bridge, the Skarrians pressing down from Linnisvale, Mereshaven having already fallen. But after the Skarrians broke through at Delmarrion's, I managed to get back here to await whatever was to come. Just Kulu and I; her mate, Kep, had died in the fighting.

Oh Vai...it was...it's such a terrible, rending time for so many here....

For days after the fall of our city, I spent nights inside here, never daring to light so much as a single candle. I was not as worried about Skarrians coming in the night as I was about our own people whose desperation for food and a safe haven could lead them to do things they wouldn't otherwise. I would tell Kulu to stay inside by the front door and come to wake me if she sensed someone outside, coming up from the Lazza or down the steps that lead past the Kojarion manse above us.

During the day we'd occasionally venture outside, hidden from below by both terrace walls my father built to a height well above his five year-old daughter's, figuring that by the time she was older she would have enough sense not to be tempted to play on the walls, and risk a fall that would break bones if not kill her.

Yare, I wasn't as clever as you, so I never thought of tying a rope around my waist, running the end through the drainage hole at the bottom of a wall, and knotting it so I could play with my dares on the wall. You gave me such a fright that time when I saw you doing just that—and neither of us knowing your sight had probably already shortened a bit then. Hardest thing for me was NOT to scream at you to get off—maybe startling you and causing the very thing I was afraid would happen.

But you had it worked out: "Galloping horses! Maima, the rope saves me if I fall off. Then, you see, it's only be a matter of climbing back up, like I'm scaling a wall in battle."

You were only a wee wain, maybe five, when you said that. Where did "galloping horses" come from? Where in hilly Milatum are there places for horses to gallop? I don't recall punishing you for doing what I'd told you not to do. I suppose I was always too lenient with you. Probably your father would have been stricter—but not much. I suspect he would have been up there with you, and then pulled ME up to show us some sailor's jig with only my nervous squeals and his laughter for the music.

I'm sorry; I was telling you about the days…after.

I reckoned that no looter—Skarrian or Milat, by night or day—would think there was anything to bother with here, and whatever might be worth the bother, not worth the effort, the steps up from the back end of the Lazza being so steep and the ones coming down from Colza's Way above not much better.

Anyway, there's little to loot here except for your boyhood books and things that would mean nothing to anyone but you and I. What little perishable food I had I put in the barrow father liked to call the springhouse he carved and dug out from the hillside. I keep the door closed with a clasp just complicated enough so that most oikoes—the feral ones—can't figure out how to get in. There's the water from the cistern on the cottage roof, though it's getting low and I have to be careful with my measures. I only light a cooking fire in the brazier during the night so the chimney smoke isn't so easily seen.

Who knows when the city shall resume any sort of…normalcy. Maybe never again. Still, I'm lucky to have survived this long when so many have not. To even be able to write this…here; a place so much smaller and more difficult—that's the word—than my Gardener's residence on Mereshaven. Some thought me foolish to keep this cottage and put up with the trouble of getting to and from it; a place where I couldn't enjoy the sightings of the royals on Mereshaven, and hear gossip first-hand; or see the sun set between the Wovens, and the Labryssons resplendent in their blue-and-green trimmed white uniforms.

Well, for most of my days I could have all that—and the ease of getting to and from the royal gardens—but I wasn't about to give up our home, even if you were living at Sulserra's; even if I rarely came home more than once a week.

When you were older I was going to tell you much more about the place in which you were born, but I never got around to doing that…and then suddenly you were twelve years-old and off to Sulserra's, the youngest ever. to go there. I was so proud of you.

In crowded Milatum it is hard to imagine a home built from empty space, but in a way your grandfather, Karev Loquin, built from less than that.

He was born on a stony impoverished island in the Shelters, one of a crop of nine. His father sold him at fourteen to a factor procuring labor for the Slagtown quarry. Karev was one of twenty-five men and youths taken from that island alone, to replace quarrymen who'd died in a recurrence of the Walking Plague that struck Linisheer particularly bad that year. He was indentured but slavery was what it was. From their pitiful wages the workers were forced to buy everything they needed from stores run by the quarry owner, and they had to pay back the money he spent to procure them.

A few years later, so the story goes, Karev caught the eye of the quarry's new owner, Kolare Kojarion, who needed men to make a terrace out of the rocky slope below his manse. Kojarion had taken a young wife to replace his first who'd died in the Walking Plague, and she was with child. He wanted a garden for them both, a place of color and fragrance from which to enjoy the magnificent view of the Queensmere, and Mereshaven to the north.

Your grandfather was one of five indentured men chosen from the quarry's workforce for this purpose. Kojarion promised to release them from their bond upon completion of the terrace. Karev and the others lived in a single room of a sair tenement, also owned by Kojarion, at the bottom of the steep hill—near where the tessaria is now.

First they had to carve out the steps leading up the hill from the Lazza, and of course past Kojarion's manse facing Colza's Way. The more progress they made, the farther they had to take the bluestone rubble away in baskets and down to wagons below. And walk back up. Vai, you know 'our' hill...imagine the work involved!—day after day, week after week.

They finished the steps in the time it took Kojarion's wife to come to term, but she died of birth-fever and the baby not long after.

What use for a terrace and garden now? Kojarion dismissed the men. But your grandfather told him that the steps should lead to something, if only a memorial to the wife and child he'd lost. Kojarion was touched by the suggestion and so Karev moved into the manse, sharing quarters with the servants.

It took your grandfather three years—pickaxe, sledge, iron wedges, hammer, baskets, a trundle cart above—to carve out the terrace and haul in soil from outside the city. He didn't know what to plant there, but by this time he'd married a woman who did, Sulania Sossule. I was never told much about her, so of course I always believed there was much more to her than everyone wanted to tell me—which made her all the more mysterious, though there was nothing mysterious about her generous and sweet nature that she passed on to my mother. Evidently Sulania's people were farmers who lost their stead near Syarra. But why she came to Milatum all by herself at eighteen, and where she learned to read and write—well, those are stories I never heard tell.

Anyway, when Kojarion became too frail for the steps, Karev and Sulania would help him to the terrace garden. And after the man died, my grandparents found out that he had bequeathed the terrace to them, making provisions that the steps, top to bottom, would forever be theirs to use.

He also left them enough money with which to build on that terrace their own small cottage. And there was one more thing he did, Vai: he sold the quarry to a prominent

Linnisheer ephor, reducing the price in exchange for giving the Loquins the municipal contract for maintaining Roishan's Gardens—which was passed on to my father, and eventually to me.

In time the cottage became crowded indeed, though for a while my parents lived elsewhere.

I remember almost nothing about my brother, Lovarr, who didn't survive his second year. My mother died when I was eleven. But I was old enough to remember her accompanying my father to Roishan's, and her helping him carve out a second, smaller terrace where he dug out the springhouse; where you liked to play with the children from the manse above us…well, at least until you had that scuffle with one of them, who called your father a low-born sailor who couldn't possibly have been a Myrcian mastlord because otherwise he wouldn't have married a gardener. Remember what I told you then? that even if he HAD been only a sailor I still would have married him, knowing full well what sailors are wont to do in other ports of call.

I so wish my father had lived long enough to meet yours; that Mott hadn't died in the shipwreck before he knew you, had been with us to see what a fine man you've become. And yes, that you might have had your own memories of him, not just mine.

Well, I suppose my having years with him was something that may not have ever happened for me, either, even if he hadn't gone down with his windwhipper, the Flury, along the Flaggy Shore, as I eventually learned. Still, I knew when I married your father that I would have to count months as years with him. In fact, I doubt that all the time we were together here would amount to but a single year.

I never regretted that; how could I? He gave me you. And for the long stretches of his absences I had my work at Roishan's, the tapestries, and my oikoes here to keep me company. Beginning a few months after you were born, I would take you with me to Roishan's, in much the same way that my father had with me.

And lucky we continued that for years, until you went to Sulserra's anyway. You know that story and how it ended! Yare, I may have saved the King's son in the Chase that borders Roishan's, but you were the one who first noticed the rabid oikoe before he leaped past that startled retainer and onto the back of the pony carrying the future king of Keshkevar!

Wouldn't that have been a tale to tell your father upon a return to Milatum! For THAT I would have bought the finest spyglass, and instead of once a week I would have waited EVERY day at the top of the steps (by the fireheart shrub in which I always hid Roak's Week candy for you), to catch sight of the Myrcian spurrose pennant flying from the Flury's mizzen as the pilot boat pulled the windwhipper toward the Lazza quay below. And waited impatiently for him to climb up the long, steep steps; and the both of us, you and I, telling the story of how I came to have that pendant hanging around my neck—the Golden Spade of the King's Own Gardener, the previous one having been found one morning drunk among border parterres of harlequin roses and sunsbreath.

You once asked me why I never married again. Oh, well, you know there were a few who paid court—including that playwright I met at Clane's Theater, when you and I were there to see the comedy that was all the rage at that time, The Braggart. What was his name?—Kesio something. His wit was certainly evident, as was the thrill of his private carriage—your mother had never been squired around in one—and also a remarkable ability to avoid looking at me square on. He'd come close—forehead, chin, ears, but my recollection is that his eyes rarely met mine.

*I don't remember giving you much of an answer to your question, except perhaps a smile and a shrug that was supposed to mean...*maybe someday.

I'm thinking now—those steps of ours—that maybe my never marrying again had something to do with them.

The steps are the most direct way to the cottage, up from the Lazza, and also the steepest. Your father could have taken the easier route along Colza's Way, most of it by a carriage he could well afford. He never did. Never once did I welcome him home when he wasn't a little out of breath from the climb.

My thought is that there are too many men—and women—quite willing to walk down steps but reluctant to go up, for whatever or whoever is at the end. Maybe that seems like an unfair sort of...test, but it wasn't.

I've met a man who I love and who feels the same way about me, but events have overtaken us. As they have all of us, those of us who still must count themselves very fortunate to be merely overtaken and not killed.

There is nothing left of Sulserra's, except a charred shell. It was set afire the last night of the siege. I can only hope you have already assumed that the edificia in Girvan will suffer the same fate when the Skarrians extend their conquests to the west—which they surely will—and that you and the other thedrals there will be far away by then. Which makes me think now of Cyalla, whom I wanted to mention anyway.

I wish her well, though she will need more than wishes to endure her assigned fate. Still, she and her sister escaped a worse one here. And I truly hope for her fair winds, because she as much as saved your life, Vai.

When you wrote that one time to tell me what happened, it was obvious to me that all you'd done was take a liking to a young, extraordinarily beautiful young woman who enjoyed talking to you about books at Sulserra's—and who just happened *to be a Demizell of the House of Keshkev.*

I never got the chance to write to you about the two times I met her on Mereshaven.

I was by Kelef's Way, with two of my gardeners in the south parterres, working the beds of meadowbride, winking jesper and staghorn. I had Bej and Avla with me. As they are still fairly young I was training them as I had Kulu and Kep, who were at the cottage. When trained, oikoes are useful in culling root-beetles that are particularly destructive to staghorn. They also find the beetles tasty, so it's a mutual benefit, though I've never quite gotten used to the crunching sound when they eat the pests.

Anyway, along comes Cyalla, reading a book, her two chaperons trailing behind her. I had no idea then that the book was one you had thought she might enjoy. Cyalla stopped, handed the book to one of the chaperons who looked as if the Demizell had just given her the spade I was using. We struck up a conversation about oikoes. Both Avla and Bej quickly took to Cyalla, who instinctively sensed that oikoes do not like an assertive, forced approach.

Now, I'd heard gossip about Cyalla being as…difficult as she was beautiful, but to me she seemed lively, curious and sweet, yet with hint of stubbornness: she kept ignoring her attendants' pointed suggestions to move on and enjoy the "brilliance and fragrance of the beds of harlequin roses down the path."

"Aren't they your favorite flower, Demizell?" said one of the chaperons.

"Why don't we let these people get back to work," said the other.

They became silent, however, when Cyalla accepted my gift to her of Bej and Avla. She was delighted, and I was both pleased and relieved since my two pairs of oikoes weren't getting along and I'd been wondering what I was going to do with Bej and Avla.

I thought no more about that afternoon—until I was summoned by the over-chamberlain of the royal household. He rebuked me for giving the oikoes to the Demizell. Oh, she did indeed adore oikoes but she'd been forbidden to have any. The chamberlain sniffily reminded me of what I perhaps should have realized: that oikoes were an inappropriate gift considering that her brother, the future king of Keshkevar, had almost been bitten and clawed by that rabid oikoe in the Chase.

But the rebuke wasn't the end of it. There was a "much more serious matter", for which it was the chamberlain's "unfortunate duty" to inform me. Seems the Loquins were getting a reputation for 'inappropriate' behavior regarding the Demizell Cyalla. That was when I found out that you had been summarily sent to the Girvan edificia because of your "highly inappropriate behavior" toward her, and for your suggesting—I was never told how that came to be known—a certain book to her, called The Enchanted Mare, *that was particularly scandalous and outrageous for a daughter of the Labrys. I WAS told that had I not been who I was, and if the Demizell hadn't insisted that any impropriety was hers alone, this matter would have had more severe consequences.*

I could do nothing about the heartache of your exile to Girvan, but I was curious to see what sort of book had prompted such outrage. Tisht! Where was the harm for Cyalla to read from a book as she strolled through the garden parterres on a beautiful day? Had you given her the kind of lewd book so popular in Gebroan, and I daresay in certain parts of Milatum?

I read the book in a quiet room off the atrium in Sulserra's, and now I realize why some squits in the royal household might consider The Enchanted Mare *more than just a robust and rouncy folk tale. The orphaned girl in the story was* ILL-TREATED; *clever and beautiful though* LAME. *She* DEFIED *her uncle and shamed his sons by taming— when no one else could—an exquisite horse they'd stolen. And then, determined to* ESCAPE *to freedom, she rode away on that horse, her plan all along. The cousins pursued her, but she* VANISHED *at a gallop before their eyes, and was* NEVER SEEN AGAIN.

I spoke to Cyalla once more in the gardens, when she told me that Bej and Avla had not been cruelly disposed of; that she had sent them—discreetly—to you.

It is very late, and I must end this. I wish with all my heart that you are safe, my dearest son, and that Avla and Bej, are doing what they can to keep you so.

I love you,

Maima

SHE FOLDED THE pages of the letter and left it on the escribore for Vaience to find. But by the time he did—*if* he did—there would probably be someone else living here, who'd just taken the cottage over, the letter tossed away. Still, you never knew, and she was glad she'd had this time with him, telling him things she hadn't before, that he should know.

Kulu had come in while she was writing, and wrapped her tail around her left ankle—the next best thing to entwining her tail with Kep's. It wasn't likely now that Kulu would find another mate. Sometimes they did when one died, but not often. And Kulu would be going with them, to where there were few, if any, oikoes. Kulu sensed she was done, and got up. She let Kulu's tail slide through her fingers, thinking that the oikoe would have no problem with the crossing, not with a tail to wrap around a branch nub, her claws gripping bark.

She extinguished the lamp and made her way to her bed chamber, and Kulu padded away to finish out the night by the cottage's front door, as its bar wasn't as stout as the other door's.

She'd always meant to fix that, but no point in doing it now; they wouldn't be here for much longer.

Banch lay on his side on the bed, head propped up on his hand, watching her. She lay down next to him, kissed him.

"Thought you'd be well away," she said.

"I couldn't. Every little sound…thinking someone's outside, somehow knows it's there. Foolish, but here I am, wide awake."

"Even if someone came, they'd never find it—Kulu's done her part."

"That she has," Banch said, smiling. "So have you, it was your idea."

The stirrup pot was in the springhouse and filled with emeralds, rubies, sunstones, flarenets, stardonyx and rare blueveil gems—all the jewels that were to have kept Queen Epona comfortably in exile in Gebroan, along with the dream of reclaiming her kingdom.

And on top of the treasure…the by-now dried-out remains of two days' worth of Kulu's leavings.

Banch grazed the back of his fingers along her cheek, then kissed her. "You were gone a long time."

"I kept thinking of things to say, and there was so much I wanted to but couldn't—about you…and us."

"You'll tell him yourself, before he even reads what you wrote. They went somewhere from Girvan, he and the others, surely; and someone along the awe will know where they went. You'll see your boy again."

She squeezed his hand, grateful for a confidence she wished she felt. She wanted to see him more than anything else but….

Not now; don't ask Banch now or we'll be arguing all night about it….

Still, she had to ask Banch sometime what she wanted to do *after* they got to Averdenn.

After the crossing, ask him then….

She turned on her other side, and gathered Banch's hand in her own.

Soon enough he fell asleep, his breathing warm on her shoulder.

You'll see your boy again….

She wanted that so much but…he *wasn't* a boy anymore; he was a man and had his own steps to take. And so did she.

There were other things she couldn't tell her son in the letter, such as whose grave it was underneath the mound in the upper terrace vegetable garden, fallow now for months. And that there was a possibility that she would be seeing the Demizell Cyalla long before he ever would.

BOOK TWO:

ANGESSA

From *DAUGHTER OF THE LABRYS*

LESS THAN A day out of Girvan the officer commanding our Labrysson escort, Symmos Korsh Mevellion, informed me that until we passed Sandsend—and possibly longer—I would be sequestered below in the cabin I shared with my sister. He listened, not without sympathy, to my protests; but he said he had his orders from the king, and patiently explained the reasons for a father's desire to ensure the safety of his eldest daughter.

There was a risk of encountering corsairs along the entire coast of Gebroan and beyond—the Ebony Isles. Symmos Mevellion didn't think it likely that pirates would dare attack a ship as formidable as ours, much less successfully, given our contingent of royal marines and Labryssons. But there remained a concern, which was why we'd sailed from Girvan with the other navy ship that had been stationed there: a faster, nimbler vessel whose primary purpose would be to maneuver between us and an enemy's, to prevent it from ramming us, should it have a snarl.

I said: "Surely in the event of an attack—which you deem unlikely—there would be plenty of time for me to get out of the way and go below."

Symmos Korsh admitted as such, but then went on about krakens, which are sometimes spotted along the Flaggy Shore between Thetis and Karsor's Bay. Thus, our ship would have lookouts posted forward to give warnings about krakens and hopefully avoid them in time.

I said: "If we collide with one, what does it matter *where* I am, above or below."

Symmos Mevellion was undeterred, and continued at length about more danger: the wind-borne spiders around the three islands across from Sandsend. It was the season for them. I'd heard about these spiders; how pious monks living on the islands would annually send aloft surplus spiders and their webs, to let the prevailing winds carry them to Sandsend and punish the people of that supposedly wicked city—as if the spiders would bite only the depraved. Though not usually fatal, a spider bite could cause a debilitating fever. I'd often wondered why someone didn't stop the monks' nasty tradition one way or another, until I learned they produced Gebroan's finest wine, and whisp made of spider silk—two of that kingdom's most lucrative exports.

But those spiders—if indeed our sails fetched any from the wind—were days away. Why keep me below until then?

Lastly there was this: our ships would not be putting into any Gebroanan port, for fear that word might have quickly spread about the "cargo" bound for Castlecliff—the cargo being two Demizells of the House of Keshkev, and one of them consigned to marry a son of the Myrcian Sanctor.

Symmos Mevellion had his orders to ensure my safety and he was impressively inspired, I'll give him that: *corsairs…kraken…wind-borne spiders… spies racing ahead of us along Gebroan's coastal Orphic Road.* But I doubt my father had particularly mentioned these.

No, Symmos Mevellion couldn't divulge the *real* reason for my sequestration: a fear that I would leap overboard, taking my life in the fashion of certain heroines in books I'd been caught reading; young women forced to accept a fate not of their choosing, and so instead entertained the notion of embracing death if they could not embrace love.

Flude! I'd stopped reading such syrupy romances long ago, but my my mother and father didn't know that—and neither did my Labrysson chaperon. But he'd seen how distraught I was in the aftermath of the tryst with Vaience.

I was annoyed about the sequestration, but mostly because Cymra was exempted from it. No, not because she, not I, would have the freedom and fresh air of the deck; rather, implicit in this was a judgment that my sister was not as important and valuable a…cargo, as I.

Dear Cymra staunchly vowed common cause: if *I* was to be kept below, pinned to the cushion, then so would *she*. For a while that common cause amounted to wretched seasickness. But soon after, I convinced her that fresh air and diversion for one sister was the next best thing for the other.

In truth, I was glad of those hours she spent on deck for I was stricken at heart by all that had happened, and there was no point in subjecting Cymra to my moodiness more than I had already.

The match with Joffreck had been arranged months before, but the more urgent need from my parents' standpoint was to get Cymra and I out of Milatum should the worst happen with the looming Skarrian threat. Better an early arrival in Castlecliff for us than possibly being trapped in Milatum. My younger sister had been shocked as we all were by the fleet's destruction, but I think she believed our mother and father—more than I—when they said that my marriage to Joffreck would be delayed until this Skarrian threat was dealt with, after which our mother and possibly Lerrist would journey to Castlecliff to be present at the wedding. At the time Cymra believed she would see them again, and father too. But I had the strong feeling we wouldn't.

In that carriage, hurrying through the Orphic Gate, accompanied by one attendant wagon, and twenty-five mounted Labryssons who would escort us to Girvan and the two navy ships stationed there, I was already grieving for my family. And perhaps all the more so because I'd been such trouble to them. They infuriated me, too, at times; but that paled with the ache that I might never see my mother and father again, or amend the estrangement with my brother Lerrist.

I loved him, and I'm sure he felt the same with me. But we'd never gotten along well. He always seemed uncomfortable around me. I think he sometimes felt that he—the eldest sibling and male—should have been the one to do the talking-back to our parents; the one to question, to bite at the leash; that as the oldest and a boy, he should be the one teasing *me*. But it was the other way around. He tried—and part of me wanted him to be successful—but he wasn't up to it. I should have let him be. Can you be cruel to an *older* brother? Occasionally I was, I admit.

Once, he tried to tease me about the time I spent reading books. My response was quick; I've never had the problem of tardiness in that regard—which I've come to realize can be a problem in its own way if you speak without a thought to the consequences of what you're saying. So that time, I said: "Lerrist, if you spent as much time with books as you do before your mirror, you'd be the most learned man in Milatum."

My brother *was* exceedingly handsome, but I think he felt he was not as intelligent as he would like to be, should be, or was *expected* to be as heir to the Labrys Throne. Humor made him uncomfortable—especially mine, which could be sharp. He often retreated from jests, perhaps because he feared he would not understand the quip or the reason why someone might laugh at it. So he seemed to hide behind the defense that he had more important things to do and think about—which undoubtedly he did as the heir apparent to the Labrys Throne. The result, however, was a young man who was overly serious. I even said to him once that he'd be even more handsome if he smiled every now and then.

I kept my mouth shut in the matter of whether Lerrist would go with us. Later, there were times when I felt almost sick about doing so—an aching self-reproach. But in that was a kind of vanity, as if I could have affected a decision that was our parents' and Lerrist's to make. Even if I had pleaded with my brother to come with us, it would not have helped. I wish he had, so that perhaps eventually he might have come to smile more, and I might have learned to keep my tongue in check.

It wasn't to be. Oh indeed, our mother wanted him to go with us, said he'd be *safer* doing so—and then realizing her mistake in telling him that, she made it worse by adding that he had a duty to look after his sisters, as it was her duty now to stay with her husband in a perilous hour.

Lerrist then was of an age where he was physically a man, no longer a youth. But that is the least measure of a grown man, and Lerrist knew it. Of course he wanted to prove himself. What man or woman does not want that?

He refused to go. "How can I become the kind of king I need to be, and wish to be, if your priorities, Mother, are my safety and…and being a nursemaid to Cyalla and Cymra?" I remember him looking so proud about these words, perhaps even the edge of disdain in his voice. He glanced at father for approval—and got it. Father nodded: "The girls will have Labryssons to ensure their safety."

But mostly in those days of sequestration, well before any of us knew what was happening at home, I thought about the young man I'd left in Girvan, and how I'd left him.

The two days of seasickness were terrible, but at least they kept my guilt sequestered as well about what I'd done at Girvan. And then the despair returned. For all I knew, a few Labryssons might have gone back to the Widow Yist's and killed him, even though I'd told them the tryst was my idea. And it was.

Perhaps that awful afternoon in Girvan should never have happened, but it did, and it began earlier with an immediate attraction to Vaience Loquin that was like nothing I'd ever felt before. I knew he felt the same and *that*, too, was different from what I'd previously experienced: there was nothing *covetous* in his eyes; I did not sense he *wanted* anything from me beyond the moment.

Others—my mother, perhaps even my brother if we'd been closer—might have said: *Oh, so you knew did you? I doubt it. What you felt was more like what a storekeeper feels when he pockets money from the best sale of the day. What you felt was nothing more than what you've always enjoyed: tithes to your beauty.* Or they might have said: *You merely felt a thrill you hadn't before—consorting with a thedral. For all their learning, they are still commoners....*

No.

I knew what I felt.

But in the ship after Girvan I kept hearing those imaginary voices—and my own.

Because of me, Vaience got sent away to a provincial edificia, probably diminishing if not ruining his prospects as a thedral. That should have warned me about further consequences if I wouldn't leave him alone. Sending his mother's oikoes to him should have been a farewell gift. I never should have gone to the Widow Yist's but I did and with a purpose in mind.

I was determined to make sure someone else besides a Myrcian prince twenty years older than I, whom I didn't want to marry, who reputedly couldn't mount a horse without help from his retainers—would make me a woman. I desperately wanted Vaience Loquin to be that man. And let Joffreck fume or pout or cast me aside after he saw the bridal sheet wasn't spotted with virginal blood.

It was obvious Vaience and I would never see each other again... afterwards. I told myself that if I was using him...well, at least I was using him in a way he'd never forget. And I'd rather he always have that claim on me— such as it was—instead of a man for whom I felt nothing. Let Vaience and I forever share that brief memory, if nothing else.

As we approached Girvan I told Cymra of my plan, and also confessed to feeling like a conniver in order to accomplish. Her vehement reaction surprised me: "Faugh! Spare me the popinall about...connivance, Cyler! Slife, you're always talking to me about making my own choices instead of having others make them for you. If you're using him...at least it's to your credit that you recognize it. You keep telling me to have faith in myself. Well, do the same; believe that what you feel for him is not skimmed from your books or the gossip of handmaidens. And never mind you've seen him only six times."

Cym felt so good about lecturing her older sister and promising her collaboration that I remember to this day her exact words.

But she was off by one: I'd met with Vaience a seventh time.

He and I had carefully arranged this particular tryst as if we were plotting a rebellion.

He would come to Mereshaven on the pretext of seeing his mother, the royal gardener. Rohaise would be working, of course, so we'd have her cottage there all to ourselves. I was confident I could sneak away from my chambers in the Kelefion—any excuse would do if a chaperon pestered me—and meet him at the cottage at the appointed early afternoon hour.

Well, Rohaise was outside, sitting on bench, sharpening a spade. She wasn't smiling and I instantly banished any thought of further subterfuge. "Yare, Vaience was as surprised to see me as you are, Demizell," she said. "I came back to get the whetstone I'd left. He's inside. The door remains open. Feel free to talk about books and the weather. I'll give you two the time it will take me to finish putting a better edge to my spade. Then I'll escort you back to the Kelefion. If anyone asks where you were, you were lost with your thoughts among the meadowbride and harlequin roses."

For some reason that…tryst was the one I was most eager to tell Cymra about, bungled as it was. I couldn't. Not that I didn't trust her. But if by chance anyone ever learned about it, Rohaise would have been summarily dismissed— at the very least.

Every other time, including the day Vaience and I first met, was at Sulserra's. We talked in a reading room off the atrium. The windows in that room were high, so neither of us could see the nearby terraces of Phelonia's Forest. But the windows were always open and we could hear the rhythmic turning of the windmill vanes powering the screw that brought water up from below.

Once I asked Vaience if this bright, lovely room—filled with book stalls and cases, escribores and comfortable chairs with arms wide enough for a glass of some beverage or another—was where he did his reading. He laughed and adjusted his spectacles. "Oh, for a while I did, until I was shaken awake in that very chair you're sitting in, by a senior thedral named Carchemion. He scowled at me, saying: 'You're not supposed to be falling asleep in the afternoon for another forty years.'

"He would have none of my excuses: the unseasonably hot weather we'd been having at the time, the lulling effect of the windmill." Vaience pointed at the windows and went on. "He said, 'Perhaps I was wrong years ago in allowing your admittance to Sulserra's at so young an age. But you're here and I'd appreciate you doing my reputation a favor and find another place for your reading and writing sessions, so that in the future you will not be tempted to confuse a working windmill with your fond memory of being rocked in a cradle.'"

Vaience laughed again, and at that moment I couldn't decide which I liked more—the story or the timbre of his laughter.

He was so different from the smug, self-satisfied courtiers I'd met at balls or by appointment; most of them—as potential suitors—seeking to impress me with their titles and plumage. And impressive they often were at first glance, much like a banquet table's rich and colorful dishes that later give you indigestion. There's truth in the Keshkan proverb: *At meeting you're judged by your clothes; at parting you're judged by your wits.*

Vaience had a peculiar tattoo—a skink, he called it—on his left wrist. For me, perhaps the most sheltered eighteen-year-old in Milatum, what was most intriguing was where he'd gotten it, a skinker's shop in the Lazza. I suppose many young men of station had tattoos, but doubtless they would have been depictions of a boast, a deed done; or a totem of some ferocious, predatory beast.

Vaience's was a single word—*Kai*.

I asked him who she was. He hesitated, looking a little embarrassed, so of course I assumed Kai had to be his first love. Then he said: "No, nothing as rouncy as that. It's…well, it's merely a reminder of a man who lived over 300 years ago." That's all he said, perhaps fearing I'd be bored with further explanation, but I insisted.

The man was a Keshkan soldier/philosopher named Auriau, who wrote only one book called *Across the Chasm*. In it he wrote about a creed he called *Kai*, which respects differences and celebrates commonality. It goes beyond what he saw as the separateness of the Keshkan Sacred Thrice, the triskell. *Kai* conjoins the circles of the Sacred Thrice, and resides where they overlap. It may be found along the shore where land meets the sea; in twilight and dawn; in the union of two people; where duty or responsibility meets self-interest; where a wealthy or knowledgeable person sees in the face of a beggar what he or she might have been.

Vaience was not surprised I'd never heard of Auriau. Most people hadn't, the man long forgotten. He'd written only the one book. He espoused no specific deity, claimed no personal connection to any. In his own words: "I am merely a soldier who has seen too much and not enough." He disappeared when he was still fairly young, Vaience said. All that was known for sure was that he sailed from Milatum, never to be seen again; nor was there any mention that Vaience could find of Auriau finishing out his days in another kingdom.

The tattoo I have now is not the same as Vaience's, nor in the same place as his. But I am getting ahead of my story.

As I said before, Vaience never tried to impress me. I made inquiries and discovered that Rohaise Loquin's son was, indeed, the youngest ever to have been admitted to Sulserra's. No, it was the other way around. *I was* the one who tried to impress *him* with my sophistication; that while my sister and I were officially Daughters of the Labrys, I wanted him to know how preposterous I thought the whole legend that so many in Milatum and elsewhere in Keshkevar believed was fact. I assumed that Vaience—a learned thedral and all the more impressively for his years—would share my disdain for all matters regarding the Labrys.

I remember him that day at Sulerra's taking a sip of wine from his glass. That he'd offered the same to a Demizell was as outrageous as the fact that I'd accepted it. Vaience put his glass down. "Well, you're right," he said. "*The Book of Labrys* makes no sense whatever to account for what Colza found here over a thousand years ago. But I think it's also beautiful. I mean, the heart and head do not…hmmm…they don't always have to be in opposition. There is a meeting place, though finding it often requires directions for which few are willing to ask, and still fewer give."

He said this conversationally, not as a tutor making a pronouncement. I was shocked and chastened—*this* from someone the same age as I? Perhaps if we hadn't just then been interrupted by the Labrysson terros in charge of my escort, who told me it was time to return to Mereshaven, I would have asked Vaience about that "meeting place", and whether it was another facet of *Kai* or…something else.

I never got the chance. Not long after that he was sent to Girvan and the edificia there that was not so much bigger than Sulserra's atrium. I never thought I'd see him again. But there was indeed a...meeting place in Girvan: the pergola at the Widow Yist's; and I needed no directions to find it. I still wanted his words, but I also wanted the man to remember as well....

About seven days into the voyage to Castlecliff, the sails of our ship did indeed fetch those wind-borne spiders. Cymra—her face and arms covered by a shawl of wisp and linsey—came down to our cabin that afternoon, and said that almost two-dozen sailors, marines and Labryssons had fallen ill from the bites of spiders that dropped from the sails and shrouds.

I'd had enough of sequestration. My Labrysson guard, posted at the bottom of the companionway, had closed the hatch above but too late as it turned out. He politely and firmly denied my request to go above—until I flicked from his shoulder a red-and-black spider that was crawling along his white cape toward his neck. The spider was the size of my thumbnail. I crushed it with the heel of my shoe with a satisfying crunch, and told the Labrysson that he needn't worry about disobeying orders since the one who'd given them was now sickened above.

Cymra and I went above to do what we could to tend to Symmos Mevellion and others similarly afflicted.

CHAPTER FIFTEEN:

BLADE-BREAKER

T HE SQUALL THAT caught them two days out of Girvan had blown itself out after a third, opening up a band of blue sky to the south and leaving a reminder of its ferocity that sung through the rigging and kept the mainsail tight as drumhead. Falca sat cross-legged against the lee rail of the canted deck, keening the falcata with the small scabbard whetstone. He stopped to wipe sea-spray off the blade, and inadvertently felt the gristly lump in the same pocket that the krael had been in.

What he wanted to do before they got to this Angessa—earlier in the afternoon they'd seen the welcome sign of gulls—was toss the fucking ear overboard, tell Blear he'd lost it in the storm. And never mind the graylock told him he must keep it; that while it had gotten Falca on board, he wouldn't truly be one of Duna Rheg's vanes until the ear was glazed and hung from his belt. "And maybe by then you'll think of a name for that blade; s'gotta have one."

Blear, the oldest of any of the crew—vanes they called themselves—had deemed it fawky that such a mazer sword didn't have a name, that being the custom in the Shelter Isles, leastways the vanes of Duna Rheg. A wondrous blade, he said; cut off Rasher's ear so clean and easy you'd think it was a link of sausage. No sawing it off, like the other vanes had to do with their hangars.

Yahh well, even good steel was little more than a long butter knife if you didn't keep the edge; nothing wondrous about that. What *was* wondrous, Falca thought, was that he still *had* the falcata Amala gave to him before they left Draica with Gurrus; that and the lock of her yellow-gold hair he'd sliced off

with the falcata before he slid her into the pool at the waterfall in the Rough
Bounds.

Amala Damarr was the only woman he'd ever loved.

She was his *kushla*, which meant 'sun-thicket' in Timberlimb Tongue.

She called him *kahyeh*...'my heart'.

They had planned to journey on to Milatum together after helping Gurrus
return the kinnet to the Isle of Shallan deep in the Rough Bounds wilderness.

Amala....

Falca reversed the whetstone for more strokes—*rasp...rasp.*

He had a penchant for 'what-ifs', a habit he never had been able to break,
because while it could distract you into trouble if you weren't careful, it could
also help get you *out* of trouble. But he couldn't help thinking now: if she had
been with him back in Girvan, would he still have gone after Vaience Loquin?
leaving her with the others?

He could hear her now. *Go, kahyeh. I'll be waiting for you in Averdenn with our
friends. Just make damn sure you come back to me—and with Ossa's son....*

Who was now below-decks, shackled by a leg to a mother-chain between
the oar-benches along with the other cullies.

Rasp...rasp.

Falca glanced up to see Duna Rheg emerging from the companionway aft
of the *Sea-Flame's* main, Kellusa following her. Duna—call her that or LadyVane
but never captain, Blear said—was pointing at the four sun-bleached vanes
stitched to the center of the faded blue mainsail, obviously reminding Kellusa
that it would have to be restitched after landfall. The vanes looked like those of
a windmill and one of them had almost ripped loose in the squall.

Falca had yet to see Duna without Kellusa at her side.

A strange pair, those two, and to look at them you'd think the greyla was
the leader here. She was the tallest of anyone on the ship but well-proportioned.
Her arms and shoulders, though not as muscular as a stoneskin male's, were still
impressive. She had black, widely-set eyes, her silver hair tied back with a gold
oval brooch, her earrings golden, too. Her skin was the color and texture of the
whetstone in Falca's hand. He'd seen the greyla tending to the edges of her own
weapon—a short-shaft glave; a Keshkan marine's weapon—by stroking it up
and down on her flat belly beneath the bandy covering her breasts. She also had
a weighted net hanging from the belt of her short trews, and on each forearm
she wore studded bronze casings.

All in all, a big handsome stoneskin female that might have made Ballast—Falca's stoneskin friend from what seemed like an age ago—forget all about his greyla mate. What was her name? *Marf Mag*, that was it. Ballast wouldn't have been intimidated in the least by Kellusa, but everyone else here was. Headbutt, the vane who'd replaced Rasher as swale, had warned Falca to knuck and nod, keep his mouth shut around Kellusa. There'd been this vane, joined up at Tantallon, made the mistake of asking Kellusa why her tits weren't as big as Duna's, and she so much smaller than Kellusa.

It was the last question he ever asked—at least that anyone understood, since he lost the tip of his tongue and most of his front teeth when Kellusa broke his jaw with a rising forearm blow to the chin the man never saw coming.

Whatever the reason the copper-haired Duna was the commander of these vanes and not Kellusa, there was no doubt she was, and that the greyla had no problem with it.

Kellusa saw Falca now, a long enough look that Falca figured he'd better acknowledge. The pair headed off toward the helmsman at the wheel, passing more vanes including the one who'd been with Rasher on the Girvan quay. Struke was his name. Falca had seen him whittling something beyond the scuttle but now he was talking to Headbutt. The swale scratched under one of the straps of his spiked helmet, and said something to which Struke nodded sullenly. Headbutt went aft and Struke scowled, brushing his gloved right hand over the bleached stripes of his dark hair, and resumed his whittling after glancing at Falca again. His one hooped earring and one glove wasn't the half of it, because he'd only had half the belly for a ruck, and of course only half the hangar he'd left on the Girvan quay.

Keep an eye on that one....

Falca finished up with the keening—two more strokes of the whetstone. As he put it away in the scabbard pocket, he noticed Blear coming up from below, the hatchway opposite Duna's cabin. The scrawny graylock was looking around, squinting, as if deciding where to dump the small, lidded bucket he carried. Then he limped toward Falca at the lee rail, the slops bucket swinging a little with the roll of the ship. It seemed odd to Falca that Blear would be emptying a waste bucket up here when he could have dumped the slops into the shithole below—but then he realized that wasn't what was in the bucket.

Falca got up as the old man approached and put the bucket down. He dabbed a red, watery eye with a forefinger of his right hand—the only finger he had on that one except for the thumb. But whatever else the years had dunned him, he hadn't lost the thickness of the hair that fell to his shoulders, swirling a bit with the wind.

"Where's it at?" he said, tapping the skein of ears tied to a leather thong at his belt, then waggling that forefinger.

Falca took the gray ear from his pocket—there were still some flecks of dried blood in the sprouting tufts of ear-hole hair—and handed it to Blear.

"They always look bigger when they're not attached," the old man said. "I would've gotten to you sooner but didn't want to waste my blue on a dead man."

"So that's it, why you were waiting."

Blear shrugged, sniffed. "Reckoned it was even odds that Strukie would've pinched your wick by now—while you were sleeping, of course. Or do it during the blow we had. But Headbutt had you below for the tantrum, outta the way, you being useless above except for why Kellusa gave you the nod back in Girvan."

"You mean Duna."

"Her too, but the Murk—"

"Wait…Murk? You mean Kellusa?"

"Isn't that what I just said?"

"She's no Murk."

"You calling me a liar?"

"You're a liar."

Blear smiled. "Last time anyone saw a Murk was a coupla hundred years ago and a long way from here."

"I didn't say I saw one. Kellusa's a stoneskin greyla. All it takes is seeing one of 'em to know the other isn't."

"And that was…where? In Draica, where you say you're from?"

"Not there."

"Yare well, we'll keep her a Murk, won't we, Breks? since that's what everyone thinks she is, seeing as how not a man on the *Sea-Flame's* seen one—or a stoneskin for that matter."

Falca shrugged. "Who'm I to tip anyone otherwise? I understand, sure: Murk, stoneskin, a big fish from the sea…doesn't matter to Duna what her deek is so long's everyone's scared of her."

"Now that's settled, here's some advice. You got wits, oyah, but best you keep 'em outta that spit-hole of yours, or someone besides the Glove is gonna start wondering more'n they are already about why you wanted on."

Falca skimmed a thumb along his fingers. "Same as everyone else."

"Not all of us."

"So this...Glove," Falca said, moving on quickly, "he's the one over there, who's been looking at us, pulling on his earring?"

"He's Duna's slider. When she chooses her Glove she makes'm wear it. Strukie's probably waiting for someone else to dun you—he's choice meat and about as smart, but that's how Duna likes her Gloves—but what I was saying was, there's others don't like you either but *they're* waiting for Strukie to make good on Rasher. They don't like you because they know they couldn't have done any better'n Rasher—and they lost money on you, betting on him to kill you. Now, let's see to putting the blue to his ear. Maybe while it's drying you can tell me why a northron like you walked up the quay like you had the Girvan garrison behind you—which is maybe why I bet on you. But between the two of us, you ain't the only one's a liar."

"I told you, I'm here to make some shine," Falca said, thinking: *Keep an eye on this one, too....*

DOMO STRUKE WASN'T making much progress carving a new handle for the caulking iron. He'd started about the same time as the Draican began honing his falcata.

Struke couldn't hear the rasping over the ship's creaking timbers, the wind whistling through the stays and sheets, the snapping of the loose canvas vane above, and Rivet droning on with the same song at the wheel.

But Struke could see the whoreson stroking the crucible steel that broke his hangar in half.

Something else broke too, that couldn't be replaced as easily as a hangar: something no one had seen before, not even Duna. Maybe suspected like Rasher did. But they all *knew* it now: that Struke was no chin-up, would rather find a way out of a ruck than stay in one, and never mind he had a blue ear hanging from his belt.

He'd quit on that quay.

Even the three sunstone jewels on the falcata's hilt—each one worth more than what he'd get for his share of the Girvan swag—shamed him, made sair his ear hoop's single ruby.

There was Blear now, putting the blue to the Draican's prize, dunking Rasher's ear in the foul-smelling pot the old skinker called his olla podruda. Letting the ear steep in the blue, gattling on to the northron all the while, then plucking it out with his clawey hand to let it dry in the heat and wind; talking to him more than he did when he glazed Struke's first ear. Which wasn't right. Only four days now since what happened and Blear talking to the Draican like he'd known him for four months.

Struke whittled a little more, looked over again. It wasn't just him who grumbled about a man sure to bring bad luck. Not only that, there was the shine lost betting on Rasher to kill the fool that came with the dawn on the Girvan quay. All the whispers since, about Struke dunning the Draican—*when you gonna do it?*—were putting him in a foul mood. As if *they* would have chinned-up on the quay with half a hangar to do it with.

Yare well, he *would* have done it after, was going to shove the Draican over the rail during the decks-awash tantrum, but it wasn't *his* fault Headbutt sent him below. And Blear only making it worse, pushing Struke to make a move, like he wanted to bet again on the Draican, make more shine.

He was still simmering about what the old man said at yesterday's three-bell's meal below, the Draican silent at the end of the board: "Oyah, Strukie here thinks he brings the salt to the table, like Rasher did, and look what happened? But who's to blame the Glove? How's he supposed to look at himself in his bronzie if his wick's snuffed."

The old gattler wouldn't lay off, calling him the prettiest fish Duna'd ever caught, still with a mouthful of teeth—and that was when Struke lifted Blear up by his neck, so enraged he couldn't get any words out, and he might have kept squeezing if Headbutt hadn't whacked him in the back of his knees. He wound up with Blear on top of him, shoved him off, everyone laughing now except for the Draican watching the whole thing and stuffing bread in his pocket.

Duna's catch? Was it his fault she chose him to replace her last Glove got killed before Struke came on the *Sea-Spider?* Which was the other thing about the Draican cob: he'd *chosen* to come on, whatever the reason. Struke *had* no choice, picked like he was, with Gyllyd, too, clinging to a hatch cover, after their merchantman foundered on the Dagger Reefs off Terenure.

Struke had a mind to slit the skinker's throat, but he couldn't do that. Blear had been with Duna as long as Kellusa had. And the graylock was also the vanes' stackler, closest they had to a medicant; and only he knew how to make what was in the olla podruda. Duna wanted ears and she wanted them blue, and the more ears you had the bigger your share of swag.

But he had to do something about the Draican, Falca Breks said he was. Too many expecting Struke to do it, but thinking he hadn't the belly. Maybe even Duna didn't think he did—she'd said not a word to him since Girvan; and before, never a day passed on the ship when she wouldn't do that, pat his crotch.

Sheer!—he didn't deserve the vanes' snorts, their headshakes behind his back. Didn't he have the best eyes of any on the ship?—Rasher putting him on the kraken-watch. He had the eyes all right, oyah, and what he'd *seen* on the fecking quay, thinking about it now, was someone shouldn't have been there…who later looked at the Girvan cullies like he wanted something from them. Seen *that*, too. Or maybe it was the other way around. Maybe he knew one of them, kin or not. Maybe the northron was taffy, but Struke didn't think so.

Whatever, there was something…*wrong* about the Draican, but all Duna and Kellusa and Blear saw was someone who knew how to use that poxy falcata—those big, quick hands.

Maybe he could find out what was fawky about him, maybe not. But all that really mattered was getting rid of the cob, and to do that Struke had to be smart about it. No one thought he was, and that probably included Duna. She wasn't slaking him ashore—never on the ship—for what was between his ears.

But he had enough wits to know that if he'd tried to do what most thought he should have by now, he'd be dead; another ear dangling from the Draican's belt. And smart enough to see the chance to kill strappy-jack when he saw it.

Probably once they got to Angessa.

But not tonight. Struke had the kraken-watch. These waters, away from the coast, the kraken surfaced most often at night, rising from the depths to scoop up the picarels. Often you could smell the kraken before you could see 'em; he had a nose, too, for that. Hadn't he already prevented one collision, two weeks after he and Gyllyd were picked up? Which caught Duna's attention, got him the Glove and the ruby hooper not long after.

Yet he had to dun the Draican soon, because maybe Duna was thinking now about taking back what she'd given him, after what happened on the Girvan quay. Maybe she'd still take 'em back after he killed the fawky Draican, but Struke didn't think she'd do that; she'd be dripping buckets for him.

And then he'd have another ear and Falca Breks' crucible steel; the sunstone gems too. And he'd give the falcata a name, like it should have, a blade like that.

Blade-breaker sounded good.

ONLY IN A dream could Vaience have gone on the ship that was taking Cyalla to Castlecliff, but the dream vanished when he awoke, someone gently shaking his shoulder.

At first he thought it was the snoring galliot captain—Chez Boaig—who lay next to him, his back turned. Maybe the man had moved in his sleep, a jostling Vaience mistook for the shoulder-shake. He rose to an elbow, squinting, as if that would help him see any better in the dark. The aft lantern was a swaying blur. But he thought he heard movement down the line of berths and hammocks: a vane coming back from a trip to the shittery after he'd stumbled past Vaience, knocking his shoulder?

Then Vaience smelled something—which wasn't sweat or piss or the stink of all the snoring, shackled captives and vanes down here. The smell was close by, and he felt for it.

A heel of bread. A thick slice of salted meat on top. His hands came away moist: the hard bread had been soaked in water.

One of the crew must have hidden food from the board, bided his time to give it to him. But why?...and why *him* of any of the captives?

For days now they'd been given only gruel with bits of meat in it. One of the prisoners had spit out a worm that would have been as long as a finger had he not bitten it in half.

Now, Vaience forced himself to eat slowly, savoring every morsel.

He lay back down, his belly nowhere near full, but better than it had been. It wasn't long before he was dreaming again:

He lay on a pallet, not planking. The bread had been soaked in wine, and there were three slices of meat, not the one. And something sweet—a golo glazed with honey? Instead of a quick shaking of his shoulder, he'd been woken by a kiss.

She was kneeling at his side, a finger to her lips, because it would not do at all to have one of the Labryssons awaken to see the Demizell Cyalla below, where she should not be. He moved her finger away and kissed her. She gently stroked his cheek and rose, and he put on his spectacles to watch her hurry away. The light was better; a lantern forward, too. And before she crept up the companionway, she turned and smiled and put her fingers to her lips again and flicked the silent message to him. He knew what it was: there would be more trysts in Castlecliff while her husband was snoring away in his bedchamber in the Sanctor's Azure Tower. But for now he'd have to taste just the honey....

CHAPTER SIXTEEN:

THE NIGHT WATCH

FALCA LEANED AGAINST the cullies' prison hut, one foot up against the stone wall, wondering if he'd get more visitors tonight than just one: Struke.

He'd been on his feet for hours, the halved Sister moons at full rise now, flanking the highest jagged remains of what had once been the keep of a promontory fortress overlooking Angessa cove. He wanted nothing more than to sit down, his back against the bar of the low door to this little prison—a long beehive-shaped hut entirely made of roughly-dressed stone blocks, is what it was.

For most of the afternoon and into early evening he'd been hauling: hauling the Girvan swag up from the ships; hauling water from the quarry pools below the fortress ruins on the headland to the small wooden house Duna shared with Kellusa on the hill above the village; and hauling more water to the only other wooden structure on this sair island, the vanes' hall. No cullies did any of the work—they were imprisoned immediately after arrival—which prompted grumbling among the crew: *why else did we kip them if not for scut work?*

Falca knew that if he sat down he'd fall asleep right off, and there was a good chance he'd never wake up, unless you counted a hangar slicing across your throat.

Headbutt had picked him for this night watch, to make sure the cullies didn't somehow escape from "the hard room", he called it; and warned him they'd better not, since the Lady Vane was in a grutchy mood, the Girvan haul of prisoners not being what she'd hoped for. "You're the eyes for tonight, Draican, up 'ere at the hard room; and for the ships below, cove-side."

Was Headbutt setting him up? Falca thought not...*probably* not. Headbutt was now the swale—thanks to Falca. So likely he'd just picked Falca because he was the newest vane.

But Struke and everyone else knew he'd be up here alone, drowsy if not asleep. And if Struke was going to do anything about...Girvan, it would be tonight, hoping for an easy skim, telling the story later about how he found the Draican asleep at his post, rightfully killed him, and took over the watch since someone had to do it the way Headbutt said.

Would Struke bring a deek or two with him? Probably...not. Duna's Glove wouldn't want to share the chivvy of killing the man who dunned Rasher.

Falca stifled the urge to yawn. *Yahh well, the wankspit comes, with or without help, keep your back to the hut....*

The hour had to be close to midnight. But still too early for...visitors. Struke would wait, and wait some more for him to fall asleep. Which was what Blear also said not to do, as if Falca didn't know that. "Some think you will, and what good then that fine blade of yours?"

Falca had asked him the obvious: "What d'you care what happens?"

The graylock tapped his two teeth and smiled. "You shined my palm before, told you that. You can't do it again, you're dead."

Which wasn't it; something else was going on. Until he found out what it was, the only thing he could trust now about Blear was that he likely wouldn't be the one paying a visit tonight with a hangar.

Falca rubbed his eyes, gripped the falcata again. He'd already used up the...swag Headbut had given him to stay awake: if only the swale knew the man he'd chosen to guard the cullies was the only vane who wanted to free them.

Falca couldn't suppress another yawn. The constancy of the *shush...shush* of waves breaking on the strand below wasn't helping. Nor the wind. Though it'd risen since he'd been up here, it still carried the warmth of the day. In Draica, even a summer wind at night had a briskness, but here it seemed like the finest of coverlets to pull over you.

Still, he was lucky. Vaience Loquin and the others had to be sweltering inside the hut which trapped the day's heat. They'd probably finished off the two jugs of water Headbutt told Rivet to put in there.

Falca kept his eyes moving, always coming back to the path leading up from the village. He tried to figure out what the snapping sound was on one of the ships below. Then he moved on to the dawnstone tower at the end of the narrow dock, and moved up...up to the brilliance of the constellations: the gauziness of the Silver Trail; the Hammer, the Cauldron and the Anvil; and the brighter Sisters.

And back to the dock; recently rebuilt, Blear said. But the tower was new, its dawnstone making it visible far out to sea, if not the skulls piled on top. They were all that remained of the few Angessa villagers who had resisted Duna's takeover of their miserable island months ago. All the others, about forty, Blear said, had been sold in Tantallon, the only port of any size in the Shelters east of Trigel. A few Angessans had hid in the fortress ruins on the headland, but not for long. Falca could see the faint glow over the ruins that came from the remains of dawnstone rampart steps, what was left of the rubble after the vanes had taken what they needed to build the cold-light little pharos at the end of the dock.

He'd earlier noticed more dawnstone ruins not far away from the cullies' hut, and figured the walk over there, the distraction, might help keep his drowsiness at bay. They weren't much bigger than the hut. Three of the six sides of the plinth were mostly rubble, and one of the three tapering, spindle-like columns had been cracked off. But the taller, thicker center column was intact, frosted at the top with spanner and gull droppings like the others.

Maybe this—whatever it was—had once been built by the islanders, a beacon for fishing boats coming in late to the cove. Nahh, that didn't make any sense; the dawnstone rubble in the ruins on the promontory would have been all the marker fishermen would have needed.

He headed back, passing the cove-side of the hut, thinking about tossing the scraps of bread in his pocket through one of the two open windows set below where the stone roof sloped in. A small child might have been able to squeeze through but not a man. But Falca only had a handful of scraps. If he tossed them through a window, likely squint-eyed Vaience would never get the food, shoved aside by the others. Much as he'd like to help the other cullies, what Falca did have had to go to Vaience—which, looking ahead, was going to be a problem. He couldn't be seen handing scraps to him, wherever he wound up—probably the promontory ruins. Maybe Duna was going to sell the cullies like she had the Angessans, but more likely they were the first of more to be culled to rebuild the fortress; why else would she and her vanes have come to this shitstep of an island? For dawnstone? Corsairs weren't in the business of selling dawnstone to Milatum or elsewhere, even if slaves were doing the hauling or quarrying.

It seemed likely she wanted a stronghold all her own, and while it would take time to rebuild Angessa's, she had a start with the luckless Girvaners inside the hut for now. And how long would a soft, thin-armed, squint-eyed thedral last up there? Never mind he was young, younger than Falca was, maybe—

He heard crying within the hut. Vaience? Probably not. On the *Sea-Flame* Falca hadn't heard him say a damn thing, though the galliot captain—Boaig was it?—had complained enough. Seemed to be that one, the burnfinger ferryman, shouting at some cullie to shut up. Which didn't work—Falca heard a slap, a surprisingly loud *crack*. Then, someone else shouted: "Leave'm alone, ya fat-arse squit!"

The crying subsided to whimpers, then all was quiet within.

And still no sign of…company. Which didn't mean Struke wasn't down there, lying awake in one of the vanes' huts, whispering to himself, maybe to others: *Not yet…he's gotta be asleep….*

Or was just sawing away? no intention of paying a visit, at least not tonight.

Maybe Duna had summoned him to her house for a slide.

If either were the case…more than enough time to free Vaience, all the cullies.

Falca glanced at the hut's door a few paces away. It was so low he'd had to crouch over when he and Rivet had gone in to unshackle the cullies, the pile of irons near the landward corner of the hut.

There was no lock on the door's stout bar.

Just lift it up….

Now might be the best chance he'd ever have.

Wait, think it through….

Maybe…*maybe* fifteen men, suddenly loose, could keep quiet. But all it would take was one vane, pissing outside the nearest hut below, to hear and raise the alarm.

Sure, we could reach the dock, get on the galliot, but where was the time to get it underway….

What about the boat down there on the strand, off to the right? Falca couldn't see it from where he was, but he had during the day, some islander's

fishing boat, now the vanes'. There'd been a couple of oars sticking out. So…
he and Vaience, maybe a couple more cullies could take it.

But the ones left behind wouldn't meekly accept their fate. All right, say
they did, kept quiet. How long would he and Vaience, a few others, last with
Falca's handful of bread scraps and no water? Even if Duna didn't come after.
Which she would. The *Sea-Flame* had passed several islands on the way here, but
getting to the nearest one—forget the mainland—might take a week or more
rowing the boat.

Tonight wasn't a good idea after all.

The next raid? *Maybe*—if Vaience was at the sweeps of the *Sea-Flame* and
not up on the headland being worked from dawn to dusk. *All right, say he's on
the ship…*Get the key to the mother-chain—somehow—and free him, all of
them, while the vanes were looting ashore, culling more men. The vanes would
probably raid some town along the Gebroanan coast, where there was no risk
of running into Skarrians. But if they raided some other place in the Shelter
Isles, Falca and everyone else would just be exchanging Angessa for another
island. And wherever the next raid might be, the vanes would take the scatboat
to get to shore, so the escapees would have to swim to freedom—only Falca
couldn't swim and Vaience probably couldn't either.

Roak's blood but he was still tempted to do it tonight…but he knew in his
gut it wasn't the time, if only because he refused to believe there wouldn't be a
better opportunity. The trick with taking your chance was *seeing* it, even if you
couldn't right off.

And all he was seeing right now was the empty path that curled up from
the village of stone huts and the timber-roofed hall. Most of the path was
hidden by the contours of this hill overlooking the cove Falca decided to leave
his post by the door to check the moon-silvered path from other vantage points
near the cullies' hut.

And…nothing; no shadowy movement on the winding path.

And…back again where he was supposed to be, everything the same: the
muffled snoring of the cullies, the *shushing* surf below and that faint knocking
on one of the ships, the empty path.

Yet something was bothering him, a burr that kept him from sheathing
the falcata.

But hadn't he just made sure no one was coming up the path, no one
hidden below a rise. He was right where he should be to see if—

That's it....

He was right where everyone would *assume* he'd be: by the door to the hut watching everything he was *supposed* to be watching—including the path leading down to the vanes' huts.

Falca pushed off the wall as if someone had shoved him hard from behind.

And even if you weren't wary of someone coming up to settle a score, you might be thinking how you'd rather be in one of the huts down there, getting your sleep.

Well away from the door, falcata in hand now, Falca kept his eyes on the side of the hut.

If he's gonna do it tonight...that's what he's thinking. Where else would the Draican be for the night watch if not in front of the hut....

Struke—with another vane, a few of them?—would stay *off* the path, not risk the chance of being seen; he'd go around, keep it quiet coming up behind the hut, close quickly.

Even if I wasn't asleep, he'd be thinking...easy skim, if he closes quickly....

Falca hurried along the side of the hut facing the strand below, stopped at the far corner, and knelt. He was beyond the pale of the odd dawnstone plinth and spindles though the strange monument wasn't far away. Likely Struke would be coming from beyond the monument or past its near side as he approached the *rear* of the hut.

Whether Struke came or not, Falca intended to spend the rest of the night where he wasn't supposed to be.

He waited, and waited longer still—standing up, then kneeling again, and looking behind frequently because maybe he'd given Struke more wits than he had, the man using the path after all—and was beginning to think that tonight wouldn't be the night.

And then there is was: a shadowy figure moving along the hillock beyond the glow of the monument.

For a moment he couldn't tell if it was Struke or someone else approaching the plinth in a crouch, now scuttling away from it, heading for the hut, no one behind him.

It was Struke, knife in his gloved right hand. No hangar.

Not here...surprise him here and he'll only back off and run....

The easy skim gone, and nothing settled tonight for either of them.

Falca quickly—and silently—went back to where he'd been by the hut's door, falcata in his left hand now. Struke would have to come around the corner of the hut, knife in his right hand—that much farther away from Falca. He gave the vane what he wanted to hear: fitful snoring much louder than the ripping and buzzing coming from inside the hut. Falca could heard the breathing now, louder than it should be, Struke anticipating a moment that hadn't happened yet: slicing the throat of a sitting, sleeping man. The breathing was so close now....

He had the length and used it, spinning around, thrusting the falcata into Struke's belly. The vane grunted, dropped the knife as Falca yanked out the falcata. Struke collapsed to his knees. Falca swung over the hand that shook toward the knife—a tight backhand slash to the neck—and stepped back. Struke fell to his side. Dark blood pulsed out of the cut. His hands twitched at his chest, and then the throes of his stuttering legs were done, and all was quiet except for Falca's hard breathing and the cullies' snoring in the hut.

He wiped the falcata on Struke's trews, picked up the knife and felt the edge—*gonna cut my throat with a dull knife*—and tossed it away. Kneeling by the body, he used the tip of the falcata to slice off just enough of the earlobe to free the jeweled hooper and then pocketed the earring.

Maybe any other vane would have taken the whole ear, but one ear was already one too many to dangle from Falca's belt. But the earring might come in handy at some point, if only as a further reminder to the other vanes of what this one failed to do.

He dragged Struke over toward the door, sat him up against the hut's wall, stuck the knife into the ground between his legs. He looked like he was sleeping, chin down at his blood-soaked chest.

Falca walked over to the dawnstone monument, sat down on the crumbled edge of the plinth.

Struke was probably it for the night. Even if any other vanes knew where he'd gone, there was little chance they'd want to see what happened to him, not after he didn't return from killing the Draican.

And for Falca little chance of falling asleep here in the glow of the dawnstone, even if he lay down on the plinth—not having just killed the Lady Vane's Glove. That wasn't because of the shakes; Falca didn't get them anymore.

You do what you have to do, someone tries to kill you.

Still...*two of them now...shide....*

Roak's teeth but he hoped that Vaience Loquin didn't turn out to be a wankspit who'd make him regret his choice at the snarls any more; and maybe

Ossa—wherever he was—sighing and thinking the same thing: that the son he never knew he had wasn't worth the going after.

Falca was still awake at dawn. But because he was sitting on the plinth, facing west, he wasn't in a position to see Headbutt or some other vane come up the path and wonder why Struke was sitting near the door instead of Falca. Nor was he in a position to see the sun rising directly over the top of the middle and highest spindle of the ancient, ruined monument.

CHAPTER SEVENTEEN:

BASKET OF RUINS

BLEAR RUBBED THE knee he'd bruised slipping on the crumbling top step of the stairway leading up to the ramparts—what was left of them. He could have easily fallen off and that would have been that, the choice taken from him. He stood up on the landing, peered over the edge—probably *there* was where he would have whumped: that heap of rubble covered by spittle-grass, weeds and wild sunsbreath.

He backed away, and after a while settled in with these ruins, trying to see what might have been.

What're you gonna call it, Duna? Castle Rheg? Castle Vanes?

For that matter, what had it *once* been called? when the four towers and the gateway rose high; when the round turris had been more than just the present single high window and the landing that, like this one on the outer wall, led to nowhere except a gimpy old man's clumsiness and fancies.

Yare well, he wasn't up here for fancies, was he?

The sea beyond was a deeper blue now with the waning afternoon. The age-coarsened stone of the jagged crenelations was still hot to the touch, though. He wiped sweat from his brow and looked out to the northeast, the direction from which Rooka should be coming with a message from Gyllyd— if not today then tomorrow—that hopefully would bring good news.

Duna called him *Raw*, for his calling sound but that wasn't the name Blear had given the stormbird fledgling when he'd captured it on a much smaller island to the west a year ago. Blear wasn't much use in helping the other vanes scour the careened hull of the *Sea-Flame*, but in the month they were on that uninhabited island, he began training Rooka to be a messenger. Heezup, who'd shown Blear the fundamentals, was at the other end, on Gyllyd's ship.

But stormbirds-as-messengers needed two handlers and either Heezup or Blear was soon going to have to pick and train a replacement.

For now, anyway, Blear had the balm of a creature with whom he could share secrets and not worry about the keeping of them.

He hadn't been overly concerned the first time, on the way to Girvan, about the spot of blood in his spit—until it happened again on the return. And this morning, more than a spot: the size of his thumbnail it was. He spent the rest of the morning in the hut, after Rivet and the others left. All the years of mixing skinker's inks? getting some inside, his fingers always stained; or inhaling the fumes? Or was it the olla podruda, preparing ear glaze?

Or just getting on in years?

Cor—he wasn't *that* old.

So what do you do? Wait until you're helpless on your pallet, coughing up every hour…waiting for the final fade? Or step off the ramparts up here…*now?*

But if you don't wait for it, when do you decide *today* is the day? How do you pick that one moment out of what remains of your life, to end it?

Duna, Kellusa—all of them, maybe even Breks—would think old Blear had slipped. And for some reason he preferred that: one final secret in a lifetime of keeping them. Was that it? Or was it not wanting to somehow taint what was to come—as if anyone would care how he crossed off; as if doing that would taint a fecking thing.

Was CastleRheg what he *hoped* would come?

Maybe the Draican would be part of it, maybe not. But so far, so good. Blear had reckoned that Struke would go after him when he did, the squit believing his nuggets were at stake. If there'd been bets taken on who'd be alive in the morning, Blear would have made more money on Breks. And more still if anyone had been foolish enough to bet that the Lady Vane would dun Breks in some way for killing her current Glove: no one knew Duna like Blear did—except Kellusa, of course.

By the time he got up to the cullies' hut, maybe half the vanes were there, and Duna not even asking Breks what had happened since it was clear enough what had: the Draican sitting Struke up against the hut, like the bloody half-brick Glove was the one who'd fallen asleep at his post.

Maybe Duna had said something before Blear got there, but all he heard was her asking Breks where it was, the hooper jewel.

"In a safer place; my pocket." Breks looking her square in the eye.

"Why didn't you take his ear?"

"One's enough."

Blear thought Duna'd want the hooper; it was hers after all. But she turned and walked away with Kellusa, telling Headbutt to have the body weighted and dropped from the end of the dock....

The mare's-tail clouds had thickened to the east, but toward the north the sky was all blue, with gulls far off the strand. There was a darker speck above them...no, a spanner not Rooka.

Still got the eyes, anyway....Though whenever Rooka did come, bringing Gyllyd's message in the wee pouch double-knotted to her leg, he'd have to hold the words away to read them. Right now on the island, the sun hanging three fingers above the horizon, there were only two others who could read, and if Duna hadn't taught Kellusa, there'd be one less.

He'd always had his letters and numbers, back when he also had all his fingers, because his father—a purser who'd jumped ship in Thetis and stayed—had taught him. He wasn't Blear then, that inevitable corruption of *blue-ear*.

His name was Carta Fallure, and he'd considered joining a theater troupe because he loved the sound of himself talking, and he was good at it. But he became a skinker after his sister married one, the man needing an apprentice who could do tattoos with words *and* numbers, that being a fashion at the time. And he also eventually became a stackler, becoming proficient in bone-setting and attendant skills. The way it happened, his sister came to him one night in a very bad way—not her husband's brutality as it turned out but one of her lovers'—and Carta was surprised to discover he had a talent for ministration. He took care of both men, *oyah*, the husband more subtly than the other, and because his grateful sister sang his praises as widely as she spread her legs, Carta found himself making more as a stackler and fixer than skinker.

Sheer! but he was a wonder in those days! Maybe on the small side, but braw and handsome enough to stroll across crowded Phrynne's Square and get second looks from the ladies, high-born and low. Yare, and *no* limp then and *all* his fingers to swagger along, and when you're tired of holding your strutter in one hand, there's always the other.

It all began to change the morning one especially bountiful lady came into his shop on Loso Lane, a peek away from the water-clock in Phrynne's Square. She said with a Trigel accent that she desired a tattoo in a discreet location so her husband wouldn't notice it from the front—which she said was all he ever saw of her anyway, and all too briefly at that. Then, she added with a smile: "Also, he's away for long periods of time. But what is important is that *I will* know it's there, my mirror and I."

Carta fancied himself a keelcat with the ladies, but this one's boldness took him aback. Still, what came out of her mouth was only a lick compared to what came out of her purse. So he set to work on what she wanted: two blue finbacks leaping toward each other in the lady's preferred location above the dimples on her shapely backside.

She paid twice what he'd asked, so impressed was she—as was Carta when she twisted around, dispensing with the modesty-sheet, to inspect his work with the mirror he provided. "You came with the highest recommendations for skill and discretion," she said. "I'm sure I won't be disappointed should I visit you a second time."

She did, and twice again over the next few months. Thrice delighted—but not for tattoos.

She never told him her name and Carta knew better than to ask.

Early one morning not long after her last visit, two sailors came in with what turned out to be broken bones—they'd evidently gotten the worst of a quayside tavern ruck the night before. A few days later, they reappeared with a request from their Trigellian captain, one Callamander Rheg, for Carta to meet with him on his ship to discuss a proposition for employment.

Carta agreed to go meet with this Rheg, at least to listen to what he had to say. Why not? He'd been having a slow week. And so he went with them, pocketing the shine the captain had given his sailors to compensate for his time away from the shop.

Much later, Carta wished he had asked more questions of Callamander Rheg, who'd been impressed by Carta's treatment of the sailors, and who needed someone of demonstrated skill to tend to ship-board misfortunes— what if those two sailors had been on the high seas, days away from repair?

Rheg's offer was so generous there was no question of refusing it. Besides, Carta was making enemies in Thetis faster than he was eliminating them so maybe it was time to get out of the fixer business.

The passage across the Bucca Strait to Trigel, the second-biggest island in the Shelters, took only a day, but required another to reach Rheg's residence on the island's south-shore. The manse, rivaling the finest in Thetis, overlooked a cove sheltering three ships. Carta was told Rheg had another residence on the north-shore, that one being more convenient to Thetis.

Two more days passed before Carta realized he was in a position from which even a talented fixer would be hard-pressed to extricate himself.

As she'd said in Thetis the morning he inked the finbacks on her glorious backside, her husband was often away on business and indeed that was the case this particular afternoon. Thus it was the manse's steward who introduced Carta to the Lady Cerrissa Rheg.

She looked as beautiful as before, though perhaps a bit more…bountiful than he'd remembered.

"Well here you are! My husband told me just the other day that he'd hired a most skillful stackler from Thetis to tend to his men. So will you be tending the birth as well?" She patted her belly.

"I…ah…uh…."

"Have you a small bird in your throat?—oh there! you've swallowed it!"

"My…em…my skill doesn't extend that far, Lady Rheg."

"Does it not?" she said, and smiled. And winked. "Well, I'm sure my usual midwife shall suffice again."

Those were the last words she ever spoke to him. He took his leave, the bird back in his throat, paused at the door to glance at her, but she had already turned away, laughing at something her handmaid had whispered to her.

Oh he'd thought about the woman many times before, wondering if she'd visit again, though he hadn't been in love with her. But he left her that day smitten, which he was sure had nothing to do with the fact that she would be bearing his child—or was it? Had she just been teasing him with…*tending the birth as well?*

That sly emphasis on the last two words.

Of course he could never again have Cerrissa Rheg in *any* sort of way, and even if he could, the woman would eat him alive morning to night—which was maybe why he later married such a placid woman who didn't know the first thing about putting birds in his throat.

He could have pleaded a change of mind to Callamander Rheg, but he stayed on, to be close to the child—her third—the only one he'd ever have. And also for the glimpses of raven-haired Cerrissa, her laughter and overheard snatches of her wit—when he was ashore, that is, at this particular Rheg manse; for Carta, too, was absent for long periods of time tending to men who he quickly found out were more than sailors.

Dark-haired Callamander must have wondered later what ancestor bequeathed to his daughter the copper hair. Carta, thanking the Fates that his own hair was dark as well, could have told him: his father was Lucidorian, a northron born in Slacere, down the Orphic coast road from Draica, and had hair the same color as Duna Rheg's.

They were dead now, all of the Rhegs except for her, killed in one terrible night: the Trigel Betrayal. All that was left was the father with his secret, and the daughter, homeless for almost three years.

Until they found Angessa.

No, not found; scavenged.

Blear found it amusing that the vanes seemed to consider themselves superior to the islanders they'd forcibly displaced, sair folk who scavenged seaweed to enrich their sair fields; who'd dug up rocks to build the walls that enclosed them; who scavenged robie shit and let it dry on the top of those walls to use as fuel; who no doubt counted a day as blessed when something useful washed up on the strand.

Scavengers, oyah, but who wasn't? wherever they were, on the land or sea; scavengers all, for shine, for flesh and the heart, for whatever else you wanted whether you needed it or not.

Which didn't mean the Angessans shouldn't have been sold.

Early on—the hall marked out for dimensions but not yet built with Gyllyd's first prize, a timber hauler bound for Milatum from Anaktora—there'd been a meeting about what to do with the islanders. Every vane could have a say if he chose; that's how these worked. Blear had his, waited for the groans to subside, the vanes expecting him to go on and on, and he did. Oh, such a fine speech it was, that followed Duna's and others like Jeppy-the-Nail, a Gebroanan who said to kill 'em all and be done with it.

"That would be a waste," Blear began. "The Lady Vane has chosen this place for what it will be one day, not for what it is now. You heard her. She calls it a basket—empty now but filled in time. Which will require much. Yare, we could work the islanders here for our purposes—but better to sell 'em for shine in our hands, and cull the sweat we'll need from others elsewhere, who won't be reminded daily of what we took from em."

That did it.

Some vanes were shouted down, five or six of them worried about having to sweat themselves if the Angessans were sold.

Blear had to smile now, despite another cough and more flecks of blood in his spit, because the one who shouted the loudest was Rasher; and also because Duna smiled at Blear, just like her mother had long ago for a different reason.

The next day the *Sea-Flame* and Gyllyd's *Cock O' The Waves* sailed for Tantallon, the Angessans bound hand and foot, crammed in the holds....

No, it didn't seem like today would be the day for Rooka and a message from Gyllyd, maybe good news about bringing more for Duna's basket. But Blear decided to wait a little longer, at least until the gloaming.

You never know....

But of course he *did* know. He'd never live to see a full basket—CastleRheg, whatever the name, resurrected from ruins, his daughter maybe the Queen of the Shelter Isles by then, her throne here of some precious wood or dawnstone or even gold. Scavenged, whatever it was made of, just as those who'd built the original fortress had scavenged what they needed. What was quarrying after all, but scavenging?

And brilliant scavengers they were. The quarries near the front of what had been the gateway provided not only a close source of stone for construction, but also served as a moat-like outer defense against a landward attack—the only possible direction given the steepness of the promontory that jutted out toward the cove and sea. Between the quarries there was only an approach so narrow that four men could scarcely walk abreast.

The quarries now were useful only as catch-basins for water. It was a chore for vanes to go down with buckets to the pools at the bottom, to fetch water left over from winter rains. Well, for now the quarries would do, but in time there would be cisterns elsewhere—in the village and those within the rebuilt fortress.

No, not a *village*; it would be a *town* by then, filled with the wives and children of a thousand vanes, not the current sixty or so, Gyllyd's crew included. And swallows to service those who hadn't wives, and some who did.

It would be a town that might someday surpass the one near the bigger Rheg manse on Trigel where they'd lost everything, and Blear—by then everyone calling him Blear, not Carta—the three fingers on his right hand and the swagger of his walk.

He'd ruptured a leg tendon jumping off an embankment as he fled from one of Hessos' soldiers who'd barely missed striking off his entire hand.

Callamander had paid the price for the arrangement he'd earlier made with Hessos, the most powerful of the Summer Princes of Trigel: in return for a cut of the profits of the by-now infamous Rhegs, Hessos agreed to look askance at their depredations, especially against Keshkan shipping in the western Isles, the Bucca Strait and along the Flaggy Shore. And to guarantee the arrangement? A marital bond between the House of Hessos and the self-styled House of Rheg: Gelkus Hessos and Duna Rheg.

If Callamander had asked his advice, Blear would have told him not to do it, but of course why would Rheg have asked his opinion? The whole thing smelled worse than his olla podruda. Rheg didn't need Hessos, though he thought he did. Was it greed? A way of gaining respectability?—which included resolving his only daughter's troublesome wildness? Blear would have told Callamander he could have found a better match for Duna than the lisping heir to Hessos' wealth, who didn't walk so much as slide his feet. And never mind Duna's reputation.

Little did anyone know that Hessos had made a better arrangement with the Keshkans, who could only have offered the Summer Prince much better terms. The plot was obvious after the fact: all Hessos had to do was eliminate the Rhegs who had so long plagued Keshkan shipping. And what better place and time for Hessos and his soldiers to accomplish the deed than the hours after the wedding.

The surprise attack came late that night, when most of the Rheg corsairs were drunk at the family manse or in the town, with only a few on the ships that had arrived for the wedding. Duna was asleep after the consummation, awoke at a disturbance to find her new husband gone from the marital bed.

Blear, Kellusa and one of Duna's two brothers came to the chamber, hurried her away. But only Blear and Kellusa survived the escape and Kellusa had to carry him the rest of the way to the *Sea-Flame*.

Out of the Rhegs' eight ships, only the *Sea-Flame* managed to get underway. On board with the survivors of the massacre, Duna was close enough to see Gelkus on the quay, surrounded by his father's soldiers, many holding torches; close enough to hear, as Blear did, Gelkus shouting about how he had intended to sell her for a tidy profit later. "But if I had known you weren't a virgin, I would never have agreed to marry you, even for the sake of a ruse."

She pulled off her wedding ring and flung it at him, shouting back: "Slide this on your cudgie; it's a better fit."

But what was hurled back made a much bigger splash in the water.

Standing at Duna's side, a scrap of rolled cloth tight around his right wrist, Blear could not have been prouder of his daughter. She did not flinch or slump to the deck. "Did you *see*?" she said. "Did you all *see* how *he* wasn't holding up my father's head? The weakling didn't kill my father; someone *else* made the toss. When I come back to Trigel, everyone will know who will be holding *his* head by his scented hair."

Ah, my daughter…would that I could live long enough to see that…but there's so much to do before you have your vengeance….

Yet the start of it was here. And he'd done his part, the fixer's last efforts. Of course, he hadn't known when he bet on the Draican against Rasher that he'd later slip the shine he won into Headbutt's hand for the favor of posting the new vane to guard the cullies. But he knew, oyah, that Struke would go after Breks up there, a coward's best chance to redeem himself in the eyes of Duna—and everyone else for that matter. And he knew which of the two would live; what happened on the Girvan quay wasn't a fluke.

He'd done what he could, Struke out of the way. The rest was up to Duna—and Falca Breks. Out of all the vanes, there wasn't a better one than the Draican strappy-jack for wits and edge. That was obvious enough to the father, and from the looks he'd seen Duna give the blue-eyed Breks, it seemed the same to the daughter.

Yare well, it was out of his hands now, but soon enough she'd realize, if she hadn't already, that as the last of the Rhegs she needed an heir, and to keep Falca Breks around at least long enough to give her one.

Blear wanted nothing more than to tell her to accomplish that first, while she was building her strength here, so that should she later fail in a reckoning with the House of Hessos, she'd have a son or daughter to avenge her death.

Over the years he told her such things as how to care for a sprained ankle or wrist; and warned her that the hardy yet beautiful sunsbreath flowers of which she'd been so fond since she was a girl, were also poisonous if ingested whole—a fixer's useful remedy—though harmless enough when a skinker ground a few dried petals to powder as a colorful ingredient in his inks.

But he never could tell her what he really wanted to.

THE SCRIM OF another island far to the west had by now halved the setting sun. Blear was about to begin his own descent, call it a day when, turning to the east again for one last look, he saw the black speck. Soon, he heard the faint, yet unmistakable *keeraw…keeraw.*

There you are, my friend, with good news for us all, I hope….

He took the stormbird's favorite food out of his pouch—a cutlass worm without the head and circular row of teeth—and draped it over the thick leather wrapping of his left arm. The big worm was by now rancid but Rooka would be hungry and wouldn't care. He was a scavenger, too.

CHAPTER EIGHTEEN:

THE GOOD NEWS

N IGHT HAD FALLEN yet Soso was still whittling by the glow of a fist-sized chunk of dawnstone between his legs. He got up as Falca approached the cullies' hut, and brushed off the shavings, threw away whatever he'd been carving, put away the knife. He was a stocky, pock-marked, three-ear vane, though lazy, what Falca had seen of him. "So, you again up 'ere," the vane said.

Falca dropped the buckets by the door. "Yahh, me again." Putting disgust into it, even though he'd nodded without complaint when Headbutt told him he'd have the night-watch again.

"Leastways you got to eat when a man should eat." Soso hefted the food bucket by the rope handle. "You brung a lot for 'em."

"Lots in there to feed. We didn't bring 'em here to starve."

"So anything left for me in the hall?"

"More than these scraps; maybe some ale, too—Duna rolled out one of the Girvan kegs."

"Twice the good news then," the vane said. He unbarred the door, took the buckets—one of them filled with water, inside while Falca stood guard outside. He could hear Soso dumping the food bucket, the cullies scrambling for the scraps, and slurping water from the other. He came out with the empty food bucket and the waste bucket. At arm's length he dumped the latter—*splosh*—not far away from where Falca stood, and tossed it back inside the hut, then closed the creaky door and barred it with an emphatic thud. "So they're all yours until tomorrow."

"Which I'll be sleeping for most of it, while you're lugging the prize timber up to the headland for the pen; you and everyone else, the cullies too."

"What're you tipping?"

"What Duna said in the hall. Where else d'you think we're gonna keep 'em all?—what's in there and what Gyllyd's bringing. She told Headbutt to get started on it tomorrow early."

"Yare well, there better be somma that ale left, fime gonna work my arse off tomorrow, doing what we brung the squits to do."

Soso left with the empty food bucket, hadn't gone far when he turned, took a few steps back up the path.

"You forget something?" Falca said.

"Only yer a fawky one."

"And how might that be?"

"You know how. Yer saying there's ale in the hall but you had nane I could smell—which anyone else woulda had some. And the pail of water so full you couldna spilled nane coming up, like it matters how much they get, food too. So how come a Draican cob's thinkin' alla that? Same one who did Rasher'n—"

"For all of that, Soso, you could be halfway to your ale by now."

"Fawky's all I'm sayin'—not that I wouldna done the same, Rasher and Struke tried to dun me."

The vane left for good this time, Falca watching him hurry down the path, the bucket swinging. Soon he was a shadow in the moonlight.

Falca carried the dawnstone rock around the side of the hut and left it to illuminate naught but weeds and spittle-grass. He also confirmed that the fishing boat was still down the strand where it had been. Back at the front of the hut, he leaned against the wall near the door, his foot up. Soso was right about the buckets, but it was the least Falca could do for all the Girvaners who wouldn't be escaping with him and Vaience Loquin.

Tonight.

The Lady Vane had made the decision for him, the message she'd received from this Gyllyd yesterday, by way of what Blear had brought into the hall this evening: a hooded and jessed stormbird that tore apart a mouse the cook had caught and saved for it, while Duna read the message.

They'd all heard the good news but the Lady Vane wanted to roll with it this evening, hence the last keg of the Girvan ale. They'd feasted on the last of the robies, too, that Kersall the cook had roasted over the fire-pit, while Duna went on about how within a year more prize ships would be taken like the one Gyllyd would be bringing into the cove very soon, possibly late afternoon tomorrow.

There'd be a dozen raids over the coming year against fishing villages in the Shelters, and towns along the Gebroanan coast from Tuleen to Thetis, and maybe even Trigel Island. More culling what was needed, and with some of the swag to come, paying for enough masons to oversee the rebuilding of what she called CastleVanes—which got roars from the men, over thirty of them at the trestle tables.

"Who will stop us?" she said in a voice that belied her size—the stormbird's wingspan was probably wider than she was tall. "Not the Keshkans! Their navy is no more, and by the time the Skarries build theirs—thinking they'll be thunder over water, too—we shall be strong enough to slap their snouts and send them whimpering back to Milatum. Who then? Gebroanans? They've always hired the Trigel Princes to do their fighting for them. But what are the Summer Princes without Keshkan ships and Keshkan marines?"

The vanes had banged banged their tankards on the table planks in approval, spilling licks of the Red Ruin ale. This was good news: shine now, shine to come. Much-needed supplies were on the way, and many more cullies to work up the ruins on the headland dawn to dusk; and women for the vanes to fuck without paying for it, and children sold in Tantallon or Thetis for coin in everyone's pockets and whatever else was needed.

All of it good news for everyone but Falca—who drank hardly at all, only tapped his tankard on the table for the show it—because there would soon be two more ships in the cove, and twice as many vanes ashore—for a while anyway, before the next raid. And once the pen for *all* the cullies was built up there on the headland, with three or four vanes guarding the lot, how would he ever cull Vaience Loquin from the herd and get him off the island...

Falca tamped down the urge to do it *now*. Too early. Too many vanes still up and about down there in the village. When he'd left the hall, the gambling games of three-star and shove were just beginning by light of the same dawnstone table-rocks as the one Soso had used for his whittling. The hall had to be empty so that when the time came later, Falca could go back and filch supplies to bring to the boat. There was no way he could have done that before, not with the hall crowded with vanes and...Duna looking at him often enough to make him uneasy, as if she suspected this night would be his last on Angessa.

Faintly, Falca could hear someone down there—probably Foosie on his battered flina—playing a lively ditty; and others singing the coarse, tavern words to go with it, hoarsely shouting the chorus: *Weevil pie, weevil pie/ save me a piece before I die....*

More vanes may have staggered off drunk to their huts, but there might be some who weren't, who might be later roused by shouts up at the cullies' hut. Falca reckoned he still had time to figure out a way of getting Vaience Loquin out of the hut without causing the other Girvaners to ruck and rumble. But he still hadn't thought of a way to do that when he saw someone coming up the path from the village.

FOOSIE SIDLED AROUND Falca after telling him, still eyeing the falcata he'd drawn out quickly before he saw who it was.

"*Shide!*" Falca cursed again.

"*Easy* now, keep it to spit, a'right?" Foosie said, his back against the door of the hut, probably thinking about what this fawky Draican had done to his last visitor up here two nights ago. "Yare, I wouldna want to go neither, trying to get a spar, the Murk in the room. But you gotta go, Breks; the Lady Vane's waitin' for yours, up at her croft."

"You're sure Headbutt said *now*; you're *sure* of that?"

"Oyah."

"Maybe you got it wrong; you said you were half-asleep."

"I was—when I heard the Murk talkin' to Headbutt outside our hut, saying the Lady Vane wants to see the Draican and not to keep her waitin'. But I *wasn't* when Headbutt tole me after she left that I'm to stand the night-watch since you, ah, won't be now. I dunno; maybe he meant it, maybe not, when he said I'm to give you the good news that you're prob'ly gonna be Duna's new Glove."

It crossed Falca's mind that maybe the little bald-headed, flap-eared vane had been sent to set him up, three or four others waiting down there to ambush him, dun him for Rasher and Struke. But if Foosie was lying he was a stiting good liar, and it made no sense, anyway: if some vanes wanted payback for those two, they would've already tried to collect.

He sheathed the falcata, walked away, and might have stepped where Soso had emptied the bucket had he not smelled it first.

Vaience Loquin wasn't going anywhere tonight, and *he* was going up to the croft the Lady Vane shared with her stoneskin greyla deek everyone thought was a Murk. What else could he do? Refuse the summons? Go on with…tonight? And when he didn't show—never mind what he'd have to do to Foosie—she and Kellusa would roust Headbutt and the vanes, and what little lead-time he and Vaience might have wouldn't last the night.

Summoned by the queen for a slide—that's how it worked, though maybe not so often this way. The Lady Vane didn't have a throne—yet—on this shit-step of an island but a queen she was, and she felt like celebrating tonight. He could slake her, sure, all she wanted; put on that Glove—but a collar and leash is what it was….

"Ehh, Breks…you gotta go now. But a word of advice about Duna."

"What, you're her spur now, too?"

"She's got tits out to Trigel, that's plain enough, but don't keep 'em pointed that way. There was one Glove who did, they say, tried to stuff her back-hole, and he's still up in the scraplands somewhere nobody knows where."

"I'll keep that in mind," Falca said, not caring a whit how Foosie might have gotten this bit of advice on how not to fuck the Lady Vane.

"I figgered you ought to know, seeing as how Struke was the Glove who replaced the one we never saw again."

CHAPTER NINETEEN:

RUN OF STONES

THE LADY VANE gestured for him to sit at one of the two chairs at the table in the middle of the croft's single room. Falca sat, Kellusa settling herself at the foot of the bed nearest to the table, the glave over her knees.

Duna could have used the other chair, but instead she pushed one of the two lanterns on the table closer toward rolled-up charts, two cups and a crystal ewer filled with some golden liquid with brown sediment at the bottom. Also on the table: a stack of three books and a single red glove. Had to be Struke's—how many other gloves could she have? She tilted a vase toward her, sniffing the yellow flower—taking her time—then moved the vase away too, and sat down, one leg up, on the edge of the table opposite Falca.

He'd been thinking that Foosie had it wrong. Sure, you have your deek keep the falcata outside, check for a dirk or sliver-heart. Maybe you'd let your hair down—and a fine coppery fall it was. But if you summon one of your vanes for a slide you probably would have smiled by now; you'd be wearing something for the dance, not your trews and half-boots and your short-sword still in the bronze-tipped scabbard at your belt.

Duna pointed at the crystal ewer, her brown eyes almost black in the low light. "A cup of quanth, Breks?"

"What's that?"

"Fermented vetch. You get a sting on your tongue at first, but it finishes sweetly. What gives quanth distinction is the addition of dried and finely crushed beetles that are found only on Laharne Island."

"Ahh…I think I'll pass, but thanks for offering."

Duna leaned over the table, shook the ewer to rouse the sediment—no doubt the crushed beetles—and poured a cup. "'Lusa doesn't like it either. Struke was very fond of it, however. He was also absurdly proud of that hooper I gave him." She took a sip of the quanth. "So I'll have it back now."

Falca took the earring out of his pocket. "I would have returned it before, had you asked." He held it out for her to take but she merely uncurled a finger from the cup and pointed: "On the glove will do."

Falca leaned back in the chair. "An earring's one thing, but why a glove?— if I may ask."

Duna shrugged. "The Red Glove is a custom of Kellusa's people, and it's become a pleasing one for me as well." She took another sip. "Are you sure you won't at least try the quanth?—it's quite good."

"I'm sure I'd find it so, without the beetles."

"Yet there were no beetles in the ale this evening. I should think that after such good news you'd have been keen to celebrate as the others did. Or were you sulking because you didn't get a share of the Girvan swag."

"I'm surprised you noticed my…mood, given the occasion, Lady Vane."

"Your…*grimness* was not hard to see. Should I be concerned?"

"Yahh well, I'm sure I would have celebrated like the others if I'd gotten any sleep the night before."

"You must have gotten plenty prior to your appearance on the Girvan quay, to so easily humiliate Struke before killing my swale."

"Am I here now to be dunned for that?"

"Why *are* you here?"

"Like that ruby earring, I would have told you before if you'd asked."

"I'm asking now."

"You could ask any man here and he'd give you my answer: empty pockets and the chance to fill them."

"Yet none of my vanes has a falcata that's probably worth as much as we took on the Girvan raid—*including* what we found in the galliot captain's cabin." Duna sipped again. "The only other falcata I've ever seen that rivals yours belonged to the son of a Summer Prince of Trigel…who also was my husband for half a day. Gelkus' falcata came from a Wolf Lord's forge in the Crumples, Tartennion's forge if I remember correctly. He uses only crucible steel and his signature is three jewels on the hilt. Gelkus' father gave him a Tartennion falcata—"

"With respect, Lady Vane, but is there a question for—"

"From whom did an empty-pockets Draican steal his Tartennion falcata?"

Here we go again....

"It was a gift."

"That sounded so weary—so I'd guess I'm not the first to ask who gave it to you."

"A woman."

Kellusa laughed; Duna didn't. "And what gave her cause to give you such a mazer gift?"

"I needed a replacement for the common blade I lost."

"Such an obliging—and wealthy—woman. Even so, it's one thing to get lucky and flaunt such a splendid blade, and quite another to know how to use the steel. I should think that with your obvious skill you could have filled those empty pockets of yours more easily than becoming a vane for the House of Rheg."

Falca shrugged. "I intended to do just that in Milatum, but then the—"

"Skarrians came to fill theirs. It's such a pity I can't thank this...Vulsa for destroying the Keshkan fleet and killing so many of the vaunted royal marines. As I said in the hall—you *were* listening, weren't you?—things will be much easier in the Shelters now. But surely, Breks, you could have sold your services to some wealthy Milat escaping to Girvan and beyond."

"Which they were gone by the time I got there."

"A disappointment for me as well; not as many cullies as I'd hoped to get. But we did acquire another ship and its captain's money-chest. And you, of course."

Duna finished her quanth, put the cup down. "So you wound up in Girvan after somehow skeltering from Milatum. I assume you *arrived* in Milatum by ship? the fare from Draica emptying your pockets, no doubt."

Falca shook his head. "Horse and foot. I did spend four days aboard the Lake Tremizene packet."

"That doesn't explain it."

"Ahh, what doesn't?"

"I heard talk of how the Draican didn't dredge his guts during the tantrum we had after the Girvan offing; how he must have been accustomed to the big breathers—what's the smile for?"

"Only that I was surprised, too." True enough, that. But he couldn't very well tell Duna the likely reason: the krael that Gurrus had given him in the

Rough Bounds to save his life after Lambrey Tallon's white rancer bit him in the leg. Who'd have thought the miracle of krael extended to preventing *seasickness*? The only other time he'd been on a blue-water ship he *had* dredged his guts during the passage to Gebroan, to where Amala had been taken by a Spirit-Lifter named Saphrax. Nor had he seen Vaience Loquin puking below during the passage here. If the soft thedral had been on any boat, it probabably was one that had only plied the water of Milatum's Queensmere.

Duna had taken the flower from the vase, was standing now, twirling the stem under her nose—as if that would enhance the fragrance—looking at him all the while. Falca stared back. "Will there be anything else, Lady Vane? *You done sweating me?*

She slid the flower stem back in the vase. "You killed my Glove, such as he was. Who was *your* last, Breks, by the way?—besides some Myrcian or Keshkan swallow. That woman who gave you the Tartennion falcata?"

Anyone else, Falca would have said, *it's none of your business*. Roak only knew why she asked the question—why she cared to know. But evidently she did, a woman who could sniff a flower one moment, and personally execute a vane the next, no reason needed. She was the Lady Vane, queen of an island—such as it was. And she had but to nod at her stoneskin deek a few paces away, and Falca might never walk out that door.

"Well?"

"No, not the woman who gave me the falcata. Another woman…in the Rough Bounds."

"Where at? that's a vasty wilderness they say."

"At a place she thought I was a fool to leave."

"Were you? Or perhaps you were a fool to leave *her*."

"She was a shadden. She—do you—"

"I know what they are."

"She would have killed me."

"For what reason?"

"She took a contract from the father of the woman who gave me the falcata. He had other hopes for his daughter than the likes of a Draican with… empty pockets." *One reason's all you get….*

"Yet you're here."

"The shadden died before she got the chance to fulfill the contract."

"You didn't kill her, then?"

"I believe that's what I just said."

"What was her name?"

"She had…I knew her as Shar Stakeen."

"The other's?"

"Amala."

"And what happened to *her*?"

"Duna, why is all this—"

"Answer the question."

"She was killed in the Rough Bounds. She—"

"That's enough. You may go now and return to your post. 'Lusa will see you out."

He got up, feeling like pushing it, taking his turn asking a question that was none of *his* business: *Why only the half-day marriage, Duna?* Instead, as he stepped aside to let Kellusa pass, his eyes strayed to the gilt title of the topmost book on the table. He couldn't read many words, but the few embossed on the cracked leather cover of that old book were three of them.

"*Run of Stones?*"

Duna seemed surprised at the question, then turned away. Falca went on. Kellusa was already unbarring the door.

"One of my brothers wrote that."

Duna was standing behind the chair in which he'd been sitting. "It's an early history of my family. Our grandfather told the stories and one of my brothers wrote them down. We were once millers on Trigel, though there are only ruins now where our windmill once stood. Farmers once brought their grist to us, to be ground into flour between upper and nether millstones. Together they are called a run of stones."

"I was curious is all."

"Perhaps you're also curious why I call my men vanes?"

"Because you want to remember that your family once made its living from the wind that turned your mill's vanes. Exc—"

"A good start, Breks, but surely someone like you can do better."

"Except that the wind now sort of turns your fortune at sea."

The Lady Vane smiled for the first time since he'd been in her croft. "And yours as well."

○

THEY HAD THEIR bedtime rituals, both for when they were on the *Sea-Flame*, and here on Angessa. And so after the Draican's departure, the door barred again, Kellusa checked the tautness of the two bronze wires stretched across the window above each of their beds. The wires, invisible at night, were tied to chimes dangling from the sides of the windows. Should any intruder try to gain entry, and brusquely disturb the wires, the chimes would wake her and Duna. The precaution wasn't solely for some disgruntled vane. Kellusa was not wholly convinced there were not still a few islanders who'd escaped and were hiding out somewhere in the scraplands, though she'd found no evidence of that in the most likely lair: the ruins at the far end of the island.

Even when the wind blew fiercely enough to hum the wires and stir the chimes, both she and Duna found that the soft music hastened sleep, never woke them; and if Duna had summoned a Glove, he never stayed long enough after to be bothered by the night music.

Usually as Kellusa was checking the wires, Duna would be loosening her hair, and combing it by the light of a single lamp as she sat on the edge of her bed. She was combing it now, though she'd unbound her hair prior to the Draican's arrival which, considering what *hadn't* happened, surprised Kellusa.

Duna had undressed, was in her knee-length gown of Gebroanan whisp. Kellusa did the same, though she put nothing on; certainly not delicate whisp that would snag on her skin. As usual, their weapons—Duna's short-sword and Kellusa's glave—lay on the floor within easy reach of the low beds. Kellusa stretched out on hers, facing Duna. The breeze wasn't much but still cooled her skin whose roughness was soft compared to a male's. Her father had once made a modest living sharpening blades of all sizes on his flat belly. That was in Sandsend, where there'd been a colony of stoneskin exiles who were originally brought in from Helveylyn to work on a second aqueduct that never was completed.

She didn't remember much else about her father, or mother for that matter, because a gang of men—roakings—kidnapped her when she was fifteen and put on a ship bound for Thetis, to be sold to a heteria known for catering to clients with…exotic tastes. Callamander's corsairs took the ship as a prize, and he brought her to Trigel and his daughter, who was about the same age as Kellusa. The idea was that in time the young but already wild Duna would have a protector, and a safe one at that—without a cudgie. She was supposed to be the stone hearth to Duna's fire, that bright hair. And so it turned out to be, especially on Duna's wedding night—which was about the only time she and Duna had not slept in the same room. And that one night remained the only time....

Duna finished with her hair, put the brush by the lantern on the small side-table between their beds, and lay down.

"Why didn't you fuck the Draican?" Kellusa said.

Duna turned to face her, head resting on her hand and elbow. "Perhaps we *did* slake each other."

It took Kellusa a moment to realize what she meant—Duna had a way of turning things into riddles. "Even so, you summoned him so you could fuck him, loosened your hair, put the Glove on the table."

"I *also* summoned him for the return of the bauble—and to get a better idea of how much trouble he'd be, because he *is* trouble."

"You knew that before, that he wasn't like Struke or any of the others."

"And Struke the handsomest of the lot. Competent enough, and his teeth were almost as white as the Draican's. Naught but a shallow bowl between his ears, but at least I knew what was in it. Unlike Falca Breks'."

"Who would give you *that* much trouble to pass on a slaking while you have him up here? You know I've had few roakings but I can recognize one that would ride as well as he talks and keeps an edge to that falcata. More's the pity for your poose, Sister."

"Oh, there's plenty of cudgies to straighten, 'Lusa, and even more soon enough when Gyllyd arrives. A spar's a spar and I'll find a decent hand's-breadth among them, but not the Draican's."

"Maybe it's just as well, since now I don't have to make a bigger Glove—the one you didn't give him was far too small for his hand. Like you said, Gyllyd will bring a better fit for it, some strappy-jack like Breks, but for all that some half-brick like Struke who talks more to your breasts than your eyes."

"Just so; who needs more for a slide? Struke was quanth without the beetles, and I'm sure *he* didn't leave in his past a wake of dead women."

Duna blew out the lantern flame and Kellusa was relieved. Enough with the Draican, at least for tonight. She rolled over on her back, wondering how she'd ever missed seeing the gap in the roof planking, the angling seam revealing a scrim of stars. Jagurtha, the ship's carpenter, had built the croft from the same prize-ship timber with which he'd roofed the hall. The mistake would have to be fixed before the rains came. A glimpse of the heavens was one thing in late summer, but a leaky roof in winter was—

"'Lusa?"

She looked over at Duna, who was still sitting on the edge of her bed. The moonlight gave her coppery hair a silver tint. Kellusa turned again to face her. "More Draican, Sister?"

"I should have left that northron on the Girvan quay, and not because he killed Rasher. I knew the man would be trouble."

This wasn't good; it wasn't like Duna to gnaw on a bone after the meat was gone. Even here she rarely did that, but never elsewhere, letting the vanes see misgivings, second-guessing. Because then they might begin to doubt her ability to keep providing a haven for them, and tankards of ale, and women to polish their cudgies; none of which they had to pay for with the swag she put in their hands.

"How could you have known then he'd be trouble?"

"Because he was *already* troubling me. Never before have I desired two completely different things to happen at the same time. I was hoping that this man who appeared in the dawn…would take Rasher's ear—and hoping he wouldn't. Yare, I told him what was required to become one of my vanes, but the moment was *his*, not mine. And with someone like this Falca Breks…there will be more of those than I care to give up."

"I understand now," Kellusa said, thinking of the wires across their windows. Then: "What shall you do about him?"

"Tomorrow we put him in with the Girvan cullies—for the time being. Tell Headbutt to post two guards, not one. And that's where Breks shall remain, even after all the others—Gyllyd's too—are up in the pen on the headland. But when we sail to Thetis for some buying and selling—"

"He's for the Blue Block, then?"

"That he is, and together with the Tartennion falcata, he alone will bring us enough to pay for the masons we'll need to oversee the work on CastleVanes."

Duna suddenly laughed.

"What, Sister?"

"Oh, just something you said earlier, about Struke. We'll hear a dozen reasons why Breks is for the Blue Block, but the true reason shall be *our* secret, 'Lusa: that he was sold into slavery because only once tonight—*once!*—did his eyes leave mine to glance at these."

She laughed again, plumping her breasts, and then put a fingertip to her lips.

FALCA HADN'T GONE far down the track that, presumably, continued on into the island's interior. He leaned against the waist-high, dry-stone wall bordering the track, feeling more...trapped than he had before, with Duna Rheg close across the table, sweating him; and her big stoneskin deek closer still off his shoulder, the glave across her knees. Sweating him like...like her run of stones, those uppers and nethers, sweated out flour from grist?

He was lucky to get out of there when he did. Luckier than some on this island—including Vaience Loquin—and countless more in Milatum who were caught between *Skarrian* stones. And he would have been one of them if not for Simi and Cofor. But so many weren't lucky. And if you thought about it... what *really* were the Fates at their Loom Eternal if not a run of stones, each with the weight of a world.

The air was warm and heavy with the scent of the sea, though much cooler than it had been inside the croft. They were sleeping now, Duna and her greyla deek, who'd kept running her hand through her short silver hair all the while.

He'd seen the faint lantern light disappear a while ago in the windows facing the cove. And down in the village—that clustering of stone beehive huts—no lights either, everyone sleeping, too; maybe even Foosie up at the cullies' prison hut. There was only the faint glow of the dawnstone table-rocks through the hall windows, and more of it up on the headland from where those rocks had been scavenged from the ruins.

He was at odds with himself about this feeling of entrapment. Where was the enveloping wilderness of the Rough Bounds to account for it? The constriction of a narrow alley in Draica? The oppressive sense of being...*under*, that he'd felt in the Skellig, even Scaldasaig for a while? What he would have given then for the sight of the celestial constellations and the Sisters.

But he knew where this feeling was coming from: there would be no way of escaping from this barren island with Ossa's son...without more killing.

He still had enough left of the night—thanks to that red glove Duna left on the table. And lucky he hadn't been *that* sort of grist for her, as he'd thought he would be coming *up* this track; as Foosie assumed he'd be, Headbutt, too. Yahh, he could have slaked her all right, whichever way she liked it—which included having Kellusa in the croft, to make sure that anything more was Duna's preference, not his.

Hadn't happened.

But Duna asking him about Amala and Shar Stakeen almost seemed like it had; as if she *had* to have those names he'd be thinking about instead of Duna Rheg.

He was glad it hadn't happened—let someone else wear the Glove, wear the collar fixed to her leash; that is until she was tired of the vane, and chose another.

But he was thinking like he was still going to be here. And he couldn't, not with Gyllyd arriving as early as late tomorrow. Which meant more blood on his hands tonight. How else to get Vaience Loquin out of that hut without killing Foosie? Couldn't dun him any other way. Rope him tight, gag him?—sure; but then you run the risk of him getting loose or working off the gag and rousing everyone before you got far enough away in the boat.

It was never easy, but sometimes it was your life or the other's—in this case Foosie. If he wasn't asleep, he'd want to know right off how it went up there, the Murk in the room watching him spar it up for the Lady Vane.

Either way the flap-eared little flinarra would never play *Weevil Pie* again. Falca didn't want to kill him any more than he wanted to wait until the morning, ambush Duna and Kellusa—killing one then the other as they came out of the croft. And become...Lord Vane? Dare any other to challenge him. Which they would. So *more* killing before the Lord Vane mysteriously vanished with the squint-eyed cullie who used to be a thedral. But before that happened, it was all too likely that *his* ear would wind up hanging from the belt of a new Lord Vane.

There had to be another way on a night that had begun with such promise—Headbutt putting him up there to guard the cullies—and then had faded with every step he took up this track toward the croft, and the prospect of having to spend the night, most of it anyway, slaking the Lady Vane a few times.

But he *hadn't* been grist for Duna's run of stones, now had he?

Only three people knew that—and Foosie wasn't one of them.

Falca pushed off the wall. Maybe he *would* be able to get Ossa's son out of here...*tonight*.

He headed down the track at a quick walk, glanced back at the dark cottage, and grinned.

Thanks for the slides tonight, Duna. You were buckets....

CHAPTER TWENTY:

BURREENS MEN

VAIENCE LOQUIN WAS fully awake at the far end of the hut when the guard shouted again: "You heard me—the one what's the eddy—get out here now!"

What choice did he have but to go?

He got up as the guard yelled—"C'mon, c'mon"—and stepped past Sterbo, jostling others: too many sprats for this crowded skillet and during the day as hot as one; like the first day, when Quoins took one of the two best spots under the windows and that was all right because he had the son who wasn't right in the head. At least Quoins didn't shove away someone to get the spot like Boaig did to Sterbo for the other window, saying he should have it since he was the galliot captain—as if that mattered now.

Outside the hut, the small, baldy corsair—vanes they called themselves—closed then barred the door, but not before Vaience heard Boaig saying it was just as well the squinty t'edral would never be returning, and now there'd be more food and water for everyone else; and Quoins saying, "Shut up, Crayfish; he takes haffa what you do." Vaience hadn't thought 'Crayfish' would stick; he'd only whispered the name to Sterbo, seeing Boaig three paces away, staring out his window with the one side-wall eye.

The other corsair was the big one he'd seen before; had a coil of rope in his hand, standing there closer to Vaience so he wasn't quite as blurry as the runty one. Vaience wasn't *that* short-sighted; he could see the three jewels on the sheathed falcata's hilt, though if he'd had his spectacles he would have been able to see if the cut of them was square, oval or round. Before he began wearing his spectacles he wasn't aware of what he was missing. He'd once thought that everyone saw the moons in their phases as he did—luminous but fuzzy—until a senior thedral noticed on his second day at Sulserra's how closely he held a book to his eyes.

The corsair with the rope told him to turn around and hold out his wrists, which seemed odd to Vaience since this Falcata could have done the tying with Baldy's sword poking his side, not his back. And odder still that Falcata was doing a poor job of it. No complaints there, but strange: if you're going to take a prisoner somewhere, wouldn't you tighten the ropes, knot them better? Vaience could have worked his wrists free in little more time than it took the corsair to draw his falcata from the scabbard, and for the other corsair to grumble to Vaience, "Maybe it's *your* lucky night, but it ain't ours."

"We're going down the path," Falcata said to Vaience, gesturing with that inward-kinked sword. "You stay to my left, three paces—let's go."

Vaience followed. What else could he do? Bolt and run? To where? Even if this place wasn't an island like they'd said, he wouldn't get far.

Lucky night?

Falcata turned and shouted back: "Remember what I said, Foosie. You keep your mouth shut about…you know…and I do the same about how you were ripping away when I came back."

"I hant forgot. But the same deal goes if I'm nodded off again when you return with the squint, which I'd bet my strings it'll be close to dawn. So we're clear?—I ain't like you with the night-watch."

"That'd cost you extra."

"Which is what?

"Play me a tune. Haven't heard *Larks on the Bough* for a long time."

"Never heard of it."

"You figure something out and we'll call it that."

They continued on down the hillock path, the big corsair at one edge of the spittle-grass, Vaience at the other, still thinking about…*lucky night*, the little vane saying it like he meant it. The only luck Vaience could think of, between now and when he supposedly would be brought back to the stone beehive hut at dawn, was that someone—Quoins probably—might have finally had enough of Crayfish and—

"Don't make me regret doing a slackhoop's job with the rope," Falcata said. "Foosie up there couldn't see it with your back turned, but he might if you did something stupid down here. So don't try anything now, Vaience; we're almost there."

⬡

IT WASN'T FAR from the path to the entrance of the small field enclosed by waist-high walls of stacked rocks. Once inside, they knelt by the sack of supplies the big corsair said he'd left earlier, on his way up to the cullies' hut to do something that he wanted to work one way, but if it hadn't he'd brought the rope to make it work another way.

They had to go quickly, had only the night, some of the morning, he said, giving his name as Falca Breks, but there was no time to waste telling Vaience how he knew his. Time enough for *all* of it, when they were away on the boat. "All you gotta know till then is that I want to skelter as much as you do, and tonight's the best chance we'll have."

Why me? What about the rest of the prisoners?

How had Breks done it up there? the other corsair clearly not knowing what he'd planned...but still talking *lucky night*, whatever that was.

It was all Vaience could do to keep his mouth shut and listen to what Breks was whispering now, because the closest of the vanes' huts were not far down the path they'd left: "We're not off the island yet. There's more of these wee fields, so after we cross through this one we'll go between the walls of the others, and then go around the bottom of the hill where we came down from. There's some kind of monument of dawnstone beyond the back of the hut, and we'll be going to the right of that and down to the strand, and the boat."

Vaience caught most of what he said though the corsair's accent was hard to understand—northron but not Myrcian. But there was only two words that mattered:

The boat....

"Could the guard see us when we get to the strand?"

"Doubt it. Foosie's at the other end of the hut. He'll be looking toward the cove; the boat's the other way and the hut blocks where we'll be. Maybe he'll be asleep but we can't count on that, so we gotta keep quiet. Muffle the oarlocks, use our shirts."

Breks hefted the bulging sack. "You ready for this?"

"Wait," Vaience whispered. "You said you had three jugs of water in there, besides all the bread and food. "They might crack or—"

"S'all right; I wrapped each one before. One more thing: there's rocks everywhere; not all of 'em pulled up for the walls. You miss seeing one, stumble and fall, you do it quiet, bite your lip."

"I've been doing that for a while, Breks."

"Yahh, so you have—and it's Falca. Let's go."

Vaience didn't stumble following him through the field, didn't fall as he clambered over the crude driftwood gate at the other end; but he did bite his lip going through the stinging nettles that filled the narrow space between the walls of the field they left and the adjacent one. Then he and Falca were in the high spittle-grass; a twisting, narrow strip of it silvered by the moonlight.

To Vaience's left rose the dark hump of the hut, at this distance blotting out a fist-sized portion of the stars. And there was the dawnstone monument Falca had mentioned, the vertical glow of it anyway. Only when they'd gotten closer could he discern the three spindles, the upper ends. The spittle-grass was sparser as they came to a ridge—a sand dune below the hillock.

And there it was, the boat, not far away to their right!

The moon ribbons—Cassena's wider—seemed to Vaience to be a path of deliverance across the water. A fuzzy path but a path nonetheless to freedom. He swallowed hard, bit his lip, lest he do now what might rouse even a sleeping Foosie, and ruin everything shouting for joy.

He slid down the dune after Falca, the stink of the tide-wrack heavy in the salty air, and as they walked quickly toward the boat, Vaience's exultation was tempered by the fact that the others were still up there, never to leave, forced to work up on the headland, the ruins—that was the rumor. He didn't care about Boaig, but Quoins, yes…and Sheffie. Even Tunty, who'd been Crayfish's swale on the galliot, deserved a better fate. But there was nothing that could be done for the others. However Falca had managed to get *him* out, the ruse couldn't have been clever enough for more. Even if it was, how to choose who goes, even if the boat was big—which it wasn't. Only a pair—no, there were two pairs of oars sticking out of the bow.

Falca reached over the rail and put the sack between the benches, then pulled on the rail to center the canted boat. Vaience helped him push it through the firm, wet sand, the *shushh…shussh* of the surf masking the effort.

When the boat was floating free in the shallows, Falca gestured for him to get in first, kept it steady. Vaience was about to sit at the fore-bench—and took a step that shouldn't have been there.

"What was that?" Falca whispered.

Vaience pulled his foot out of the bottom of the boat. "The bottom's rotten."

He was surprised he said it softly; he felt like shouting with frustration.

Falca sank his head into the rail, the useless boat rocking as Vaience got out. He leaned back over the rail to get the sack, but Falca grabbed it first, slung it over his shoulder.

"What now?" Vaience whispered

"Only one thing to do, and—"

"No, I'm not going back, wait for another chance that may not happen. You said yourself that this—"

"We're neither of us going back."

"What then?"

"We run for it until we run out of island It's not that big, what I heard. Wherever we hole up they'll probably find us, but maybe that'll be later, not sooner, and that's something anyway."

"So be it then."

"I've always hated those fucking words, but sometimes that's all you have."

Something nagged at Vaience as they began wading back through the shallows, and then he realized what it was. "Falca, I just—"

"Shhh, not so loud—yahh?"

"They know about the boat; they've seen it, right?"

"Sure they have."

"But what if they *don't*. We sink it farther out. They'll think we've escaped in it."

"So they don't search the island. That'll give us time to figure out some other way off. Vaience, you've short sight and long wits—quick now, before the stiting thing sinks where it is."

Falca hurriedly left to put the sack on the strand, then helped Vaience with the boat. Chest-deep water was as far as they got. Falca shoved the oars at an angle through the hole in the bottom. Hopefully the tide-change wouldn't float the oars free.

They sloshed through the surf, crossed the strand, pawed their way up to the top of the dune, and kneeled more or less where they'd gone down, the glow of the dawnstone monument to their right now, and above. Falca didn't glance back, maybe because there was nothing they could do now if the moonlight revealed any sign of the sunken boat. Vaience looked back. Perhaps if he'd had his spectacles he would have seen something. But for once he was glad he wasn't wearing them.

"We have to move around the huts and beyond," Falca whispered. "After them and the hall, there's a track that may continue on. For now, it's between the fields again for us. Can't be so many we'll get lost."

THEY DIDN'T, GOING around the last of the outer fields, brushing through more spittle-grass and nettles. Falca seemed sure they'd come to the track. Maybe he could see it, but for Vaience the only indication was fewer weeds where they were standing than along the wall that sloped down this rise.

Falca was looking down the track. Vaience squinted: off to his right and below, a smudgy gray shape; seemed to be a small building, half-hidden by a swelling of the hill. "Is someone coming up?"

"No…I think we're all right for now," Falca said, and for the first time in a while he wasn't whispering. "Looks like it worked after all. No light in the croft."

"Croft? Whose croft?"

"Duna's. The Lady Vane. The one who ganged you in Girvan, has that copper hair which is gonna catch fire once she finds out she's been dunned a fool. That's where I was earlier tonight. Duna likes her slides and for some reason she had me summoned from the hut. and Foosie had to take over the watch."

"What happened?"

"Nothing except a lot of talk and then she showed me the door. I hope she won't snap his strings tomorrow; Foosie's not a bad sort, as these vanes go."

"You've lost me."

Falca shifted the sack to his other shoulder. "I played Foosie a song, said the *other* kind of nothing happened with the Lady Vane; told him she kicked me out, ordered me to bring her someone who *could* lift his lumber. Even going to the boat I was worried maybe Foosie had got to thinking why Duna would want some skinny, half-starved thedral who probably hasn't yet spit his muck—with a woman that is. But I was betting that even if Foosie thought that fawky, he wouldn't leave his post to see if I *was* outside her croft, waiting while you spit yours out five or six times till dawn like I used to do—we'd better move on now."

So there it was, his *lucky night*, and Falca had said it all without a grin—at least Vaience didn't see one. As they walked abreast, he wondered how old this northron was, guessed he couldn't be more than twenty-six or so. And at what point in the last half of his life did he come by that falcata? And what…*song* had he played to get it? In the meantime, there was the fact that *he*—he wasn't *that* skinny and felt better than he should have, considering— had spent almost half of his eighteen years at Sulserra's; and yare, maybe he'd missed out on a few…*songs*, but you'd think by now he'd have heard it called *spitting your muck*, which he'd been close to doing just that for the first time with Cyalla at the Widow Yist's. Hard as the spine of a book he was, and she'd seen that, how could she not? Spitting your muck? Well, it was that… but later maybe they'd have called it something else; no, he was *sure* of it. By now Cyalla would be…where? Roak's awe? With Castlecliff and her husband-to-be a few days away….

He'd fallen behind and hurried to catch up. "Falca, do you know where this track leads?"

"Have no idea," he said, "but one thing's for sure: we'll know it when we get there."

THE TRACK LEVELED off after awhile, then began to rise again, enough for Vaience to feel it in his legs; and by the time they reached the crest Falca, too, was breathing hard. But they didn't stop to rest since there didn't seem to be any more hills ahead, the horizon of stars unbroken.

Still, this wasn't flatland. Vaience had the sense of being surrounded by undulating terrain that seemed in the moonlight to be a kind of rough sea, the swells of shelving rock silently crashing and rising again, yet somehow parting for the winding track. The terrain hadn't been defined before, at least for Vaience, but it was now, maybe because of the wide fissure—no, it was bigger than that, a crevice—that extended alongside the track; a cleft in the land, darker than the night.

Falca saw it much more clearly than Vaience. "Looks like it's angling toward the track up ahead. Might make a good hiding place, and probably there's plenty more of those in this scrapland, but hidey-holes won't get us off the island."

"*Burreens of Brann,*" Vaience said, almost to himself:

"What?"

"Nothing."

"You said, Burreens of Brann."

"Things jump into my head. It's a book of verse, a favorite of mine. Brann's a town in the Coombs, which is about as far away from scrapland as you can get. You said 'scrapland' so I—"

"Ahh, help me jump here, Vaience—if we're in what there isn't any in this Brann, then—"

"I should have kept my mouth shut. We're not on an evening stroll along the Terraces next to Sulserra's, discussing poets like Cenachie who wrote the book two hundred years ago."

That seemed the end of it, Falca suddenly quiet.

They walked on. Then he said: "I still don't understand."

"Burreen is an old Keshkan word for outlaw. You said hiding place, too— which is what outlaws need, which made me think that's what we are now."

"He knew about outlaws, this Cenachie?"

"I doubt it, first-hand, anyway. He was a famously lame innkeeper in Milatum—Linnishill—so maybe he embellished a traveler's—"

Falca tagged Vaience's shoulder. "Hold up."

"What's the matter?"

"There's something ahead and it's not the track we've been following."

IT WAS A silent bridge arching over no burbling stream, only a wide crevice into which the Sisters' moonlight did not venture far. And beyond the bridge, winding through more of the burreens, there was what appeared to be a road, a uniformly gray ribbon that merged ahead into the darkness.

Falca went over the bridge first, saying that it was his turn to put his foot through something, if the hump of the bridge proved as useless as the boat's hull. When he came back he confirmed the fact of a road beyond, about three strides wide, with narrow, ankle-high shoulders.

It sounded to Vaience like a processional, but why would it begin…here?

He had to agree with Falca, however: most likely the road had once begun at the cove, but the islanders had scavenged the flat stones of the road to build their beehive huts. Clearly they hadn't built the road or the bridge—why would they rip up their own road? The bridge, then, was as far as they'd gotten, or needed to.

The tops of both its sides were adorned with a series of stone curls, and as Vaience brushed a hand over the ones to his left, they seemed to him like waves caught at the moment of descent. At the apex of the bridge the faint yet unmistakable glow of dawnstone rose from the deep gap between the ascending and descending succession of the stone waves. "There's another one on the other side, too," Falca said. "They put them right above where the keystone of the arch is below, I'm guessing."

Something of dawnstone must have filled the deep gaps, but whatever it was had been knocked off, toppled into the crevice below, or scavenged. All that remained in the gaps—Vaience and Falca took turns feeling the nearest one—was a rough, circular nub.

As he walked down the bridge, Vaience ran a hand over the second descending series of curls, which had been carved in the opposite direction from the first. "They didn't have to do all that, any of it," Vaience said. "Whoever they were."

"Yahh, none of it helps you cross over, does it? And this road—how fancy do you have to make a path across an island that's mostly burreens and fields so poor you need to pull up rocks and add seaweed to what's left. Makes you wonder why some people do more than they have to…but if they didn't then it'd be a lot harder for everyone to get to where they are."

What Falca said seemed to Vaience almost as strange as the stone waves of the bridge—and stranger still coming from a corsair. He said nothing, though, and they continued on, their footfalls quieter now; no more scuffing along a track. Would this road lead to…well, all roads led to…*something*. And on this island that could mean another village on a strand beyond the burreens, that *might* have an abandoned boat whose hull wasn't rotten.

But he didn't want to get his hopes up with this road…nor with the boat they'd sunk. Because if that ruse hadn't worked, the vanes would be looking elsewhere, and if they got this far they'd surely see the path he and Falca were taking through the weeds and spittle-grass growing in profusion on the road.

"I saw another fawky thing on a bridge once," Falca said. "Not the bridge itself, nothing at all like the ones in Milatum, but—"

"You've been there?"

"Not for long. This bridge was in the Banishlands—that's in eastern Lucidor, past the city of Bastia, on the way to the Rough Bounds wilderness. It's what you'd expect there, timber-built, and the river it crossed was wide and quick. You won't find your burreens in the Banishlands, but you will the other kind. That's what I was then, me and the two I was with: runagates.

"You see, the three of us had met someone else before—this was on the way to Bastia. We didn't know his name or why he was an outlaw, one of your poet's burreens. Found that out later. But we saw him again as we approached that bridge in the Banishlands. He was already on it, about halfway, when two horsemen rode up to the other end. He shouted at them to wait until he had crossed, but they only laughed, the scuts, and spurred their horses on.

"Now here's the fawky part: there wasn't room enough for all of 'em on the bridge. We thought the man would scurry back, or press himself against the railing and hope he wouldn't be trampled. But he stood there in the middle of the bridge, and when the horses came close, they reared up, throwing the riders into the river."

"What did he do, the burreen?"

"Went on as if nothing had happened."

"Was this magic, Falca? You said you found out later why he was an outlaw, so was he a magist as well? Not that I believe they exist."

"Neither do I. He was many things. He'd killed a man who'd harmed someone he loved. He was a bloodsnare hunter on his way to the Rough Bounds—it was the scent of bloodsnares that caused the terror in the horses. And before he made his living hunting 'snares he sold to the aulost dens of Lucidor, he was the mastlord of a Myrcian windwhipper. He was also your father."

Vaience stopped, as if another crevice had suddenly opened at his feet and there was no bridge to cross it.

CROSS IT HE DID.

There was another bridge and they crossed this one, too, after stopping to rest; and by now Vaience knew much more than measures, the distances Falca Breks had traveled to wind up here: from Draica to the Rough Bounds; and then south through Myrcia to Milatum, the city which was all Vaience had ever known except for Girvan and now this island and all the books he'd read and copied—lines of words that took him to places to which even Falca Breks had never been.

Still, there were measures and distances and then some; Falca had said as much: however far he'd traveled couldn't be as far as Vaience had this night.

First came shock and disbelief, but even before they rested at the second bridge—Kyria's Lyre, the brightest constellation in the heavens over his shoulder—Vaience knew it was all true. He felt no anger that the father he never met—a man who'd never known he had a son—never returned to Milatum after surviving the shipwreck off Gebroan's Flaggy Shore. But he did feel a kind of numbing, pervasive sadness that was so different from those moments after his mother would tell him this or that about his father: stories about a man who'd died long ago. But he hadn't; he'd been alive until very recently, though far away.

Very likely the tales would all be ending here. His mother would never know now what Falca had told him: that her husband had spoken of her in the moments before he died at this Scaldasaig; that he'd been so ashamed of his marital duplicity—another wife in Castlecliff—and the fact of the horrific facial brand he'd suffered before his release from the Sanctor's prison, that he'd created a new name and life.

So many tales: the bloodsnare hunting in the Rough Bounds; the searching for the daughter who hadn't been in Castlecliff when he returned from many years of forced military service and captivity in Gebroan. She'd been sold to the Cassenite cult and Mott Demoul had killed the man who did it—self-defense—but still enough of a crime to get him branded; the man was well-known. Mott never found his daughter until it was too late, their reunion a matter of hours; less time than it had taken Vaience and Falca to escape this far along a road that had its own long-ago tale.

I had a sister; a half-sister, anyway....

Falca said she'd taken another name, too, but not the reason for it.

HE SETTLED IN against a platform or dais, whatever it was, Falca sitting close by, leaning against what had been part of the roof that had collapsed, the jagged opening a scar of stars. Moonlight spilled across rubble they had to step over coming into what Vaience thought of as the Road-builders' Temple.

They'd heard the end of the island well before the rising road ended: a faint crashing that grew louder the closer they came to a spur of the burreens that blacked out the lower hanging constellations. But the spur materialized as a building, and then ruins perched at the edge of a cliff, because the sound they heard wasn't the sighing of waves breaking upon a strand.

This was an assault upon a bastion and close enough for Vaience to feel on his face the rising mist wafting through a wide, broadly arched doorway behind him. Whatever lay beyond could only lead to a precipice, the very end of it all, and what did it matter if the ruse of the sunken fishing boat at the other end of the island had worked or not: they had only four days' worth of food and water in the sack, maybe more if they were careful—not much time to find a way off of Angessa. And then what?

"Falca?"

"Yahh?"

"There's not much of a chance, is there?...that we'll find an abandoned village...and a boat."

"Tomorrow we'll see how much of this side of the island is cliffs...but no, probably not."

"You knew it before, didn't you. That's why..."

"I was going to tell you everything as we pulled on the oars of that boat—which I should have checked before."

"Even if you had we'd still have wound up here. So thank you for telling me, for getting me out of that place. Here's better than there."

"For us both."

"What you told me, though—it wasn't everything."

Falca had drawn his falcata coming in, just in case. Now he placed it on top of the sack which lay between them.

Vaience persisted: "You didn't say much about, well...about...*why*—in Girvan."

"Your father was the finest man I've ever met, not that I've been in the sort of places to find better. You're his son. He saved my life and that of a woman a little younger than you."

"It's a long way to go to repay a debt."

"I didn't start out thinking that; I didn't know you existed. Call it that now, but it isn't repaid, not yet. We have to decide on some things in the morning, like which way to go—left or right since we seem to have only two choices now."

"You didn't tell me how he died at Scaldasaig."

"Roak's throat, Vaience; you've gotta be as duffed as I am."

"And about my…sister."

"I've said enough."

"Please, I'd like to know."

"Vaience…we need to get some sleep."

"Tell me."

He did, after more silence and a sigh in the dark.

THE EDGE OF the dais was too uncomfortable now, so Vaience lay alongside it, on his side, an outstretched arm for a pillow, and stared at the fuzzy, almost indistinguishable stars framed by the gray vault of the temple's arched doorway.

Could he have done it, made the choice his father had? Taking one life to save two? Forcing his daughter off the parapet of Scaldasaig's keep—and then stepping off himself—to save Falca Breks and Raleva Barra from what his shadden daughter had planned to do to them, to get and keep the secret of krael for herself and her father and no one else.

What were such choices but…*hunters?* You might live out your life eluding them, yet never knowing they were out there somewhere, either pursuing you or hidden, waiting to spring at you.

Or even Falca's: using the last piece of that krael to save the life of someone he didn't know, instead of keeping it for when *he* would need it, and a man like him surely would, never mind his favorite song apparently was sentimental— *Larks on the Bough.* And then getting on a ship of corsairs.

"Couldn't let the krael go to waste, now could I?" Falca had said. Vaience hadn't seen the smile but he heard it in his voice.

What kind of men could make such choices? Part of him wanted to find out if he was of that breed. and the rest of him hoped he'd never have to confront the hunters. What were the measures of each, within him? Well, there was no sense in dwelling on that, since he'd probably be finding out soon enough.

As for names, there was no need for him to choose between Mott Demoul or Ossa Vere, and Flury Demoul or Shar Stakeen. They would always be father and sister—such as she was, or rather came to be: a shadden. From what he'd read about the cult—which supposedly began hundreds of years ago with the last of the Orphics—shaddens were to burreens what senior thedrals at Sulserra's were to first-year edificiates.

Vaience listened to the waves pounding against the cliff as yet unseen beyond the door behind him. But tomorrow, before they left here, he'd see just how close it was.

"Falca?"

"I thought you were asleep."

"*Larks on the Bough*...that doesn't seem like a song that would be a favorite of someone like you."

"I liked it once, that's all. Amala did too, very much."

"That woman you spoke of? who was—"

"We heard a flinarra play it at Rhysellia's Gardens in Draica, long before we left the city. It was a courting song, but we didn't know that at the time."

Chapter Twenty-One:

ROAK'S THROAT

FALCA WOKE TO warmth on his face, the not-so-distant roar of crashing waves, and a crick in his neck. He knuckled his eyes, looked over at Vaience. Still sleeping. The angle of light shafts piercing gaps in the roof hinted at the hour: mid-morning.

Probably the dream more than the glare of sunlight had awakened him and still lingered....

He and Vaience running out of food and water...going back to the village to steal what they could...seeing two more ships in the cove...and Gyllyd leading one of the captives off a ship, a tall black-haired woman, and Vaience whispering is that her?...and he said it was, and they had to go...go now, because his sister was talking to Duna and Gyllyd, pointing in their direction, all three smiling, Gyllyd's grin revealing the same blue gums as Lambrey Tallon's....

Falca couldn't remember the last time he'd had a sweat-dream. The breeze funneling through this place during the night should have cooled him off. And what *was* this place? Vaience thought it a ruined temple; otherwise why would a well-built road and two over-dressed bridges lead to something unimportant?

He could easily have fallen back to sleep; shutting his eyes only for a moment would do it. He got up instead, took a look around before heading to the disheveled entryway. Small temple or manse, it was mostly rubble now, with a partially caved-in roof and a spanner's nest atop a fallen lintel. The empty windows had notches for shutters? long since scavenged for the wood, no doubt. Two doorways, each flanked by top-to-bottom niches in the wall opposite the tumbled roof, probably led to smaller rooms than this big one, but what was the point in checking them?

Falca stood to the side of the entryway, and peered out.

A lone spanner swooped over the empty road and the tell-tale pattern of the path they'd taken the night before through the spittle-grass. Well, nothing he or Vaience could do about that. But still, the reassuring thing was the empty road that ran straight to the steps leading up to a weed-choked courtyard and the circular stubs of dawnstone—six of them—that he assumed had once had enough height to mark a formal way into the building.

He kept his eyes, though, on a far speck—was it the second bridge? Hard to tell. Maybe some outcrop of rock in the surrounding scrapland. It didn't move, and that's all that mattered.

Maybe it worked, sinking the stiting boat....

Yet that ruse in itself was no escape, only gave them a little more time. On the road he thought of a way they *might* get off the island. But it was absurdly risky, and he'd shifted his hope that the track, then road, would lead to an abandoned shore-side village and maybe they'd find something to make a raft like the one he, Gurrus, Ossa and Styada had built in the Rough Bounds, never mind it was only to cross a river.

So much for that pinch of hope.

Still no one on the road.

Tonight there would be—he and Vaience.

Falca hadn't told him yet...but they had to go back to Duna's croft.

The door would be barred, and they couldn't go through windows and not wake up Duna and her deek. Without surprise, there was *no* chance. He and Vaience would have to hunker outside, keeping awake until they came out in the morning. Falca saw it in his mind now: Kellusa first, a leg-strike to give him time for Duna, subdue her, Vaience taking over while he finished off the greyla. Have to kill her. No way around that. And then maybe the even riskier part of the plan: walking into the village with Duna a hostage, and walking on to the dock and the *Sea-Flame* and its scat-boat. Plenty of rope on the *Sea-Flame* to tie up Duna, but they'd also need more food and water to put in the scat-boat. Vanes would have to bring the supplies...*Follow us all the way to Gebroan, you want, but keep your distance. We'll leave her on the shore....*

And once there, run for it.

The plan would never work, but it was better than the other option: slowly dying here from thirst and hunger.

Yahh well, there was *another* way, the first one he'd thought of; and a song it was, especially for all the cullies he and Vaience had to leave behind. And it *might* have worked—but he'd thought of it too late, long after they'd sunk the boat. Which at the time had seemed like a good—

"Falca? Take a look at this."

He turned, and there was Vaience on his hands and knees, his face a hand's-breadth from the floor where he'd been sleeping at the edge of the dais. Falca walked over, kicking away a chunk of the roof instead of stepping over it.

"What am I s'posed to be looking at besides you looking—"

"Move the sack, will you?"

"—Like you're looking for the spectacles you lost in—"

"There, that's enough. See? It continues. Do you see it?"

"Sure—if something was there."

"It's what isn't," Vaience said, kneeling now. "This dais here…the plinth… it's not aligned. It's askew."

"Compared to what?—rubble?"

"See how the squares of the mosaic flooring are set? You brush them off, they're—"

"Blue and red, I'm seeing that."

"Well, when I woke up I noticed the edge of this plinth is at an angle that doesn't match the set of the floor. It's skewed."

"So…."

"So whoever built this temple…don't you think they would have matched the front of this plinth to the square of the mosaic pattern. Why do poor work here but not out there?"

Falca didn't say what was on his mind—that not everything was lined up like the words in a book—because Vaience had a point.

Falca came closer, knelt, brushed his hand over more of the mosaic squares. "Em…all right…yahh, that *is* fawky." he said, and got up. "Something must've moved the plinth—maybe that long piece of the roof over there when it fell—but that plinth is thick."

"Yare, and how does it move the plinth *away* from where it was, when it's falling more or less directly down?"

Vaience stood. "There's something else that's strange." Squinting, he pointed to an angle in the plinth, half-hidden by rubble. "I couldn't see it last night…but this plinth just might have more than four sides."

"Which would mean…what?"

"I don't know but we should find out, clear away more rubble."

"Let's clear away, then," Falca said.

If nothing else it was something to do before he had to tell Vaience about tonight, and then plan the ambush, show him a few things that might keep him alive in a ruck.

But by the time they'd worked up a sweat, he'd forgotten about that

"You were right," he said. "And that monument near the hut?—the plinth had six sides, too. Someone likes the number."

"Maybe just a coincidence, but in Milatum as well: the base of the Wovens on Mereshaven, and the Labrys inside the citadel. I've never seen it but—what are you staring at?"

"That crack, right where the plinth meets the floor—I just noticed it. About as long as my arm. See it?"

Vaience moved closer, leaned over. "Now I do…that's a straight-line crack. Seems to get wider before it disappears under the big piece of the roof we didn't move."

"That's what I'm seeing, too," Falca said, and went over to the end of it. "You'd think by now it would've filled up." He scuffed dust and bits of debris into the crack with the side of his boot. And again. Vaience did the same.

The crack didn't fill up.

"If that's a crack," Vaience said, "it's a deep one."

"One way to find out—I'll be right back."

Falca returned with the falcata and slowly thrust it into the crack—to the hilt. "Looks like we have some *down*…down there, my friend."

Vaience grinned.

THE PIECE OF rubble was about six feet long. Grunting, they lifted it up at one end, then shoved it away. It fell with a crash, and they had to retreat for a few moments to let the dust settle.

The crack was now a black wedge the width of Falca's hand.

"You realize we've got to find out what's down there," Vaience said.

And wouldn't it be a help at Duna's tomorrow morning if what's down there is a few Angessans escaped the fate of the others…which is about as likely as—

"Falca?"

"Sure, but we can't stay for long, don't want any surprises when we come back up. I didn't see anyone before but that was then, and we've been at this for a while. I'll go see if we're still all right."

He picked his way through debris to the entryway—and quickly darted to one side.

Shide!

He glanced back at Vaience, gestured for him to stay back.

They weren't that close, but close enough for him to see the spot of her copper hair, Kellusa striding beside her; the glave, Duna's sword, the vanes' hangars glinting in the late-morning sun.

She'd brought them all it seemed for the road that had offered hope the night before—enough anyway to walk past the feeling that maybe he and Vaience should find some outcrop of rock close by the road, and wait until the morning to see if the vanes were coming-after, and not count on the sunken boat; because if it didn't work, a furious Duna—dunned a fool—would be taking a lot of vanes with her, leaving only a few at the cove...

Only moments for this as Falca scuttled back to Vaience—who was just emerging from the portal beyond the plinth. "What we thought," he said. "A courtyard, more rubble. A cliff."

"They'll be here soon—this plinth better move."

"Did before; it's a lid."

"We gotta push where the crack's widest."

They bent down, pushed straight off, pushed hard, thinking the lid wouldn't move easily. So did Vaience.

It was like pushing a table chair.

Vaience might have fallen off the edge of the maw if Falca hadn't grabbed him by the scruff at his shirt and pulled him back. He leaned over.

"Steps!...we got steps!"

He quickly went down four of them, shivering with the upwelling of cool, dank air. "Get the sack."

"It's gotten."

"This lid opened...it's gotta...must be a...*there* it is!" He reached for the handle carved out of the underside of the plinth. It didn't close as easily as it had opened, but Falca was still surprised the stone lid moved at all. Was it that smooth stripping set in the floor?—on the underside of the plinth, too.

He couldn't see Vaience's face though he was near enough to smell his breath.

He warned Vaience he was drawing the falcata. A blind man's tapper is what it was now.

"Did they see you earlier, you think?" Vaience said.

"Doubt it, where they were, looking in from the sunlight. But they knew where we went, our trail through the weeds."

"We didn't leave anything up there, though. They'll think we saw them, took off. Even if they don't, we're safe for now. They could move the plinth like we did, but only if they *know* it moves, which they *don't* because if they'd come here before, all they would've seen was the plinth half-covered by rubble."

"Now *there's* some grist," Falca said.

"Grist?"

"Never mind." *Duna's run of stones. She's the fucking runner above, and down there's the nether....*

"We still should go down," Vaience said.

"Yahh, what's a little more...*down*. That'll give 'em time to leave and be looking for us everywhere else. Then we come back up." *And I'll tell you about tonight....*

After taking a few more steps, Falca decided against using the falcata as a tapper—better to feel for the sides of the passage with both hands. The steps were steep and narrow and the greater risk was becoming disoriented in the blackness. Lose your balance and there'd be one more for the tomb below— what else could the steps lead to but a tomb? And so, carefully now: *feel for the edge of a step, that's it, make sure the next is there....*

Falca slid his hands along the walls of the passage that seemed even narrower than the one below Sulserra's. In places the walls seemed roughly dressed rather than naturally formed. But he had the overall impression this was a fissure, something of the burreens.

Since Scaldasaig it seemed like he'd spent more time...*below* than above, breathing air so dank you could chew it first; and feeling the traps-and-squeezes, one poxy hand pressing against your chest, and the other pushing your innards up your gullet.

He smeared the complaint on the passage wall, because he and Vaience would be getting dead now if not for this gullet. Still, the Fates and their fucking Loom were having their fun with gullets...*and this time, why not let's put Shar Stakeen's brother behind—*

"Falca?—why'd you stop?"

"Jammed my fingers—something on the wall. Feels like…maybe a torch-butt. It's…empty, not that we've anything to light it with if it wasn't."

"Why do you take a torch and not put it back for the next time?"

"Maybe because someone knew there wouldn't be a next time?—it's gotta be a tomb down there."

"If it is…why fix a torch-butt to the wall in the first place? when you can just take a torch down with you—that is if you're not carrying the body."

"Which maybe I'm wrong about the tomb. Why go to all this trouble when you can just say what you gotta say at the cliff, and slide'm over the edge, like you do in Milatum."

"How do you know about the Eight Steps?"

"Someone told me when we were below 'em, in a short-cut to the Reef of Bones—which I hope this isn't."

And down…down they went, step by step, shivering more now in the chillier air; the only sounds their breathing, the tapping of Falca's scabbard on the steps, and the muffled *chunk-chunk* of the water jugs in the sack Vaience was carrying—which reminded Falca of how thirsty he was, and hungry. The last time they'd had anything was late the night before, after he'd said as much as he was going to say about Shar Stakeen—which *didn't* include telling Vaience that before he discovered she was a shadden, he'd slaked his sister in an embrasure on the ramparts of Scaldasaig's keep as the last of the flokas who'd survived the battle flew away from the carnage around Lake Shallan; and then again in a—

"Falca? shouldn't the air be worse than it is?"

"It's bad enough, your stink and mine."

"No…something else."

"Whatever it is…the krael's probably the reason. Heightens the senses for a while afterwards, and you had yours a lot more recently than I did."

"I was meaning to ask you about that—if it can do so much, why didn't it heal—"

"Your eyes?—I don't know. Your father and I…we knew a woman and her daughter who were both *blind*…took a lot of the krael…but it didn't help."

"What were their names?"

"Laineth and Sovay. If there were any who deserved a nod from the Fates, it was those two."

"What happened to them?"

"They—"

Falca was thrown off balance by a step that wasn't there. He slid his foot ahead, felt Vaience close at his back. "What is it?"

"We're outta steps." Falca grazed the fingers of his right hand along the rough wall. "The passage seems to be angling away." He drew the falcata, felt ahead with it...*tink*...*tink*.

If there was something ahead that the temple-builders wanted protected—and they had the means to cross the dead-fall trap they'd devised—here was the place for it.

Falca's caution vanished as he made a slow turn.

The faint glow wasn't enough to appreciably soften the darkness, but it was enough to reveal the end of this passage that now stretched ahead on a decline.

"That...shouldn't be there," Falca whispered.

"Someone's down here."

They crept ahead. The passage trailed down, and angled still more to the left. Falca blew on his right hand to warm the grip for the falcata. There was no room here for the arc of a strike. It would be a straight-on thrust—if it came to that. Until he saw what he faced—maybe more than just one man?—he wasn't going to leave the protection of the passage for more open space.

Roak's throat!—is it a few Angessans after all?

He strained to hear voices—any sound; heard nothing from beyond the end of the passage, now a ragged silhouette that narrowed almost to a point at the top. He suddenly felt disoriented. Despite the lack of voices, this seemed all too familiar: the breathing behind him, the constriction of the passage, the light at the end...getting brighter...and the unmistakable tang of the sea.

Below Sulserra's.

The moment passed at the entrance to the chamber, and he let out the breath he hadn't realized he'd been holding.

No need for the falcata. But only on the third try did he manage to slide it scabbard-home.

"They light tombs after all," Vaience whispered.

"They did more than that—look over there."

Chapter Twenty-Two:

THE SIXERS

T HEY SAT ON the pile of thin hides next to the boat, and to keep warm they'd draped a few over their shoulders. Between them, at their feet, two dawnstone rods lay across the sack of food and water jugs and the four pages Vaience called an artifact.

The dawnstone rods had been leaning near the entrance to this sea-cave. Five more were scattered around the chamber that was scarcely more than a widening of the crevice that led down to this…tomb.

The rods were the same size, almost as long as Falca's arm and perhaps half the thickness of his wrist. He'd held cold light in his hands before—chunks of dawnstone and lunelings—but he wondered why these rods of dawnstone seemed different. Was it because their polished, glistening smoothness was no more necessary to their purpose than the wave-like curls on the bridges?

Why not just bring a piece of dawnstone to where you needed light?—as Soso had done at the hut—for building the boat that would ensure your escape from your enemies, whoever they'd been. And not just one boat; Falca was certain there'd been another in here.

There was nothing more they could do now but wait for the night, take the boat and leave; leaving as well the unanswered question of why the man and woman here had stayed. A decision made hundreds of years ago—probably much more—now gave Falca and Vaience the chance to keep on. And hope they'd miss the rocks out there which could rip apart the boat before they got to the open sea.

FALCA HAD APPROACHED the boat expecting another rotten hull—the Fates had their songs, too; surely after having had their laughs with the first boat, they'd want to enjoy more of the same despair of foundered hope from him and Vaience.

The boat lay slightly keel-canted, to Falca's eye slightly wider and longer than the other one Vaience put his foot through, with a splayed double-prow like a strange sort of open fish-mouth, the top part of the jaw protruding over the lower. Looking for signs of rot or holes in the hull, he and Vaience ran their dawnstone rods along its length, both sides. The prow and keel seemed to be all of one piece. And it wasn't wood—couldn't be—or the boat would have been a pile of moist, clumpy dust. Nor was it metal. The keel, ribs and rails appeared to be made of bone, to which were stitched sections of some sort of skin or dressed hide, the seams sealed with Roak-knows-what. Three paddles—had to be bone, too—leaned against one of the two thwarts.

Stitching hide to bone? You'd think the builders of everything else on Angessa that wasn't dry-stacked huts of stone, had used the customary iron tools; you don't build a fortress, road and bridges and a temple and carve out steps, without metal tools.

But Falca and Vaience had found none—nor what might once have been iron tools—in what looked like a work area in the middle of the sea-cave chamber. They found scraps of hide and bone, coils of thick cord; they found long, thick needles and variously sized implements suitable for cutting and puncturing; they found four of what looked like a stalker's serrated mandibles, except these had grips for the hand. They found lesser amounts of most of these in an open area of the chamber that seemed to indicate another boat had been built.

Wherever that boat had gone, its builders had taken it out of here by way of a jagged opening that led steeply down from the chamber. And when they'd pushed or carried the boat to the water's edge, and made their farewells to the man and woman left behind, while waves crashed against the rocks out there, had they seen the same sunlight of an early afternoon, as Falca and Vaience had?

They'd talked it over: which was worse?—leaving now and possibly having Duna and her slew dogs seeing them and hurrying back to the cove and the *Sea-Flame* and sooner or later overtaking their prey? Or waiting until nightfall and having only the light of the Sisters and the constellations to avoid those rocks?

Whichever, the boat had to be moved from where it lay, and in doing so, they were astounded by how light it was—and then worried that it was *too* light, too flimsy; the thickness of the smooth hide of the hull not even that of a little finger. And while the stitched seams were sealed, would they *remain* watertight? All you could do was assume that the boat-builders knew what they were doing; wouldn't have made a boat of animal skin that would get waterlogged or otherwise prove impractical for a sea voyage to…wherever they went.

Falca didn't mention to Vaience that *other* option for escape, the riskiest of all: Duna's croft.

They decided to leave at night. By then they'd have gotten much-needed sleep, if such could be had down here, in a tomb.

The ones-who-were-left-behind lay on the biggest stack of hides on the far side of the chamber across from the boat. They lay together; what had once been their clothes now only patterned scabs upon their bones. The skeletal arm of the smaller, shorter of the two hung over the edge of the stack. She—*was she female?*—lay on her back. Her mate in death was on his side, one arm draped over her. Under the hand of his other arm was what appeared to be… pages of some paper that *should* have gone to dust, too, like the boat.

Vaience, bending over closely, had slid them out from under the hand, and whispered an apology for dislodging the bones. Four blank pages—but Falca had to agree with him after he felt them that they were slightly rough, as if someone had etched lines of writing on the fawky paper.

VAIENCE CLAMPED THE dawnstone rod between his knees and slowly moved one of the pages in front of it—this way and that, up and down; maybe some trick of light and shadow might reveal what was written. After trying the other three to no avail, he put them down on the sack, and sighed.

"It makes no sense, Falca. I can *feel* the writing, line after line. I just can't *see* it. I know there's coy ink that shows only when a certain kind of wash is applied that reveals the words. But if they used that, why bother to etch them on this…paper? which isn't paper at all. There's the skensy we used at Sulserra's and the Widow's, and paper that's animal skin, but that's thin. This is thicker, though not by much."

"And we're sitting on more of it," Falca said. "Seems about the thickness for what they used to make the boat."

"Perhaps for writing they scraped the hides thinner."

"Still probably the same—the only things that haven't decayed down here."

"We keep saying *they*, Falca. Who were...*they*, I wonder."

"Maybe what's above us wasn't a temple but an edificia."

"You think that because of four pages of writing we can't see?"

"And the boats—the one we *can* see over there, and the one we can't, that left."

"What do they have to do with an edificia?"

"Well, I've told you much, my friend, but not how lucky I was to escape from Milatum."

"I NEVER KNEW about it," Vaience said softly. "But I wasn't a senior thedral at Sulserra's—and then I...had to leave."

"Yahh, I overhead a few things about that at the Widow's."

"I knew what I was doing, and so did Cyalla but—"

"Sure she did; she chose you. We're the ones get picked, even if we think it's the other way 'round."

"I'll keep that in mind for the next Demizell I meet," Vaience said.

Falca smiled; he couldn't see Vaience's—the hide draped over his head and shoulders was in the way—but it was in his voice. Then more: "Cyalla just came into Sulserra's one day. She came back. And again. We met only six or seven times. Once we—well, never mind that. We very much enjoyed each other's company. We talked like you do when you lose track of the time. Cyalla could have been anyone of spirit and wit—"

"Except she just wasn't *anyone*."

"Yare well, I had no intention of fleeing at the sight of her, scurrying away and hiding in the scriptorum for fear of consequences."

"Nor at the Widow Yist's."

"Even if there hadn't been...consequences, we knew we'd never see each other again. She despaired about having to go to Castlcliff, but she had to, of course. And looking back, lucky she did—the Skarrians. I only wish I'd had the chance to wish her well in her new life there, but now...well, she has only Cymra left. And a husband-to-be who's twice her age. At least there's the edificia in Castlecliff. They can be places to find solace, too. But they don't last forever. Castlecliff's first edificia was also burned, destroyed."

"Like this one—if that's what it was."

"Whatever *they* called their thedrals, there couldn't have been many of them, from the size of what's above. At Sulserra's there were over a hundred of us if you include everyone who worked and lived there. But here? Maybe a dozen—which probably means *all* of them must have known about…this." Vaience swept his arm around.

"Gotta be hard keeping a secret in so small a place," Falca said, "and they all would have been needed to carve out the passage, the steps—whatever else had to be done. And however they did it wasn't with stiting *bone* tools."

"We're back to what happened at Sulserra's, aren't we?—keeping the secret."

"Yahh, I doubt that anyone else on the other side of the island, in that fortress—when it *was* one—knew about what was below this wee edificia."

"But *everyone* on the island would've had to help build the road and bridges," Vaience said. "The thedrals here would've needed regular deliveries of food and supplies from the other side."

"It's a head-scratcher, you think about why they just didn't put their edificia in the fortress, keep their books and scrolls in what they thought was a safe place—until you realize that if they'd done that—"

"They would have been trapped, everything lost."

"I s'pose they *could* have made a secret way out of the fortress, but with an enemy's ships crowding the cove, soldiers everywhere, your chances of escaping would be much worse than *here*."

"Yare, if Sulserra's was on Mereshaven, say—or in the citadel—there's no way out of a besieged city. Makes me wonder about the similarities of…*here* and *there*; that maybe what's *here* is more than a people separated by hundreds of years having the same idea."

"Keep going."

"Maybe *they* reprised what they had done *there*…in Milatum—no, that's too far-fetched."

"Ahh, maybe not, Vaience—what you said above. Maybe the six-sides here and there aren't a coincidence."

"You just named them."

"I did?"

"The Sixers. Some of them may have just been thedrals, but many others were builders. Who knows, maybe they built the Five Bridges, too."

"Roak's balls, why not? And while we're at it...our Sixers must have left Milatum—or whatever they called it then—either willingly or they were forced to skelter...or there was a war."

"Hmmm...so the survivors sought refuge here, another island, and there couldn't have been too many survivors—this island is smaller than any one of Milatum's Linnises. But if there were *more* Sixers, those must have scattered to other places. All we know...well, not really"—Vaience laughed—"is that some *were* here, however long that was. For twenty years? Fifty? A hundred? And only a handful escaped, our *thedral* Sixers."

"But not back to Milatum."

"No, not there," Vaience said, and pulled the hide off his head, obviously getting excited about the speculation. "Falca...it's...it's hard to imagine, but this all must have happened *before* Colza came to a ring of islands where the only things *not* in ruins were the five bridges linking them, and the strange structures that were eventually called the Labrys and the Wovens. *All* of this before *Roak*. Before there *were* Six Kingdoms."

Falca had his dawnstone rod in his hands now, tapped it on the scoury floor of the chamber. "And whoever the Sixers' *enemy* was, the fucking Skarrians weren't it. But I bet those poxy pages would tell us." He lifted the rod, pointing. "And maybe who *they* were, those two over there, and why they didn't leave. They must have been badly wounded. Or just one of them was, and the other would not abandon him...or her. I wish we...it would be a good thing to know their names—why are you looking at me like that?"

"Yare, it would be a good thing," Vaience said softly.

FALCA SAT ON the hide he'd folded and placed on the floor, his back against the pile, a dawnstone rod across his legs. Vaience lay above, asleep, his feet hanging over the corner of the stack.

Neither of them would be getting much sleep before night fell, but a few hours each would be something, anyway. Later, on the water, they could take turns again, and by then Falca would know which stars and constellations would be their guides. Vaience said he knew them. There had been an observatory at Sulserra's, and as a novice edificiate he'd been required to know them all, their seasonal journeys through the heavens, and the provenance of any mythology associated with them.

Falca knew some of them by different names, and surely the Sixers had called them something else. But for practical purposes at night, Vaience knew which would help keep them true to the northwest and the coast of Gebroan. And while they might be blurry to him without his spectacles, he knew where they were and could point them out for Falca to see clearly. And not only the stars and constellations.

Falca would first see the scrim of an island on the horizon, hopefully within a few days; they'd need to replenish their food and water before continuing on. Roak bless *any* landfall, but the closer it was to the Gebroanan side of the Girvan awe the better. Thetis, farther up the coast, was the goal, and Falca would rather blister his feet walking there than arrive at its very harbor, with hands so ruined by paddling they would take a week to heal. But Thetis it was, and the edificia there; and let the thedrals puzzle over the fawky pages Vaience would be bringing them.

They would also be taking some of the hides for shelter on the boat—the sun would be merciless—as well as two of the long serrated tools: at some point—on the hoped-for mid-journey island or on the road to Thetis—Vaience might need a slashing weapon. And having an extra one was a good idea.

What had *they* taken with them, the Sixers who'd left in the other boat? Had there been a third boat as well? And what was *their* hoped-for destination? It was bewildering for Falca to think that the Sixers on this island could no more find refuge in Milatum than he and Vaience could a thousand years later.

And what must the men—and women?—in that second boat have felt leaving the last two. Had they pleaded with them to come? Or had it been something else, closer to abandonment, for whatever the reason.

Those two....

The man was on his side, facing in Falca's direction, his head above the woman's; so likely the last thing he saw before he died was the boat that would so many years later give a thedral and a rapparee from Draica a chance to escape.

Falca hadn't realized it before but the man's arm that was draped over the woman might mean that she'd been closer to dying than he.

The memory was upon him so quickly he had no chance to fend it off:

The morning with Amala at the waterfall in the Rough Bounds, a day that had begun so wonderfully—until the Wardens surprised and overwhelmed them. In the silence of this tomb he could hear his screams and hers not far away, as Lambrey Tallon pressed the deadly white rancer on his leg. He was already dying when Maldan Hoster stabbed her with the falcata, but he crawled toward her, through the shallow water sluicing over the shelving rock below the waterfall, hoping only to reach her before the rancer poison completely stiffened his body and then killed him. He watched her die....

Was it those two over there, reviving the memory of that terrible morning, that had given him the feeling that there was something else he was missing here? Or was it simply all the questions that could never be answered about this place? The feeling had the urgency of...looking over your shoulder to see if someone was following you, coming after you. Now, Falca *did* look over his shoulder, and chided himself because how could anyone have been hiding all this time in the shadows of this chamber.

Or maybe....

He got up quickly, dawnstone rod in his hand, and at the entrance drew his falcata, listened for the sounds of them coming down the steps, their breathing, whispers. Who would be first?—Duna or Kellusa? Headbutt? Or some other vane to whom the Fates had whispered above: *See how rubble has been tossed aside, the dust disturbed—move the plinth, you'll find steps. The ones you seek are down below....*

Falca heard nothing except the shout in his mind, shouting at Vaience to wake up—*push the boat to the water!*—and seeing himself killing the lead vane, then another to block the passage enough to give himself time to bolt to the boat, picking up the sack on the way, and fighting off the closest pursuers as Vaience frantically paddled the boat toward the open sea.

It wasn't the silence that reassured Falca but the certainty that if the Fates had indeed whispered to the hunters above, they would have done so long before.

He left the entrance, and as he was sheathing the falcata, he noticed something glinting in the dust, not far from the side of the stack of hides where the two Sixers lay. He nudged it with the end of the dawnstone road, then knelt to pick it up.

The ring's band was gold, and within the oval setting glistened a blueveil gem. Lambrey Tallon had one, set in a brooch; said it was worth what he'd had to do to get it, even though the blueveil gem was scarcely bigger than a peppercorn. But this one, a blueveil *this* size—here was a fortune in your hand.

The ring had slipped off a dangling finger of the woman. How long had it taken for her flesh to decay? so that in one moment of one day out of all the thousands, the ring had finally slipped off her finger and plunked to the floor—

the only sound in here for a thousand years—and remained half-hidden in the dust, lodged against a rough little wrinkle in the chamber's floor.

He stood, put the ring in his pocket, and whispered to her: "I'm sorry. Forgive me, but my friend and I will need it in Gebroan."

They had no money. But even a poor sale of the ring would fill two pouches of gold: one for Vaience on the day they parted ways; and one for Falca, to pay for homeward passage to Draica, with enough left over to buy a small manse in Beckon, Falconwrist or...*no, not Heart Hill.* He couldn't bear daily reminders of where Amala had once lived.

If he ever got to Draica, that is.

If he and Vaience ever got to the coast of Gebroan.

Would the last thing he heard, the food and water long gone and no land in sight, be the laughter of the Fates: *What good did it do to rob the tomb? All this way from Draica and you're still a rapparee....*

And so fucking what if he was? Who *wouldn't* take what was there if he could, and not hurting anyone with the reive? He and Vaience were going to need that ring in Gebroan—and the Sixer's boat to *get* to the coast. There was no getting anywhere *above*, not with Duna and thirty vanes up there, hunting for them—

But there is...that's it....

Maybe it wouldn't have worked the night before, when he'd had the... *what-if* on the road. But it might tomorrow.

Now wouldn't that *be a reive....*

He got up from the stack of hides, thinking about it, walked past the boat. At the water's edge the lowering afternoon light shadowed the spuming rocks out there. At night, if he and Vaience couldn't steer the boat clear of those spurs and snags, the escape—and the reive—might be over before it began.

We leave earlier then. Twilight. Rouse Vaience now? Nahh, let him sleep longer....

There was time enough to tell him, after he got his own rest—if he could now—that maybe they wouldn't have to paddle the Sixers' last boat to Gebroan after all.

Chapter Twenty-Three:

WHAT'S WHAT

E XHAUSTED, WET, PALMS chafed from paddling halfway around the island, Falca sat against the boat, Vaience next to him, head lolled back at the rail. The thedral's softer hands had gotten the worst of it, so he'd had to push at the stern with a shoulder as Falca pulled at the bow to get the boat across the strand to the bottom of the dune.

The marker of the dawnstone spindles on the hillock above the dune had been Falca's guide for the landfall—but if he'd seen in the gray light of near-dawn that Gyllyd's two ships had arrived, there would have been no landfall.

At least the boat was off the open strand, where it might have more easily been seen by an early-rising vane fetching something from the *Sea-Flame*, or by the cullies' guard preferring to piss along the seaward-facing side of the hut.

The wind had picked up now but for most of the night the Sisters' ribbons shimmered upon a lightly treading sea. Still, he and Vaience almost hadn't made it beyond the breakers below that almost-vertical cliff, losing control of the boat, unable to avoid two spurs of rock. Falca was sure the side of the boat would be pierced, ripped open. But the Sixers had known their business; the stitched hides were tough. And as Falca and Vaience struggled to keep the boat pointing into the turmoil of the surf, they realized the purpose for the strange, overhanging prow: breaking those waves.

Soon enough we'll find out if it's been for naught....

But it did seem likely that at first light Duna would be taking most if not all of the vanes for a second day of hunting. After what had happened, she wouldn't be in a mood to call it off, letting Falca and Vaience merely die of thirst wherever they'd be holed up in the burreens, or on some other strand to the west or east. Surely the Lady Vane would want the satisfaction of capturing them *and* the added pleasure of choosing the most painful way to kill them. She'd be confident about eventually finding the escapees: there was no way off the island…or so she thought.

She and her men would have come back to the village for the night, so that's where they were now. But not for long.

In thinking it through before he and Vaience set out in the boat, neither of them could come up with a good reason why a skillet-hot Duna would not take all her vanes for the hunt. Why keep even five or six at the cove just to sit around? As far as Falca knew, neither she nor anyone else was worried about a threat from other corsairs. She'd keep a guard at the hut, of course; and old Blear would stay. Maybe one other vane. But even if Duna left five or six others, chances were still good that Falca and the cullies could handle them. The prisoners might be in sair condition, but the prospect of freedom would make up for that—hopefully.

Weapons? There'd be the guard's hangar to give to the most eager of the cullies. Worst came to worse, there were the Sixer tools. But surely on the *Sea-Flame* and galliot there'd be enough things to use as weapons if a few vanes tried to prevent them from setting fire to one ship and sailing off in the other.

What am I missing here? Falca thought. *Gyllyd's arrival?*

But he wasn't here *now*, and within an hour of freeing the prisoners, they'd all be away. Even if—homeward bound—Gyllyd saw a sail on the horizon, would he give chase? Not likely.

And so what if he saw distant smoke rising from Angessa? He'd press on, alarmed, sure. But as long as he didn't see the galliot leaving, they'd be all right. Gyllyd would be low on supplies and water after his own hunting, his crew divided between his ship and the prize. By the time Duna told him what had happened and they resupplied Gyllyd's ships and set out in pursuit of the galliot….

We'll be all right…probably….

He rose to a knee.

"Is it time, then?" Vaience murmured.

Falca nodded. In a crouch he walked past Vaience, knelt near the boat's stern and looked beyond the strand. To the west and north, the sea was a fretted sheet of iron.

"Anything out there?"

"Nothing—where's Terenure?"

"Southeast of Milatum on the coast—why?"

"It's the direction he's s'posed to be coming from, Gyllyd. So he'd be bearing 'round from the east. All we can do is hope we see that when we're well away."

"Anyone at the dock?"

Falca scuttled back. "Can't see it from here. We're beyond the curve in the strand so I'd have to go farther out to check—and if anyone is at the ships, he could see *me*. And then we're arse-up over the turd barrel."

Vaience ticked his head up at the dune. "So how far beyond that to see what's what?"

"Up this side of the hill, belly it up near the spindles. Could be a while before I can make sure about the vanes, see if they're leaving, get a count."

"If it's good?"

"More waiting, to make damn stiting sure it is. Then longer still, or it's—"

"The turd barrel."

"Yahh, they've gotta be far enough away they can't hear anyone shouting— Blear in the village is all it would take to bring 'em back at a run."

"What about the hut's guard?"

"After I cosh him, he gets locked in the hut after the others are out. If the count's good, he can shout all he fucking wants."

"You know I'm coming with you, right?"

"Vaience…that's not…Look, s'pose I'm off by three or four vanes? If there's a ruck, how're you gonna see what's coming at you, much less hold a—"

"I'm not staying here, Falca. Maybe I couldn't barely mark Duna from Foosie at a hundred paces but my hands are a little better; good enough to carry another sack of supplies from that hall—we'll need all that's there. Maybe I can't swing a blade right now, but I can do that."

Falca squared him in those short-sighted eyes, which squared him back. *You're Ossa's son, all right….*

"Stay close," Falca said. "Let's go."

BLEAR STOOD ON the hillock, facing the quay, Rooka's talon-leather draped over his shoulder like a scullery cloth—well, whatever it was. He coughed, spit. No blood in the gobbet. *That*, anyway, was something.

They must have found butts of caulking pitch on the *Sea-Flame*, emptied the contents aft, because that's where the sheets of flame were highest above the taffrail, at the mizzen shrouds and spars now, black smoke drifting in. Blear covered his mouth and nose with the end of the talon-leather that had saved his life, his arm anyway.

All of them were aboard the galliot except for the four at the oars of the gig, the tow-line taut, slowly pulling the blunt bow of the ship around in the offing. The thick smoke obscured much, but it looked like most of the cullies were at the lee-rail amidships, probably with buckets of water, ready to douse the cinders blown across the quay from the *Sea-Flame*.

And Breks? Blear's last glimpse of the Draican was when he and the thedral were hauling a boat over the lee-rail—and it couldn't have been the scat-boat from the *Sea-Flame*, which would have required four men to lift it up and over.

He's getting away with it...making a fool of my daughter, all of us....

Blear tried to summon up the rage that *should* be there, burning within him as surely as the *Sea-Flame*. But here was the strangest thing: he felt like he'd bet again on the Draican—and won. If anything, a smile was closer to his lips than curses; that and a whisper of apology to his daughter.

He hadn't *in fact* betrayed her but what else was he doing now except staring at evidence to the contrary. Which would have to be kept be a secret, hidden behind the curses he'd manufacture upon her return—which would be too late to salvage a fecking thing.

He looked back at the village below, though he knew he'd have heard the shouts of thirty-odd running vanes, Duna and Kellusa in the lead. Maybe she was on her way, having seen the smoke even before Jagurtha located her out there in the scrapland or the western strands. It was much more likely, however, that Rooka had found her first.

Even at this distance he could hear the crackling of the fire. Smoke billowed thickly, but the in-shore breeze was now wafting more of it away from him, so he dropped the mask of Rooka's talon-leather from his mouth and nose.

Most of the rigging was gone, spars ablaze, the flames licking at the bow. Duna's figurehead—carved in her likeness, the back-swept tresses brightly painted, her renowned bosom the color of sea-foam—would soon be gone.

Yare well, she could have another made for the *Sea-Flame*'s replacement; perhaps Gyllyd's prize.

And the cullies he'd taken would more than replace those lost. Still, his daughter would never soon forget this day, or Falca Breks.

Blear had never seen her so wrathful. She wouldn't have listened to him anyway—or so he told himself now. He'd heard her that morning, fuming to Kellusa about how, *how* did Breks know she intended to sell him in Thetis—*can he read minds, too?*

Everyone but Jagurtha and Blear, of course—how could the old man keep up with his limp?—would be going to hunt him down, she shouted at the vanes. And only calming down a little when Foosie saw the faint outline of the boat sunk off the strand; Foosie probably saving his life with that, because that brought her boil to a simmer, telling everyone that the Draican wasn't as clever as he thought, trying to make them all think he and the thedral had escaped by sea.

Blear had a mind to speak up then, remind her to be careful not to underestimate Breks. But even if he had she likely would've said that was why she was taking thirty men to hunt him down.

He was surprised it didn't occur to her to ask for Rooka's help in finding the escapees. But he'd kept his mouth shut there, too, and he knew why: Rooka would locate them, he had no doubt about that. All it would take was the stormbird seeing a twitch of movement in a hiding place below, an exposed arm or leg…and he'd begin his tight, descending spiral to mark the location.

And by now Breks would be stretched out on the four-square by the hall—the thedral waiting his turn—like basted meat waiting for the spit; Duna too incensed to sell him for the Blue Block.

Jagurtha said he'd never made a four-square but he'd seen one in Karsor's Bay and what remained of a criminal, shackled to its timbers, after the Gebroanan sun had cooked him for a week.

"Just so," Duna said. "You'll have plenty of time to think about how you'll go about making ours while you're guarding the cullies."

She'd been sure she would corner Breks somewhere on the far end of the island, if not the ruins. Kellusa agreed with her that would be the place to begin the hunt, Breks and the other one wanting to get as far away as possible, and as quickly as they could.

In hindsight both were wrong. But that first morning and again earlier today, Blear had a strong suspicion that the Draican was a lot closer than those cliff-side ruins, yet he'd said nothing. Because whether the ruse of the sunken boat had worked or not, Breks couldn't have stolen enough food and water from the hall to last more than a week. Maybe he thought he'd find a way off the island at its far end. Maybe not. But the man had more than enough wits to reckon the woman he'd made a fool of would bring every vane she had to find him; that his best chance was where he *knew* there was the means to escape from Angessa.

So what did Breks do? He did what Blear would have done: as soon as he saw the scrapland, he hid off the road, someplace where he could see it without being seen, and mark the passing vanes, counting 'em all, so he'd know how many Duna had left at the cove.

Blear could have said all this to her; it was on the tip of his tongue....

Sheer...maybe he *would* have spoken up if he hadn't heard her mention early on that she intended to sell him on the Blue Block in Thetis. What a *waste* that would have been; never mind the fat, clinking purse of siller. Such a waste for the House of Rheg. Duna could get more ships and coffles of cullies to replace those she'd lost, but she'd never find a man like Falca Breks to give her an heir, and stand by her side and help her fight and outwit all those who stood in her way.

Yare well, that had been *his* hope for his daughter, not hers. Still, she must have taken the Draican's measure as quickly as Blear had. Why else would she have summoned him to her croft if not to give him the Glove?—he'd heard Foosie tipping about that, oyah. Yet she decided to sell him on the Blue Block. What had happened up there?

Blear glanced again the empty village.

Ah, my daughter...what did you fear?

So what now?—Gyllyd?

There was only one ship out there, the cullies hauling up the gig. Two spanners wheeled above the galliot as the patched mainsail dropped. They'd soon be tacking north, then bearing off west. Gebroan. Tuleen, maybe Thetis. Karsor's Bay was too far up the coast. They'd want the closest landfall for what they'd taken—and hadn't—from Angessa.

Breks had taken something else, too—the kind of swag you couldn't put in a chest. But Blear didn't reckon the man would be bragging about how he'd done it, making fools of them all. He wouldn't be doing that, not on the galliot, not in some tavern in Thetis, or any on the way back to Draica. He had a gob on him, the strappy-jack did; but he wasn't a mouthy yape like Rasher, or a half-brick like Struke. If either of them had appeared that dawn on the Girvan quay, soon enough everyone would have known why.

Which Blear, even now, wondered why the Draican had wanted to join the *Sea-Flame*.

Possibly the thedral had something to do with it, or else Breks wouldn't have freed him first. Still, the best way to do that would have been to accept the Glove, soften Duna as hard as he could, and in time she probably would have released the thedral—what was one less cullie when many more were coming? It couldn't be that Breks had changed his mind. Duna wouldn't have told him that night he was bound for the Blue Block…and then let him walk out the door.

Blear had no doubt that by the time Gyllyd arrived she'd still be angry, vowing to take the hunt over the water, to every town along the Gebroan coast—from Tuleen to Karsor's Bay—and maybe even to Trigel. She might find the galliot and its captain, that splay-eyed, pendant-lipped gallybagger—but Breks would be long gone. And a man like him could offer his crucible steel to any patroon or princeling in Sandsend, move on to Myrcia, and by the time he got back to Draica he'd have enough shine to fill another chest like the one he knew—every man did—was at the Lady Vane's croft.

Which was about all that Breks *didn't* take, though Blear doubted—even odds here—that fact would cool Duna's skillet. Breks had been too smart to waste time getting it, not knowing if Duna was about to appear over the hill. And there were more important things to take for the run to Gebroan—you couldn't eat or drink the shine. Which was what he told Boaig, the galliot captain, adding that if he wanted it so badly, he could damn well go get it but they weren't going to wait for him.

And even odds here, too, whether Blear would tell Duna that. But there were some things he *could* say. He *had* been in the hall for his morning meal and the scraps for Rooka, and unaware of what was happening up on the hill above the cove. Coming out of the hall—three steps and a cough—and there they were: seven of them running toward him, Breks in the lead, steel out, Boaig brandishing a hangar. Jagurtha's, who else's?

Blear did the only thing he could do at that point, which certainly wasn't trying to skelter. Maybe they heard his command to Rooka, maybe not: *Duna, find Duna*. But they saw the sudden lofting of wings from his arm, oyah.

Boaig wanted to kill him, shouting that someone was going to pay for the corsairs robbing him, taking his ship. But the thedral stepped in front of him. *He's an old man, and even if the bird finds the others, it can't give them wings to fly back......*

Which was true enough.

Best leave it at that for Duna.

But of course the eddy didn't say that about no wings for Duna's vanes, though he did step in front of Boaig *after* the yape tried to kill him. The thedral was closer to Blear than Breks was, or any of the others; but no one was close enough to stop Boaig—who would've cleaved Blear's head with the hangar if he hadn't reflexively raised his forearm.

A vicious strike...and for all its impact, Boaig would have done better tapping Blear's wrist with a spoon.

He'd stared at his arm, then the ground where it should have been, then at Boaig. A saltswallow could have flown into his mouth. The thedral was the first to react, stepping in front of Boaig and his yellow teeth and wayward eye, the man seemingly stunned that he still gripped a blade and not a spoon. Breks was staring at Blear's leathered forearm, as if he'd seen Duna and thirty vanes suddenly appear. Then he walked over to Boaig and took the hangar from him as easily as he might have plucked a sunsbreath petal. He handed it to one of the cullies gathered round, who ran a thumb along the hangar's edge, shaking his head before flinging the blade's away.

Blear heard Breks' commands as whispers, but they couldn't have been, everyone quickly scattering: four cullies to the hall; Boaig, looking back once, toward the cove.

This much Blear could tell his daughter: how they all left; how soon enough he limped up to the hut on the hill, expecting to find Jagurtha dead. Breks, however, had only locked him in the hut.

"Maybe I better go with 'em—Duna'll kill me fer—"

"So might *they*. But she prob'ly won't—someone's got to carve her a new figurehead. Garn now, go find her—and make sure you're blowing hard when you do."

The wind had changed direction bringing more smoke toward the hill. Flames tongued out of the oar-sweep holes. There was no point in watching the *Sea-Flame* burn to the waterline, or the galliot bearing off in the distance, its sail the only one on the horizon.

As Blear limped slowly down the hill, he thrice folded Rooka's talon-leather around his wrist and forearm, the end under, corners tucked in. Sooner or later the stormbird would be returning. Blear had always known it wasn't common leather. If it had been, by now Rooka's talons would've scarred it, and if it was only some kind of densely woven cloth, it would've been pierced and cut.

A *kinnet*.

That's what he'd heard Breks call it as he and the thedral walked away from the hall, the last to leave for the cove, Breks arm over a butt of water on his shoulder, and Rasher's ear gone from his belt.

Whatever a *kinnet* was, it had sentiment for Blear and maybe Rooka, too. While highly intelligent, stormbirds were difficult to train for return. Yet Blear hadn't had the slightest problem with him. He'd been hatched upon this... kinnet in the nest from which Blear took him as a fledgling—Roak knew where the mother and father had gotten it. They hadn't been there, presumably killed elsewhere. Rooka had been barely alive, his sibling dead.

At first it had been a swaddling cloth as Blear nursed Rooka back to health. And then it became something to wrap around his forearm and wrist—a thin, supple yet tough greave to protect his flesh from the stormbird's talons. Rooka gripped harder than the first stormbird Blear had trained, a female who'd died of the red molt at two years. Blear believed—sentiment again—that Rooka's grip was how he expressed affection or gratitude.

As had Falca Breks, clasping Blear's shoulder before he turned and left with the thedral.

Gratitude? For what? Gattling on when few others would talk to him? A few obvious words of warning about Struke? What an old man might have counseled the Lady Vane but didn't? Breks couldn't have known about that.

But that's what it was: a gesture of thanks. Which was only another piece to the northron's puzzle. Yare well, someone *else* would have to fit the pieces together, though the Draican would have to stay in one place long enough for that to happen. Blear gave that even odds, though he wouldn't have put money on a bet, not this time.

CHAPTER TWENTY-FOUR:

UNDER THE STARS

V AIENCE SAT FACING aft on the overturned hull of the Sixers' boat, leaning with every roll of the galliot. There had been no room for the boat except toward the bow, prow and stern to the narrowing bulwarks. The gig was bigger, stowed in its usual place forward of the main, over the hatch of the *Lysidia's* single hold.

So far, all that had happened—Falca would take over at dawn so Vaience could get some sleep—was the rat. Vaience saw it as a blur of shadowy movement along the lee bulwark, but more clearly when it detoured into the moonlight, coming close to the sack near where Falca lay sleeping. He poked the sack with the kraken's claw—what they were calling it—and the rat skittered away.

But it had come back, and again Vaience defended what little food remained in the sack, along with the other precious artifact: the pages. That was the rat's last foray; probably it had found a way below decks where all the food was. Crayfish had insisted the supplies taken from the hall be kept below, lest the Girvaners help themselves to it between the appointed mealtimes. More likely he wanted to do just that himself.

For a while the swale at the wheel, Tunty, had been talking to Shillik, whom Boaig had posted in front of the companionway hatch. Maybe Shillik had fallen asleep, maybe not. But Vaience had heard no more talk, only Tunty singing a song, *Kegs of Eggs*, that must have had as many verses as the number of stars of Kyria's Lyre over the southern horizon. There was more music in Falca honing his falcata than Tunty's voice, and blessedly the swale had stopped about the same time the rat reappeared. Vaience had found Tunty more amenable than Boaig's other crewmen, Shillik and Nails, partly because it was clear Tunty thought the captain had all the worth of a soup ladle with a hole in it.

The eleven Girvaners were aft, clustered by the taffrail, not below—Crayfish's order—so Vaience heard only the loudest brays, whistles and rattles of snoring. No retching though, not even Sheffie, who'd had the worst of it before the sea relaxed somewhat with the rising of the moons.

But no, nothing eventful so far on this, the second night after their escape, with Quoins saying this afternoon that they were five days out from Thetis, maybe four if the wind shifted more from the south. Vaience wished he'd mentioned earlier to Falca that Quoins had once been a blue-water sailor. If he had, likely Falca would have made sure Crayfish stayed on Angessa, and never mind the *Lysidia* was his ship.

Boaig couldn't be trusted. And Crayfish, in his cabin below—the door surely barred—doubtless didn't trust the man who'd freed him. Falca had his falcata but Boaig had another hangar now, and so did Tunty, Shillik and Nails who found three of the blades on the *Sea-Flame* and one on the galliot. Quoins and Sterbo had belaying pins, should there be trouble. Probably wouldn't be, but it was all too evident that Boaig was still angry about the sea-chest of money and what happened with that old corsair—being humiliated in front of his crew. And he'd been livid when Vaience and Falca, ignoring his order to leave the Sixers' boat on the strand, had hauled it aboard the galliot, Crayfish glaring at them, chewing furiously on his thick lower lip.

Boaig probably *was* the sort—a coward really—who preferred to nurse his grievances rather than act on them, but probably wasn't good enough. So Vaience and Falca had to be vigilant until they were off the *Lysidia*. Which was why Vaience sat on the boat's hull instead of sitting against it next to Falca, where the *shushing* of the ship's passage and the rhythmic creaking and groaning of the mast might lull him to sleep.

He had to stay awake. Even without his spectacles he damn well could see a big shadow approaching in the moonlight from aft, from where any trouble would come, and kick Falca awake and swing out with the kraken's claw. The blisters were gone. Because of the krael?

Fortunate he was to be on a ship bound for Thetis, because he should be where Cyalla doubtless thought he was: buried in thedrals' cemetery behind the Widow Yist's. But he wasn't because a stranger happened to be there; happened to hear a whispered conversation—and had something called krael in his pocket.

How do you measure such luck? You couldn't, no more than you could measure randomness, which Auriau considered as much of an element as the air.

Auriau.

If he was here now he, too, would be keeping his eyes moving, though for him shadows would be distinct, the constellations not blurry, because how could you be a soldier with short sight. But Auriau had also been a philosopher, devoting an entire chapter in *Across the Chasm* to randomness and luck. He was far from being a grutchy, distempered sage, but obviously he'd been rankled by self-satisfied people who asserted that one created one's good luck.

Falca had saved Vaience's life *twice* now, and what part had a thedral with soft hands—but not as soft as they once were—played in that? Other than having a father whom Falca had grown close to in the brief time they were together.

Auriau posed the questions: What was so threatening about accepting that good luck—or bad—was merely a function of randomness? How did the acceptance of the element of randomness diminish one's existence? To be sure, striving was all—but there was no guaranteed reward for the effort in creating good will, or certainty of consequences for the bad. Call it randomness; call it the Fates working at at their Loom Eternal—there were no celestial scales that measured the disbursement.

Vaience tapped the kraken's claw on the deck, seeing shadows aft but none were moving.

But there *was* a measure to what you did with your disbursement—the essence of Auriau's *kai*—and Vaience was still stunned by how generous his had been, even before the events at Girvan.

In his entire life—at the cottage above the Lazza, at Sulserra's—never once had he fallen asleep wondering what might happen if he did. In Falca's world—what Vaience knew about his past—the assumption was that someone would always be hunting you, whether you knew his name or not. And that's why you had a deek, Falca said, explaining what that was: someone you could trust with your life, so you could expect to wake up.

The hard part was picking a deek you *could* trust. Something told Vaience that maybe for Falca that hadn't always been the case, because no matter how careful you were…you couldn't entirely be sure of the other. But Vaience's father—Mott Demoul, later Ossa Vere—had surely been a deek you could trust with your life. Or maybe Falca had been one for him. Didn't matter, did it? who was older and who younger.

And all of it playing out under the stars; Kyria's Lyre—what Falca called the Silver Trail—the most brilliant of them all, save perhaps the Cauldron, higher in the northern sky. He'd asked Vaience on the boat why there were three different names down here for one constellation—Kyria's Lyre…the Thousand Strings…Heaven's Bridge. Well, only in Milatum were people so querulous and feisty they couldn't agree on a single name.

Vaience chided himself now because what could have played out while he was lost in thought was a single deadly fate. But he'd been moving his eyes all the while and nothing had changed: no shadow darting behind the gig or mast, though Tunty had switched now to loud humming—or was it the wind? Falca, stretched out along the rail of the boat, had shifted to his right side now—and somehow had made the turn with the falcata still in his hand, the point of the inward-curving blade resting against the folded…kinnet he was using as the thinnest of pillows.

It was kraken-skin—same as what the old hawker corsair had wrapped around his forearm. Still, Falca had tried to cut it with the falcata, a much keener blade than Boaig's hangar.

Nary a scratch.

Falca reckoned that the etching of the pages was done by a needle or stylus made of kraken-bone—what else could do it if even a steel edge sharp enough to shave with couldn't slice kraken-skin?

He handed Vaience the long, claw-like tool. "This will have to do, the point is sharp enough. Write something on the skin."

Vaience did, clumsily, using both hands, Falca stretching the skin tightly on the deck.

"What did you write?" he said.

"Your name and mine—and Cyalla's," Vaience replied, though of course they couldn't be seen.

Falca took a water jug from the sack, along with the pages, and splashed water on the hide.

"Now they can," he said, and smiled: "So *that's* who we all are."

Water. Just water. And more words on the pages. Vaience had no idea what they said. The lettering was like nothing he'd ever seen before, and he doubted very much the thedrals in Thetis would know what they said, either.

And then, by the time the smoke from the *Sea-Flame* was a dark smudge against the welkin sky, Falca began a tale of a room in a hostelry overlooking Sciamachon's fountain in Draica. He'd shared the room with Amala Damarr and the Timberlimb priest, Gurrus, who had something he called a kinnet that Falca first thought was a stable blanket—but which he found out later was kraken-skin.

And by the time the night had deepened, the wake of the *Lysidia* streaming with phosphorescence, Falca ended the tale at Scaldasaig, where Gurrus' kinnet remained, the only one left of all the kinnets that had once comprised a tapestry that depicted the exodus of the Sixers from...*here* to *there*—Falca was sure of it; as surely as he, and now Vaience, knew now why the old corsair, Blear, still had his arm.

They talked for a long time the first night, sitting on the boat's hull, facing aft, long after Boaig had paused at the companionway, to stare at the two of them before going below. There could be no doubt that Sixers must have lived not only in Milatum and on Angessa, but also on the island in Lake Shallan long before the Wardens built Scaldasaig; and little doubt that the Sixers were not only builders and thedrals but also the makers of a kraken-skin tapestry revered by the Timberlimbs; Kelvoi they called themselves.

Yet there were other names, too, and Vaience wished he could have known them as more than just names, the ones who died at Scaldasaig or on the way there: Amala Damarr and Gurrus—who'd stolen the kinnet from the Tapestry and never could return it though he desperately wanted to because the Tapestry had disappeared. And his father—most of all his father. And yes, even his sister.

But all that remained was a tale and artifacts; what the Sixers had left behind. Including the five bridges of Milatum. What else could their cables and woven spans have been made of than kraken-skin? And a lot of it...from a time when there were many more kraken in the sea, and possibly bigger than the lake-kraken of Shallan.

How had they been hunted and killed? Or did the kraken shed their skins somewhere? Or was there a place known only to the Sixers where the kraken went to die?

The Sixers must have woven or braided the cables of Milatum's bridges, all of them cut by tools such as the two kraken-claws Vaience and Falca had taken from the chamber. But were they even that? Perhaps the claws were merely… teeth, fashioned as cutting tools.

And why had the Sixers *made* them from kraken-skin? Why not bridges of stone? Because unlike stone, kraken-skin could neither be cut nor burned?

So many questions, including where Blear—who didn't seem to have known what he was using to protect his forearm from the stormbird's talons—got his scrap of kraken-skin.

But the bridges—how long had it taken for each to be built? Five years? Ten? And how many workers had been needed? And where were the Sixers' descendants? If they hadn't all been killed by their enemy, had the survivors gone back whence they came? For that matter, whence the enemy?

That night, Vaience said he'd take the night watch, if only because he wouldn't be getting much sleep with so many questions they'd posed to one another; questions with so few answers.

"The older you get, you're s'posed to have less of one and more of the other—isn't that how it's set up?" Falca had said with a faint smile.

"Not if you're a thedral," Vaience said, playing along. "If you're not careful, you're going to wind up as the oldest novice in the history of Draica's edificia—there is one there, right?"

"In the Tidesback district. I'd pass it every now and then, but it wasn't in my bricks…my, ah…working territory. I never stepped foot in it—what's to steal? Books? Where's the mark in a thedral with empty pockets."

Vaience could feel the stitching of the kraken-skin as he slid off the boat. He stretched and paced the beam of the galliot—only once did he misjudge the roll of the ship. At the lee rail for the second time, he saw someone else standing farther aft, leaning against the bulwark, behind the ratlines. He couldn't tell who it was, but he watched long enough to make sure the man wasn't coming forward. And then he was gone. Probably a Girvaner who couldn't sleep.

Three more nights of this watch, maybe four…and then Thetis…and the edificia. Falca's third in what?—three weeks? And up till then, not a one.

Where's the mark in a thedral with empty pockets?

Vaience smiled. There would be no marks in Thetis either—just the sweat of bringing a boat to the edificia there.

They couldn't leave the Sixer boat on the quay for someone to steal. So they'd have to carry it through the streets to get to the edificia, which evidently was adjacent to the water-clock in Phrynne's Square. Vaience had never been there but Iolus had, said the thedrals received a yearly stipend for maintaining the clock. Heard they got four times what the Girvan thedrals received for the campanile contract, Iolus complaining that filling a small basin with water once a day was hardly commensurate with ringing a bell every hour from dawn to midnight.

And once the boat was there, the thedrals would surely want to put it on display, given its provenance. Vaience was confident they would offer accommodations, considering the gift of the artifacts given to them.

But not that blueveil ring.

However exquisite the wedding ring Cyalla would soon be wearing, Vaience doubted it could match what Falca had found.

He wondered again why Falca had told him. He could have kept it for himself and Vaience would never have known. Falca could have bid him farewell an hour after they brought the boat to the edificia, and within another he could have sold the ring, keeping all of the money.

He'd asked Falca what he was going to do with his half after they sold the ring.

"Go somewhere the Lady Vane won't find me."

"Passage home to Draica?"

"Yahh, that would do it—you?"

"Buy a pair of spectacles—and a spare."

Falca laughed. "That's all? You're gonna have a *lot* left over, my friend."

"I'll think of a way to spend the rest of it," he said, though he already knew. Getting his mother out of Milatum.

There was no point in dwelling on the worst of what might have happened to her, the King's Own Gardener trapped on Mereshaven. Even if she hadn't been, she probably was unable to escape the city before the gates were closed. She had the working residence on Mereshaven, but she'd kept their home on Linnisheer. So…she *might* have managed to get there before things got bad. The cottage was secluded. It would be a refuge—but for how long?

He planned to spend his share of the ring money for passage from Thetis to Milatum, and back again. And having enough money wasn't the worry; it was a matter of *when* he could do it.

When would Milatum return to a semblance of normalcy?

Normalcy?

How could he even think in terms of normalcy after thousands had died and were wounded in the siege and aftermath? Never mind everything else such as the burning of Sulserra's...playhouses closed...sullen streets. No more the summer races on the city wall's allure, the king giving laurels to the winner in Labrys Hall; no more the joyous fetes and routs of Roak's Week, Cauldron's Day, the Night of the Mistra; no more the sky coming alive over the Queensmere with the scrybing of kites.

Normalcy?

How long would it take people to move on from shock and the mourning for those who had not survived? But they would move on in time; they still had to eat and return to their trades, even as they suffered from depredations and dealt with the conquerors and their adherence to Tholos, that vile creed. Surely the Skarrians hadn't conquered the city to keep it sealed forever.

Still, how long would it be before Myrcian and Gebroanan merchant ships would again be passing through the Cleave? Months could pass before the owners of those ships—and their captains and crews—decided that dealing with the Skarrians was worth the risk. Assuming of course the Skarrians didn't alter the terms and traffs of trading more to their own benefit. And that was only the commercial aspect. For all Vaience knew, events might already be moving toward war between Gebroan and Skarrian Keshkevar.

I have to get her out as soon as I can....

And he had to believe he could, that she'd survived; that he'd find her somewhere—either at the Linnisheer home or elsewhere.

Yare, she could take care of herself; she'd had to—the both of them—for many years. She was a resourceful. She would do what she had to do to survive. But for how long? What if things did *not* get better for a long time and she herself couldn't find a way out?—like thousands of others who were also desperate to escape the city.

What if he couldn't get there—and out again with her—for many months?

It might already be too late to help her.

He'd exchange in a heartbeat the artifacts, his share of the ring—everything he had—for at least *knowing* he'd done all he could to get her out before it was too late.

There was nothing he could do now, and he turned away from the rail to see the scuttling shadow of the rat, that bold rat again approaching the sack that lay against the overturned boat.

But maybe there *was* a way to get her out…and soon.

Maybe he was looking at it right now.

CHAPTER TWENTY-FIVE:

THE DEEK

FALCA TOOK ONE last look around.

Thimble was sitting against the bulwark amidships, mending his trews with his legs still in them, talking to Nails. Shillik had the wheel now. Boaig stood behind him, his back to the weather rail, wiping his forehead with a blue cloth, then the back of his neck, what there was of one. He stuffed the sweat-rag into a pocket, glanced over at the Girvaners clustered as usual along the taffrail, shook his head. Disgusted that his swale was over there, passing the time with Quoins? Or was it that Sheffie had one of Tunty's slingstones in front of an eye, peering through the hole in the middle, his playful shrieks far louder and discordant than the creaking of the galliot's single mast and the groaning of her timbers.

For most of the morning they'd had a vagrant sea, but the wind had since picked up, now coming off the larboard quarter, and the *Lysidia* rushed along under a cloudless sky in mid-afternoon, sittin' high, as the sailors said.

There was no point in waiting any longer; everything was as good as it was going to get.

Falca nodded at Vaience. They slid off the overturned boat.

Crayfish saw them as they came around the gig, his hand moving to the hilt of the hangar tucked into his belt.

"Whadda you want, Breks?" Boaig grumbled, the wayward eye aligned to Vaience who stopped slightly behind Falca and to his left.

"A matter of mutual interest."

"We don't have any."

"Except the arrival in Thetis."

"What about it?"

"Something best discussed privately." Falca nodded at Shillik.

"No, you'll tell me here."

"Ahh, I strongly suggest your cabin, Captain," Falca said, and ticked his head back at the Girvaners. He thumbed his fingers a few times, slowly, so Crayfish would be sure to notice.

"Shillik's deaf in one ear, and those yapes can't hear us—say your piece."

"They're too close," Vaience said.

"Was I talking to you, Squint?"

"You're talking to both of us."

Falca kept his voice low: "What he meant was they might get suspicious if they see us talking here a while. You aren't the only one who doesn't think we have anything in common."

Boaig stared at him, rubbed the right side of his nose where the veins were. He sniffed. "Ehh, all right. You go below first, meet me outside my cabin—just you."

"Wait now, it was *my* idea; I should be included," Vaience whined, acting his part. Falca had told him Crayfish, if he went for it, wouldn't want to be outnumbered below.

"No," Boaig said. "Just Breks—and with an empty scabbard."

Falca feigned a protest: "What about you, your hangar?"

Boaig smiled. "Stays with me."

Falca had expected this, too. He sighed, frowned, said: "All right; you're the captain, your cabin."

There were a few names for what Vaience had proposed to do, but to Falca it was a reive. And unless the snatch was a rap 'n rip or straight-on cosh—not the best way to go about this, he and Vaience had decided—you had to make the mark feel like he had the upper-hand. Until he didn't.

Falca handed the falcata to Vaience, who still looked impressively annoyed at not being included. "I'll be back for it soon enough," he said, "after Captain Boaig and I have finished with our…business." Whispering the last word.

He headed for the companionway hatch, sweat tickling down from his armpit, right side. The kinnet didn't fit all the way around, though Vaience had tightened and knotted the laces sliced from a hide with the claw, then poked through the holes pierced in the hide: three holes, chest to waist; the tailoring done behind the Sixer boat. He hoped he wouldn't need the protection of the kraken-skin, but it would almost be worth it to see Boaig's reaction again… almost.

○

BETWEEN THEM, HANGING by a beam-hook over the table in the small, sour-smelling cabin, a lantern swung gently with the ship's movement. Boaig blocked the shaft of light slanting in from the window directly behind him, but another splayed across what had to be a sizable amount of the supplies taken from the vanes' hall. Standing where he was, short, thick arms folded, Crayfish couldn't see the rat scurry over his berth—a corner of the coverlet neatly folded over—and disappear behind a butt of water.

He scratched his beard. "Let's hear it."

Falca dropped his hands from the low beam, and stepped to a corner of the table, and helped himself to a swig of water from the flagon set with its girdle on the table. He wiped his mouth with the back of his hand.

"I see no reason why you and I can't make a profit from the, ahh…from the *cargo* up there." He raised a finger.

"You're forgetting this is *my* ship, so the cargo—"

"Is mine, since I supplied you with it—and yahh, you're welcome—not to mention I *also* gave you back your ship. Shall we agree, then, that we share an interest in making a profit once we arrive in Thetis?"

Boaig snorted. "You've a fancy tongue, Breks, but where was your concern about my profits back on that scab of an island?"

"You'd be looking at *no* profits if Duna Rheg had returned before you ransacked her croft, looking for the shine she stole from you. But here's your chance to make up for what you lost. Don't tell me you think what I'm proposing hasn't already crossed your mind—you being a man of business."

Boaig showed his yellow teeth, the smile confirming what Falca suspected. But Crayfish was too cagey at this point to admit it. "Is that what *you* are, Breks? a man of business?"

"Some have said that, sure, in Draica."

"A long way from here."

"What's *here*, Captain, is the two of us wanting to pick up where we left off: selling the cargo in Thetis. And also the boat you didn't want the eddy and I to bring aboard." There, he got that in, as Vaience suggested.

"You won't get much for it."

"You're probably right, but selling it wasn't the only reason for taking it."

"Which would be?"

"It may be only four or five days to Thetis, but I think you'd agree that it's always best to have...options, should—"

"And what would your *option* be if I don't agree to this."

Falca shrugged. "No shine for either of us in Thetis. You need me to help you...ah, *handle* the cargo. Are you confident about all your crew—your swale, for instance. From what I've seen he—"

"You need me just as much."

"S'why we're chatting."

Boaig leaned over the table, the backs of his hands hairy as paws. "What'd be the split?"

"Half each...after your crew gets theirs, whatever points you think."

"What about the eddy?"

"What about him?"

"You didn't mention his cut."

"He's not here so how's he gonna know he won't be getting one? In Thetis, after he's helped us, we'll sell him, too. And I'm not worried about what the squinter's gonna do when he finds out we dunned him." He laughed but it wasn't what Boaig thought; Falca was thinking of Vaience, outside the cabin door now, like they'd planned, but hoping he maybe hadn't heard that last.

"Yare well, maybe he thinks he's getting a share, but who ever heard of an eddy who cares about shine to begin with—seems fawky."

Falca had to step quickly here: "This one does. Quivs too, the keelcat. She's something else, he said; met her in Girvan. Only she took her backside to Castlecliff and he needs siller to get there. Which I have better use for—and I'm talking about the both of us."

"You better be," Boaig said, leaning farther over his side of the table, as if those hairy-knuckled fists were a lot bigger than they were.

All right, enough of this....

Falca glanced down to make sure the table wasn't bolted to the floor. *That'll work....*

"We should get back up now, Captain. Are we agreed, then?" he said, moving to the table edge. He slid his fingers underneath.

"Agreed," Boaig said. "When we're a day out from Thetis, we'll talk again, work out the details, which includes you dunning Tunty when the time comes." He stood, rubbing his tiny paws. "I—we—got better use for *his* share, too… thinks he's the salt at table."

"Now that you mention it…" Falca said, and heaved up.

Flagon, cup, hourglass, trencher, utensils skidded back toward Boaig, who gave a startled squeal. Falca kept low, shoved the flat of the table against him, ramming him against a narrow shelf below the slanting windows. Boaig had almost pulled the hangar free from his belt when Falca punched him in the mouth so hard his head spun, a yellow tooth *tinking* against a window. And again—left hand this time—splitting Boaig's lower lip.

Crayfish slumped, eyes rolling white.

Falca pulled the table away, grabbed the hangar from Boaig's hand, and then yanked off the coverlet on his berth. Falca tossed the hangar toward the door—quicker to rip the bedsheet lengthwise. He rolled up the halves, and tied Boaig's ankles and wrists, saving enough of the linsey for a gag he stuffed into the fester's bloody mouth. Crayfish was just now coming around, eyelids fluttering, groans muffled…*mmmphh…mmmphh….*

Falca knelt, breathing hard. He could have finished the business much sooner…but where was the song in that?

He stood, feeling a throbbing high on the side of his forehead, and only now remembered he'd banged it on the low-hanging lamp. Boaig was groaning louder but there'd be no problem with him. The crew? Before, mulling it over, Vaience didn't reckon Tunty, anyway, would be fashed about a rucked-out Crayfish, and after what Boaig said about him that seemed certain. The others? Vaience said none had seemed especially loyal to Boaig, except maybe Shillik. Besides, the *Lysidia* wasn't a Keshkan navy tresreme; the crew weren't royal marines.

Still, better to keep the hangar for the time being instead of tossing it out a window. Hangar in his hand, Falca unbarred the door, opened it a crack, expecting anything but hoping Vaience would be out there, like they'd planned.

He was, stepped inside, saying: "I was worrying a little; you were in there a while—so *that's* what it was: you moved some furniture."

"You hear anything else?"

"Not much."

"Good. I…em…got a wee bit carried away."

They exchanged blades.

"What am I supposed to do with this?" Vaience said.

"You'll know if you have to do it," Falca said. "The wankspit might've been the easy part. Convincing the others to take us to Milatum and—"

"Wait, did you say…*us?*"

"Yahh, I'm going with you."

"Falca…you just got *out* of Milatum. I wasn't expecting you to go back *in* with me."

He grinned. "I wouldn't be much of a deek if I didn't, now would I?"

THEY WERE A mismatched pair, Tunty and Quoins, standing side-by-side a few steps back from the companionway hatch: Quoins the taller, with the chest and arms of a dock-heave; the swale slender but sinewy. The wind had picked with the waning afternoon, ruffling Quoins baggy trews and the ends of the sling hanging loosely from around Tunty's neck.

Falca, coming up first, didn't sense an immediate threat here from either man. Even so, they loomed as solid a presence as the capstan behind them.

"You two were below a while," Tunty said.

Quoins scratched his grey-flecked beard at the jawline. "Two blades and no Crayfish—what's the skim?"

Falca glanced over at the Girvaners. With the exception of Sheffie, all were looking toward the companionway. Quoins' burly son had a hand in front of his face, was loudly talking to it, as if giving his fingers instructions to block out the lowering sun. "It's about them," Falca said, pointing, and then gave the rest of it—mostly.

"*Cargo?*" Quoins said. "The gallybagger called us *cargo?*"

"Yahh. I couldn't believe it myself when I heard that," Falca said.

Tunty shrugged. "Doesn't surprise me—so he's not dead?"

"Coshed and bound with his bedsheet, is all," Falca said. "He'll need proper rope and a guard."

Quoins shook his head. "I still don't think he coulda got us all to the Blue Block, even with help."

"Like I said, for our half I was supposed to dun you and Tunty. After that he figured the others would be an easy."

"The ship's yours now," Vaience said. "Everyone's—to sell, divide the proceeds, whatever you decide."

Tunty pointed down. "What do we do about him?"

"That's up to y'all," Falca said. "Me?—I'd let the fester off somewhere he'll have a long walk to Thetis, instead of selling him there like he wanted to do to everyone over there. How much could you get for'm anyway?"

"Whadda you mean it's up to us?" Quoins said. "We sell'm—which I ain't kin to neither—we do that and it's more siller for you, too. Either way, I s'pose you want that half from us now, since you did what some of the rest of us were only grutching about wanting to do."

Vaience shook his head. "We don't want half. We want—"

Quoins guffawed. "You ain't getting *more* than that."

"Yare, might be hard to convince everyone to give you even half," Tunty said.

"Not if we're not in Thetis to collect it."

"What're you tipping?" Quoins said.

"What I was about to say: we want you to take us to Milatum," Vaience said.

Tunty barked a laugh. Shillik, at the wheel, turned around.

"Not *into* Milatum. Off the Cleave. At night. We'll take the boat we brought aboard."

"You canna be serious!"

"But they are, Quoins, or my sling's an arse-wipe—look at 'em!" Tunty pointed at Falca. "You coshed Crayfish for *that*?"

"We're going to Milatum, Tunty," Vaience said.

Falca nodded. "Just let us off, s'all you have to do."

"Look, maybe if it was up to *me*—"

"Isn't it?" Falca said. "*You're* the captain now."

"I reckon I am but…" He looked at Quoins.

"I s'pose it's you or me, Tunty. But yer the swale. I got no burr with you taking over, except maybe you'll shut up with yer singin', with all else you'll have to do. Anyway, I got Sheffie to look after."

"It's me, then. All right. That's one thing settled. The other thing…maybe it's the least we can do, Breks, what you did before and now. We'll have enough food and water to get us back to Girvan or Tuleen, maybe a little farther west. But the way things are…we *all* gotta have a say, we do this or not."

"They'll wanta know the reason for't," Quoins said. "So would I."

He and Tunty were looking at Falca, who shook his head. It was up to Vaience if he wanted to tell them.

"A personal matter," Vaience said.

"Which it is for us, too," Quoins said, "seeing as how we're adding a few more days getting home to Girvan, if that's what it still is."

"I doubt the reason would change anyone's vote from no to yes."

"Whatever the show of hands is," Tunty said, "that's what it is— understood?"

"You're the captain now," Vaience said, and glanced at Falca who knew what the look was for: *We still have the ring as a last resort….*

Falca's nod was more for Vaience than Tunty. He hoped they wouldn't have to use the persuasion of the blueveil ring in his pocket if the vote was shy. Give it to Tunty or Quoins? Sure. Either one likely could be trusted to keep the ring safe until it could be sold, the shine shared out. But there were others who might have a different idea, a ring like that. A lot could happen in the days ahead, including a few men asking why they had to keep on to Milatum now that the ring was theirs.

TUNTY VOTED YES; his three crewmen no, including Shillik and four Girvaners. Falca was surprised Quoins was a yes; he figured Quoins would want to get his son home as soon as possible. He was a strong-looking youth, a few years younger than Vaience, but there was no brawn between his ears.

"What now, Tunty?" a Girvaner asked. Harkells, a naysayer.

Before Tunty could reply, Vaience said: "Sheffie hasn't voted yet."

"He's three staves short of a barrel, that one," Thimble whispered near the taffrail gangway. "He don't count."

Quoins drew the belaying pin from his belt, but Tunty stepped in front of him, a hand gripping his wrist, saying: "Breaking bones won't break the tie." Then he walked over to Thimble, said something Falca couldn't hear, but when Tunty turned away, Thimble's smirk was gone.

Wyrrion, another Girvaner: "Thimble ain't right for gobbin' it, but he is, Tunty. The boy don't know what we're doing; he's been picking weevils outta that biscuit all the while, and eatin' 'em."

"Then we tell him," Falca said.

"Won't do no good."

"He's been through as much as you or anyone else on this ship. He gets his say."

"Fa, why're they all looking at me?" Sheffie said.

Quoins knelt at his side, put a hand over the biscuit Sheffie held. "Lissena me now." He pointed at Falca and Vaience. "Those two want to go somewhere. Some of us want to let 'em; some of us don't. We're counting hands to decide. You need to let us know what you choose, a' right?"

"What'd you choose, Fa?"

"Don't matter what I did. You get your own say about we let 'em go or not."

"They keep to the boat but I know who they are. The big one got us outta the stoney pen."

"That he did."

"Then he should go where he wants—should I raise my hand now?"

"Yare, now's the time."

"Didn't you say they both want to go?"

"That's right."

"Then I should raise two hands, Fa."

"Might seem so but the way this counting works, there's only one of you, Sheffie—so one hand's enough."

THAT NIGHT, ON his way to relieve Vaience—who'd taken the first watch below to make sure Boaig stayed put—Falca stopped by the helm. Tunty had the wheel again.

"Don't worry, Breks. We're on course for Milatum, north by northeast."

"Who's worrying?—except that for all I know you could have us bearing west."

"Now why would I go against what we chose? 'Specially seeing as how I'll have a little extra shine with you two gone. Oh, by the way, we decided something else while you and the eddy were roping up Crayfish."

"Which is?"

"After Milatum we're for Girvan, keep in the offing to see what's what. Most of us have family still there, leastways when we got kipped."

"And you?"

"No one in particular but I s'pose she's gone up the awe like we'd planned. If the Skarries came like a lot said they would, we'll all of us head north, too. Averdenn's the best bet to sell the ship if we can. But you, how're you getting out of Milatum, or isn't that part of it?"

"Same way we're getting in."

"Then what?"

"Probably Averdenn. Both of us have friends said they were going there."

"Yare well, I hope you ain't thinking of paddling that far."

"We'll get there, one way or the other."

"Something tells me you will, Breks."

"It's Falca—so how'd you wind up with Crayfish?"

"Fecking Skarries. I'd heard Boaig was a swinkin' gallybagger, but I signed on anyway to keep myself in a little shine while I was waiting for another berth I'd been promised; a cog that makes the run from Milatum to Sandsend, points between. Only it never showed in Girvan. Prob'ly never got out of Milatum."

"And before then?"

"Ah, lots of reasons for going to sea if that's what you're asking. One of 'em's having your family on the losing side of a war between princes. That was on Trigel."

"You were one of those Trigel slingers?—I've heard about them."

"What I was, was twelve years-old; the stones and sling I have were my father's. He lived all his life half a day's walk to the harbor at Slitten Mar and never once stepped foot on a ship. It's my luck Duna Rheg's prize crew didn't do nothing with them except maybe use the stones to play a game of spoils on the way to that fecking island.

"For a cutling, I got to be good with the sling, but I'm outta practice—not much use for a sling on a ship. Now my father, he could crack a man's skull at two hundred paces but a sling's not much good at night, and that's when they came. My sister and I...the only reason why we escaped was...we weren't there; my mother had sent us to hide out in the Ramna Stacks."

What was there to say to that? Moments passed. Sea spume sprayed over the weather rail. There was a nimbus around the Sisters. Tunty probably knew what that meant, but Falca didn't.

"Maybe in Averdenn you could show me how it's done—the sling."

"Yare, I could do that, but we all gotta there."

Falca slapped the rail. "I'm below now. Keep us north by northeast, will you?"

"Don't you worry, Falca. We're sittin' high."

He wasn't two rolling steps away when Tunty called after. "So how much did you leave in Milatum?—I'm curious, is all."

"Leave?"

"The swag you left there, and why you didn't take it with you before."

"Not what you think."

"No? Don't worry, now—if I wanted to sell my vote for a share of what you left and'll bring out, you woulda known, oyah."

"Unfinished business, Tunty."

"That's *Captain* Tunturrion, if you please," he said, a wink in his voice. "Telio Tunturrion. So…let's have it: what unfinished business?"

"Someone's there we gotta get out."

"Ah…and who might she be, then?"

"Someone I've wanted to meet for a while."

"Does that mean she's the *eddy's* jolie?—I'd have bet my sling and my other stones too, that she was yours."

Falca smiled. "Captain Tunty, I think that's enough fish in your chowder for now."

Chapter Twenty-Six:

DERE FATHER

KOLL PRASTAGI SAT at the sloping escribore by a south-facing window of the three-storey manse, one of many that looked out upon red-bricked Scunder Square. He figured that if you could afford such a place, you also did things like give names to the rooms of your residence and so Koll, in a whim of possession, had named this one the Mask Room: on the wall opposite the three windows with fancy cut-glass borders hung a dozen masks of all colors—some full, some half; some with furry faces of animals and others with out-sized human features. Probably whoever lived here had worn them for the Night of the Mistra.

Everyone, young and old, put on a mask for that festival, though of course only the wealthy could afford masks like these; most people just put a sack over their heads, with holes for eyes, nose and mouth. Yola and Cashol had forbid him to do the same, made him shutter the open window of his upstairs garret, but through a crack he'd glimpsed revelers going by on the street below. Cashol said it was for his own good—"you can hide your face but not your hands"— because on the Night of the Mistra, with everyone disguised, anything could happen. But wasn't that the point? Koll said he'd wear gloves to mask his hands, but Yola said she wasn't about to make six-fingered gloves to be worn only once a year.

And probably whoever had lived in this manse had worn some of these masks to balls and costume routs. Surely they'd been invited to such on Mereshaven, the king and queen pointing with delight or amazement at this costume or that mask. The people who lived here certainly wouldn't have had a long carriage ride to Mereshaven: from where Koll sat he could see—beyond the expanse of the square and the dawnstone risers of the King's Terrace—the graceful cables of Colza's Bridge that spanned the northern channel of the Queensmere and linked the royal isle to Scunder Square and Linnisvale.

Given the manse's closeness to Mereshaven, maybe the owner had been an ephor, but Koll guessed he'd been a prominent—what were they called?—playwrights, that was it. Wrote for theaters, not that he'd ever been in one. Koll had found all the tools of that trade in this very room.

Whoever the owner was, one thing was certain: he and his family wouldn't be going to any more Mistras or fetes; no one would be. The Priaptor and his priests would see to all that. So the people who'd lived here must have fled before the siege, or more likely had been killed. Either way, they'd left food that still hadn't spoiled in the cellar, and bottles of wine.

Koll had been lucky to find such lodgings in which to hide out and wait for the Priaptor to make an appearance in the square. Surely, Koll had thought, Vulsa Hork, the conqueror of Milatum—now Tholosia—would say something to his new subjects at some point from the top of the King's Terrace.

And he had, just hours ago.

Koll knew he couldn't stay here for long. Sooner or later a Skarrian officer would take it over, or maybe some of those red-caped priests would move in—purisees, that's what they were called. But even if had to give up his new home after a few days, it would have served his purpose.

Better get to it then.

He had everything he needed.

He had a glass—crystal it was—of unwatered wine and he took a sip now. He had sunlight coming into his Mask Room. Had the Priaptor appreciated the beauty of this day of all days?—beyond the satisfaction of knowing what he'd accomplished, and all that he would in time, now that Milatum was his. Reveled in the heat as Koll had in the square a few hours ago? Probably not. He'd been sweating under that shiny, stalker shell armor he'd been wearing, wiping his brow several times as he spoke from the top-most tier of the magnificent Terraces that made a jest of Koll's Mount in the Skellig.

The Priaptor hadn't *actually* wiped his brow himself, since in one hand he held what he said was a Gavilor, the steel of the warhammer bright as silver in the early afternoon sun; and in the other what he said was a vial of Slevaig's sacred ashes—whatever that was—which he flung in the direction of all those Milat youths line up in the square, to consecrate the sacrifices they would make as future soldiers of Tholosia.

So, his hands full, someone else had to wipe the sweat from his brow.

Koll had his own vial on the upper shelf of the escribore: a vial of ink. And he had his pick of quills from a canister—more crystal—next to the vial. He'd found a ream of parchment in a cabinet but he didn't intend to use any. After all, a few sheets of paper might blow away or be trashed as litter.

Any cruppie in the Skellig, or a boney—even the Mitoll himself—had to be resourceful to survive; thus Koll had taken down a painting from a light blue wall of the Mask Room. A beautiful rendered and doubtless valuable painting of Colza's Bridge at twilight, and in the backround the ramparts of the royal citadel, the Kelefion, and the tops of those two monumental statues, the Wovens.

Koll had everything he needed: the back of the canvas painting to write on; the pair of gullyman's gloves atop the bag of shims he might need later to get back into the Skellig; and resting on the gloves the two fingers of a Milat he'd followed from the square after the Priaptor had finished with his speech.

It had been a quick kill in an alley off a street shadowed by the aqueduct overhead: a thrust with his Mitoll's dagger into the man's side, and a slice across the neck. The man, not so much older than Koll, had seen him but clearly didn't think Koll was a threat given the bandages around his hands. How could the man have known his hands hadn't been wounded on the walls or in the streets.

He had everything he needed—including the Eye of Tholos that hung from his neck by a common leather cord.

He dipped the quill in the vial of ink and began:

Dere Father,

I hope these words are not so small you cant reed them but they have to all fit on the back of this painting.

Did you see me in the Skware today?

I am sorry there were not many people there to lissen to you. Except for the Culled Yuths. You said there were five hundred of them and sum were crying bekawz they were going away from home here. Maybe I shud have been crying too since I wuz seeing you for the furst time. Being a baby duz not count. I wuz smiling.

I wuz very close to you. I cud have shouted and not loud and you cud have herd me. I had to be careful bekawz of the soljurs around the bottom of the Terraces where you were on top with the preests and that yuth. He looked younger than me and he stood next to you and had your yellow hair so he must be your other son. Am I rite?

Sum of the soljurs looked at me but they did nuthing. Why wud they think I wud try and hurt you, father? I wuz smiling. And how cud I hurt you? My hands had Bandages around them I made from strips of a shirt. Maybe you saw the Bandages and thawt my hands were hurt in the Battul here. They were not. I hurt them myself and I've given you the proof with this letter.

I no now what you did many years ago, father. And I understand you wud have to kill Me if any Skarrian new what you did. Maybe I am dangeruss to you but do not worry. See the Fingers I cut from my hands? If I did not do that I wud be killed by a preest, or put in one of the Iron Wikkets I have seen around the city, burning alive peeple who refuze to worship Tholos as Skarrians do. And burn alive those who are not Pure, who are deformed like I wuz or diseezed.

I am no longer deformed. The scars will heal. Unless you look close you wud not no I had extra fingers.

It wuz beautiful to hear your voice for the First Time. It wuz deep and did not become high like a womans when it rose. But I did have trubble understanding sum of what you said. Skarrians talk like they have a mouthful of spit. I wud have talked that way too, rite?

There wuz a farrener near me. Wearing only a cloth around his waist and his hands were bound with stalker silk. I think it wuz stalker silk bekawz it did not look like rope. I wondered why he had not already been burned alive in an Iron Wikket bekawz his mouth was diseesed with Blue Gums. Two soljurs, an officer and a preest guarded him. They looked like they were waiting for you to finish speeking and when you did the Purisee hurried to you before you left on the stalker to go back to your Home on Meershaven across the Bridge.

I wuz kuriuss to hear what the preest said to you. I cud not. But I did hear what the preest said when he came back to the farrener. He said that you wud see him on Meershaven, and you wud decide if what this Blue Gums told the preest and officer interested you. Blue Gums said to the preest that you wud not regret it, and that is when the Purisee slapped his face and said it was not up to him to say what the Priaptor wud or wud not regret.

I am still kuriuss about what it waz that mite interest you about a diseesed farrener. Did it, Father? Or did you feed Blue Gums to a stalker on Meershaven?

I no you wud have lissened to me had I been taken to you like Blue Gums wuz. I am shure you wud be interested in what I told you. What Father wud not be interested in what happened to his son after he said goodbye to him when he wuz an Impure baby with six fingers on each hand. You wud have been interested and lissened, and then you wud have killed me. So this is better.

Me? I was interested in everything you said about the Culled Yuths. The furst of many Cullings to come from Tholosia and other places in Keshkevar, you said. How when they are older and finished with their Purificashun and Traning they will do Grate things as soljurs in Battuls to come. They will fite in the name of Tholarsh, the most Pure and Blest servant of everlasting Tholos.

It is a wonderfull idea. Sum of the Yuths were crying like I said. Did you hear them crying? They will hate you for sending them away to that camp outside the city. But do not worry. I no they will stop their crying in time. They will no only what they have becum and not remember who they were.

Evun the boy will, who broke away from the others when his mother ran tord him from the crowd. She wuz shouting his name. I forget what it wuz. But he will forget her because he has to forget or he wud burn up like he wuz in an Iron Wikket.

The mother wuz lucky. You cud have ordered a soljur to kill her on the spot insted of asking her to be brung to you. I cud not hear what you said to her before the soljurs took her away. I did not have to hear that because I can gess what you said. Wash her and bring her to me later. Am I rite? I wunce said the same things when women were brawt to me in the Skellig. I am shure that sum of those women had sons they wud never see again like the woman in the Sqware.

I am gessing her son was 8 years old. Others were older. Maybe 12. I did not see any yuth who wuz as old as I wuz when I had to leeve my home in Slagtown in Linisheer.

That is where they went to live, the ones you gave me to long ago.

Do you remember the names, Father?

They were Yola and Cashol Prastagi.

They said I wuz named after what is a high hill in Skarria? A koll. Did you name me or did they?

I did not find out who I reely wuz until I wuz 14.

They were mostly good to me. She wuz a seemstriss so I had clothes she made. He wuz a gullyman. I gess it wuz one of the few job besides working in the Quarry that he could get. He wuz a Skarrian like you but I herd him say to others that he was from Atalisia. They call them slags here.

I wuz never hungry and for a few years they paid for a tuter to come to our home. They said that wuz better than being edjukated with others because in a skool I wud have been teezed and bullied for my hands. So the tuter tawt me my numbers and how to reed and rite and about Milatum and Keshkevar.

Maybe it does not seem like I lerned well but this letter is the furst thing I have written in 8 years. I hope you are not dissapointed in me, Father. But when the tuter left because Yola and Cashol said they ran out of money, he said it was too bad because I had more wits than anyone else he ever tawt.

Are you interested in what happened next when I wuz 14?

One night when Yola and Cashol thawt I wuz asleep, I got up and saw them counting money on the table and I cud have gone back to my room but I did not. I suprized them and asked where they got all that shine when we were living in Slagtown and they had no money any more for the tuter. I am not gleggy. I new where they got it. They kep for themselves sum of what you sent them for me every too years. Several times I saw the man who gave it to them and herd them all talking. I am shure you gesst they wud probly take a little. But there wuz a LOT of money on the table, Father. They told me to go back to bed. I wud not, bekawz there was something else on the table. It was the jeweled Eye of Tholos, they said, with two holes in it for a strong cord.

Yola and Cashol tole me you were a highborn Skarrian but the Law there said you had to leeve me out to die and be eaten by flenx because I was an Impure baby. They said you cud not do that so you paid them to take me away to where it wud not matter if I was Impure.

I wanted to go find you in Skarria. I said I wud cut off a finger on each hand so no one there wud no I was born Impure. I said I wud take some of your money to find you. They said no and I wuz too young anyway.

I went to get a nife from the kitchen shelf and Cashol tried to stop me. He turned around to shout at Yola to stop screaming and when he turned to face me again I cut him across the throat. I wud have killed Yola too but she wuz crying in a corner of the room and did not try to stop me when I took all the money that wuz mine anyway. Before I left I asked her more about what the round jewel thing wuz for and she said it wuz the Eye of Tholos which preests give to Pure highborn parents to titely bind to a baby's forehead and in time it makes a lasting mark of Purity. I asked.why they did that. She wuz still wimpering and crying but she said that Skarrians beleeve the world must be seen not just through the eyes a person is born with, but through another that lets you see the world as Tholos wishes.

I did not get far, Father.

I made the mistake of showing too much of the shine when I tried to buy what I needed to go far away to find you. A nob saw me. Why else wud a yuth have so much money except he is a theeving rapperee with 6 fingers on each hand to take more of what is not his? That is what he said. He hit me when I said he had only 10 and he wuz going to steel what wuz not his.

He took me to the Skellig. But he did not find the Eye of Tholos which I hid in my fist and later put in a place where I had to take it out only once or twice a day, at leest until I became the Mitoll and rose to the Mount 4 years after I went below into the Skellig. The

Mount is not as high as where you were today, but high enuff to be Lord of the cruppees and my Boneys, as you are for all above. You wud have bin so prowd of me for rising to the Mount, and using my 6 fingers and the Eye of Tholos to help me do what had to be dun. As you did.

Shurely by now a preest or someone has told you about the Skellig. No? It was a Quarry long ago but they built over it. It is all yours now, Father, to do with it what you want. But you must no you probly saved my life again. Bekawz if you had not come to Milatum, there is a gud chance someone else wud have become the Mitoll instead of me. He wuz one of the last cruppees brawt down into the Skellig. He wuz from Drica, and killed my First Bone to get back his crooked sword and made a ruck happen with the cruppees. But the nobs opened the hatch when you came, maybe because they needed men for the Battul above. The Dricans name wuz Falka Breks and he was the last to leeve and he thawt I never wud, because he locked the hatch. But as you can see, I left, oyah. You are the Priaptor, Father, as I wuz the Mitoll and both of us have secrets, do we not?

There is not much more room to rite.

I am now like everyone else. But if you ever see someone who reminds you of me, will you look at his hands? Will you look closely to see where he might have cut off two fingers? Well, almost like everyone else beckawz I still have the Eye of Tholos, if not the mark it wuz supposed to make on me. Like it made on your other son's forehead. I wuz close enough to see that today.

I am happy the city is yours, Father. But pleez be careful. It cud still be danguruss. Maybe you shud send your other son away forever to save him like you did with me. But then who wud take your place as Priaptor of the Skarrian army and in the name of Tholos and all that is Pure become Lord of Tholosia you call it now and all Keshkevar?

You must have been prowd of your other son as he stood next to you on this beautiful day, his golden hair brite as the sun. But has he dun much to receeve your adorashun? Once you get this, will you be proud of me, too, Father? Or will you think I am something to be got rid of? Something to shovel into a gullyman's cart.

Your furst son,

Koll

CHAPTER TWENTY-SEVEN:

THE LAST WARDEN

L AMBREY TALLON WANTED to believe it a good sign that two hours must have passed since four soldiers and a red-caped priest led him up to this tower room in Mereshaven's citadel. Still, he had to be ready if Vulsa Hork proved to be more of a fool than he looked, and dismissed Tallon's offer—and his life.

If that proved to be the case Lambrey Tallon—who not so long ago had been a favored comitor of Lucidor's King's Own Wardens—decided he would kill himself rather suffer the fate of those Milat prisoners below whom he'd seen earlier being fed alive to three...vairgs, the Skarries called them; beasts that looked much like the white rancer that should have killed Falca Breks in the Rough Bounds three months ago—except these vairgs were black, each one bigger than a horse.

And so the first thing he'd done after the soldiers and priest left him here was open the diamond-paned window, not an easy thing to do when your hands were bound. They'd tied his wrists with thick stalker silk but that wouldn't hinder a quick plunge through the window before they could take him away to endure a far worse death.

Tallon stood before the window, wearing only the loincloth the Skarries had forced him to wear, stripping everything else from him at the barbican on the mainland side of the causeway that spanned the east channel of the Kingsmere. He'd been sweating all the way across and sweating as he listened to the Priaptor in the square; then in the citadel forced to wash before his audience with the new ruler of Milatum. But he was sweating again now though not as much as before; night had fallen.

The last time his wrists had been bound was on his way to the River Rhys prison hulk outside of Draica. A prisoner then, a prisoner now. And Falca Breks at the fucking center of it all; the only difference was that Tallon had come willingly to Milatum.

He couldn't stop feeding on the rancid meat of Breks' long-ago betrayal in Draica, and then the disaster at Scaldasaig. And he blamed his one-time deek for another kind of stain on his life: at the end of his audience with Vulsa Hork, the Priaptor had asked, pointing to his mouth: "What caused *that*, Comitor Tallon?"

"The effects of rife, a more potent kind of scrape that was smuggled into the prison where I spent five years. The rife helped me to survive."

"You still take this…rife?"

"No, but the effects were permanent."

"So, out of weakness you found strength. Perhaps that will be as long-lasting," the Priaptor said, and ordered him taken away. Had it been a good sign that a guard, upon a nod from Vulsa, had cut the noose of stalker silk around his neck, and again where it was knotted to the bonds at his wrists?

Skarrian soldiers—not a runt among them—had trussed him up at the barbican after he'd first told a sentry, then an officer, then what turned out to be a priest, that he had very important information for the Priaptor. The silk came from a handler of one of the two vairgs outside the barbican, who prodded the beast to make it produce a length of silk. Tallon had never before heard anything like the slithery…*haaassss*…of that silk coming out of the thing, the smell of the silk it shit something between sour wine and rotten eggs.

The night air was warm yet cooler than inside this tower room, and pungent with smoke from the myriad torches below and the stench of what had to be scores of vairgs and thousands of Skarrian soldiers bivouacked on the royal isle of the now-deposed House of Keshkev. Had to be that many, the stink of it; probably a significant part of the Priaptor's troops posted elsewhere in the city. *Tholosia* now; Vulsa had corrected Tallon when he'd said *Milatum*.

He detected the fragrance of the gardens he'd seen surrounding most of the citadel—and couldn't help but shake his head at the idiocy of gardens around a citadel. Not that he cared about their fate, but the soft, decadent royals of House of Keshkev had gotten what they deserved: Skarrian soldiers pissing in the trampled garden parterres.

In the distance to the west and silvered by moonlight, Mereshaven's two monumental statues—he'd glimpsed them on his way to the citadel—rose to an impressive height, their shoulders at the level of his prison cell.

Which, so far, was just that.

And if he had to plunge through the window, better to wind up as broken bones and tendered meat than alive and encased in a shroud of vairg silk, gagging for breath, his only hope to suffocate before the thing began sucking out his blood.

Tallon turned to face the door of his cell though kept by the window. Should Vulsa decide against him, there was at least this: Shar Stakeen would likely suffer a worse fate when she got to Milatum.

And she would be arriving very soon—unless Feccan had been wrong.

But he couldn't have been—and never mind that Tallon hadn't caught up to her afterwards. If Feccan *had* been wrong he'd still be alive, and Tallon and his optio would be somewhere far away, still seeking employment, trying to sell their swords.

They hadn't had much luck doing that in Myrcia after he and Feccan and the other four Wardens had fled from Scaldasaig. Myrcian memories of the last war were longer than they'd thought. No provincial nobles wanted to buy the services of six Wardens from Lucidor.

So they'd kept on south, riding into northern Keshkevar. They'd found work all right in Arzardys—an on-going feud between two brothers over the inheritance from their father, a wealthy nobleman—a kennard, as such were called Keshkevar. It was a vicious squabble, not worth the siller: Vopel and Giff killed; Gaimar and Sciber captured and presumably executed.

Tallon and Feccan, his loyal optio since well before Scaldasaig, rode on south, past the Lake Tremizene shore-side city of Maraine. Late one afternoon they came to the town of Crobost. And there they heard the news of events farther south, in Milatum. The Skarrians hardly needed the help of two runagate Wardens, so Tallon figured he and Feccan could try Syarra, across across Lake Tremizene to the west. He'd heard that the people in that area hated Myrcians as much as Keshkans.

You'd think the Fates would've had their attention elsewhere than this sair shore-side town. What were the chances that the woman who obviously worked the tavern's second-floor swallow's nest, looked uncannily like a skinnier, older, and less handsome version of Shar Stakeen; who kept her dark hair long, not short.

She glanced at the pot-man who had to be her spur. Maybe she rolled her eyes because it was too early in the evening, but what Tallon saw was: *just my luck—the stickler's got blue gums....*

The spur finger-tapped his lips. "It'll be extra, you want to kiss her."

"That's not what I'm paying for," Tallon said.

He hadn't gotten any of that from Shar Stakeen in Scaldasaig, not that he wanted it. What he got, for too brief a time, was slaking from a woman unlike any he'd had before. He'd used and discarded women—paid for or not—almost as beautiful as Shar Stakeen, but he hadn't wanted to discard *her* after he and his men found her by a river not far from Scaldasaig.

He didn't believe a word of what she said by way of explaining why she was alone in the Rough Bounds. Maybe discovering the truth behind her lies was a reason why he didn't just fuck her and be done with her. But as it happened, she as much as discarded *him* before he could force her secrets from her and possess them, too. And worse: later, from a distance, watching with his five men the ruin of his hopes for Scaldasaig, he'd seen her on a tower with someone who should have been dead from that white rancer's bite.

Their horses stabled, Feccan had been outside the tavern, awaiting his turn to slick his cudgie with the swallow's dew. Maybe if Tallon hadn't been fucking her so roughly he might have heard his optio's shouts.

Tallon found him bleeding out, his hands drenched with blood from the knife that had pierced his leg in the worst place, the blood pooling at the corner of the horse trough by the public well across from the tavern. Before he died, Feccan managed to whisper: "It was her...your quiv."

He got the rest from a man who'd rushed into the tavern for help, and Tallon pieced it together.

Having recognized Shar Stakeen as the woman on horseback who was letting her mount drink at the trough, Feccan must have walked toward her, stagger-axe in hand.

The man said the woman had quickly left, keeping on south along the road through town.

Feccan died because of him, and Tallon knew then that what Shar Stakeen had kept hidden from Tallon was something that sooner or later would have killed him. Whatever else she was, she knew how to throw a knife—from the saddle of her horse, no less.

Comitor Lambrey Tallon gave his optio his due—a sworn Warden's pyre—such as it was in this shit-smear of a Keshkan town, though all the while he was thinking about his killer.

Why had Shar Stakeen parted ways with Breks? What was she doing this far south, far from Scaldasaig where he'd seen her last? Clearly she was not going back north. But there was nothing farther south except the end of Lake Tremizene and the bigger town of Carrick, which the Skarrians would doubtless soon be occupying.

Milatum had to be her destination. But why would she be going there? Surely she'd learned, as Tallon did, what had happened there. The news would have spread quickly up the lake to Maraine or even Arzardys by now.

And then, as he'd stepped away from Feccan's pyre, he knew.

She intended to *sell* something in Milatum, something that would ensure her safety if she lived long enough to peddle it.

Scaldasaig.

The fortress that Culldred Hoster, the Warden Allarch, had built in the southern wilds of the Rough Bounds, that he boasted would become the bone-in-the-throat of Myrcia.

She was going to sell information: the existence and location of the magnificent lake-isle castle that should have been the keystone to the arch of Culldred Hoster's dream of ruling a *seventh* kingdom; a dream that Lambrey Tallon would in time have seized for his own from Culldred's feckless sons and their abomination of a mother.

And then...disaster. Tallon didn't know exactly what happened—he wasn't at Scaldasaig until the very end—but he knew who'd done it, annihilating 4,000 Wardens: Falca Breks and possibly Shar Stakeen and hundreds of the Timberlimb slaves they had freed—and the kraken of Lake Shallan.

Now, that boast would be Falca Breks'—if he gained enough time to get the men he needed, because the castle was still probably only garrisoned by survivors of the Timberlimbs whose labor had built it.

Neither Myrcia's Cascade Throne nor Lucidor's Cross Keys knew of Scaldasaig, so for Breks it would be a matter of filling an almost-empty fortress before they did. Which he would; there were enough outlaws in the surrounding

Rough Bounds for him to recruit and begin his plundering forays into Myrcia, using Scaldasaig as his base—Culldred's plan.

Roak only knew why she and Breks had a falling out. Betrayal? Shar Stakeen planning all along to sell the secret of Scaldasaig, preferring to live elsewhere in luxury for the rest of her life.

Whatever the reason, she'd skaved Breks. And while that gave Tallon a twitch of pleasure, it still didn't make up for what she'd done—and was *going* to do: push her peddler's cart to Milatum and the Skarrians.

He had to give the woman her due, because the Skarries would have been *his* first choice if he'd skeltered from Scaldasaig with a mind to sell what he knew. They had once failed to conquer Myrcia, but with Scaldasaig in their possession, they'd have the base to eventually cut Myrcia in half, and recover the eastern provinces that had once been part of Skarria.

Of course, when she left Scaldasaig she hadn't known that Milatum and much of Keshkevar was now in Skarrian hands or would be soon. But surely she'd figured the House of Keshkev would be very interested in buying. After all, didn't Keshkevar have a score to settle with the Cascade Throne? having lost a war with Myrcia over control of the Lakes province.

What did it matter now, anyway? Skarrian gold would shine as much as the House of Keshkev's would have.

But Shar Stakeen wasn't the only one who knew where Scaldasaig was.

Feccan's pyre was still blazing when Lambrey Tallon rode hard after her that night.

HE STOOD WHEN the door creaked open.

Four of them came in, backlit by two torches held by the rearmost Skarrians: three soldiers and an officer with the same mark Vulsa and most of the others in Labrys Hall had on their foreheads. He gestured to one of the torchbearers to leave it in a bracket next to the door.

"Put his kit on the table," the officer said, smiling at Tallon. "And leave, all of you. Wait for me outside."

They saluted, fists to heart then forehead, the last closing the door behind him.

Tallon stepped away from the window.

The Skarrian officer was sized well, like most Skarrians Tallon had seen. Broad face, all his teeth. Maybe it was the torchlight, but his hair plaits seemed almost white. Unlike his men he wore no mesh helmet. His vairg-shell breastplate glistening over a black tunic. A war-axe hung from his belt.

He moved to the table, waved his hand as if in offering. "Your uniform has been washed, boots polished. What you came here with is hardly suitable for southern Keshkevar. Our homeland cannot boast of such splendid weather, but we are making adjustments, as I'm sure a Lucidorian like you will have to as well. I'd suggest cutting off half the length of your trews, but for now, your wrist-ropes." He withdrew a dagger from a bootsleeve. "Turn around, Comitor."

Why polish the boots of a man about to be killed?

Tallon turned around.

Four cuts and the Skarrian had the silk in his hands. As Tallon faced him again, the officer said: "The Priaptor wished me to express his concern that you were not overly discomfited."

"Yahh well, silk's better than iron."

"Just so. Of course, iron has its uses, but silk is more convenient than shackles and stronger than rope. For every vairg that climbed Tholosia's walls, there were ten men beneath, gripping this." He tossed the silk on the table, then hefted Tallon's double-headed stagger-axe, running a thumb over the edge of one of the blades. "Tell me, do Warden officers sharpen their own, or is that a task for a subordinate?

"Every Warden regardless of rank is—or was—responsible for his own weapons."

"As it should be," the officer said, and put the stagger-axe back on top of Tallon's uniform. He smiled. "Though it seems I'm to be responsible for you and yours. My name is Scylux Kullerioc. As of tonight I'm detached as First Blade of the 2nd skirriton of the Priaptor's Ghosts."

"Skirriton?"

"A thousand men. The 2nd had the honor of breaching the northern wall of the city—in the Linnisvale district. I was not present in Labrys Hall for your audience with the Priaptor. However, I've been informed of the...intriguing aspects of your proposal and assigned to convey to you the Priaptor's decisions regarding it. I will also be accompanying you to this...Scaldasasig."

"You alone?"

"And twenty other picked soldiers, as well as two purisees...our priests. Such a number was deemed sufficient for the mission but not so large as to attract undue attention as we cross through Myrcia. Obviously we shall avoid as much contact as possible with the locals, riding at night."

*This one's as polished as his armor....*Tallon wondered if there were other reasons—besides his silky smoothness—for this particular Skarrian officer to be assigned to him. He said, getting right to it: "I would recommend another number of soldiers...but what's most important is haste—when do we leave? As I stressed to Vulsa, time is—"

"The *Priaptor* understands that. We leave in seven days. Should your information be as you have said, we shall return quickly and then consider the next step. You estimated two months for the return here?"

"At most."

"Good. By that time the Tholarsh should have arrived."

"The...Tholarsh?"

"Keeper of the Nimbus. Most Pure of Tholos, whom we all serve. We are anticipating his arrival from Zakros within two months to consecrate the Priaptor's victory." Kullerioc lowered his voice: "Perhaps I overstep my authority to speak for him but I would imagine that the matter of Scaldasaig would require the Tholarsh's blessing. But I am sure he would see the... potential of the opportunity you have—"

"Excuse me, but how does receiving a *blessing* help—"

"Careful, Comitor. There are others close to the Priaptor who see a plot in your presence here, not opportunity."

"And who would *they* be?"

"How does one see what lies over and beyond the hill? The answer may be obvious to most: climb to its top. But some men choose to see by other means."

"So your *priests* then—why didn't you just say that instead of posing a fucking riddle?"

"Comitor Tallon, you parry with dismaying intemperance considering your empty hands. Your impatience to gain the better ground here requires forces you do not now possess. The situation is thus: while Tholosia is well-in-hand, we are still engaged in securing outlying territory to the north and west. In fact, the Priaptor has just sent a full skirriton to take Girvan, a particularly important objective. My point is that an expedition in force through Myrcia to take Scaldasaig will require additional troops from those karls still in Skarria. That will take more—"

"The passing of time blesses nothing. If the Priaptor gives me—gives us—a hundred of your best men, we'll take Scaldasaig within a month of our leaving here. Send a few back with the news, and your Tholarsh will have *two* victories to consecrate."

"Only a hundred, Comitor? From what I understand, this fortress is—"

"Defended by one man, a crouch-alley from Draica I know all too well, and some Timberlimbs who—"

"At least it was when you left there."

"And still is—believe that. If it isn't, your men can kill me before returning. The Priaptor will have lost very little. But I'm telling you, a hundred of your men can take it—and hold it until more arrive."

Kullerioc smiled. "You pose your own riddle: how Scaldasaig was taken in the first place."

"By a ruse and circumstances that could never happen again," Tallon said. *If Falca Breks can do it, so can I*….He added: "And once we have it, the Myrcians will deplete their forces in central Myrcia to try and counter the threat posed by Skarrian possession of Scaldasaig. Which will then allow the Priaptor to slash the belly of Myrcia with those additional troops from your homeland. Boldness, First Blade Kullerioc. Strike first, before others can."

"It is fortunate that you did not lecture the conqueror of Milatum on boldness, Comitor."

Kullerioc ran his hand over the stagger-axe. "Why are you so impatient to gain something that will never be yours?"

"I told the Priaptor when he asked about that."

"Which was what?—as I said I was not present."

"He asked me what reward I sought in return for this prize that could lead to the gutting of an enemy he will have to fight sooner or later."

"I was informed only that the Priaptor was sufficiently impressed with your willingness to forego…compensation."

"There are only two things I ask for: the opportunity to kill this man, Falca Breks, and the immediate custody of a woman who will be arriving in Mil—in Tholosia—within a day or two. And with the same offer I have given the Priaptor."

"How do you know this?"

"We were...I know her, is all."

"It would seem then that you are either a poor hunter or faster rider than she; certainly more eager."

"She must have tarried somewhere after she murdered my optio in the north. But she *will* be here and she is not to be trusted. The woman was with the man, Breks, when he took Scaldasaig."

"So, your reward would only be resolution of...personal matters?"

"I would accept, of course, whatever else the Priaptor deems appropriate for my service."

Except execution after I've led him to Scaldasaig....

Avoiding that would be a challenge, but he had time to think of a way to succeed in that, too, before or after he killed Breks.

"Very well," Kullerioc said. "I will pass on your thoughts to the Priaptor. The guards outside will tend to your needs as required."

"Two guards is it?"

Kullerioc smiled. "You require more?"

"Surely you can't regard me as a prisoner if you've given back my weapon."

"The Priaptor would not want anything happen to you."

"He doesn't trust his guards to ensure my safety?"

"I believe I've already mentioned to you that there are some who may not share his belief in your potential value to Skarria."

"And you?"

"I follow orders, Comitor. But yes. And I would even venture to say that what you've told me would convince anyone who doubted the...purity of your intentions; there are few things more pure than vengeance."

"You would have risen high in the Wardens, First Blade Kullerioc."

"Perhaps, then, you might at some point tell me more about them. Is it true that after Lucidor's war with Myrcia they were disbanded?"

"Most of them. The rest were exiled far from Draica."

"Prowess ever threatens the weak. Still, such a lineage, dating back to the Orphics. Fine soldiers, your Wardens."

"They were."

"Then I am all the more interested—perhaps lessons to be learned. Always the most useful habit," he said, glancing at Tallon's mouth before he walked to the door.

"I almost forgot...this woman who we will apprehend and bring to you here...."

"Her name is Shar Stakeen. Myrcian by birth, I believe. She will be traveling alone. She is taller than average, has black hair and eyes."

"A common enough description."

"The woman is anything but common. She can be…dangerous."

"Oh I think we'll be able to handle her—anything else?"

Besides a dark beauty to match her talent for killing and betrayal?

"No."

"Then we shall talk again soon, Comitor. There is much to be discussed before we leave." At the door Kullerioc paused. "Dangerous? How dangerous can a woman be who's traveling alone?"

"Maybe because she has to be if she is."

"I"m sure vairg silk will suffice for her as well."

Tallon stared at the closed door after he left, listening to him talking briefly with the guards.

Vairg silk would indeed suffice while he had his fill of Shar Stakeen in this room. But when he gave her to First Blade Kullerioc's 2nd skirriton of the Priaptor's Ghosts?

Maybe the silk around her wrists would still be be necessary while the first fifty soldiers had *their* fill of her.

But not after that.

CHAPTER TWENTY-EIGHT:

GULLYMAN

L ONG AFTER THE rising of the moons Koll Prastagi remained at the open window of the Mask Room, marking the pattern and timing of the Skarrian patrol—five soldiers, two with torches—making what was now their third circuit of Scunder Square.

He'd planned his route to the King's Terrace and the timing of it—when the patrol was on the west side of the square, the Terrace being on the east. He'd picked out the dark mask of a grotesque, hairy animal that had never existed, to cover the paleness of his face. He'd cut the canvas from the painting's frame, rolled it up into a scroll, put the fingers inside, and tied off the ends with lengths of long hair he plucked from the mask-animal's chin.

But he couldn't do it: take the scrolled-up letter to the King's Terrace.

He'd been so excited about a beautiful ending to a beautiful day that he hadn't thought it through—which angered him now because he hadn't survived this long by not thinking something through.

The letter would be thrown away as trash; what he'd written on the outside—TO MY FATHER, PRIAPTOR OF THOLOSIA—dismissed as a prank. And even if the letter *was* brought to his father in the citadel on Mereshaven, chances were good that it would be read first by others, maybe even one of those priests. And that would likely mean his father would be executed.

Was that what Koll really wanted for the blood-father who saved his life long ago, risking his own should some priest have discovered he'd broken a strict law by not leaving a corrupted infant son for flenx to devour? True, the father had as much as killed the son's other life, forcing him from the Mitoll's Mount and all that he'd achieved...unlike the *other* son who'd surely done nothing comparable to deserve a place at the father's side.

Because his father had conquered Milatum, Koll could never go back to the Skellig. Just the one time, soon, to get the swag he'd had to leave; never again after that. The Skellig would no longer be *his*. And already he was missing the Mount as he'd never missed the only other home he'd known.

He was the last Mitoll of the House of Skellig; there would be no others. The Skellig would never again be filled with cruppies whose lives were *his* to rule. He'd heard the Skarrians did not imprison even lesser criminals; they executed them as they did the undesirable, the unwanted, the impure.

His father thought he'd deposed just one king from the Labrys Throne, but there'd been another Below on the throne of the Mount.

CRUPPIES BELIEVED THE Mount was only a high mound of slag left over from the time when the Skellig had been a quarry, before the Milats lidded it over, the roof becoming the cruppies' heaven.

But the Mount was in fact the leavings of a tunnel excavated long ago.

As Mitoll, Koll had plenty of time to think about the tunnel previous Mitolls had bequeathed him.

The cruppies who'd carved it out must have been worked to death or killed by their Mitoll to keep the secret. And over the years, if someone found out about it, he didn't live long enough to pass on the secret, or act upon it.

The tunnel's entrance was far behind the Mount where no one was allowed except fettered female cruppies. Koll chose his boneys for their stupidity and demonstrated loyalty. Only once had he thought a boney suspected the existence of a tunnel hidden somewhere behind the Mount, and that same day he killed him.

Still, he'd wondered how such a secret could have been kept over the years, passed on from one Mitoll to the next, whether the succession was violent or not—which in Koll's case had been a bloody one.

But then he realized how beautifully crafted was the secret: what cruppie or boney could possibly believe in the existence of a tunnel if the Mitoll never left? What loonzie fool would *want* to remain Below if there was a means to escape?

As far as Koll ever knew, no Mitoll had disappeared and never returned.

Because why *would* you? when you were king of the Skellig, with life-or-death power over your subjects; when you had the best of what could be had Below; when you knew you *could* leave whenever you wanted for a day or two— the Mount guarded by your boneys—and get from Above what you couldn't Below, then return to your throne.

And Koll would do that. Sometimes just for an hour at the tunnel's exit, to feel the wind coming in off the Kingsmere, breathe in its richness, taste its salt.

And sometimes for much longer.

He never used his Mitoll's tithes and swag to *buy* better food, drink and women Above. Why should he? knowing he had a refuge where no nob would think to look; where there were no consequences for what he did Above— except for the one time that got him sent to the Skellig at fourteen.

Meresguard nobs were only shims in his pocket: occasionally he'd do favors for the mersers stationed in the castlet above the Skellig in return for others, such as the Draican's falcata he gave Rekkie as a reward for his loyalty.

The commander of the castlet above, Kydar Bezellion, had been particularly appreciative of his talents. He'd informed Koll in the usual way of a problem he couldn't risk resolving himself: getting rid of his bed-swerve of a wife and her lover to make room for his own. Which Koll did one night at Bezellion's home in the Shirrets neighborhood not far from the Glass Gardens, while the nob officer was on duty at the castlet, of course. Later, Koll didn't tell him he enjoyed the distraught quiv before he killed her, not that Bezellion would have been angry.

Without a doubt he must have wondered how Koll did it, or arranged to have the pair murdered. But Bezellion didn't ask, didn't want to know. After all, the Meresguard officer might need the Mitoll's services again.

A beautiful thing…such a beautiful thing that tunnel, much better than any woman.

Like the Chute, it led to Linnisheer's southern escarpment facing the Kingsmere, but unlike the Chute the tunnel's exit was only about ten feet below the bottom of the city wall. Yet there was no chance anyone might see it, certainly no ships heading to or from the Cleave.

Three rocks—big but not too big to be moved by one man—blocked most of the exit. You would have to be squarely in front of it to know what it was. And little risk, either, that someone would climb down during the brief period of time Koll was outside the Skellig.

And also not much of a chance someone above could see the deep slots carved out of the escarpment and in the wall. Koll didn't really need the two augor-bone shims for handholds—there were slots for feet and hands—but he used the shims occasionally when the wind blew fiercely off the Kingsmere. Always—going up or down—he climbed at night, caressed by the Sisters, timing his forays to avoid the routine but infrequent nob patrols on the broad allure of the wall.

His BEAUTIFUL REFUGE was gone, as was his earlier intention to bring to the King's Terrace the letter and fingers and hoping they got to his father.

Koll heard the sound of the approaching patrol, the tread and voices of the soldiers growing louder; churgs, the Milats called them. And he'd heard Skarrian soldiers call *them* slorries, after the fish-sauce, not that Koll ever had much of that. Cashol and Yola hated the foul-smelling sloritsa Milats slathered on everything.

Which was he—churg or slorrie? Skarria-born yet living for almost all his life in Milatum.

The soldiers slowly passed beneath the manse's second-floor window. Koll heard laughter—something about how many priests it took to purify the same arsehole.

What was he going to do now?

He'd been so focused on everything else—biding his time in the tunnel… then cautiously making his way through the city at night, avoiding patrols, to set himself up for a hoped-for glimpse of his father…then getting the fingers… then thinking about what he'd put in the letter—that he hadn't given much thought to what he would do *after* tonight.

He couldn't go back to the Skellig.

Stay in Milatum? *Excuse me, father—Tholosia….*

He had gloves to hide his hands, a better pair of gloves he'd had made on one of his forays into the city. But wearing them in the heat of summer would arouse suspicion, regardless of the work he'd have to find once his Mitoll's swag ran out.

He could *leave* the city, make for Gebroan. But that would be risky: there would be guards not only at Linnisheer's Orphic Gate, but also at the outer gatehouse at the end of the causeway that spanned the Narrows. Either place, what if the guards searched his sack of swag? They'd confiscate it, which would be bad enough. But they also might wonder why he needed gloves to carry a sack of shine over his shoulder.

How do you replace the beauty of the Skellig?

Below, his deformity had set him apart, and in some ways had helped his rise to the Mitoll's Mount.

An Iron Wicket rumbled across Scunder Square.

There *had* to be another refuge for someone who once was king of the Skellig.

But where?

I'm missing something here….

Maybe it wasn't a…*place* after all.

And then he realized what it was.

It's me….

A belief he could survive Above as he had Below, and for longer than a day or two at a time.

It's me….

The refuge of who he was…the beauty of his deformity, his impurity, and…wasn't there also a kind of beauty in daring to stay in a place where he'd be killed for it?

He was no longer the Mitoll of anything, but he could still be the Lord of *Himself*. Which, after all, was why he'd had the mazer idea of sending someone *else's* fingers to his blood-father and not his own.

And wasn't there beauty, too, in choosing for himself the time when he might eventually leave Tholosia and—

Why didn't I think of it before? I don't have to risk the gates. I can leave by ship….

But in the meantime, how does the impure, adopted son of a Skarrian-born peasant survive without hiding?

There it is…like father, like son….

A gullyman.

Beautiful….

Yare, he had the gloves for it, bigger of course than the ones Cashol—a small man for a Skarrian—wore, and always left outside by the door, on top of his shoes. Not once had anyone stolen the gloves or shoes. Even in their poor neighborhood of Scatterleg in Linnisheer, who'd want the gloves and shoes of a man who spaded shit, garbage, offal and tannery reeks into a cart and dumped the waste into the nearest gullet, day after day?

Cashol wasn't a man to crack his thin lips with a smile but he did that one time he took Koll with him on his rounds. There were over thirty gullets in the city, half of them off Colza's Way, out of sight, yet close enough to that busy thoroughfare that linked all the bridges except the one from Linnisvale to Mereshaven.

He was one of eight gullymen who worked Linnisheer, from Mago's Bridge to Delmarrion's. From what Koll remembered, the gullets were about the size of the Skellig's ventilation chutes, into which people sometimes dropped food and clothing for a cruppie relative—and occasionally things no one wanted, such as a baby still bloody from birth and squeezed through the ventilation grate.

Each of the gullets, Cashol told Koll, led to a broadening channel which sloped down beneath the city to the escarpment upon which the city wall had been built. Where the channel opened, the waste slid and dripped into the Kingsmere, to be dispersed by waves crashing against the rocks below.

The more Koll thought about being a gullyman the more beautiful the idea seemed.

The churgs were their masters now, but slorries still needed gullymen.

No one could have given Cashol-the-gullyman much notice back when he pushed his cart from one gullet to the next, rake and shovel sticking out of the cart. So why should it be any different for Koll, who had no intention of actually doing the shoveling and raking and dumping. For all anyone would know, he'd just emptied his cart. He could make his own sort of rounds, carefully and quickly picking up things he needed or wanted, maybe even discarded food if it wasn't too spoiled.

So where would he get a gullyman's cart? Cashol's was long gone, but Koll could find another abandoned somewhere during the siege—a shovel and rake, too. And if not?

That was easy to think through.

Where there were gullets there'd be gullymen soon enough, and all Koll would have to do is wait for one to show, follow him on his rounds until he was done for the day, and follow him home. So what if it wasn't much of one? So what if he had a family? So what if he killed them all? Who would miss a gullyman and his family? or wonder where they'd gone in a city where bodies were still being disposed of daily. Few would care that someone else was living at that home—though they might wonder why the man wore such fine gloves for a gullyman's work, or ask him if the churgs were paying or forcing him to do it.

Even a lowly gullyman could have dreams.

Cashol Prastagi probably had been waiting only until his adopted son was a little older before abandoning him, taking Yola and most of the money a powerful Skarrian karl named Vulsa Hork had sent to him year after year to care for and educate the son he'd saved from the belly of a flenx.

And Koll, too, could have a gullyman's dreams.

Maybe someday in the months to come he'd be somewhere along Colza's Way, pushing his cart along with his gloved hands, the Eye of Tholos hanging from a cord around his neck, hidden beneath his shirt. And there he'd be: his father, the Priaptor, surrounded by a bodyguard of soldiers with plaited hair and glistening stalker shell armor, making his own rounds of Tholosia.

And from the back of the crowd, partially hidden by a cart, someone would throw a scroll tied off at the ends and weighted by two fingers hidden inside. There was at least a chance it would be given directly to the Priaptor by a soldier who would've seen written on the outside of the scroll: *FOR THE PRIAPTOR OF THOLOSIA*. Even if the soldier couldn't read, he might give it to the Priaptor or someone who could—where's the threat in a rolled-up painting?

No one would think a lowly gullyman had thrown it.

And then?

If he didn't have much left from the swag, he could steal what he needed to sell for his passage on a ship leaving Tholosia for…did it matter where?

Until then, gullyman's cart.

Time enough to find one after he went back to the Skellig to retrieve his Mitoll's swag. But for now, Koll Prastagi wanted to enjoy the last of the food and wine here in the manse overlooking Scunder Square, and maybe if he was lucky, catch another glimpse of his father coming from Mereshaven across Colza's Bridge with his escort of soldiers, his other son on a stalker, as always right beside him.

Here was another dream, though far more fanciful: making his gullyman rounds with his golden-haired brother parceled out in the cart, and dropping him piece by piece into gullets from Mago's Bridge at one end of Linnisheer, to Delmarrion's at the other.

BOOK THREE:
KRAKEN'S CLAW

From *DAUGHTER OF THE LABRYS*

A ND SO I did not learn until much later about my mother's fate and what she set in motion that night, hidden from the Skarrians in a Lazza warehouse.

It is a common enough observation that few plans issued by commanders prior to a campaign or battle survive intact, regardless of whether such plans are clever with feints and deception or a need for the blunt force of a hammer blow. Perhaps some are devised out of despair, others from anger at an outrage—and my mother surely felt all of that. But far fewer plans have also been issued out of love—for a husband, for her children, for her people. I was not there with her but this I know…as I know that her Labrysson escort was sworn to die to protect her and carry out her last command—all but one as it turned out.

The news about Milatum's fall arrived in Castlecliff before Cymra and I did: ours was a landfall of sorrow for all of our people who had died in the siege and those who had to live under the boot of the Skarrian Priaptor and the priests of Tholos.

It was a landfall of guilt, knowing that I had escaped only because of a marriage I didn't want; and shame at my distress with that—when so many had suffered a far worse fate.

And I felt a confusion bordering on self-loathing: I was so fortunate in my birth, yet I'd wished a station in life where I might freely choose for my first lover a commoner so sweet and learned for one so young, too young to have become an expert in the art of telling someone what she wanted to hear for his own gain.

This, too, made landfall at the royal quay adjacent to Heap O' Heads, Castlecliff's harbor district south of the falls: the lingering pain that I'd probably caused his death, and regret that I'd not known him longer. He may have been formed in what many people consider the soft world of an edifica, but I did not sense this man of my years was soft, ineffectual and weak.

The day after our arrival, escorted by six of my white-uniformed Labryssons and accompanied by Cymra, I was summoned to River Hall in the citadel of Falls Keep for an audience with Sanctor Urias, and presumably my husband-to-be, Joffreck.

Besides the usual retainers, seneschals, chamberlains, lickspigots and ten of the Sanctor's household guard of stoneskins in the wings, there was Urias on his Cascade Throne and his queen, Belliflor, sitting on the lesser next to him at the end of an azure-and-gold mosaic processional of spurroses.

Urias silenced a brace of trumpeters with a backhand wave and beckoned me forward. And as he proceeded to perfunctorily offer his condolences about my family and events in Milatum, I found myself hoping that Joffrek at least hadn't inherited his father's tiny and closely spaced eyes. I say hope because it soon became apparent that Joffreck was not in attendance. I would have to wait to see if the rumors of his immense girth were just that.

It did not go well after Urias expressed his wish that the voyage hadn't been overly tedious for my sister and I and then formally welcomed me, his future daughter-in-law, to Myrcia.

"My desire is that you shall come to appreciate not the least of what Castlecliff has to offer to one as beautiful as we were assured you would be; who has been baking in Milatum's oven for twenty years." This last came with a wink. *Ha ha ha....*

"I believe she comes with eighteen, my dear," Belliflor said loudly.

"Oh...yes, of course—you're quite right; indeed she does," Urias said, clearly annoyed his wife hadn't corrected him with a whisper. "Perhaps her impressive bearing is responsible for my mistake."

"You are most gracious, Eminence," I said, "though surely such an inconsequential mistake has more to do with the consequential matters the Sanctor of Myrcia must have on his mind—but I believe you were about to tell me a bit of what Castlecliff has to offer; something regarding the lack of ovens here?"

The queen laughed, which wobbled her dumpling wattle. "Perhaps she has twenty after all, Urias."

"As I was about to say…my hope, Demizell, is that you'll come to appreciate how the ever-present mist from our magnificent waterfall helps preserve the beauty of a woman's complexion."

"Oh, *that*. Well, I'm sure I will come to appreciate the cold, boiling mist of your waterfall here as much as I did Milatum's warm sea-breezes." I forced a smile: "Especially in the company of Joffreck—and where might he be?"

I found out soon enough that the father had long made a sport of demeaning and apologizing generally for his son. In the case of Joffreck's absence from the Azure Hall that day, the Sanctor informed me that a "situation" had recently occurred along the northern border with Lucidor, and he'd sent Joffreck to "assist" the commander of the Gardac troops he'd dispatched to quell the disturbance.

"Depending on the severity of this trouble," Urias said, "it could be several months before his return. I understand this must disappoint you as much as it did Joffreck, but it is for the best."

Indeed.

It was all I could do to refrain from smiling at this reprieve.

The Sanctor smiled, too—was that a *jeweled* tooth-cap he caressed with the tip of his tongue?—and motioned me closer, to the side of his throne, well away from Belliflor who was in any event peering at her fingernails, as if lamenting the work of a manicurist she'd just dismissed for a poor effort.

Little did I know that within moments I would be feeling sorry for Joffreck, but at that point I assumed this was to be a show of the 'common touch' that Urias supposedly had. He drew me still closer, tugging at my sleeve. Where to look?—at the age-spots on the back of his hand or his beady eyes?

"Consider the delay a wedding gift," he whispered.

I chose the age-spots. "A wedding gift, Eminence?"

"When I was seeking a match for my son, your virginal beauty came highly recommended, though there were caveats regarding your bountiful…spirit. On both counts you have exceeded my expectations. And also if I may say, the Demizell Cymra. She is an unexpected pleasure, but then most pleasures are sweeter when that's the case, are they not?"

If he hadn't been gripping my arm so tightly, I would have snatched it away. "It would be more of a pleasure to hear of this wedding gift than my sister."

"Of course," he said, his smile more a leer. "I was about to confide to you, my future daughter, that as a father weary of his son's campaigns at the dining table, I can only wish for success in the other I mentioned. May he not wear out the horses required to get him to a...particular campaign. When he does return—" and here Urias paused, as if that was in doubt—"your wedding gift is a hopefully hardened and triumphant Joffreck. We shall see if he is fit enough to ride on top of a renowned Keshkan mare and not under. I would prefer to avoid the humiliation of my son crushing her to death on their wedding night, or expiring from the exertion of planting his seed in her."

He let my arm go, and as I drew away from him in shock—for once speechless—he made louder recommendations for all to hear: "So a warm welcome to you, Demizell Cyalla. And while you await Joffreck's return please enjoy our Spurrose Gardens, you and your lovely sister; and walks along the Falls Promenade and, again, the beneficial effects of the spume from the cascade below. For diversion there's our many theaters—Cloon's has the most accomplished players. And you'll certainly find more in our magnificent, royally endowed edificia, Cyalla—I have heard of your passion for the written word."

PERHAPS THE EMINENTLY disgusting Urias had only been titillating himself in the only way still possible for him, but I was in no mood to give him the benefit of the doubt, especially given Joffreck's suspiciously arranged absence. Even before Cymra and I talked the matter over that night, I asked Symmos Mevellion to double the Labrysson guard outside the door to our chambers on the third floor of the Azure Tower, and made it clear that in my absence no one else's orders would supersede my own that Cymra should never be left alone, with *anyone*—and that included the Sanctor Urias himself.

That neither Cymra nor I would go anywhere without an escort of Labryssons was, of course, a given. Mevellion said he'd planned for a six-man escort, at all times.

I told him to double that, too.

As far as my husband-to-be, I felt as sorry for him as I was repulsed by his father. Poor Joffreck had probably long abandoned the campaign of being the kind of son his father might respect.

Cymra wanted to leave immediately—as did I. Any other city would do for exile—Draica...Carvorran in Helveylyn...Sandsend. But we were effectively trapped here. Our fetters might be velvet but fetters they were.

We'd never get out of Roak's Awe, Castlecliff's long channel to the sea. We might steal away on our two ships at night, but Urias would soon be alerted and send riders or signals from Castlecliff to the castlet where Roak's Awe narrows, and Joomey's Chain there would be winched tight above the waves to prevent our escape. Our Labryssons were fiercely loyal; there was just not enough of them. Their purpose had not been to fight hundreds of Urias' soldiers.

In those first days in Castlecliff there were some who sought to elevate their status at the expense of ours—such a tiresome fact of life whatever the venue— by suggesting that the Skarrians would not have found such quick success, if at all, against Castlecliff. On one occasion, at a fete in the Hall of Convocation, a politician—they're called Convocators here—said as much. I replied that if not for a miner's son named Lukan Barra, and the unforeseen intervention of an Erseiyr, Castlecliff would have fallen even more quickly than Milatum to Gorta Hork, whom I subsequently learned had been the grandfather of Vulsa.

Just that morning in the edificia—admittedly larger than ours was in Milatum—I'd come across Lukan Barra's recollections about his part in the victory that evidently was still celebrated in Castlecliff. I read this fascinating book over the objections of a sniffy thedral who thought it not suitable for the future wife of one of the Sanctor's sons.

Still, while I silenced that smug politician, there were others who subsequently stepped up to the trough. One in particular, the castellan of Falls Keep, prattled on about how Castlecliff is perceived as the 'male' to Milatum's 'female'; the thundering waterfall evoking the power of the city—as opposed to Milatum and its ring of islands surrounding the 'female' water of the Queensmere. "Navel of the World, indeed!" he exclaimed. "And aren't your biggest statues of women? Where is the stature of your men down there?"

I looked him up and down: "Perhaps in the steel of their tools that shaped such monumental figures." I turned away from his reddened face before he could respond with the riposte I'd already thought of for him: *And what would a Demizell such as you, know of a man's steel?*

And after him, yet another. Oh, I should have known that the edificia's Master Thedral who was in attendance, would have been informed of my insistence on reading Lukan Barra's book. I don't think this Gisgo Levole merely thought to impress me with his knowledge of Milatum when he commented: "It's my understanding that Pelagia's outstretched arms point in the direction of your two heroically licentious districts."

He was, of course, referring to the Snarlshome quayside where the Keshkan fleet was berthed to the east of the Cleave in Linnismorn; and the Lazza, for merchant ships, in Linnisheer to the west.

"*My* licentious districts, Master Levole?" I replied. "Well, I suppose they once were, though I can hardly boast about our having *two* to your one here in Castlecliff; the Carcass, is it?"

I couldn't help myself, playing to other ears besides Levole's—and perhaps my sister's too; she was not far away: "But I'm curious," I said, squinching my eyebrows. "*Which* are you asking me to recommend should the Skarrians vacate the city, allowing you make your pilgrim's journey? Or do you consider yourself heroic enough to sample the temptations of both?"

I lived all my life seeing Pelagia every day from my south-facing chambers in the Kelefion, though her immensity can only be fully appreciated much closer, when one is either entering or leaving the Queensmere by ship.

And beyond her, more distantly, rises our Neskayuna. She is much smaller than Pelagia yet still imposing. She guards the Cleave, the main entrance into the Queensmere and the city and thence Mereshaven, the royal isle…the home I thought I'd never see again in those days of Castlecliff.

Neskayuna was Kinnion's queen.

Such an odd pair, those two, and of all the past royals of the House of Keshkev, my favorites.

He was the fourteenth king after Colza. Given his deeds, it's a shame he is best known for his withered left arm that so embarrassed an otherwise physically imposing and handsome man, or so it is written. Kinnion-the-Stick he was called, though doubtless not to his face.

Neskayuna was more than a prominent patron of what came to be Sulserra's edificia. I've read that after the disastrous defeat of the Keshkan fleet by the Gebroanans' at Bucca Straits, Neskayuna roused her husband from despair and urged him to personally assume command of the war in which Keshkevar ultimately prevailed and reclaimed its territory east of the Girvan Awe.

That the famously slender Neskayuna also bore him *ten* children…well, there are few women—and I'm one of them—who would not place *that* achievement alongside Kinnion's subsequent victory west of Tantallon against the combined fleets of Gebroan and the Summer Princes of Trigel.

Not surprisingly, perhaps, she preceded him in death; but by the time Kinnion died, his memorial to her was completed: around an iron frame encased in bluestone sculpture she remains with us now, rising from her waist in the center of a six-sided islet that alone took four years to construct in the middle of the Kingsmere entrance to the Cleave. Waist-to-head she rises eight times the height of a man, her outstretched arms resting on the base of the islet, her hands gripping the ends of chains longer than the Cleave is wide at that point. The chains lead to capstan chambers within the escarpment on either side of the channel.

When I heard my father tell me of these chambers years ago I asked him to take me there, to those circular stairs within that descend from bartizans, one each on the wall to either side of the entrance to the Cleave. He refused my request as unseemly for a young Demizell—though of course when I was older I disobeyed him and saw for myself what would happen in the event of a sea-borne attack on Milatum: men would wind the capstan, and Neskayuna's chain would tighten from both ends to a height of four feet above the water level, thus preventing access to the Cleave and the Queensmere beyond. At all other times the chain remains slack, allowing naval and commercial traffic.

So yes, I was thinking about chains at Castlecliff—my own; Joomey's, whoever he was; and Neskayuna's.

Now it has become fanciful for some to believe that she came magically alive, and lowered the chains for Vaience Loquin and Falca Breks the night they entered the Cleave. That may well become legend someday, but I know for a fact the Skarrians kept Neskayuna's chains taut after the conquest of my home.

I know for a fact the two men could not risk even whispers as they passed under her chain, crouching low in their boat, and saw the evidence of the earlier fighting along the ramparts above the Cleave and around the greater heights by Mago's Bridge, where the Cleave is narrowest. The bands of dawnstone inlay on either side of the channel illuminated this grisly evidence, as they otherwise would the passage of ships at night.

Of course, I did not see all this but I know that the steep, rocky slopes of the Cleave had caught the dying—Milats and Skarrians alike—as they fell from the walls. The two men surely stifled coughs from the stench, though by then the Skarrians had retrieved their own dead, and salvaged whatever weapons that hadn't sunk into the water. But they left the Milat dead and the remains of burned stalkers and charred firehoops and broken pikes and twisted lengths of stalker silk used to climb the sides of the Cleave.

And still Vaience Loquin and Falca Breks dared not talk even though the bridge they passed under was far above them, passing as well the Skarrian sentries posted at either end of the bridge. Once the two men had gained the Queensmere they rested in the dawnstone glow of Pelagia.

She rises from an otherwise unoccupied islet off the northeastern headland of Linnisheer, her height rivaling that of the Wovens, if not the latter's mystery and age. As with the big island districts of the Linnises, the heights of this much smaller island were once reduced to expand its periphery, and so at high tide it appears as if Pelagia is rising from the very Queensmere.

Sculpted of dawnstone, she is the protector of all who take to the sea, and while many do not believe in her powers, there are few who do not at least nod in her direction as they leave for the Kingsmere and the blue-water beyond, or do so upon a safe return. If I had left Milatum by ship I would have done this, too. As it was that night, both Cymra and I made our nods for Pelagia's blessing in my chamber.

And I know for a fact that the Skarrians had fastened stalker silk, gray in the moonlight, that bound Pelagia's neck, raised arms and waist; the ends of the silk ropes wrapped around spurs of rock at the islet's northern end, awaiting only the arrival of timber or iron bars to twist and tighten the silk and bring all of her down.

The Skarrians were no doubt offended by Pelagia's unclothed form; certainly it is well-known they tolerate no idols to manifest their loathsome beliefs other than the living idol of their Tholarsh, the appointed messenger of Tholos. I know for a fact, too, that the Skarrians had wrapped stalker silk around the Wovens on Mereshaven. But these two huge figures had so far in history defied destruction, as they were not made of any kind of stone. They leaned and swayed but did not break and could not be burned.

It was only until I was older—my fifteenth year—that there came a winter storm so ferocious that I saw, from my chambers in the Kelefion, the Wovens lean and sway in a tempest powerful enough to shatter window glass in Labrys Hall. When I was younger my sister and I—and certain children of our household and favored ephors—would play tag up, down, around and over the Wovens' plinth and race through their legs to avoid getting caught.

Recollections, whether spoken or written, always carry the thread for embroidery. And so I'll always believe Pelagia offered a blessing for what came later to Falca Breks, when that night he and Vaience Loquin were only grateful for their safe passage through the Cleave.

CHAPTER TWENTY-NINE:

HOMECOMING

T HEY HADN'T DARED stop to rest in the Cleave but they did soon after
they entered the Queensmere. Falca, in the stern, rolled his shoulders and
neck, stretched fingers cramped from gripping the paddle, wiped at the saltwater spray on his face. The boat rocked gently, the waves here nothing like the
riffs out on the Kingsmere, where Tunty had tacked the *Lysidia* around to the
east of Pharos Island to let them off.

They couldn't rest for too much longer; already the boat was drifting
toward the red-and-gold light shimmering upon the water surrounding the islet
from which Pelagia rose far into the night, the hands of her outstretched arms
seemingly weighing the very heavens above, despite the silk ropes stretching
down from her wrists and neck.

Pelagia would be their first marker, Vaience had said; where they had to
turn to the west and Linisheer. And they did, heading away from the Cleave and
Mago's Bridge and the not-so-distant torches of Skarrian sentries on the outer
flanks of the massive towers at either end of the bridge.

At all the bridges this night there'd be more of them, especially at the one
leading to the royal isle at the northern end of the Queensmere. Falca couldn't
see that bridge, Colza's, as it was hidden by Mereshaven. But there were plenty
of torches—pinpricks of light—marking the ramparts of the citadel.

They'd be everywhere this night, the Skarrians and their torches: patrolling the
districts, the city wall itself, enforcing a curfew. But it was the bridges that counted:
control the bridges that linked the Linnises and Mereshaven, control the city.

Falca paddled on, he to the right, Vaience the left: lean, stab the water, pull, recover, stab again. He felt the rhythm of the moment, the soothing *shushing* of the kraken-skin boat. How many times in his life had he been aware of that rhythm?—when all that mattered were the moments that wouldn't last very long. But while they did you could forget that life was too often little more than a continual striving to replace what had been lost.

He'd forgotten on Harro Scapp's corry, gliding along Motessin's Moat in Lucidor with Amala and Gurrus, enroute to Bastia; forgotten on that early morning tryst with Amala below the waterfall in the Rough Bounds, the most beautiful place he'd ever seen—until the Wardens came. And yahh, Vaience's sister, those hours with her atop the turris of Scaldasaig...before he knew who Shar Stakeen really was, what she was after.

And now, more moments. Maybe he was a fool—Milatum had done its best to kill him and still might—but right *now*, Vaience's deek for this, Falca was exactly where he wanted to be. Never mind he was soaked from the spray of the waves and so tired he kept stabbing poorly with the paddle and—

"There it is," Vaience said, over his shoulder. He stopped paddling, pointed ahead.

The westernmost windmill of Linnisheer.

Vaience probably saw it only as a blur but that was enough.

He'd said this windmill would be the closest marker for the cottage tucked into the rocky hillside above the Lazza, below a manse fronting Colza's Way. His home was a little east of the windmill yet still close enough to hear at night. The mill's vanes were disengaged from their gearing at night, when there was no grist to grind or wagons to pull up from the Lazza to the leveled heights of Linnisheer, but the vanes still turned with a rising wind, the rumbly sound sometimes more of a *squeak-squeak* in the winter after a rain. What Falca heard now was a faint, rhythmic *tick...tick...tick*, and he asked Vaience how long it would take to get from the Lazza quayside up to the cottage.

"At night?—perhaps an hour. But I haven't done that—going back up—since I was a boy, and of course it was during the day when the Lazza was crowded."

He would sneak away from the cottage when he saw a windwhipper flying the Myrcian azure-and-gold, coming into the Lazza docks: the kind of ship his mother said his father had commanded. He did it three times without Rohaise finding out, but never again after the fourth, when he saw her waiting for him at the landing halfway down the long steps—the way you got to the Lazza or back home. She told him never to do it again. And he didn't—not because she forbade him but because of the tears in her eyes.

"Well, however long it takes us is what it is," Falca said, thinking that one thing was certain: they wouldn't be spending any time on the wharf, waiting for a windwhipper to tie off, and asking the first sailor coming down the gangplank if the mastlord's name was Mott Demoul.

THEY PADDLED SO closely past the ships that Falca could have tapped rudders with the end of his paddle. So far they'd gone by maybe twenty of the Lazza's wharves and about twelve merchantmen—galliots like the *Lysidia*, oared cogs and holkas, and one three-masted windwhipper. There should have been more ships but many must have fled before the Cleave was chained.

The air smelled of brine, pitch and the nightsoil stench of bilge and piss. Ships creaked and groaned. Wavelets slapped against hulls. They were careful now with the paddling as they kept on toward the western end of the Lazza, but Falca wasn't too worried about a ship's night-watch hearing them—why post a watch to guard cargo the Skarrians had probably looted?

Nor was he concerned that any Skarrians patrolling the darkened quay would see them, low and dark in the water. The ships berthed alongside the flanks of the wharves mostly blocked their passage from view. But even if there were patrols enforcing the curfew they likely wouldn't be looking *out* toward the Queensmere, nor would there be any sentries posted at the end of the wharves. What was there to see on the water this deep into the night?

Then he noticed a brightening portion of the windmill—their marker. Vaience apparently didn't see it, so Falca leaned forward and whispered: "I think we have company coming down from above."

A dozen quick strokes got them to the stern of a seemingly deserted cog; at least there came no shout from the taffrail. Vaience held on to the rudder to keep their boat from knocking against the hull. There were no other ships berthed on the facing side of the opposite wharf, so Falca could see the top half of a dock-ganger's tipcart on the quay above the sea wall.

They won't be checking the wharves....

No, the Skarries would keep to the quay, maybe glance toward the water, but their attention would be on the warehouses and alleys. And they'd likely keep on going down the quay where there was another ramp like the one at this end, Vaience had said, that led up past the eastern windmill and then to Colza's Way. They wouldn't be stopping…unless there was a reason to halt.

At first, Falca didn't hear them over his breathing, the lapping of water, the creaking cog and the rumbling of the windmill. But they were coming closer…and what he could see of the quay gradually brightened as torchlight flickered on the stone warehouses fronting the quayside.

Three of them passed by, two carrying torches that burnished mesh helmets, stalker shell breastplates, and war-axes hanging from their belts. A stalker followed and Falca hoped that the *eeeyisss* sound it made was something other than the sensing of prey.

This one had to be even bigger than the dead one he'd crawled under on the city wall allure, with a larger constellation of red eyes—and it had a rider. Unlike the three Skarrians in the van, the rider's hair was black as the beast and not flailed. He poked his hideous mount with a barbed prod and the thing stepped over the ganger's cart, the bristly hair on its legs moving it aside with a squeaking of wheels.

Two more Skarrians followed. One of them stopped to pick up something from the quay, then tossed it away. Whatever had caught his attention skipped over the seawall, splashing into the water near the bow hawser of the cog.

Torchlight receded as slowly as it had appeared. Moonlight reclaimed the broad Lazza quay.

They paddled on to the end of the last wharf, and with rope taken from the *Lysidia*, tied the boat off at one of two rusty rings set into the stone. They'd already decided they couldn't leave the boat anywhere else but tucked alongside one of the berthed ships. There'd been a few smaller ships berthed at the ends of wharves, but none here. Anyone on the dock couldn't see their little boat unless he was at the very end, and looked down. Nor could anyone on the deck of the nearest ship see the boat; only from the Queensmere could their boat be seen. And what ships would be coming in?—the Cleave was chained.

So it wasn't likely someone would steal the boat before they'd be leaving, the *three* of them—tomorrow night? The only other thing they could do was take the paddles, which Falca did, clasping them over his shoulder. If they encountered trouble ahead, and Falca had to draw his falcata…someone taking the boat would be the least of worries.

The steps up to the wharf were slimy and Falca whispered a caution to Vaience behind him, since he had the sack containing food they'd taken from the *Lysidia*, and the Sixer claws, pages and a hide.

They kept low on the wharf and knelt when they came to the edge of the quay.

Falca saw no one in the immediate area, only the quick shadow of a rat scurrying across the bricks from the nearest wharf. It disappeared under a wagon with a broken axle, a wheel leaning against the side of a warehouse. The bay door was open; probably the Skarrians had confiscated the contents of the warehouse.

But down the quay....

"The torches are stopping," Falca whispered.

"Are they coming back?"

"Don't seem to be...they're...going across the quay—are there steps there, up from the Lazza?"

"Yare, up to Colza's Way, past the west end of Slagtown. Bigger, what everyone uses, not ours."

"We're all right then. We're not going up there."

"No, but they might be making a turn back into the Lazza, along Reek Street."

"Where's that?"

"Where we have to cross to get to Limekilns and then Flunt Street, which runs along the entire backside of the Lazza, where the hill begins. Runs west to east like the quay."

"So if they come along, we wait for 'em to pass. Must be plenty of places to hide, anything'll do."

"Anything is what's here: tenements, sailors' boards, deadfall dens, forges, factories—"

"You said our steps begin at a...tessaria."

"Behind it—and don't worry, you'll see the factory before I do. If she's still there."

"*She?*"

"Out in front. A mosaic figure of a woman...as naked as Pelagia. At the time she made quite an impression on me."

THE SKARRIAN PATROL must have kept going up to Slagtown: the only thing they saw on the way to the Flunt Street tessaria was a pair of oikoes scrounging for grain at a capstan mill. And the only person who saw *them* was a woman leaning out of a second-floor window of an apartment that had to be a brothel because she softly called out, saying she'd take them both for the price of one.

Given the patrols Falca wasn't surprised the streets were deserted; who wanted to risk execution for violating the curfew? Still, it was strange to see no one about. The Lazza was Milatum's Catchall or Slidetown. And even at this hour there should have been many more swallows leaning over brothel balconies, whistling and clicking their tongues and otherwise mooching their wares; and soused galloons stumbling out of taverns and deadfall dens and into the streets where there'd be the leavings or beginnings of sailors' rucks; and on every other corner someone selling Milatum's skid or spiced flush, which Falca had heard was as potent as Draica's scrape.

Little Pelagia was there, all right—as a heap of painted tessera rubble and sculpted stone. But a marker for the tessaria, nonetheless.

The alley at the side of the single-story factory was lined on one side with open barrels of mosaic chips and pallets of brick on the other, leaving little room for Vaience and Falca to weave through. The alley ended abruptly, intersecting with an embankment that materialized as a wall as high as Falca was tall. The hillside loomed steeply beyond the wall, its upper reaches bathed more generously by the Sisters.

"Where are they, our steps?" Falca said. "All I see is this wall."

"They're coming up. There wasn't any slide-wall when my great-grandfather carved out the steps; that came later—so did the rockslide that crashed through."

"All this time and the break was never fixed?"

"You'd think it would have been, but it's always been here, the hole-in-the-wall."

THEY STOPPED TO rest where Rohaise had waited for her boy that time long ago, the landing scarcely more than a broadening of the steps.

Falca had been thinking the steps would be just that. But these were little more than notches in the rock. He leaned on the paddles and wiped the sweat from his forehead.

Vaience, too, was breathing like a bellows. "It's…not far up now."

He'd heard that before…*in the Rough Bounds wilderness, Ossa far above him in the tree canopy village, urging him on as he clung to the cuts the Timberlimbs had made in the towering mothertree, before he decided there was naught to do but keep on climbing as Ossa and Gurrus had done.*

And from Lukan Barra—or was it his his wife, Rui? or Raleva—when they were climbing up the ruins of the tower that had the fine view of the Barras' home across the lake, this the day before he left to journey south to Milatum. They'd all given up trying to convince Falca to stay. But still, someone—Lannid or Tolo?—tried again, saying that Milatum's a long way to go to see someone you've never met before. And Lukan, Raleva's grandfather, saying: "That may be so—but it also depends on who the person is you wish to find."

They climbed on, Vaience in the lead, a little quicker now, the sack bouncing on his back, the Sixer claw-like tools clicking against each other.

He can't see beyond the length of his arm, Falca thought, *but when you're this close to home maybe you don't have to….*

Vaience had said there were two terraces in front and below the cottage, and a springhouse hewn out of the rock in the lower. And there was the first, bordered by a waist-high wall that intersected with the final steps. Then, another that seemed slightly higher, that bordered the wider, upper terrace where Rohaise kept her garden.

And there it was, the cottage.

Two windows flanked the yellow door.

She must have painted it herself…more than once over the years.

The door was yellow, Falca, Roh's favorite color, but it hadn't been painted in a while and the sun had bleached it almost white; so I said when I got back I'd give it a fresh coat. But I never did….

The windows were dark…but why wouldn't they be?—she was sleeping.

Vaience had hurried ahead. Falca hung back. This wasn't his home, nor Rohaise his mother. The moment should be Vaience's.

Falca glanced off to his right…and saw in the overgrown and shadowed upper terrace garden what Vaience with his sair eyes had missed.

A body.

Leastways someone's legs sticking out of the high weeds. One foot looked tiny and misshapen; the other with a boot no woman would wear.

Falca dropped the paddles, drew his falcata. "Vaience….wait!"

But he was already at the door, the sack at his feet. "Falca…it's open."

He pushed the door wide open, calling out: "Maima? Maima, it's me."

Then, to Falca who'd bolted to his side: "She wouldn't leave it open at night. She isn't here."

Falca put a hand on his friend's shoulder: "Someone is. Over there, by the terrace wall."

CHAPTER THIRTY:

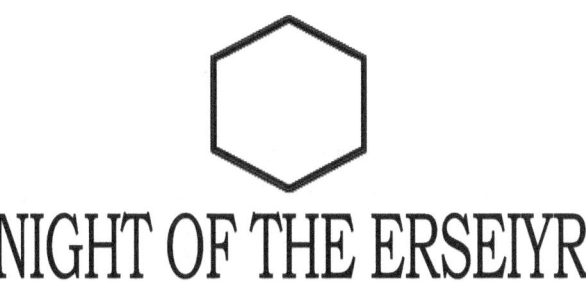

NIGHT OF THE ERSEIYR

F ALCA AWOKE TO brightness that revealed everything lamplight had not the night before.

He lay on a quilt he'd found in a chest in Rohaise's bedchamber, and folded the coverlet over to fit the space between a table and the hearth in which a cooking pot still hung from an iron strap.

She'd painted the sill of the window yellow, too, but the stone walls of the room were a light green, the bathtub in the corner patterned with a colorful mosaic of leaping fish. Domestic necessaries filled the shelves of the high cupboard next to her bedchamber door. She'd hung tapestries on the walls: one of oikoes, tails entwined; another of a path winding through a wild garden; the third of a three-masted, white-hulled ship on the Queensmere. If Falca hadn't stared at that one the longest, he probably wouldn't have noticed the tiny lizard crawling from the wall onto the tapestry, changing its skin from light green to Queensmere blue.

Everything seemed as it should be—except for her absence, the empty flower vase on the table…and what was outside: the low but unmistakable mound in the fallow, weed-choked garden; the grave Falca had only noticed when he and Vaience had gone back to the scavenged corpse of the man.

Later, he'd seen Vaience reading a letter by lamplight in his room, and knew it must have been from his mother. Falca closed the door, and after a while the scrim of light vanished from its bottom edge. He couldn't get to sleep on the quilt, though he was very tired. He heard Vaience open the door, moonlight casting him in shadow.

"My mother left a letter for me," he said. "She…it's as if she knew something was going to happen. She said she wanted to tell me things she hadn't before, that she'd met a man. He must have been with her when it happened… but knowing her…she would have gone out with him. He must have killed the one out there but not before she…and then he buried her and left. Why would he want to stay here after…I would have left, too."

"Vaience…I'm so sorry."

"I knew there might only be a slim chance."

He went back into his room and closed the creaky door….

Something wasn't right, though. Falca had the burr last night, but last night hadn't been the time to mention it to Vaience. The feeling was stronger now. Was it just the empty cottage? That she had been here? That they'd been too late coming back?

No…but all he could do now was dispose of the body somehow, and he might as well get that over with. He couldn't leave it out there rotting so close to Rohaise's grave, even for a day—before they left. Tonight? That was up to Vaience…but what was the point in staying here now?

Falca got up, put on his chasers, unbarred the door and went out, taking the falcata with him. He leaned the scabbard next to the door, not far from the garden hoe she'd left against the cottage wall, near the pipe that led down from the roof cistern to a spigot. At least he could use the hoe to scrape earth over the dead man. The morning had warmed the handle.

The sun was high in the blue. A few gulls screeched a protest, lifting off the body as he approached. Flies scattered, but many still crawled over the corpse. There wasn't much meat left. Much bigger scavengers—feral oikoes and dogs—had stripped away most of the flesh down to the bones, leaving only scraps of clothing and that single boot. The other one lay nearby, the leather gnawed at…beside something glinting in the weeds.

A hangar.

Falca had missed seeing it last night in this part of the terrace garden that Rohaise obviously hadn't tended in a while. Nor had he seen the extent to which the knee-high weeds had been trampled elsewhere. Had he missed anything else?

The other body lay farther along the stone wall that formed the boundary of this upper terrace, and a few bold, returning gulls led him to it.

There wasn't much left of this one either, another man. For some reason scavengers hadn't gnawed the sandals off the feet. A hangar lay at the base of the wall, the end of it broken off.

Two bodies…two swords….

Another man made it even more probable that Rohaise had been overwhelmed in the ruck outside before her companion could kill the second man. Falca sighed hard, looked away—and that's when he saw what seemed to be the handle of a…spade? in the weeds on the far side of the grave mound.

The shaft near the blade lay over what looked like—

Can't be….

He squatted down, pulled it out.

Roak's throat, what's that doing here?

It certainly didn't come from the cottage. How likely was it that Rohaise would have a heavy bronze door-dog in the shape of a stiffened phallus and balls for the knocker?

Three men, then—not likely one of the men would have been wielding a hangar *and* a door-dog.

Came up from the Lazza, where sticklers clapped them on brothel doors—at least they did in Slidetown in Draica; he'd clapped a few himself.

Three men…including Door-dog….

The third crouch-alley must have gotten away.

Unscathed?

Maybe not. The spade should have been leaning against the cottage next to the hoe.

Falca lifted the spade near the collar, turned it this way and that….

Maybe Rohaise hadn't worked this garden in a while—too busy on Mereshaven working the royal gardens—but she kept the edge of her spade here sharp. And there were unmistakable brown splotches near the keen edge, both sides.

Dried blood.

He checked the hangars and the door-dog.

No blood on them. And none on either of the hangars or the—

"Falca, what've you got there?"

He turned to see Vaience in the cottage doorway. He was wearing the spare spectacles he'd said he always kept here.

Falca smiled. "I think your mother got away."

THEY PUT THE evidence on top of the terrace wall. Vaience used the hoe to pull the remains of the men together at the far end of the garden and then Falca took over, scraping earth and weeds over the bodies as Vaience brushed away pestering flies. Without much flesh left to rot, the stench wasn't terrible but Falca breathed through his mouth anyway. He was sweating buckets by the time he finished.

He put the hoe back against the cottage and then the both of them drank warm water from the cistern spigot. Vaience wiped his mouth off with the back of a hand, and Falca noticed again the skink he had on the inside of his wrist: three letters. *KAI*. Probably all the thedrals had it, whatever it meant.

"You really think that's what happened?" Vaience said.

Falca nodded. "And whoever he was—the man your mother was with— she chose well. He kills two of them while she's grabs the spade and swings at Door-dog. *And* connects. They *both* chose well. Good as the man was, taking on all three would have been tough. They were a pair that night—those festers had to have come up at night."

"We never had any problems when it was just her and I here. The Lazza is what it is, everyone desperate now, but if you don't know the steps are there… well, maybe it isn't so puzzling: they could have come *down* the steps from Colza's Way. But…we're not wrong about this, are we?"

"It's the *spade*, Vaience. It had to have been used over there *before* the attack. Otherwise—"

"The bloodstains would have been scoured off digging the grave."

"And if either your mother or her companion had been badly wounded or killed, there'd be blood on a hangar or both. Whatever we're missing about what happened…she's alive…somewhere out there. Maybe both of them."

"They must have left in a hurry—but that isn't surprising."

Falca shook his head. "They couldn't know if the one who got away might bring more men to settle the score."

Vaience pushed up the bronze, oval frame of his spectacles and walked over to the low mound of the grave. "There's this too—what *isn't* here. Take a look."

Halfway over, Falca guessed: "No marker."

"And there *would* be if this was my mother's. Her man would have left something. But if there was a third person with them that night, who was killed in the attack, you have to wonder why they didn't put a marker on the grave for him…or her."

"Like you said, they left quickly."

"Or maybe you don't leave a marker if it's a stranger—but if they didn't know him, how likely is it they'd allow him to stay with them in the cottage?"

"Could've been someone badly wounded in the fighting."

"My mother would have marked the grave—I don't know, Falca, it's almost as if they deliberately chose not to."

"Whatever happened, whoever it is they buried…the grave needs a marker."

"I'll cut some of that fireheart over there," Vaience said. "I'd rather use your falcata, if I may."

"Sure, it's by the door."

Vaience flung the hangar far over both terrace walls. Somewhere on the steep hillside it landed with a faint, ringing clatter.

Vaience got the sword, walked over to the bush that rose above the end of the upper terrace wall by the steps. He easily cut off three stems, each with palm-sized, reddish-yellow blossoms. After putting the stems on the grave he slid the falcata home in the scabbard and rejoined Falca at the wall.

"That'll do fine for whoever it is," Falca said.

"She planted that—the fireheart—from a seedling before I was born. It wasn't until I was older that it occurred to me why she put it *there*, close by the top of the steps. It would have been much easier to tuck it in somewhere in the upper garden terrace." Vaience pushed up his spectacles. "As it was, she had to build a deep container for it to grow, using rocks she collected from the hillside or prised loose—see how well she fitted the rocks together? Filled it with earth from the garden. At least she didn't have to carry the soil far, from Roishan's Gardens below Delmarrion's Bridge, like my great-grandfather had to for the terraces he carved out, because there was no earth here then to grow anything."

"You ever ask her why exactly…there?"

"Never did, but I came to think it was so that my father could see it coming up the steps. She did say it needed a lot of water; why firehearts aren't all that common in ordinary places elsewhere. So she made it my responsibility to care for it—before I went off to Sulserra's, anyway. Showed me how to prune it. I remember asking her if that was to make the blossoms bigger. She said that was so, and then winked, telling me that looks are one thing, but careful trimming also makes the fragrance better—you know, hoping I'll hear more than what she was saying."

Falca laughed. "Maybe she's right. What do we know? She's the gardener."

"Yare well, all I know is that filling a pitcher of water from the spigot and watering the bush was easy enough for a six, seven year-old—but trimming? I was lucky I didn't kill it. But she never said a word about the butchering, other than next time cut the stems lower, or higher; something to do with where the buds are."

⬡

FALCA LAY AWAKE on the quilt that night, thinking about what he and Vaience had decided.

Which bothered him and he didn't quite know why. It wasn't like he'd objected to what Vaience had suggested; far from it. They'd talked it through. He'd agreed. And while there was a risk of the boat not being where they'd left it, the plan made sense: wait a week for Rohaise to return to the cottage, with or without this man of hers. Possibly they would, if only to get what they'd left here. There was still food in the larder—dried sprats, a loaf of bread hard enough to use as a club; and in the springhouse sealed jars of pirlo and posca, a round of moldy cheese.

It was Vaience who'd said there was no point in searching for her. She could be anywhere in Linnisheer. So a week. Waiting any longer and they'd be out of food—and run the risk that something would happen to the boat. If it was gone, they'd be trapped here like everyone else.

He turned on his side, facing the door. The cottage was warm and he would have liked to unlatch and open the window, let in the night breeze, but he couldn't do that.

So what was it?—this burr. A smirking reminder from the Fates that you could be trapped Above—wind and sun in your face—as surely as you could be trapped Below in the foul dankness of the Skellig.

No, something else....

Was it Vaience talking about wanting to do something about...out there? About the "fecking Skarrian culchies"—what had to be the first time Falca had heard his friend curse. Maybe in his mind Vaience was seeing himself as a thedral springing from the pages of a story, becoming a man of the burreens or forest verge, who could strike at the whoresons and then vanish into a refuge... and come out again to strike again.

Vaience didn't want to leave empty-handed after waiting a week.

Neither did Falca.

They'd come here to get Rohaise out. Vaience had even said it: "I feel like I'd be abandoning her...even though I *know* what she'd say if she knew. She always thought she was too lenient with me, but she can be hard-headed, tougher than I'll ever be. She'd say, 'What good would it do for *both* of us to be trapped here. If you have a chance to escape, then *that's* what you ought to do.'"

And wasn't that what *he'd* always done? what he was best at? Escaped from Draica with Amala and Gurrus...and below Scaldasaig with Shar Stakeen. He still couldn't believe it—slaking Vaience's *sister*. Half-sister, anyway. And escaped the Skellig with Cofor. And below Sulserra's, with Simi and her boy, too. And Angessa....

And he would do it again in a week.

More than anything else he hoped that Sixer boat would be full. But if it wasn't, if Rohaise Loquin and her man didn't return....

He could tell himself he tried.

So could Vaience.

Wasn't that good enough?

It *should* be enough.

But it's not and—

The Sisters' moonlight dimmed momentarily in the room.

He'd been lying on his back, not looking at the window...and something had caused the brief darkening. Lost in his brooding had he closed his eyes? Or maybe swiftly moving clouds had obscured Cassena and Suaila.

That's probably it....

But he knew he'd never get to sleep until he eliminated the other possibility: someone was outside and had passed by the window.

There were two reasons why he kept the falcata on the edge of the quilt: the two men half-buried out there at the far end of the upper terrace. What if more quay-stompers had come up from the Lazza?

He got up, falcata in hand, and went into Vaience's room to wake him up.

VAIENCE TOOK A kraken's claw from the sack on the table and led Falca to the rear of the cottage, unbarring the door.

"Better I go first," Falca said. It didn't matter if someone just outside heard the whisper; he would have heard the bar creak up on its pin, and would be ready.

If someone *had* gone around the cottage, was waiting for them, Falca reckoned he'd be to the right to give himself a better arc for a strike. Likely the scut'd be right-handed, set to swing a hangar or another stiting door-dog, whatever he had. In the dark you had a better chance of connecting with a swing than stab. But if there were *two* of them....

Defted with both hands, Falca switched the falcata to his left. He quickly opened the door, bolted to his right to quickly move inside the arc of a swing.

None came.

As far as he could tell, the narrow area between the cottage and the hillside was empty; at least no one was silhouetted by the moonlight beyond the end of the cottage. With Vaience close behind, Falca hurried to its corner. To his right the steps began again, rising steeply toward the manse above the cottage. He saw no shadows in that direction or in the other, only the end of the upper terrace wall and the top of the fireheart bush that marked where the steps continued down the hillside.

Was that all Rohaise and her man had seen, too? They'd been here. Vaience guessed that they must have been alerted by his mother's oikoe. So they crept around the cottage to surprise the intrudeers. Otherwise they likely couldn't have done what they did.

But something wasn't right. If anyone was on the other side of the cottage, wouldn't there be sounds by now?—the thumping of a shoulder at the door, the breaking of window glass.

Still, Rohaise and her man probably hadn't heard anything either; they'd surprised the men before broken windows or a busted door.

Falca crept ahead, keeping close to the side of the cottage. At the front corner he stopped again, peered around.

The Sisters, high above distant Mereshaven, bathed the upper terrace with moonlight.

No one was hiding in the weeds, in the shadow cast by the terrace wall, on the other side of the cottage, or on the lower terrace.

No shadows fleeing down the steps.

The wind was brisk, carrying from the west the rumbling of the windmill's vanes. Of course it seemed louder than usual; he was outside, not in the cottage.

The wind…that would have done it, scudding silver-tinged clouds across the moons.

But there were no clouds.

"C'mon Vaience, let's go back in. I must have imagined it."

FALCA LAY ON his side on the quilt, staring at the moonlit window. He couldn't shake the feeling that he *hadn't* imagined it; hadn't mistaken closing his eyes for a moment with someone outside, passing by the window and obscuring the moonlight.

It happened again.

He rose quickly, falcata in hand; was at the side of the window heartbeats after the passing of the shadow. He heard nothing out there, no whispering, only the faint rumbling of the windmill.

This time he wasn't going to roust Vaience. If there was more than one intruder out there, chances are he would have heard…*something*. One man he could handle. And if there was *still* no one out there…he'd rather Vaience not know he was still seeing things that weren't there.

Falca went out the same way as before. Same slow, same careful.

Same…everything.

No one lurking anywhere.

He sat against the cottage door, falcata across his legs, thinking that if it had happened twice now, maybe it would again; and *this* time, out here, there would be no paned window glass, no *nothing* to prevent him from finding out if he was loonzie or not.

A dark, angular shadow glided in front of the Sisters. The night darkened, then lightened again as the shadow moved on, briefly extinguishing stars and then the constellation of the Silver Trail.

Only one thing could do that.

An Erseiyr.

And it had to have been close to chasten the brightness of the Sisters.

He'd never seen one before—during the day or night. Lukan Barra and Rui Ravenstone had…and experienced much more than only a sighting of the legendary Erseiyr.

Falca got up, sanity intact, grinning for the song of it because he could live out the remainder of his life and not see one again. He walked to the terrace wall, as if that would bring him closer to a reappearance of the Erseiyr—*an Erseiyr!*—crossing the Sister moons.

Had there been just the one? Or had its mate, too, been circling around the night sky over Milatum? Raleva had said Erseiyrs mated for life. Lives that some said were immortal. Whether that was true or not—how could mere mortals know?—it was what she believed, and Lukan and Rui as well.

Falca wished now that he had rousted Vaience so he could have seen it. Falca thought of getting him up now, but he didn't want to miss another sighting.

He waited a while but it didn't happen again: no Erseiyr, nothing celestial; only the pinpricks of lights of the Skarrian torches on Mereshaven, a curfew patrol down in the Lazza; the torches at the near ends of Delmarrion's Bridge to the west and Mago's to the east.

He went back inside the cottage, lay down on the quilt, again staring at the window, thinking about what it must have been like to *ride* an Erseiyr as Lukan Barra had done long ago, tucked into a fold of its vast carapace....

And so, in his dream that night, Falca did.

CHAPTER THIRTY-ONE:

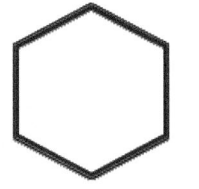

BRINE FOR THE PICKLE BARREL

U PON AWAKENING HE thought it must have been a dream—but there was the kraken's claw leaning near the door where Vaience had left it.

So I did go outside again....

He clasped his hands behind his head, wondering if it was the same Erseiyr who took Lukan from Shadow Mountain to Castlecliff. What was the name?—Rixizzix, that was it. Lukan was a graylock now, a prominent steadman east of Stagfall, and famous—at least to Myrcians. He'd written a book about what had happened long ago but he kept no copy at the stead, nor had he told Falca about how he came to befriend an Erseiyr. But Raleva did. It had crossed Falca's mind that the whole of it was an impressive man's even more impressive imagination, but there was no doubting the fact that without Rixizzix's intervention at Castlecliff, site of the historic landfall of Roak, Cassena and their Sixteen Ships, Myrcia's capitol would have fallen to the Skarrians.

Falca wanted to believe the Erseiyr he'd seen—sort of—was Lukan Barra's Rixizzix. Maybe it wasn't but...what was any Ersieyr doing this far south, momentarily blocking Milatum's moonlight?

Not once, but twice....

Did it mean anything?

Roak's teeth, if there was a time to begin believing in portents and omens...*this* was it.

Falca knew little about Erseiyrs other than what Raleva had told him, but he doubted that the fabled creatures flew around looking for opportunities to befriend and help mere mortals.

Still, hadn't Gurrus told him that his Kelvoi people believed that Erseiyrs hunted for kraken—what else could kill them? So that was probably it, the Erseiyr hunting for kraken in the southern reaches of the Farther Water.

But whatever the reason for an Erseiyr over Milatum, it had nothing to do with anything else.

Milatum was on its own now.

Then, Castlecliff hadn't yet been captured. Rixizzix had swept the Skarrians from the walls, destroyed their siege engines in a tempest of wings, beak and talons.

Regardless, it was too late for Milatum: thousands of Skarrians were already *in* the city.

Maybe by the time he and Vaience were graylocks like Lukan, someone would have gathered an army to besiege Milatum—and a fucking big one to cover the staggering losses. Surrounded by water and beyond the reach of siege engines the city's walls would remain intact—Milatum was basically a larger version of Scaldasaig, wasn't it?

So this army would have to ferry troops across the encircling Kingsmere as the Skarrians had done. But the attackers would have no stalkers to climb the escarpment and the wall, bringing up the assault troops. But there'd be plenty of stalkers *on* the wall's parapet, waiting for them.

So...you blockade the entire city, starve out the whoresons? Yahh—and starve out everyone else too. What then? Get inside the city by ship?

There were only two channels to bring in your troops: the Cleave to the south and the passage between Linnisvale and Linnishill in the north. That one, too, probably had a chain that could be stretched across the mouth of the channel. Even if men got into the channels with boats that could be hauled over the chains—as Falca and Vaience had slipped *under* with their very small boat—those soldiers wouldn't last long. Never mind the withering fire of archers from the ramparts lining the channel walls; few men would get past the bridges that spanned the Cleave and the other channel. The Skarrians would pack the bridges with more archers just as they would defend the bridges that linked the Linnises, in the unlikely event that enough attackers got into the city to begin assaulting the bridges.

One bloody assault after another.

No getting around that....

To take the city, you'd have to take the bridges. And as with the Milats, the Skarrians would have no other choice but to defend them; you couldn't set fire to them or cut the cables with steel—no matter how keen the edge—and bring them down. There'd be no time to demolish the massive bluestone anchor towers at the ends of each one.

Why am I even thinking about all this?

Milatum wasn't *his* city—unless you counted the days in the Skellig as a prisoner, a crappie; trapped below—

Unless....

Falca rose to an elbow, staring right at the answer.

Vaience had left it by the door.

One of the tools...the claws they brought from Angessa.

What the Sixers must have used long ago to cut the kraken-skin they used to make the cables and weave the road they supported. Falca had crossed over two of the bridges on his way to Linnisheer that first day in Milatum: Phodry's and then Mago's, which later he and Vaience, in the kraken-skin boat, had passed under in the Cleave.

Control the bridges and you control Milatum....

Without the bridges the Skarrians on each of the Linnises would be trapped where they were. Yahh, and so would everyone else...but who knows what might happen if the bridges came down?

Even Phodry's and Delmarrion's. These spanned gardens below, where once there had been channels of water. So Ossa told him, talking about the city he'd never see again—nor Rohaise Loquin:

She said some king, long after Colza, had wanted to make it more difficult for an enemy to attack the city. So the east and west channels were filled in, the outer wall extended. Anywhere else, Falca, that would be enough. But the Milats, they planted gardens below these two bridges. When I met Rohaise Loquin, she had dirt under her fingernails, a laugh of campanile bells at noon—and the municipal contract for maintaining the garden, Roishan's it was called, below Delmarrion's Bridge, just as her father had....

And just as gardens could be planted, bridges could be replaced, even bridges that have stood for two thousand years.

"So do it, then. Use the...kraken claws, take 'em all down, and...."

And suddenly he was glad Vaience hadn't heard the whisper.

It was fucking *loonzie*.

You're staved, you know that? Shide....

A rapparee from Draica and a bespectacled thedral...bringing down the bridges of Milatum?

He felt disgusted with himself for even thinking about it. There was as much chance of that happening as...as there was befriending Rixizzix to save *Milatum* this time.

Making fools of Duna Rheg and her vanes was one thing; sneaking back into Milatum and avoiding curfew patrols another.

But *this* was something else again.

Bring down *all five* bridges?

How about just *one?* But even with only one they'd *still* have to get past the Skarrians sentries at one end...at night...and cut enough of the cables to bring it down before they were overwhelmed and killed either by the sentries or the collapsing bridge.

And would the destruction of a single bridge make a difference?

Falca put on his chasers, got up and sat at the table. He picked up one of the golos they'd brought in from the springhouse, took a bite. Mushy. He rolled it away. They all were probably mushy.

There's nothing for it....

This wagon didn't have wheels, never mind a horse to pull it.

All they could do was wait the week and leave—with or without Rohaise and her man in the boat—and then get to the coast like before, tramp to Averdenn.

Then...back to Draica—where else?—with half the proceeds of the blueveil ring, his safekeep fat with shine. And if he wasn't careful he'd get soft by degrees in some manse in fashionable Beckon or Falconwrist and one day realize his life had become little more than the counting of his money, the polishing of his phaeton and the grooming of its matched pairs of horses—all those *things* he'd once wanted so badly when he didn't know any better; when he measured a good day by how much coin he'd reived from Timberlimb refugees who sold scrape along the canals....

Falca heard Vaience stirring in his room and soon the thedral came out, yawning.

Vaience scraped back the other chair, sat down, glanced at the once-bitten golo on the table.

"It was an Erseiyr dunning the moonlight," Falca said.

Vaience nodded.

"What, you saw it too?"

"I couldn't sleep either. I mean, if someone like *you* thought there was something out there, then there *had* to be. Well, there wasn't. But you must have seen *something*. Then I heard you getting up again, and went to my window. And there you were. And there *it* was, crossing the moons. What else could do that on a cloudless night except an Erseiyr. Never seen one before, but I've read about people who did."

"I never saw one either before last—"

"Falca, why are looking like that golo's given you a gut-ache?"

"COR! NO WONDER," Vaience said.

"I wasn't going to tell you. Forget I said a fucking thing."

"Too late for that now." Vaience scraped back the chair, got up, went to the door, unbarred it, opened it wide to a wafting of warmer air. He leaned against the edge, took off his spectacles and polished the lenses with a cloth he took from the back pocket of his trews, twice holding up the spectacles in the morning light to see what he missed. He put them back on, stuffed the cloth back in his pocket and folded his arms.

"I'd guess that if we told ten people what you just told me, half of them would say—despite what's happened—half would say not to do it. Even if we could. They'd say—"

"'You're loonzie'."

"Yare, that, too. But they'd also say the bridges were here before the Skarrians came—and the bridges will still be here when they leave."

"Maybe that's what they'd say—until a daughter or wife caught the eye of a Skarrie as she was crossing Mago's Bridge at noon; or a son or husband got fed to a stalker because he said the wrong thing at the wrong time. We brought back Sixer artifacts from Angessa. But that's all the bridges really are, too. They could be rebuilt—stone would have to do."

Vaience turned away from the door. "That's what the *other* half might say—what you're saying now. What I'd say, too, if I was crazy. Leave a few bridges, of course. Maybe most of them." He picked up the kraken's claw and tapped it against the door sill. "Like you said, all we could possibly take down is one."

"What I *said* is that we'd have no chance for even *one*, which if we *did* should be the one to Mereshaven."

"Colza's Bridge."

"Which would be the most heavily guarded of them all."

"Well, yes…and no."

"*No?* What d'you mean, no?"

"I've been on that bridge twice, both times during the day, of course; once to visit my mother—she'd gotten permission to show me around Mereshaven."

"The other time?"

"It had to do with Cyalla."

"Now there's a song I'd like to hear sometime—but what about Colza's Bridge *not* being heavily guarded?"

"There are gates of solid bronze just off the bridge at either end. I saw the winches needed to open and close them."

"Which there aren't any gates on the other bridges, just Skarrian sentries at the ends."

"Right. So at night the gates on Colza's would presumably be closed," Vaience said. "Now there is a lesser, postern gate with a narrow squint. But that, too, would probably be closed."

"And only opened if some Skarrie needed to go one way or the other in the dead of night. So it's possible no sentries would be on the bridge itself, yahh? Why would there be? seeing as how the bridge is secure at both ends."

"Especially the far end, on Linnisvale. It's more fortified, has flanking towers.

"The Mereshaven end doesn't?"

Vaience shook his head. "It's a formal entrance to the royal isle, not a defensive one. Designed to impress and it does. There *are* watchtowers along the ring-road. But Mereshaven doesn't even have a wall around it."

"A thousand years since Colza and no one thought it might be a good idea to build a wall around the royal nest?"

"A few kings did, I'm sure, but then Scunder famously said that while the wall around the city was necessary to discourage external enemies, what need was there for wall around *Mereshaven?* As long as the kings and queens of the House of Keshkev ruled justly, there would no reason for them to fear their own people, and thus no reason for a wall."

"Ah, sounds like he was polishing the shovel."

Vaience smiled. "It was said the real reason was that Scunder's queen didn't want a high wall obstructing her view of the Queensmere as she strolled along the ring-road—which she named after herself, by the way: Livy's Walk."

"Which means there's no wall or sentry's parapet by the Mereshaven gate—but what *is* there?"

"Hmmm…well, there's the continuation of the road between the two anchor towers for the bridge—we're on solid ground now. There *are* walls on either side of the passage—the approach to the Triskell Gate. The usual arrow loops, I suppose. The Triskell Gate takes up most of the facing wall at the end. Both times I was there, half of the gate was open, but there's that smaller postern gate within one of the halves. Once you're through, you're in a roofed colonnade. Between the columns you can see the Ephoria off to your right."

"What's that?"

"Where the ephors convened. Politicians."

"Probably the Skarries are using it for barracks—all right, go on."

"So you walk to the end of the colonnade and you see the sitting statue of Colza. More dawnstone. It's huge—the plinth alone is a man's height. He's facing the gate, holding the Scroll of Wisdom in his left hand, the Spear of Victory in his right. Both are supposed to be solid gold. If so, I doubt he's holding them now."

"Can you draw a map of it all?"

"A map?"

"Not all of it—just up to the Triskell Gate. We'll need a map to plan this."

"Wait…*what?* We're going to do it?"

"Isn't that what we've been talking about?"

Rohaise hadn't used for the letter all of the skensy Vaience brought occasionally from Sulserra's, where the paper was exclusively made. By the time he finished making the map, his fingertips were smudged with ink. He and Falca spent the rest of the afternoon going over the map, devising a plan, marking their route across the Queensmere to Colza's Bridge.

They agreed: if the boat wasn't where they'd left it, they'd have to find another small one down there along the wharves of the Lazza quay; getting to Colza's Bridge on foot was out of the question. They would have to go over Delmarrion's Bridge, somehow getting past the Skarrian sentries there, and then keep on through Linnisvale, avoiding curfew patrols. Even if they *did* manage to do that, Vaience didn't think it possible they could climb down the escarpment near the bridge. The inner bluff of the Queensmere might be less formidable than the other which rose up from the outer Kingsmere, but it would still be a difficult descent—all the more so without being seen by the sentries posted by the gate at the Linnisvale end of the bridge.

Climbing back *up* to the level of the bridge, either along the span or at one end of it…*that* was a problem that could only be solved once they were there. And to *get* there they needed a boat—which they'd need getting *away*, to return to the Lazza.

And once back at the cottage…wait to see if it had all been for naught.

They left the map on the table where Vaience had drawn it, went outside to drink water from the cistern spigot. And then they walked over to the terrace wall.

The Skarrians had been busy all the while. There were two ships—one large, one smaller—berthed at Pelagia's islet. The soldiers were tiny specks moving about the ends of the web-like tracery of stalker silk they'd use to rip off her head and outstretched arms.

"If we can do this, Falca…will it make a difference…filling the streets with people?"

"That's the map I wish we could draw. So much depends on how many of the whoresons are on Mereshaven and maybe if that hard turd himself is there, this Vulsa—but where else would he be?"

"Like you said, it's cutting off the head of the beast."

"Giving it a bloody hinge, anyway. They'll be trapped, the festers, and maybe a lot of their fucking stalkers—for a while. Hopefully long enough for people to realize that a lot of Skarries are trapped."

Falca nodded at Mereshaven in the distance. "All that smoke…maybe that means there *are* a lot of 'em garrisoned there. The more that are trapped there, the fewer to kill people *there* and *there*." He pointed to the northwest and the east. "And *here*." He jabbed a finger on the top of the terrace wall.

"If there *are* risings in the Linneses."

"*That's* the brine in the pickle barrel—what happens when the word spreads that someone's dunned Colza's Bridge, and that a full barrel of Skarries are trapped on Mereshaven."

"You reckoned a third of them, but I still think that's optimistic. That many men are not needed there. Vulsa would have dispersed more around the Linnises."

"You're right."

"You changed your mind?"

Falca shrugged. "While you were doing the map I got thinking that the city couldn't be the wankspit's only concern. If I were him, once I'd put the lid on the kettle here, I would have sent some of my troops outside the city, to the west and north, to grab Girvan and Carrick. I passed through Carrick on my way here. Girvan's important, where it is, but so's Carrick, seems to me."

"I'd say so: it's the key to the north and the Lakes—Keshkevar's part of them anyway. What about the southeast east? Terenure's bigger than Girvan and Carrick."

"Vulsa wouldn't worry about that. He's already come that way. It's already in his pocket. All that matters now is how many of them are *in* the city—first things first. Colza's Bridge."

"That reminds me," Vaience said, and turned from the wall. "I need the rest of the string I used to roll up the map."

"For what?"

"To tie the stems of these." He pointed a finger at his spectacles. "I can't be losing my eyes climbing up to Colza's Bridge tonight."

CHAPTER THIRTY-TWO:

LENDREE'S MEAT

GABEEKA LENDREE SAT away from the fire to wait for his spitted meat to finish roasting; waiting, too, for shadows to move across the moonlit strand below.

For the week he'd been hiding in the royal Chase, Lendree slept during the day, keeping watch at night for Banch Redallion and his woman. Seeing the Erseiyr twice the night before, momentarily disrupting the moon ribbons shimmering on the Kingsmere Narrows, might have been a marvel for some but Lendree could not have cared less about such a rare event.

Killing Redallion and taking what surely he'd be carrying—*that* was all he cared about.

Lendree was confident he would come into the Chase at night, as had Lendree himself. Redallion, too, would not want the daytime risk of people seeing him unlocking one of the two Quillons gates, probably Shimsinnion's—never mind Skarrians nearby or on the allure of the city wall.

Lendree had chosen his refuge and vantage point carefully—and the place to make a fire to roast his meat. If anyone on the mainland shore across the Narrows happened to be looking east to Milatum, he would see a spot of light. But not any Skarrians patrolling the parapet of the city wall, who might look west over the darker-than-night forest of the Chase—twice as large as Mereshaven it was—that extended beyond the escarpment, wall and Linnisvale proper.

He'd made the fire in the lee of a wooded rise overlooking the strand, the only one in Milatum, and that only possible because sand had to be annually imported from Gebroan at great expense to replace what was washed away. Just so Rhakotis and Epona, maybe their Demizell brats, and the usual attending lickspigots could walk on a strand while a Labrysson escort scuffed along behind them. Lendree had once commanded such a detachment. For all that he could have imagined then that he'd be back here—the House of Keshkev washed away like so much sand after a storm—the Erseiyr last night might as well have pissed on Milatum and called it rain.

Or imagined that in a month he would be in Syarra with Queen Epona's jewels, which had to be a hefty portion of the entire royal collection.

But for that to happen, Banch Redallion had to appear on the strand with the jewels, ready to make his swim across the Narrows. Probably he'd have the little stallion chest containing the jewels inside a common sack.

Tonight?

It was a fine night for a swim—Lendree's that is. Scarcely a rustle in the leaves of the swingbacks and hackhards on the rise, so the Narrows wouldn't be rough.

Redallion would see the fire, but he'd likely ignore it, thinking it was some Milat taken refuge in the Chase. But Lendree didn't want him to ignore it, so he intended to call out softly. *Over here, Ikonos...Are you hungry? Would you like some roasted oikoe before we swim across?*

Redallion might ask why him why hadn't already swum across, as per his instructions, but Lendree could finesse that. There was no reason why Redallion should be suspicious; he didn't—couldn't—know it was Lendree who'd sent the three quay-stompers up to the woman's cottage.

He hoped Redallion would bring the woman because he'd like to crease her, *oyah*, after he killed Redallion. But to do that—given what she'd done to Sepsull at the cottage—he'd best knock her senseless before he fucked her.

Then, after he killed her, on to the strand after he cut down a few saplings and tied them together with strips of clothing from Redallion and the woman. A crude raft but it could carry his boots, the jewels and two Labrysson's swords—Lendree's and Redallion's. At some point on the mainland he'd sell Redallion's for what he'd need to get to Syarra.

Lendree's mouth was watering at the smell and sizzle of the cooking meat Cor! he was famished. He'd been careful with the food he'd brought with him a week ago but it was almost gone. He walked over to the fire, poked at the oikoe with his sword to see if it was ready. Not quite.

He caught it late in the afternoon. Luckily, the oikoe was a young one, a kiff, its fur still a tannish-white; no musk yet. An easy kill, the oikoe alone and listless. Its parents had probably been killed by a snagwolf—the Chase had been stocked with them for the hunting pleasure of the Mereshaven elite, and for Labrysson training—or possibly by Milats who sneaked into the Chase to hide from the Skarrians.

He assumed some people had gotten in through the Chase's custodial gate after the merser guards had abandoned it, and before the Skarrians posted their own. The royals used the two Quillons gates, which needed no guards because they were always locked—and only a Labrysson carried the means to unlock them.

Lendree hadn't seen anyone else yet but there was a lot of forest in the Chase and he kept well away from its paths that were doubtless patrolled by Skarrians. He'd been concerned initially that the churgs would mount sweeps in force through the Chase but evidently they hadn't. Even so, he'd excavated a burrow, covering it with leafy branches for the hours he slept. Lendree had tested it and was confident that unless someone came within ten feet or so, he wouldn't recognize the lair for what it was. And Lendree hadn't ever been told he snored.

He also had never had oikoe meat before.

He'd dragged the kiff back by its long tail, cut off the head, then knotted the tail over a low-hanging branch. What a pleasure to watch the blood drain! Then the skinning of the hide with his Labrysson's sword. By the time the gloaming faded to night and a few points of light appeared on the darkened, distant scar of the causeway that led from the Orphic Gate to the mainland, the oikoe's drippings began to sizzle in the fire he'd made....

The meat had to be done now—close enough anyway.

He sliced off a haunch.

Hot…hot. He let it cool a bit, flipping the meat from one hand then the other, licking his fingers.

He bit off a mouthful. Greasy but delicious.

Of course it was. Young and tender, not like the other fecking oikoe—no kiff there—that ruined his original plan for Redallion; why Lendree was still here after a week. Because of *that* oikoe Redallion still had the jewels that were intended to keep Epona comfortably in exile. Yare well, she had her exile now, in a place where she'd never need them.

There was only one man who would be enjoying an exile fit for a king—and it wasn't going to be Ikonos Banch Redallion.

GABEEKA LENDREE HAD been second-in-command of the forty Labryssons Rhakotis ordered to take his queen out of the city, hurry to Girvan and then up the awe to the safety of Averdenn. When the king made his decision the siege had just begun. The Labrysson Archos, Sullinion, told him the Skarrians hadn't yet blocked the Orphic Gate and the causeway that led to Humberton on the mainland and the Girvan road. The churgs had attacked from the east and while they would soon be at the Cleave—its entrance chained—there was no way they'd be able to get farther west in time to threaten Queen Epona's escape.

Lendree had seen her weeping as she stepped into the blue-and-white phaeton at the gates of the Kelefion. He'd found out later from one of his men in Labrys Hall that her tears had begun in anger, that she had refused to go; that she wanted to remain at the side of her husband and son, come what may. Her vehemence evidently subsided to acceptance after Rhakotis told her he'd chosen Ikonos Banch Redallion to command her Labrysson escort.

Lendree had seethed all the way through Linnisvale, his anger finding the edge of his sword when he should have been using the flat of it to help clear the route along Colza's Way. Of all the Labrysson officers the king could have chosen—including the older Lendree—he'd chosen the jumped-up Redallion who, not all *that* long ago, had been waving to adoring crowds in the Palestra. However uncommon his skill in leaping over charging augors and landing on his feet, the man was still just a fecking...*acrobat*.

That night the Queen and her Labrysson escort hurried to the Orphic Gate, were halfway across the causeway when a Meresguard rider from Humberton told them that the Skarrians had landed in force outside the town.

Sullinion, the king's younger brother, had been wrong.

They had to go back, but not to Mereshaven, Redallion saying that by the time they did that the Skarrians might already be threatening it. He had another plan to which the Queen agreed.

"Do what you must, Banch," Lendree heard her say.

Do what you must...Banch....

Not Ikonos, or Redallion.

Banch....

What, was he creasing Epona on the sly?

Do what you must?

They left the phaeton and horses by the Orphic Gate, stuffed their white Labrysson tunics down the nearest gullet. By the time they got to the Lazza, everyone was dressed as if they belonged there—except, of course, for the swords. And the Queen? Four Labryssons escorted her into a tenement; she came out looking like a shopkeeper's wife.

Do what you must?

By Redallion's plan, that meant hiding in the Lazza, in separate but close groups. And hoping for a Milat victory. But if that didn't happen, Redallion said they'd find carts and trundles and over the course of a few days, by groups of twos and threes— their swords hidden on the underside of the carts, secured with nailed leather straps— they'd make their way across Delmarrion's Bridge to Linnisvale. Then, at night, alternating between Quillons Gates, each group would enter the Chase. Redallion himself, posing as the son of the shopkeeper's wife, would go last with her. And if all went well, the Labryssons would have made a raft to take the shopkeeper's wife across the Narrows to the mainland, the Labryssons swimming alongside. Which they could do, no problem there. Labryssons were required to learn how to swim ever since King Othellion's only legitimate son—celebrating his seventh birthday—had drowned in the Queensmere after he fell from the larger royal barge.

And then on to the castlet at Averdenn, where presumably the 500-man royal garrison at Girvan would have gone, since they'd have no chance of defeating the Skarrians when they inevitably marched on Girvan.

This...*this* was the best that...*do-whatever-you-must-Banch* could come up with?

Faugh! What rot from the once-famous augeron who as much as killed his wife in front of 30,000 people in the Palestra.

Then again, Redallion had *another* plan, didn't he?

Oyah....

Lendree never saw what happened at the Truff Row warehouse in the Lazza, the night word came that the Skarrians had taken the city; that their red-and-black stalker battle flag could be seen on the Kelefion.

Only Redallion knew what really happened. He summoned Lendree— his symmos and second-in-command—from the Iron Petal forge; and also

Loguvar, the terros and third officer, from another hiding place in a mason's workshop on Limekilns Lane.

There had been fifteen men with Redallion—and Queen Epona alone in her makeshift quarters behind a row of carpets stacked shoulder-high. As Redallion spoke to him and Loguvar, Lendree kept thinking that the Ikonos could easily have killed her himself without anyone seeing the deed. Redallion was clearly shaken—*the Queen has taken her life*—but he also might have looked troubled if he'd just murdered her.

Still, what a fine story he told! Lesperria himself, the bard of Clane's, couldn't have written better lines for him to deliver onstage.

The Queen had summoned him, Redallion said. She had a dagger in one hand, the point snagged on the common duvelin she wore. Rhakotis had given it to her through the window of the phaeton; Lendree saw him do it. The flaring end of the dagger's grip had the Keshkan triskell in gold and stardonyx, the tips of the short quillons set with rubies. A hand-held fortune—and many more in the big pouch of jewels Rhakotis then gave her by way of a footman who needed two hands to place it within the carriage.

Redallion said he pleaded with the Queen not to do what she obviously intended, but she had made up her mind: her husband and son would be dead soon, if they weren't already. It was her desire to join them.

Redallion said *this*, Redallion said *that*...Redallion said he tried to dissuade her, pleading with her that after she was safely in Averdenn the word would spread the Queen was still alive, and thousands of Keshkans would rally around her, and before the year was out an army would be marching on Milatum to take back the city.

Redallion said she silenced him with something she hadn't yet told her husband: "I have been bleeding where a woman of my age should not bleed any more."

What a poignant touch *that* was! the frankness of it making it almost plausible since the queen was well-known for bluntness. And so very convenient for Redallion.

Supposedly Epona then said: "I am dying but my daughters are not." She gave Redallion jewels—so he *said*. "Use these to get to Castlecliff and bribe who you must to get my daughters away and thence to Averdenn. Many more of my people will rise for them than their dead mother."

Supposedly the Queen stabbed herself, angling the blade up into her heart.

She now had to be buried.

Redallion had a plan for that, too.

He told Loguvar and Lendree that he knew where they could lay the Queen to rest. It was above the Lazza. Behind Stoma's tessaria which had the wee Pelagia out front, there were steps that led up the steep hillside to a cottage; said he'd been there a few times, seen the terraces of earth, the view of the Queensmere and Mereshaven.

It's the best we can do for our Queen since we can't tuck her into eternity at Cauldron's End....

How convenient: his woman's cottage.

The home of the King's Own Gardener: Rohaise Loquin.

Lendree had seen enough of her on Mereshaven to wonder how she managed to keep the parterres of Tulemia's Gardens blooming without throwing tantrums at her three-score spademen and weed-pullers. He'd seen her catch the eye of even the younger Labryssons though she was old enough to evidently have a grown son. Seems she'd been a widow for a long time which, considering her beauty, was surprising. But that was the rumor.

Labryssons could not marry but otherwise they were free to slake themselves elsewhere in Milatum, usually at one of the more exclusive hetarias in Linnisvale. Lendree didn't like their strict rules or the expense, and most of all the looks he got, before...and after a slide. So what if his cudgie wasn't... what you might expect for a man with his thick proportions.

Chell-the-Smell—who had to be ordered to bathe—had once jested that Lendree could make a lot of coin hiring himself out as a dock bollard on the Lazza quay. Redallion had overheard the quip in the barracks and silenced The Smell in passing with his own jibe about Chell's dainty feet and short fingers. What bothered Lendree most was not Chell's jibe but Redallion quickly coming to his defense while Lendree was still assembling an insult.

Still, he considered himself reasonably handsome, and was confident that Rohaise Loquin would be attracted to a Labrysson symmos with an excellent family pedigree, and who was about to be promoted to the rank of ikonos.

Until he wasn't.

Until he found out she had a lover who'd been promoted instead of him.

Who never let the jewels out of his sight after Epona *supposedly* killed herself.

One by one that night, they all knelt before the dead Queen, whispering a Labrysson's Three Vows, the ones Lendree had first uttered ten years before

Redallion had—no, it was eleven. Ikonos Redallion was the last to whisper his in that warehouse and then he took the jewels, hefted the Queen's body over his shoulder and left with three others who presumably would take their turns carrying her up the steps. The last Lendree saw of Redallion, Epona's dangling hand was knocking against the big pouch of jewels tightly knotted to his belt.

Loguvar and the two other Labryssons who went with him, came back without him. Redallion's orders, repeated to Loguvar up there, hadn't changed, the men still for the Chase. And Redallion would be doing so later, with the jewels. Then the swim across the Narrows and on to Averdenn, where they'd take ship for Castlecliff. Epona had given her last command and Redallion intended to fulfill it.

So he *said*.

No one else, even Loguvar, seemed to share Lendree's certainty, which he kept to himself, that they'd never see Ikonos Redallion again—though he did say to Loguvar that it seemed odd the Ikonos hadn't come back with the others.

"Not if you'd seen that woman."

"I have."

"Then you can't blame him," Loguvar said, "for wanting some time with her; he'll never see her again."

Lendree had turned away in disgust. Couldn't the terros—all of the men— *see* what Redallion was doing? smell the stench of betrayal? How could they not see that what the acrobat intended was to spend four or five days up there alone, creasing the woman and then—with or without the her—make his own swim across the Narrows at night, avoiding any Labryssons waiting for him. Or more likely, he'd wait in the Chase until they had to assume the Skarrians killed him, took the jewels. And *then* make his swim. And skelter off to the north with a fortune to last three lifetimes, to the Lakes—Syarra or Ascalon. Anywhere *but* Averdenn.

With Queen Epona dead, it was every man for himself—and Redallion had been the first to know it. Getting to the Chase...and then across the Narrows...and then to Averdenn?

Lendree doubted that more than a few Labryssons would make it all the way. But he was sure Redallion didn't care if *anyone* did. Epona's last command? Even if the swinker hadn't murdered her for the jewels, her command was such that only a half-brick would believe it possible to fulfill. What?—a few Labryssons were supposed to show up in Castlecliff, dispensing bribes and kidnapping the wife of a Sanctor's son? The Myrcians would keep the bribes *and* the Demizells and kill the Keshkans. Even if the Labryssons did get the princesses out, eluding the pursuit of the Sanctor's stoneskin guard and oh, a few *thousand* Gardacs wasn't likely. It was a long way back to Averdenn. By ship? They wouldn't get past the chains across Roak's Awe.

Whatever else he was, Redallion *wasn't* a half-brick; he knew Epona's last command was a death-sentence.

The House of Keshkev was no more and with that, Lendree believed, so were a Labrysson's vows.

Yare, it was every man for himself now, and better someone have the royal swag who truly deserved it.

And that wasn't Banch Redallion, who began as a fecking awning-boy, helping furl and unfurl as necessary the shade for summer spectacles in the Palestra. And when the cutling wasn't doing that he'd been mucking augor stables. The story of how he got his chance in the Palestra's Oval amounted to one thing.

Luck.

He turned out to be a very good augeron; Lendree had to give him that: the first to leap three augors, and live. Crowds loved him before and after he married the only non-Keshkan augeron ever to perform in the Oval. From Gebroan she was. They were so popular Rhakotis hosted a reception for them after their wedding—in the Palestra, where else? The rumor that she was the daughter of a Sandsend hetera was especially rouncy because heteras rarely made such a mistake.

Oh, they were a pair all right.

Didn't end so well for them, though, did it.

Some said the fault was hers not his, because of her condition. The second augor in line—mandibles sharpened as they always were—slashed her across the belly, almost cutting her in half while Redallion was still in the air. But it was Redallion's fault, had to be: a tardy prompt to his wife. Why else did he quit the ring if not from guilt at causing her death and that of the child she was carrying. Anyway, if he hadn't known she was heavy, he should have. Three months along was the word but that, of course, was only a bloody guess.

He disappeared for two years; no one knew where. When he returned he petitioned the king for an appointment to the Labryssons. At thirty he was well past the usual age of a falding. Rhakotis granted his request; riots would probably have ensued if he hadn't. But Redallion didn't begin as a first-year Labrysson recruit. Rhakotis gave him the rank of terros to start.

When a young Gabeeka Lendree was a falding, patrolling Livy's Walk at night, or standing watch over the Cauldron's End tombs of Keshkan kings and queens on a drizzling winter's day, the younger Banch Redallion had been enjoying the assorted rewards of his freakish ability to leap augors.

Lendree did not expect deafening applause for his loyalty to the House of Keshkev. For five generations the Lendrees had sent their eldest sons to serve as Labryssons, and he'd been the last.

But loyalty and duty should count for something.

Faugh! Where was Redallion's when he abandoned his men so Rohaise Loquin could poose-polish his cudgie up at her cottage?

Loyalty? Where was the loyalty to *him* four months ago? after what he did at Aknanore. And did he complain about that? No! But even now he still seethed with rage about the slight.

A band of outlaws hiding out in the Forest of Aknanore had been holding for ransom the king's cousin, the High Kennard of Phaistos. They'd abducted him and his wife shortly after the couple began the journey to Milatum for the Roak's Week festivities, killing all but one of the twelve-man escort.

Lendree was the ranking symmos of the 3rd Labrysson triskalon—200 men strong and commanded by Ikonos Lysando Berrusis—that Rhakotis sent to Aknanore without any ransom money. His orders: save the High Kennard and his wife if possible but witihout fail kill the outlaws and spike their heads at the Phaistos gate.

With the help soldiers from the Phaistos garrison the 3rd spiked twenty-two. And lost almost as many Labryssons doing so, including Berrusis. When he was mortally wounded—a spiddard bolt through his left eye—Lendree took over and later spiked the heads of the three brigands he'd killed, after the Labryssons brought the bodies of the High Kennard and his wife back to Phaistos for burial.

His reward upon returning to Milatum?

Banch Redallion, ranking symmos of the 2nd, was promoted to Ikonos of the 3rd, replacing Berrusis.

In what crucible of battle had the acrobat proved himself? At the cottage, slaking Rohaise Loquin while Lendree was killing outlaws? Or later, at the warehouse in which he probably murdered Epona?

The morning after Loguvar and the others returned from the cottage, Lendree began sending out the men by twos and threes, every other hour, as Redallion had ordered. Then, that afternoon, he left too—ostensibly to see whether the Labryssons in the other hiding places had found enough carts or trundles. He never came back. By nightfall he'd hired four Lazza street-busters in a deadfall den the Skarrians hadn't yet closed. He had to kill one who tried to take his money, but three would do. After all, there was only Redallion and the woman up there.

Looking back, he should have either gone up himself or gone with them. But at the time he reckoned: why risk something happening to himself in the ruck? He had too much to lose if Redallion got lucky and wounded him. These dock-heaves were expendable; Lendree was not.

Two of them had hangars and one, Sepsull, had a door-dog he'd found in a Slake Street gutter.

Lendree kept it simple for the three, telling them only that he required their services to resolve a personal matter. He gave them the directions, said they were to quickly break into the cottage; surprise was all. Subdue the man and woman there—coshing if necessary but no killing. Tie them up with whatever they found there and send one man down the steps to let Lendree know. He would be waiting halfway up the steps. As soon as he saw they'd done as ordered, they'd get the other half of the money, their services no longer required.

Redallion would surely have temporarily hidden the jewels. But one way or the other, Lendree would force them to divulge the whereabouts of the cache.

How was he to know the woman kept an oikoe up there?

Sepsull was the one who stumbled down the steps, stinking of musk, feverishly scratching his musk-bloated and bloody face, whining about how the woman caught him with the edge of a spade after the oikoe—"*thet dairty t'ing*"—sprayed him, then leaped at Raff. Maybe Kefartha had wounded the man, Sepsull wasn't sure.

As Lendree raced up the steps he heard Sepsull retching.

He didn't bother checking to see if Raff and Kefartha were still alive. The front door of the cottage was open. So was the other one in the back, where Redallion and the woman—and her fecking oikoe—must have sneaked out, gone around, to surprise the men.

There was no point hunting for the jewels in the dark; Redallion would probably have taken them anyway. And no point either to go after him and the woman. They'd be holed up somewhere soon, not wanting to risk the curfew, Skarrians seeing them. Which *he* might be if he moved about, hunting for the pair.

Whether Redallion was wounded or not, likely after what had happened he wouldn't try to get to the Chase. But Lendree had to believe he would, sooner or later.

Sepsull was gone when Lendree went back down the steps. The worthless yape—bleeding and sick as he was from the oikoe musk—had correctly assumed Lendree would have killed him for the botched job.

Lendree wasted no time leaving the deadfall den the next morning.

He found what he needed at a tannery not far from the tessaria, whose workers were dead or had yet to resume their trade. He dumped the hides from the trundle cart but saved several, making the necessary cuts in the leather— and the bottom of the cart—with tools he found in the tannery. When he was finished he had a basket tightly knotted to the underside of the cart, which held his Labrysson's sword. He kept his money pouch on him. Probably the Skarrians would be satisfied with taking his money and not search the cart. And why would they look underneath? when all there was *in* the cart was a jug of water and food—hard bread, hoodle and dried fish in a sack—and a couple of hides that hid the exposed thongs of the basket.

Delmarrion's Bridge was swarming with churgs: ten of them and a stalker on the Linnsheer side. Lendree expected about the same at the other end. The black stalker was wrapping silk around a dead man. Five cocoons hung from the branches of the swingbacks and redshanks that lined the center of Colza's Way. Nearby, dozens of Milats—enough to reach from one lamppost to the next—had lined up in front of a wagon filled with provisions. A sair lot they were, dregs of Linnisheer. The air carried a stench of burning flesh and smoke from a cresset of coals.

Some of the Labryssons who'd gone from their hiding places to forage had seen this...branding. Evidently, in exchange for food—what the Skarrians called the 'Mercy of Tholos', the churgs required you to suffer a brand, which signified loyalty to their Tholarsh and their Priaptor, this Vulsa. Or some such popinall. The oval-shaped brand, marking the Eye of Tholos they called it, was seared into the back of the right hand.

A shrieking woman, dressed in better clothes than Epona wore when she died, had just been branded. The Skarrian with the iron grabbed her wrist, plunged her hand into a bucket of water, told her she was purified, shoved a parcel of food into her chest, pushed her out of the way, and waggled his fingers for the next-in-line to come forward.

As Lendree approached the bridge in the shade of the massive cable towers, one of the churgs looked into the cart, checked the sack, took his money, and waved him on. Lendree asked him what the cocooned men had done to wind up as stalker feed.

"The windmill. They ruined the workings inside last night. Someone did. Don't matter who pays the price so long's it's paid—now g'arn with you, slorrie."

Lendree pushed the cart ahead onto the woven road, thinking there was indeed a price to be paid, and Banch Redallion was going to pay it.

Yare, the Skarrians were indeed scum but soon enough that wouldn't be his worry anymore. They were also clever. Mercy Wagons? The food was free but it, too, came with a price: the brand marked you as a collaborator, never mind your hunger. Brand by brand the churgs would divide the people of Milatum. Loyalty? In the end, to whom would you be more loyal if you had the fecking Eye of Tholos on the back of your hand? The Skarrians who gave you food? or your fellow Milats who beat you or killed your husband or wife in reprisal?

For the rest of the day Lendree pushed the cart back and forth along Colza's Way in Linnisvale, in the general area between the two Quillons gates in the city wall not far to the west. As the evening faded, the curfew drawing nigh, he pushed the cart into a side street off Colza's Way, then into an alley. He lay under the cart for hours, waiting until the night had deepened, and then slid out his sword from the slim leather basket.

Before he approached the nearest Quillons gate he made sure no one was about, nor any Skarrians above on this particular stretch of the city wall's parapet. Even so, he walked—didn't run—to the gate itself: the eye—a living eye—was very good at noticing sudden movement.

He slotted one of his Labrysson sword's quillons—either one would do for a key—and turned it to the right. No need to open the gate fully, as of course any Labrysson would have done to let in horses and the royal arses sitting on them. He slipped through, closed the gate, pausing with satisfaction when he heard it lock, then took the wide, graveled path that wound down the bluff toward the forest verge. The moonlight was low, the moons bitten: Cassena and Suaila would be chaste for a few days more. But even so he walked slowly, mindful of his shadow on the white gravel and a Skarrian patrol that might be passing on the wall.

GABEEKA LENDREE GNAWED the last of the oikoe's leg meat and tossed the bone away, wondering if it would be tonight. If it was, he'd be ready. This time the woman—if Redallion couldn't bear to leave the quiv behind—wouldn't have a spade or oikoe handy. Neither one was what you'd take for a swim across the Narrows.

CHAPTER THIRTY-THREE:

COLZA'S BRIDGE

AT THE SAME time Gabeeka Lendree extinguished the fire that cooked the oikoe kiff, and Lambrey Tallon spilled his muck to the image behind his closed eyes of a bound and bruised Shar Stakeen bent over the bed in his chamber in the Kelefion, his cudgie buried in her bottom-hole, Falca was wondering if maybe Rixizzix had decided to intervene on behalf of the Skarrians this time.

Sure seemed like it.

Paddling out from the Lazza quay, he and Vaience had the boon of a southern breeze but about halfway across the Queensmere the wind suddenly rose and shifted, coming from the east, dashing any hope of resting now. They had to dig hard at the same lee rail or the wind would scud them toward the west and the Linnisvale shore.

There was no shadow moving across the Sisters and constellations but still…it was as if Rixizzix was having a flurry-of-wings tantrum somewhere off to the east—or whatever an Erseiyr did when grutchy—and was trying to keep two men in a kraken-skin boat from getting to where they had to go.

Falca was drenched from the spray of roused waves—a warm-water soaking but a soaking nonetheless.

He kept on, his back and shoulders aching; Vaience, in the bow, keeping on.

Dig, pull hard, recover, dig again….

Falca didn't dare pause to wipe salt-spray from his eyes.

It seemed that all he'd been doing in the past few weeks was paddling across water at night, water you could drown in, not like in Draica where all you had to worry about was stepping over puddles; though sure, if you fell into a filthy canal, its sides slick with moss, you wouldn't be climbing back out.

Vaience had never sailed from Linnisheer to the Cut—Cusheen's Cut, the northern channel between Linnisvale and Linnishill. But he'd heard you could do it in two hours at most, so he reckoned they might be able to paddle the boat to the north end of Mereshaven in about the same time, seeing as how they wouldn't be going as far at the Cut.

Well, thanks to fucking Rixizzix, they had to've been at it for more than two hours.

Dig, pull hard, recover, dig again…and yahh, do it now before it's too late: apologize to Lukan's Erseiyr because just maybe he *was* out there in the night and hadn't changed sides after all.

AND MAYBE IT worked…or maybe it was just reaching Mereshaven's rocky leeshore, but they were finally able to rest.

Falca could see two of the watchtowers Vaience had said were spaced around the perimeter of the island. Its bluff, though harder to discern, didn't seem to be as formidable as elsewhere in Milatum.

The torchlight that had appeared as bright pinpricks from Linnisheer now loomed large enough to cast shadows on the battlements of the watchtowers that were linked by Livy's Walk, that ring-road around the perimeter of Mereshaven above a low escarpment. Vaience had gone entirely around the island once with Rohaise, by way of the ring-road. She'd been the King's Own Gardener for only a month and eager to show her son the splendors of her new home-away-from-home, Vaience said. She also—a smile here—couldn't pass by a weed that needed pulling along the shoulder of the road's finely crushed marble.

Falca could see neither the road nor sentries on the nearest two watchtowers. There was another that seemed to be bigger than these, to the west of south-facing Coomion's Cove where the royal vessels were still berthed. He could make the two ships, possibly excursion barges from the huge size of the sterns which dwarfed that of a third ship, possibly a tresreme.

They stayed close to the sheltering shore as they passed the two towers. Sentries would be looking out at the moon-silvered Queensmere and not below—so Falca hoped, anyway. A few times Vaience had to use his paddle to fend the boat away from jagged boulders, one of them the size of the boat itself. Once they growled upon a submerged, shelving rock. Falca had to get out, sloshing in water up to his ankles to free the boat.

Slowly they moved northward. After a while came the dark, elevated strip of the narrow aqueduct that spanned the channel between Linnisvale and Mereshaven. Vaience earlier had said the aqueduct began in the foothills of the Skysheaves far to the west of Milatum, crossed the Kingsmere north of the city and diverted in Linnisvale; one branch then spanning the Queensmere channel to provide water for Mereshaven. He estimated it was about two hundred feet west of Colza's Bridge. Broad arches supported the aqueduct, its foundations rising from several islets in the channel.

Falca stopped paddling, as did Vaience moments later.

Here was another square watchtower where the aqueduct continued on to the interior of Mereshaven. The tower was higher than the others and seemingly built over the aqueduct itself. A few torches on the tower's near parapet provided enough illumination to cast a sheen on the water by the islet closest to Falca and Vaience, where they'd planned to observe the bridge and mark the route of their climb at its Mereshaven end.

From here they couldn't see where they had to go. But if they tarried too long at the islet, they risked a sentry spotting them; maybe not a big risk but they'd come too far, gotten this close, to chance it. Where there were torches, there'd be sentries.

Vaience turned to Falca, paddle in one hand, and pointed up at the tower, shaking his head—as if in apology for not remembering the aqueduct tower. Falca silently cursed the Skarrians for posting men up there. What, were they worried about Milats scurrying like rats along the aqueduct to swarm into Mereshaven, or poison the water?

Then he realized what he and Vaience could do. He pointed toward the islet, and fingered a circular motion. Vaience touched his forehead with the heel of his palm: *Of course....*

They paddled farther out into the channel, away from the watchtower, and had to put some muscle into their strokes—Falca could feel the funneling of the east-wind through the channel as well as the strong current. On the far side of this closest of the aqueduct's islets, he glimpsed the form of someone slumped against the bottom of the foundation arch. Three spits away he was, the close-cropped head tilted...as if curious why two men in a boat were here in the dead of night, when it didn't matter anymore.

Vaience leaned back, whispered: "A Labrysson."

Falca had heard of them...the royal guard...wore white tunics. Down here, this Labrysson's was gray, with darker splotches.

He'd probably been wounded in the battle for the bridge, fell off, got swept away, and with what little strength he had left, crawled out of the water to lean against the foundation stone for his final hours.

Falca and Vaience continued on past more bloated, stinking corpses floating in the water or snagged on rocks. Falca's paddle got snarled in the plaits of a Skarrian's. Vaience had to push away two more Labryssons with his.

They stopped near the end of the islet but had to occasionally paddle to recover their covert position given the funneling wind and current. Vaience turned again, said softly: "The middle tower of the bridge...it's closer toward Linnisvale than I remembered. More work for us."

"Maybe worse for them...after," Falca whispered back.

There was a faint glow of torchlight behind the middle tower of the bridge above, and the two at each end. But the three had mates on the far side of the bridge. So the torches were bracketed on the inward faces of the six. Falca couldn't see the gates at the bridge ends, but thanks to Vaience's map he saw them in his mind, the gates that had been added long after the Sixers built the bridge.

But what mattered was that at this hour the Skarrians would likely not be posted on the bridge side of the gates—and that patrols across the bridge would be infrequent.

So far...nothing. No moving torches.

Falca could barely discern the thick cables angling down from near the top of the middle bridge-tower to the anchor towers at the ends of the span. Yet even these seemed to be bigger than those of the two bridges he'd crossed after his arrival in Milatum, marveling at the woven road surfaces of each and the cables supporting them. Then again, Colza's Bridge, Vaience had said, was probably longer than Mago's that spanned the Cleave. Before, Falca hadn't noted the spacing of the thinner vertical cables that connected the top cables to the bridge road itself—why would he have at that point? But Vaience estimated the spacing at about the length of an arm for these strings, they were called.

Strings of a monumental lyre, fit for a god to play.

"She's playin' today, ain't she?" the vendor said, taking Falca's Myrcian coin for a cup of blige and a trencher of hoodle. A famished Falca had just crossed over the bridge into Linnismorn, and stopped at the first vendor's cart he'd come to. The breeze swirled away the smoke from the brazier and flapped the edges of the man's skimmer cap. Falca asked, "Who's playing what?" The vendor replied, "Why, it's Kyria playing the bridge—this one's Phodry's but she plays 'em all." And winked at Falca—obviously a northron—before he turned his attention to other customers....

Now, she was playing the strings of Colza's Bridge.

How many strings would have to be cut? At least half of them—both sides of the bridge, from Mereshaven to the middle tower. Vaience guessed they'd have to each cut perhaps...fifty. The spacing of the strings meant *time*, and once they were on the bridge there wouldn't have much of it. But more time on the bridge to cut more strings also meant a bigger chasm for the Skarrians to gape at later—if all went well.

It was hard to tell down here on the water—the aqueduct and the bridge blocked much of the moonlight—but Vaience seemed to have correctly remembered the steepness and height of the Mereshaven escarpment off to their right: the climb up to the end of the bridge didn't appear to be too daunting. Even so, it'dbe all fours going up.

They'd ruled out a climb up to the Linnisvale end of the bridge. Likely the Skarrians would post more sentries to guard the outer bridge gate from where any threat to Mereshaven would come.

They'd also ruled out getting up to the bridge from the middle tower and its foundation islet. Vaience thought he remembered—what he drew on the map—that its elevation was lower than Linnisvale's and Mereshaven's. So the bottom cables of the bridge road were set at their elevations, passing through the middle tower at a height a man couldn't possibly reach. Falca and Vaience could climb up to the top of the isle but they couldn't scale the tower.

So it had to be Mereshaven, climbing up the slope to where it met the bridge road. The Mereshaven bridge towers were set back, the upper and lower cables of the road passing through the upper elevation of the towers, presumably anchored deep within them though probably beyond, into the very guts of the island; no one knew.

Falca had the map in his mind now: given the positioning of the cables the bridge was wider than the road between the towers. The Mereshaven gate was near the end of the bridge road, where the Skarrian sentries would be on the other side of the solid gates. Two of them? Three? Maybe four if for some reason half the main gate needed to be opened. If not, opening the postern gate within the main to let someone through wouldn't require more than one of two sentries. How many would come charging out of the postern once they realized half the bridge was sinking into the channel? Didn't matter, did it. He and Vaience would be back on the boat by then.

If all went well.

Falca leaned forward, tapped Vaience's shoulder. He nodded but didn't turn around. They began paddling again and soon were deeper into the passage, moving as silently as smoke. The keening of Kyria playing the lyre of the bridge above masked the sound of their breathing and the splashes of their paddles in the black water.

THE BOAT SCRITCHED upon shoaling rock.

Vaience got out first. Falca handed him the Claws and the coiled clothesline rope they'd brought. Vaience carefully put those aside and steadied the boat for Falca to get out. They pulled the boat out and away from the water, up the scree but not too far, and didn't overturn the boat. If there was close pursuit afterwards, they needed to quickly slide the boat into the water.

They knelt by the Claws and rope, had to crane their necks to look up at the bridge. There came no shouts from the watchtower behind them, only the humming of the wind through the strings. Still no moving torches, no sentries. If some Skarrian was pissing through the strings, he wasn't doing it from the side of the bridge that mattered now. No faint sounds of footfalls, not that there would be; the bridge road was made of woven kraken-skin, not timber or stone.

They helped each other with the Claws, tightly wrapping two lengths of clotheslines around each other's backs, and knotting them. Vaience made sure his spectacles were tight, the kitchen knife he'd taken from the cottage secure at his belt. Falca did the same for his scabbard and falcata.

Falca took the lead as they began the climb. They had to crawl, careful not to dislodge a rock, send it tumbling down the slope to splash in the water. But he hadn't gone far when he did just that—a skid of his foot. Luckily the rock missed Vaience—at least he didn't cry out—and Falca heard only a faint splash.

They stopped twice to rest and listen for Skarrians above. Maybe there'd be no sentries posted on the bridge at this time of night but that didn't mean a couple wouldn't occasionally patrol the bridge, probably doing so from the Mereshaven end.

At the top of the rocky slope they crouched low, resting again, and then made their way over to the bridge road. The massive cable tower loomed high to their right, blocking most of the constellation of Kyria's Lyre.

Falca cursed silently. The bridge road seemed to be too high, a fact confirmed when he stood under it, raised his arm and couldn't touch the lower cable that presumably was spliced or braided into the road itself, however the Sixers had done it.

Shide, all right then….

He laced his fingers together so he could boost Vaience—who shook his head and formed his own basket: *Better I boost you up….*

Falca nodded. Maybe Vaience felt he had the strength for that but not for pulling the heavier Falca up onto the bridge. But would skinny Vaience have the muscle for the boost?

He did, even managing to lift a little, grunting, the hand-basket quivering, before Falca grabbed one of the strings and pulled himself up to the bridge road. He squeezed between two strings—a tight fit for someone his size—the scabbard snagging momentarily. He wiped his hands dry of sweat—hoping Vaience was doing the same now—and lay down on his belly, long arms reaching down to clasp Vaience's hands and slowly, straining hard, pulled him up as he rose to his knees. Only when Vaience was on his own, an arm wrapped around a string, did he let go. Vaience stepped through with more room to spare than Falca had.

They scuttled to the nearby tower and rested where the taut lower cable disappeared into the stone. When their breathing had quieted they freed the Claws with Vaience's knife. Falca balled up the clothesline and hid it close to the wall, under the cable.

He took the lead again, moving toward the far corner of this anchor tower, Claw in his left hand, his right sliding along the tower wall. Whatever the depth of its immense stone blocks, the seams between them were so tight he could hardly feel them: the mazer Sixers weren't just cutters and weavers of kraken-skin.

At the corner now, Vaience kneeling behind him, Falca listened for… anything…anyone in the passage, the short avenue of crushed dawnstone that led to the Triskell Gate. There was no sentry in the shadows directly across the avenue or by the other anchor tower. The passage between the towers was narrower than the bridge road itself, off to Falca's left. At this hour, there'd be no Skarries peering through the arrow loops in the walls linking the anchor towers to the facing wall of the Triskell Gate.

Falca peeked around the corner.

Nor was there a sentry posted at the end of the passage, only the faintest glow of torches above the other side of the gate—and that of Colza's statue beyond, rising over the level of the colonnade roof. Vaience had remembered correctly, too, about the gate's height: roughly twenty feet. And also about Skarrian looting: the gold triskells at the top of each gate-half—symbols of the House of Keshkev—were gone. All that remained were the jagged settings.

Again: how many sentries on the other side of the solid bronze gate? Call it…*six*..at most. So soon after, maybe four chasing them down to the boat, and one staying at the postern and another running to alert others…at the Ephoria barracks? But with luck…the Skarries wouldn't see them. Stunned, they might not even think to look for men in the night. How could *men* dun the bridge?

Only one way to find out….

Falca turned to Vaience, nodded, made a cutting motion with his Claw.

Nothing needed to be said now. He was to take the east side of the bridge, Vaience the west. Each would stay as close to the strings as possible, the better to shield their run to the middle tower where they'd begin and work their way back toward Mereshaven, where hopefully they could cut the lower, thicker cables of the bridge. And then hurry down to the boat for the escape.

Now they had to cut one of the strings to see if these vertical cables *could* be severed. The strings—leastways those he'd grabbed—were a little smaller around than the grip of his falcata. But how long would it take to cut one with the Claw? The longer that took—

Falca heard a raspy, sliding sound off to his right.

A shaft of torchlight appeared in the passage.

He and Vaience scurried back along the tower wall, spun around the corner.

The gate sentries couldn't have heard them, not through all that bronze. No one on the watchtower could have seen them here; maybe before…the boat. But there'd have been shouts then.

A patrol…they'll only walk the bridge, come back, close the postern again….

But Falca had to be sure it was only a patrol doing just that.

He risked a look around the corner.

There were two of them, one holding the torch to his side, the flames brazen in the wind. The other dragged a woman by a rope tied around her ankles. They passed close to where Falca and Vaience had been, continued on, the woman's naked body sliding over the seam where the bridge road merged with the stone at the end of the passage. The Skarrian dragging the woman was complaining about how the "ganchy Capes" just dumped her at the gate. "Like it's *our* job to get rid of their meat."

They didn't go far before the Skarrie with the rope slid her between two strings.

Falca heard a faint splash over the humming of the strings. He ducked back, as the soldiers began talking again:

"I had this same one two days ago, before the Capes took her from us. Could have been *mine* the slorrie draff sliced half-off."

"Which glipe lost it?"

"What does it matter, Gashkie? He's a Four-eye, they said—like *that* make's losing his bolt somehow worse."

"But how'd she sneak a blade into the Capes' barracks?"

"T'wasn't—didn't you hear when the two of 'em brought her over? Shard of glass. Hid it in her mouth."

Almost as quickly as it flared in Falca, the urge left him to kill these two. He looked at Vaience, who was shaking his head. *Can't.* ...The Skarrians had left the postern open and likely there was another sentry on the other side. Even if Falca could silently kill these two, another sentry would soon wonder what was taking them so long to get rid of the Milat woman.

When the postern closed, darkening the passage, he and Vaience crept back to where they'd been, then walked onto the bridge, Falca still thinking about the woman, but he had to get what happened out of his mind.

They separated, Vaience darting to the west side of the bridge where the Skarrians had dumped the woman, and Falca to the east. He walked quickly, no sound to his footfalls on the kraken-skin surface of the bridge. He was almost halfway to the middle tower when he stopped, gripping a thrumming string.

He'd forgotten—Vaience, too—about what they'd planned: cutting one of the strings back there to see if it could be cut and how long it would take.

No point doing that now.

He hurried on. The wind seemed to be stronger, playing the strings louder.

If a patrol was sent out now from either gate, he and Vaience would be trapped. He looked all around—and up, even though he knew the bridge tower ahead wasn't the kind of tower that had a parapet and a sentry posted on it. The watchtower? Too far away now for a Skarrie there to see them easily through the strings—at least until they got to the mid-channel tower where two torches were set in brackets on the inner wall, the flames dancing in the wind. All was dark beyond the pale of that light; darkness all the way to the Linnisvale end of the bridge and a nimbus of torchlight above the gate.

Vaience was already at the south corner of the tower, the torches fringing him with light.

They were supposed to signal each other at this point, begin the cutting together. Vaience waved his Claw; Falca his.

He'd have to backhand the cuts, unlike Vaience.

Falca wrapped his hand around the closest string, feeling the tight braiding. He pulled. It didn't move. The cable-string couldn't have been much tauter a thousand years ago.

Cut or swing? Or saw through something that no steel could cut nor fire burn, that was scarcely thicker than the shaft of Lannid Hoster's strutter?

Would there be a popping sound? A snap-back from the tension?

He shielded his eyes with a forearm, pressed the Claw against the string.

It might have been a stem of Rohaise Loquin's fireheart for all the effort it took Falca to cut the kraken-skin cable.

Maybe there'd been a sound but he couldn't hear it above the song Kyria was playing, the bridge her lyre. Nor did Falca hear the longer length of the cut string slapping hard against his elbow, but he felt the sting of it before the wind swirled the cable away.

He cut another…and another.

He quickly moved on: one backhand slice after another, a trembling beneath his feet now.

A glance across the bridge: Vaience a shadow, a moving shadow in the moonlight. He wouldn't have forgotten the crucial thing: it would be a race to keep ahead of the bridge—this half of the bridge—as it slowly gave way in their wake.

The Linnisvale gate was still dark.

So was the one that mattered now: the Triskell Gate.

He soon had the rhythm for this harvesting and quickened his pace.

The torches on the middle tower revealed the shadow of the slowly deepening vale in the bridge road, the ever-fainter illumination catching the swirling strings Falca and Vaience had cut, though they still remained attached to the top cables.

Even if the Linnisvale gate suddenly opened and sentries appeared, the middle tower was as far as they would get, though they could still shout the alarm for those at the Triskell Gate.

But both gates were still closed. What could anyone have heard? Nothing, except maybe a puzzling diminishing of the keening of Colza's Bridge.

Falca kept slashing at the strings with the Claw. He was sweating now. With each stroke he shielded his eyes. Wild strings slapped his arm, shoulder, snaking over the top of his head.

Halfway there...no, more than that.

When would the Skarries hear it?—the *absence* of the sound that had always been there?

The strings proved ever easier to cut. Fewer and fewer to bear the weight of the sagging road, so more tension. It seemed he had to do little more now than touch a string to sever it. Would the remaining ones snap before he and Vaience got back, beyond the road?

He was running now to outrun the sagging.

And there was Vaience, running, too....

In the dark, the towers blocking most of the Sisters' light, it was hard to tell who first reached the corner of their respective towers.

We did it! You grinning now, my friend? I hope you fucking are....

The passage ahead leading to the Triskell Gate was still dark.

It wouldn't be when the bridge fully collapsed.

They weren't done yet.

The sagging bridge, half of it, was still being held up by the two lower cables, one on each side, to which the strings had been attached; what had probably kept the bridge road from routinely swaying.

The drooping lower cable that disappeared into the tower was much thicker than the vertical strings. He expected to have to saw at it with the Claw...but it parted as easily as meat sliced from a roast.

The kraken-skin cable slithered away, unleashed from the ages.

As Falca's side of the bridge fell, it was caught by the east wind, a sail now that swept down the slope under the end of the road, taking more rocks with it into the water. Vaience's side sheared away, twisting in the wind, the cable writhing, scouring more rocks into the seething channel.

For a stricken moment, Falca thought Vaience had been swept away from the other side of the passage—*no, there he is!* Waiting for him. Falca waved a hand—"*Go!…GO!*"—then bolted after him…as the postern gate opened.

Falca ran along the northern wall of the anchor tower, leaping over the cable Vaience had cut. He couldn't see him below or hear his scrabbling descent over the shouting of the Skarrians in the gate passage. They couldn't have seen him; he'd gotten across the passage, the entryway to the Triskell Gate before the first of them rushed out. They wouldn't immediately link the fall of the bridge to men in the night. There'd be enough time to escape in the boat and so what if they *did* see the boat, or hear the splashes of frantic paddling? They weren't going to swim after. Still, better not to be seen or heard. *So when we're in the boat—*

Falca took it too fast.

He slipped, his feet skidding out from under him on the scree of the slope…lost his balance and tumbled, the Claw flying from his hand. He heard the splash below, a moment before his right shoulder slammed into an outcrop of rock, his head hitting another….

The next thing he heard was Vaience whispering at his side.

"Falca! We have to go! It's gone. Come *on*, quickly!"

His right shoulder throbbed. He had to use his left arm to push himself up to his knees. His head felt like a bucket of sand, someone beating it with sledgehammer.

"Ahh…all right…but they—"

"No time, we have to go—*now!*"

"Give me a—where's the boat?"

"It's gone. The bridge swept it away."

CHAPTER THIRTY-FOUR:

ROH'S BOOTS

T HERE WAS NO strand, only a pittance of spliny shore splotched with moonlight and the shadows of rocks, some so large Falca and Vaience couldn't clamber over them, had to wade into the shallows to get around. High overhead the aqueduct slashed across the Anvil and the Cauldron; the adjacent tower on its far side blocking out the smaller Sister, Suaila.

They hadn't gone far when a Skarrian war-trumpet sounded—*ko-wahh*... *ko-wahh*...*ko-wahh*—the alarm echoing from the gate area.

Falca could only hope the trumpet's braying had diverted the attention of any sentry on the tower's ramparts; if he'd looked down he would have seen moving shadows.

Falca kept the falcata in its scabbard; hadn't lost that, anyway, in the tumble. He needed his good left arm to brace himself against the slippery rocks as he followed Vaience. The dizziness had subsided and with a clearer head came the realization that even if no Skarries had seen him they wouldn't be gaping at the collapsed bridge for long. Gathering torches would reveal the severed strings writhing in the wind, and the cut, bitter ends of the bigger, lower cables. The Skarries would know someone, *somehow* had done that—and couldn't be too far away.

He didn't hear shouts or splashes behind him, but sure as his duffed right shoulder the scuts would be coming after. Many of them would be searching along Mereshaven's northern shore, but some would also be coming *this* way, around to the west and then south. There was no escape now, only keeping on…and then making a stand. He was good with his left hand, so he'd make ruck of it before they overwhelmed him and Vaience and—

Falca slipped on a rock, fell into the warm Queensmere water, but Vaience turned at the splash, stretched out a hand, tightly clasping Falca's left, and pulled him out.

And on they went; Falca dripping, chasers squelching, right shoulder throbbing; his scabbard and the Claw in Vaience's hand ticking and skeering against a rock jutting here, another there; and still no sound of pursuit, only the strains of their own breathing and the lapping of water against the dark, tumbled shore which fractured the Sisters' ribbons glistening upon the Queensmere.

VAIENCE THEN FALCA squeezed past the inner face of a rocky outcrop that leaned into the shallows. They needed to rest, and hunkered down behind the boulder. Falca massaged his shoulder as he looked past the rising end of the crag that pointed out over the Queensmere to the south and Linnisheer, as if the answer was obvious: *You think you're trapped but there's your skelter-way—all you have to do is swim….*

Vaience pushed up his spectacles. "How is it?"

"Better." Falca raised his arm to the level of his chin before pain flared. "Could be worse—we should be dead by now."

"Maybe they didn't see the boat out in the channel, wherever it wound up; made them think we escaped."

"Yahh, who stays close to the pocket after its picked? For all they know maybe we're off to pick another one."

"Would that we were—you know there's no point in going farther, not with all those torches up ahead at the cove."

Falca scuffed a stone into the water. "Shide, didn't think it through, Vaience."

"Neither did I."

"Too late now but we should have realized they wouldn't be trapped, not with those ships there. The fucking barges and the tresreme are their way out. They'll take as many men as they figure they'll need to get to the Linnises, help crush any risings. They'll do it because they can't know there *won't* be any. They weren't the only ones woken up by that rouser trumpet."

"Yare, by dawn there'll be a lot of people in Scunder Square. Word will spread fast from there, one way or the other. But whatever happens after that… we did it, Falca." He grinned. "We picked it clean, didn't we?"

Falca bounced his left fist off Vaience's knee: "We surely did, my friend."

There was no point in adding what Vaience must also know: that it was likely all for naught.

"Now we gotta find a way to get off this rock—any ideas?"

"Besides stealing a 300-foot barge or a sixy-oar tresreme?—and while we're at it, setting the others adrift?"

"Wouldn't *that* be a pocket to pick."

"Falca, I wasn't—"

"But you're heading in the right direction, seeing as how we don't have any other—unless you can swim, which I can't. We can't go back the way we came. But…what if we wait until they get on those ships—which they will, right? They don't want to be trapped here. So this Vulsa…if you were him, would you give the order?"

"I'd already have done that."

"So would I. A show of force where it might be needed, and surely retaliation for what happened."

"Both of which can't be done here," Vaience said.

"There's the throw. But at the very *least* you're moving a few thousand of your men to where they can be more easily supplied in the days and weeks to come. Now…there'll still be sentries over there but less of 'em with the ships gone. So why don't we go over to that cove tonight, see if there's something we can use to get to Linnishill or Linnisvale—Roak's balls, *anything* that floats could even get us back to Linnisheer."

"But they might *not* leave tonight, what's left of it."

"Tomorrow night, then; or the next.

"That means staying here for a day or two—out in the open."

"Then we go *up* this bluff while we still have the dark, find somewhere to hide during the day."

"There's a lot of them up there, Falca."

"Which most of 'em are either on the north side of the island, gawking at a floating pile of kraken-skin, or waiting for the dawn to get on those ships at the cove. There has to be somewhere we can hole up…it's all we can do now—what's the grin for?"

"I know where the *somewhere* is."

It took Falca a moment; then he grinned too. "But it could be—"

"In which case we'll have to find another burrow for the night. Or maybe not—they have the entire island—the citadel, all three Labrysson barracks, the Ephoria. Why would they garrison the cottage of the King's Own Gardener with only two or three men?"

○

"...BUT THERE'S NO sense in putting you in harm's way," First Blade Scylux Kullerioc was saying. The torchlight behind him brightened the edges of his dark plaited hair; they all didn't have the yellow. "You'll be staying here until we return. Given what has happened, I think it best to post another guard outside."

Lambrey Tallon leaned over the table, fists clenched. He closed his eyes momentarily. Maybe he was still asleep, hadn't been woken by the blast of the war-trumpet, was dreaming all of it: the guard coming in with the torch, then Kullerioc with the news that had turned everything to soft turds.

Another soldier barged past the one behind Kullerioc who stood on the other side of the table.

"Why is another—" Tallon began.

The Skarrian officer held up his hand, cutting him off, and leaned over to hear the soldier's whisper, then nodded. "Tell Karl Genazeret I shall be there shortly." The soldier saluted and left.

"You were saying, Comitor?"

"I was about to ask you why I'm considered even more of a prisoner."

"The Priaptor does not regard you as a prisoner."

"*Three* guards now?"

"A precaution. While the plans for Scaldasaig must obviously be delayed indefinitely, you remain of significant value to the Priaptor."

"That doesn't answer my question."

Kullerioc turned to the soldier behind him: "Leave us. And close the door."

The First Blade heaved a sigh in the darkened chamber. "You remain insufferable, Comitor Tallon. You seem to think that what has occurred tonight is but a mere affront to *you*. It took us an hour to find two soldiers who could swim across the channel and tell our men on the other side to send runners to inform the Priaptor who is, as I said, in Linnisheer—fortunately or regrettably. You should be—"

"You said precaution—where's the need for *precaution*? You're expecting a thousand Milats to swim across to—"

"Are you as willfully forgetful as you are arrogant and rude? I thought I was clear on this before: there were few—besides the Priaptor and myself— who saw your value and still do. As I was leaving to come here, Karl Genazeret's attending purisee mentioned the suspicious coincidence of your recent arrival with what has happ—"

"*Coincidence?* What has one to do with the—"

"I'll accept your thanks now, Comitor, for pointing out to the karl's *Four-eye* purisee the absurdity of suspecting a link between the two events. Blessed Tholos always reveals the truth, which was confirmed by the fact that you were here where you should be when I arrived. Your complicity in what happened tonight is as likely as an Erseiyr's, which—"

"What? An *Erseiyr?*"

"Some of our men said they saw the beast flying across the moons two nights ago; that's the rumor in the ranks: that only an Erseiyr could have swept away over half of the bridge. And to some of my superiors—and purisees—a Lucidorian Warden who's a traitor to his king is as rare a sighting as an Erseiyr. Have you ever seen one?"

"No." *A fucking Erseiyr?—these Skarrians are as loonzie as Cassenites....*

"Neither have I, though unfortunately many of our grandfathers did, at Castlecliff—including the Priaptor's who commanded the army that invaded Myrcia, was on the verge of taking Castlecliff...and then an Erseiyr swept a third of his men from the walls of the city, and scattered the rest."

"Arse-hairs. I'm sorry, First Blade Kullerioc, but from what I know about it, the attack was made at night, during a severe storm. Naturally—typically for them—the Myrcians attributed divine intervention for their victory, and just as inevitably your Skarrians claimed the same to excuse their failure."

"It was a long time ago, but that, of course, only gives legend and belief more time to sweep away the facts of the matter which, in this case, *do* include survivors' accounts of siege engines being toppled and swept away like so much chaff. It must have been quite a tempest that night.

"But we still have ours to deal with—including the fact that, yes, it is foolishness to believe an Erseiyr was responsible for what happened *tonight.*

Why, its wings alone would have spanned the entire bridge. The sentries at the gate evidently thought it could only have been an Erseiyr but they were executed anyway for their failure to see or hear anything prior to the collapse of the bridge."

Kullerioc paused at the door. "The additional guard is necessary, Comitor. As for the *other* tempest, no one has seen this woman of yours who was supposed to have arrived in Tholosia by now. A pity. From what you said earlier, I would have enjoyed my turn with her—after yours, of course. Perhaps she may yet show up."

Moonlight reclaimed the room after First Blade Kullerioc left. He must have muttered something to a guard outside because Tallon heard laughter.

Wankspit...stuff your plaits up your arsehole. Loonzie scuts, all of 'em....

He pounded the table with a fist, his drinking cup clinking against the ewer. He swept both from the table, water splashing his hand, the vessels crashing against a wall. Two strides to the window...and he felt like smashing that, too. He took deep breaths, hands spread out on the sill, pushing against it, as if he could dun this tower chamber like the fucking bridge.

First Scaldasaig...and now this....

And where *was* the quiv? She should have gotten here by now. He wasn't wrong about her intentions; there was no other possible explanation for why she'd been in Keshkevar, travelling south.

Perhaps she may yet show up—the prissjack saying it like he was talking about another sighting of the Erseiyr.

If...*when* she did, he'd have to be satisfied with making her pay the price for what she'd done—betraying him at Scaldasaig, spreading her legs for Breks— and by the time he got done with *her*, Kullerioc might as well fuck a mattress.

Scaldasiag *delayed indefinitely...*

That meant months. Maybe even a year.

Vulsa would have other things on his mind, such as finding the ones whose magic—whatever it was—had brought down a bridge that had been there when Colza was still sucking at Cassena's tit. Even on the streets of Draica, Tallon had heard of Milatum's fabled bridges. Tonight's disaster wasn't merely the ambush of a Skarrian patrol. *Tonight* could have serious consequences, trapping thousands of soldiers on Mereshaven—at least until this Genazeret got them off.

Vulsa wouldn't believe the rot about the Erseiyr. The Milats who'd somehow halved the bridge had come by boat—how else?—and they'd escaped the same way, were surely still in the city. Vulsa would double the postings on the other bridges so they couldn't do it again. Hunting them down could take weeks or months in a city of Milatum's size. And the rebuilding of the bridge would take more time. Over half of it was in the water, Kullerioc said. An entire new span would be needed—and how do you join stone or timber to what was left? Something you have no idea what it is.

And there was the visit by the Tholarsh in a few months, the High Priest of Tholos or whatever the fuck he was, coming all the way from Skarria to consecrate the victory. Tallon—and Vulsa—could have given him the gift of Scaldasaig too, not just Milatum. But now, Vulsa's ambitions might have soured—never mind what Kullerioc said: the Priaptor still probably didn't even know yet what had happened.

Tallon cleared his throat and spit, not caring where the gobbet landed.

So while he was stuck here, Breks would be recruiting Rough Bounds outlaws to garrison Scaldasasig, and adding to his personal bodyguard of Timberlimbs.

And Shar Stakeen?

He couldn't get it out of his mind why she hadn't showed. Did she change her mind? or was it something else? A woman like that—Feccan's killer—anything was possible. She was *all* of what you saw—swallow's dew, yes—and *some* of who she'd *said* she was…which had to be the *half* of who she *really* was.

Riding away from that town had she figured—correctly—that Tallon would pursue her to Milatum, and so turned those blackpool eyes north to Castlecliff, the Sanctor there? Maybe a better bet after all, seeing as how she was Myrcian. Not so for Tallon, a Lucidorian and hated Warden, had he gone there to sell Scaldasaig.

He felt trapped here—the River Rhys prison hulk again—with nothing to do except seeing in his mind again Falca Breks and Shar Stakeen together on that tower rampart of Scaldasaig, the fortress Breks' now and not Culldred's and his favorite Warden officer's who would surely have led the first campaign into Myrcia to carve off the first meat of a Seventh Kingdom.

He rubbed his lips which, even after all these years, still tingled when his blood was up—all that rife smuggled into the River Rhys prison hulk.

Tallon wanted to bolt out of this room, kill the guards, escape from this prison cell—that's what it was—and hunt down Shar Stakeen before it was too late, before she got to Castlecliff.

He had nothing left—except peddling Scaldasaig to someone else.

But breaking out of here would only confirm the loonzie suspicion that he had something to do with…tonight. And there was no way off Mereshaven now except at the cove, by early morning the ships crammed with soldiers who'd be useless here so get 'em where they might be needed. Even if he could somehow sneak aboard one of them, what then? The city gates would be sealed, at least for a while. He'd still be trapped, and there would be one more to be hunted down for what he'd done tonight.

She was far away that night, beyond the Shelter Isles, seeking kraken that rose close to the deep water's surface to feed. She would be able to see the riffles and sense the krakens' heat, so different from the heat of the sun or the thermals above cities. Basking her wings in that peculiar heat was a pleasure for her, as it had been recently. She knew the source of that heat, but unlike her mate—who would soon be flying south to join her—humans held no particular interest for her, certainly not as sustenance. There were many of them—hence their collective heat and that which they otherwise produced, like fire—but individually not worth even the minimal effort of hunting; in all the ages they never had been. Always they were but specks upon the land and at night only the tiniest of shadows; at the remove of distance and indifference, nothing more than that.

But shadows also breathe and have names, and that night two of the many on Mereshaven lay on their bellies at the top of the bluff that was not as steep as the other they'd climbed earlier. One of the shadows had the worst of the climb for he was hurt, though not badly. The other knew the way; it was his time to lead, though neither had said as much.

They waited, hidden in high grass, for the stalker and its rider to pass on the ring-road. There was no question of taking the same direction though that was the shorter route to their destination. To do so they would have to pass two watchtowers farther down the road, and then one at the cove. Already the stalker-rider had stopped at the first of the towers to give his message to sentries shadowed by torchlight, and to more shadows at the cove.

They crossed the ring-road, their shoes crunching on its ribbon of crushed white marble that showed gray in the moonlight. They hurried across a meadow and up a shallow slope to the loggia that formed the outer wall and walkway encircling Cauldron's End, the royal tombs. Within, the dome of the mausoleum gleamed with spiraling inlays of dawnstone that gave the impression that the dome was rising to the heavens.

They didn't think there would be sentries posted at the entrance of Cauldron's End— why guard what had already been looted? Still, they moved cautiously around the loggia.

The processional that linked the tombs with Kelef's Way was empty, and tempted them to take it. The avenue was farther away from the Kelefion—the citadel—and a quicker way to their destination. But there was no cover. And once they got closer to Kelef's Way—which passed through the royal gardens, linking the citadel and its promenade to the cove—they could be seen.

There would be cover in the sundered garden parterres. These were closer to the Kelefion, but unlike what they saw in the high windows, ramparts and gate towers of the looming citadel, there were no flaring torches or signs of soldiers bivouacked among the parterres and now alerted to the night's emergency.

The nearest encampment seemed to be to the west of the Wovens—and a large one, given the glow of torches, evidence the soldiers had received orders to move out. There would be more encampments to the north, nearer the fallen bridge, in addition to the Labrysson barracks, the Ephoria and the citadel itself.

Still, they had to get through the darkened, ruined gardens before all the soldiers began moving south to the cove along the ring-road and Kelef's Way.

But there was no cover in the gardens either, other than what might hide the shadows of crawling men, and they couldn't crawl the rest of the way. The parterres had been obliterated in the assault upon the citadel, and what little remained of sunsbreath, staghorn, harlequin roses and snowdrop; of meadowbride, tryony and blush-my-lady; of allyssum, mare's-tail and fireheart; of sylphium, yellowsark and winking jesper…had withered from lack of watering and so too their scents.

Yet there was a way through: the stream that began at the pool and cascade at the end of the aqueduct and meandered on through the garden.

The two shadows slid over its banks and into the stream and began to wade through the waist-high water, pushing aside debris.

As they neared the wide, shallow arch of the stone footbridge that spanned the stream they heard the approach of tramping boots on the promenade bricks: soldiers coming from the Kelefion's south gate.

The two waded quickly ahead and hid under the bridge and waited for the soldiers to pass overhead; at least ten of them from the sound of their footfalls. Torchlight shone on the stream at either end of the arching refuge. But before it faded, the one who'd led the other this far remembered the walk he'd taken with his mother through the gardens that were her responsibility, strolling along the path adjacent to the winding stream. Mother and son had stopped where the path intersected with Kelef's Way, very near this same bridge with its triskell keystones, and enjoyed a beverage served by a royal householder, and chilled from a block of ice the size of a bathing tub. They had no other flavor to choose from except honey, that being the favorite of the king.

Now the shadows cautiously emerged from underneath the bridge and hurried on, as quickly as is possible wading through water. The stream wound through the last of the east gardens but they had to leave it at a footbridge smaller and lower than the other.

They were very tired, and their trews were drenched, dripping water, and so they didn't move quickly along the path by the stream that continued on to a silvery, oval pool as large as a pond, that supplied water to the royal isle's tilling fields and vineyards and livestock byres and all who had worked here until recently, their common labor and mundane dwellings hidden from view of the once-royal gardens and all but the parapets of the Kelefion by copses of trees to the north and south of the pool.

The shadows moved around the pool, closer now...almost there. The Sisters' light notwithstanding, all was dark except for a single torch on a watchtower by the ring-road that ran past a row of dwellings behind a single, bigger white-washed cottage....

THEY CROUCHED BY a hand-cranked water-screw used to lift water from the pond and into the nearby spigot-wagon—the Skarrians had probably butchered and eaten the horse that pulled it. The wagon-tongue was the only thing now between Falca and Vaience and the cottage.

Rohaise Loquin's working home had a pitched roof, and two dormers. Flower boxes rested on windowsills. The door was partially opened—maybe a good sign, maybe not.

They crept around the spigot-wagon, knelt by a rear wheel, close enough to see a pair of boots off to the side of the door. Moonlight revealed a bronze plate, set in the lintel and embossed with the royal triskell. Vaience got up and Falca winced pulling him back; he had the falcata in his left hand. Vaience pointed at the boots, then his chest. *They're hers....*

Falca held up his right hand. *And maybe they're a Skarrie's...Wait....*

Rohaise certainly wasn't in there, and they couldn't know for sure if a few Skarries weren't.

Throw a boot, see what happens....

It was all Falca could think of, short of going in without knowing—and that wasn't a good idea. He went ahead. Vaience, Claw in hand, didn't wait, was behind him when Falca saw that the boots were not a man's size. But he underhanded one into the cottage anyway, heard two thumps...and nothing more.

They went inside.

The Skarrians had ransacked the cottage of the King's Own Gardener.

There was no point in climbing the stairs to check above: if there were no Skarrians on the first floor, there'd be none on the second. A cupboard had been pulled away from a wall, chest drawers pulled out, contents dumped. The looters had overturned the mattress in Rohaise's bedchamber and the dining table, two of the four chairs tossed to a corner. "As if the whoresons couldn't see there's nothing underneath," Vaience muttered. "Scuts…wankspits."

Weary though he was, Falca had to smile: he couldn't have said it any better.

He wasn't thirsty; they'd scooped up mouthfuls of water from the pond. Hadn't tasted good but it wasn't foul. Maybe tomorrow see if there was any food left in the cottage.

They kept the door open—better to leave it as they found it. Each cleared a space on the flagged floor to lie down. Dropped wet trews over the chairs.

Falca's right shoulder still ached but he expected he wouldn't have a problem crossing over.

He did, as usual.

Too exhausted? Sometimes that's how it was.

For a long time he stared at the boot he'd tossed in. It had hit the overturned table now squarely in the shaft of moonlight coming in the doorway. Vaience was asleep. A good thing he didn't snore, nor did Falca; at least Amala and others had never told him he did. But maybe he did and wouldn't *that* amuse the High Fates at the Loom Eternal: letting the crouch-alley from Draica have the rest of a night he'd never forget—and then make sure a Skarrian passing by the cottage in the morning heard the snoring within.

Maybe he *should* close the door after all.

But Falca didn't think they'd be coming this way from the Labrysson barracks and also probably the encampment on the adjacent training ground. Vaience said Rohaise had pointed out the barracks and the gyrus on their walk around Mereshaven, took them two hours he said. So plenty of them up there—he and Vaience had seen the torch-glow in the distance when they'd gotten out of the stream. But the bridge that crossed it there was small, the woods and pond blocking that way—nahh, the Skarries would take the ring-road to get to the cove.

So it could work, the plan—assuming the garrison troops here, most of 'em, would be leaving.

They will, he told himself again. Why stay *here*, when you're gonna be needed *there*?

Tomorrow night then or the following, he and Vaience would make their way down to the southern-most woods bordering the fields. And from there they could observe what was going on at the cove and then…find something to get them off the island.

But right now he had to put the boot back where it belonged.

Which he did, mating it with the other one outside.

Much better; just as Rohaise Loquin left them after a day's work in the gardens…before everything changed, for everyone.

He kept the door open.

By the time he finally fell asleep, dawn was breaking.

CHAPTER THIRTY-FIVE:

SPIT IN THE CAULDRON

THE SMELL OF smoke had awakened Lambrey Tallon, but the chamber pot saved his life.

He had the bucket in his hands, was about to heave his morning piss out the window…when the door to the room burst open, a Skarrian's yellow plaits swinging as he lifted the axe for a strike, another Skarrian behind him.

Tallon flung the swill—most of yesterday's, too—into the soldier's face. He pawed his eyes, giving Tallon time to swing the bucket at his right wrist. The Skarrian grunted, dropped the axe, bent over to get it, one hand swiping his eyes. Tallon kneed him in the jaw, shoved him back, the soldier behind stumbling against the table. He grabbed two fistfuls of plaits and whirled, sending the first Skarrian crashing into the window. The second had a short-sword, tried to go around the table. Tallon pushed it hard, trapping him against the door, which slammed shut on a third Skarrian.

Short-sword wasn't a soldier, hadn't the stalker-shell breastplate. Skimmed hair, a string of balls dangling from his neck: a purisee. Tallon ducked as the priest scythed over the table, snatched the axe from the floor. The table scraped as the purisee tried to get around but Tallon was quicker, shoved it against him, the priest's second swing narrowly missing his fingers. Before he could recover and strike again, Tallon leaped onto the table, knees jabbing into the belly, and struck the right shoulder with the flat of the axe, and again before the purisee dropped the sword, which skidded off the table. Tallon slid his hand up the axe shaft, pressed the blade against the throat.

Hard, heaving breaths: "Who...sent you?"

"They're dead."

"What? Who's—"

"All who went...with the ships. *You* killed them."

The table shuddered: the third Skarrian ramming the door, trying to get in.

"You...wanted Tholosia all along...the other place...a lie. Before you send me to the Purest Embrace...how did you do it? Are you a Thread?"

"Whatever the fuck a a Thread is...tell your Tholos the Erseiyr did it for me."

Tallon slit the throat, got off him, yanked back the table, pulled the priest away by the cord around his neck. The balls were stalker eyes, he remembered. He ripped free the cord as the third Skarrian barged in with his own axe, pushing at the table. Tallon threw the eyes to distract him and one-handed the axe into the groin, nicking the bottom edge of the stalker-shell breastplate. He jerked out the axe as the soldier fell, and finished him off at the neck.

So stupid....

A Warden wouldn't have come in leading with his weapon, especially an axe; would've kept it back, ready to strike. And the plaits. Vain idiots. Only something to grab, you're in close. And when you're dead, something for your killer to use to pull you out of the way, which was when Tallon heard breaking glass—the first Skarrian slowly backing out of the shattered window, twisted seams of the diamond panes snagging plaits smeared with blood from his face and neck.

Tallon thought he'd sent him crashing all the way through, not that he'd had the time to make sure. He did now with no more effort than tipping a wheelbarrow...and saw that he might not have face the consequences for killing three Skarrians.

The windows of the tower chamber faced the west. Not far away from the two monumental figures was evidence the priest might not have been talking nonsense.

The *shushing* of water from the cascading terminus of the aqueduct was much fainter than the roar of the other waterfall and ledges far away in the Rough Bounds where he'd left Breks—so he assumed—as dead as his golden-haired woman. These were man-made ledges that stepped down from on high, the water glistening through wisps of smoke in a pool that branched off toward the citadel and again to a meandering stream.

At least fifty Skarrians clotted the pool, and almost as many were climbing up the narrow ledges through the succession of cascades. Tallon leaned over the windowsill, careful about the remaining jags of glass, to get a better look.

There had to be another fifty Skarrians atop the aqueduct itself, splashing through the channel.

More distantly, one of them fell from where where the northern run of the aqueduct approached a tower. And beyond the statues that faced the west, more smoke drifted across the Queensmere.

They're dead...all who went with the ships....

These Skarrians then—the last of the few hundred left behind on Mereshaven?—were trying to escape the only way they could, by way of the aqueduct that crossed over the northern channel near the useless bridge the loonzie priest thought he'd wrecked.

How did you do it....

Lambrey Tallon quickly turned away from the window, found his boots, laced them with bloody fingers, grabbed the short-sword and the axe.

There was only one place to find out what had happened, see how bad it was.

⬡

"THEY DID IT after all. Spit in the Cauldron."

Falca didn't smile after he said it; nor did Vaience, standing next to him on the half-drum watchtower.

There were too many dead and dying out there, and some of them Milats.

The Queensmere, rimmed by the cropped hills of the Linnises, seemed to Falca nothing if not a vast, smoking cauldron.

The night before he'd asked why the royal tombs were called Cauldron's End. Vaience said that after the death of a king or queen the Cauldron—Roak's gift to his son, Colza—was taken from Labrys Hall in the Kelefion to Scunder Square for one day, so that people could pay their respects in passing, tossing into the Cauldron whatever gift they wished, valuable or not.

And if the monarch had not been esteemed or beloved?

People could spit into the Cauldron or toss in dung. For that *one* day only you could deposit a fistful of offal or trash scooped from a gullyman's cart without fear of repercussion by a merser or Labrysson. Then the Cauldron was brought to Cauldron's End and emptied in the royal's tomb, though of course *foul* contents were emptied elsewhere. After the Cauldron was cleaned and returned to its customary place by the thrones in Labrys Hall, it served as a reminder to the new monarch that he always had a choice of legacies....

They'd missed it all, sleeping through the morning, oblivious to the tramping of Skarrian boots along the ring-road—Roak only knew how many passed by: maybe a thousand men from the Labrysson barracks and gyrus encampment alone, never mind soldiers from those encampments west of the citadel; all of them tramping to the barges and tresreme berthed at Coomion's Cove.

Vaience woke first, roused Falca. They cautiously went outside. The smoke seemed to be drifting in from the south. All was quiet. They saw no one on the Kelefion's ramparts or the nearest of its towers, and hurried to the rear of the cottage, then on to the row of dwellings of gardeners and tilthmen, and crossed over the deserted ring-road to the empty watchtower beyond.

There must have been a hundred vessels of all sizes on the Queensmere, maybe half of them blackened, smoking husks in the distance. Vaience reckoned it had begun with the fishing boats from their base in Linnishill near Cusheen's Cut, where people could have seen what happened to Colza's Bridge; where the news would first have reached.

The two royal barges and the tresreme still burned, the flames blanched by the brightness of the day. From what Falca could see through the patchy smoke, they'd gotten about halfway across the Queensmere before the fireboats converged on them.

But what about that *other* tresreme—a second one—*see it burning there?* Could only have come from Snarlshome below the inner bluffs of Linnismorn, one of the few ships of the fleet that hadn't been destroyed when it all began. Must have been sent out to help the others that left the cove, packed to the rails with Skarrians and stalkers. And *there*...see those two bigger ships? just to the north of Pelagia? Those two—cogs or galliots like the *Lysidia*—they must've gotten away from the Lazza wharves; both of 'em probably already burning when one blocked the path of the barges and tresreme...and then the other rammed the second tresreme.

At this distance Falca couldn't mark the killing that had to still be going on: Milats in late-arriving boats clubbing, gaffing Skarrians clinging to whatever they'd managed to throw overboard to escape their burning vessels; Milats flinging fishing nets over survivors to ensnare them, haul them into the water, not out of it.

If there were hundreds of Skarrians still alive, had to be many more who'd drowned. And the Milats—those who weren't late arrivals, who had set their boats afire and jumped into the water before collisions, or tossed pitch-smeared torches onto the decks of the huge barges and tresremes—how many of them had perished?

It seemed to Falca a small, *small* thing to have merely cut the kraken-skin cables of an empty bridge under the cover of night.

About ten fishing boats were heading toward the cove, others tacking toward the east and west; a bearing that would take them around Mereshaven to…what?—the channel between the island and Linnisvale? By now there was probably fighting going on around the still-intact northern half of Colza's Bridge and Scunder Square. Those were the only places where the Skarrians who hadn't gone on the barges and tresreme could hope to escape from Mereshaven.

"Falca?—I don't see any of them around the Kelefion, at least the south-facing battlements and towers. Do you?"

He stepped back, looked past Vaience toward the citadel, its white-washed walls and blue-and-white-banded towers. The citadel was not close but still, he could have glimpsed movement had he seen it, soldiers passing by embrasures.

"Not a one," he said. "But maybe not surprising—who wants to make a last stand which sooner or later's only gonna end one way."

"Or defend an empty throne," Vaience said. "If Vulsa was on a barge or the tresreme…he's dead."

"I'm thinking it won't stay empty for long, the citadel. After the Skarries—what's left of 'em—have skeltered back to where they came from, someone else is gonna wind up there and the rucks to claim it will be bloody, and not a drop of it Skarrian. It'll be Milat against Milat. Or some lord out in the hinters, thinking only *his* arse fits the throne."

Vaience was looking away at the citadel, as if he didn't want to hear anymore.

Falca frowned at himself. *Should have kept my mouth shut.…*

Now wasn't the time to talk about…*after*; not when the *now* was still here. Which for them meant the cove where those boats'd be coming in.

"Vaience, if there's any Skarrians down there at the cove, maybe we can help make sure none of 'em get on any, yahh?"

They left the watchtower, but Vaience was still looking at the citadel. As they were about to cross the ring-road and head south toward the cove, he was *still* looking at it.

"Ah, you seeing something over there I'm not?"

"I'm thinking it could be much sooner, Falca."

"What...sooner?"

"What you said, about someone winding up in the Kelefion...claiming the Labrys Throne. It may as well be one of us—we're here, *they're* gone. And we have this."

Vaience held up the kraken's claw.

IT TOOK LAMBREY TALLON but one circuit of the tower's parapet— embrasure to embrasure—to see that he was a garrison of *one* for the entire citadel; the courtyards, wallwalks and the other towers all deserted.

No Skarrians, anyway, would be coming back to Mereshaven.

They were finished or would be soon.

A few weeks as masters of Milatum...and the hoops are off the barrel.

He dropped the axe and sword on the embrasure, one *clang* then another.

From here he'd seen the fighting, the three red-and-black standards in the salient of the square north of the bridge.

And now only one.

The aqueduct pool and ledges were empty, but on the aqueduct channel itself, high over the fighting below, the last of the Mereshaven Skarrians were escaping the city. Maybe lucky for now, but how do you climb down from an aqueduct?

The pall over the Queensmere was the most sickening evidence of disaster, but there was more: smoke rising from a dozen places elsewhere.

All because of the fucking bridge....

And all it took was one Milat seeing it slumped in the water and even an idiot could figure out that the Skarrians on Mereshaven would be trapped for a while. Fear—or the lack of it—can spread quickly. Tallon had seen that happen even before Scaldasaig.

The Milat rabble had lost their fear, and so they'd taken out weapons they'd hidden. If they hadn't any, they picked up weapons from dead Skarrians...who might kill two or three Milats for every soldier they lost, but they didn't have the numbers to prevail, not when an entire city had lost its fear of them in the space of a morning.

Somewhere out there, First Blade Kullerioc and his Priaptor were fighting for their lives if they weren't dead already. But the Milat rabble were fighting not just for their lives, but also for their city, their wives and children.

Forget help from outside—the men Vulsa had sent to secure the territory around the city, confident he had his boot on Milatum's neck. Those soldiers wouldn't arrive in time, wouldn't be enough of them anyway. Soon enough the rabble would take back the city gates—even now, over there to the east, that thick column of smoke....

All because of a fucking bridge...it's Scaldasaig all over again....

And the thing of it was...he'd done it; turned piss to wine...come here with a plan that would have put Shar Stakeen and Breks under *his* boot...only a matter of days for her; a month or two for him at Scaldasaig. Who would have stopped him? Not Breks and his mottles fit for their trees not ramparts. Not the small detachment of Skarrians Vulsa would have sent with the only man who knew where Scaldasaig was. With luck and a handful of Rough Bounds outlaws or Wardens—*all* the Wardens couldn't have died up there—he could have taken back Scaldasaig, crossing the lake at night...climbing the walls....

What did he have now? Only the priest's sword and the axe to kill a few Milats when the first of them arrived on Mereshaven, before they killed him. All this way, to die at—

No...no...you're looking at this all wrong...you're not one of them....

They didn't know he'd been dealing with Vulsa, any of the Skarrians. The Milats would see he wasn't one of them. He still had his Warden's cingulet. The guards had taken his Warden stagger-axe after all, probably on orders of the priest so he'd be unarmed for the kill. But he could ditch the Skarrian weapons—

No, keep them; show them you've killed your share...tell them you were captured....

So why was a Warden from Lucidor was so far from home? *Why?* Well, seems the Skarrians wanted to know the same thing but before they could find out, they had more pressing matters to attend to, didn't they. And he escaped—after all, he was a Warden comitor—the proof of it in the tower chambers: the two corpses, the shattered window.

Sure, when Mereshaven was overrun with Milats, he'd be as jubilant as they were. And then he'd leave on one of the boats, the cove filled with boats soon enough.

And not long after he'd be walking out the gate and over the causeway with nothing in his pockets, nothing to show for it all except the priest's sword to sell in service to some noble of the Lakes, like he and Feccan were going to do. And back to where he started, nothing gained for all the humiliation: kneeling before Vulsa in Labrys Hall, wrists bound, the Priaptor's thick fingers tapping on his throne's jeweled armrests, the man undecided about feeding him to a stalker or listening to more of what this traitorous Warden from Lucidor was saying about a magnificent fortress called Scaldasaig; while next to him his taffy son sniffed at the ends of his plaits as if trying to decide which smelled better; and Tallon still on his knees, not all that close to the huge Cauldron to the right of the lesser throne in which the son sat, but close enough to the mocking memory of Falca Breks at his side when the Draican street seer had given Tallon an absurdly fanciful prediction that had amused him nonetheless because, after all, it had cost him only the copper coin he'd plunked in the old beggar's cup. Breks did the same and moved on, and Tallon remembered wondering why it had bothered him—such a small thing, really—that Breks hadn't waited to hear what he'd paid for, as if hearing a prediction, however preposterous, was a sign of a mind as soft as a scullion's sponge and—

And he has Scaldasaig now. And what do I have? Nothing....

Unless....

Roak's balls and a dog to lick 'em...maybe I do, old man....

Lambrey Tallon grabbed the axe and sword.

QUICKLY NOW, DOWN the spiraling steps in the gut of the tower, the stairwell so narrow the blades of the axe and sword scraped against stone. He was sure there'd be posterns to the floors...and there it was, the first. Probably led to a corridor and the royal residences. And down, going so fast he felt a little dizzy by the time he passed a postern of another floor.

The next? No, likely the top three floors were for the chambers used for royals, chamberlains and other select householders. Below that wouldn't be Labrys Hall; he remembered the long, grand staircase that led up to the Hall; a different priest than the one he killed, accompanying him with the guards, slapping him, telling him how he should act in the presence of Vulsa Hork, the Priaptor and Hammer of Tholos.

So the floor after that.

He hurried on, his thoughts in the van, to the days ahead when he'd walk out of Milatum, pockets full of jewels prised from the throne, where Vulsa once sat, deciding his fate.

All right, not *all* of them. Wouldn't be possible to carry them all. But more than enough to spend whatever it took to find Shar Stakeen and have his fill of her and afterwards see if she'd rather keep her secrets or her fingers…and more than enough to buy the services of runagates in Myrcia and Rough Bounds outlaws…and take back Scaldasaig by stealth…and kill Breks. And train the best of the lot as Wardens, recruit more, train them…and in time he'd have what Culldred Hoster never lived to see thanks to Falca Breks: a 7th Kingdom.

So he'd stuff his pockets with jewels, stuff his cheeks with two bigger jewels like he'd once stuffed in rife…and find some place outside the citadel to temporarily hide the jewels before he stole one of the boats that would soon be coming to Mereshaven. He could handle a boat—all he had to do was get it across the Queensmere. Do it tonight, while the Milat scum were vandalizing the island, probably taking what remained of the throne's jewels—and cursing the Skarrians for stealing the others.

He'd figure some way to get out of the city with the jewels….

Tallon paused at the fourth postern. *Had* to be this one.

He belted the sword, felt better with the axe. Not a Warden's stagger, but it would do. In the unlikely event there were Skarrians in the Hall…he could handle two or three; any more and he'd have to think of something else.

He pulled up the bronze gill-latch, opened the heavy wooden door. A moment's creaking. Listened. No voices. No one with the same idea as his, unless they'd already done it.

He was right; this was the one. After the confines of the passages between the floors, he could sense the vastness of Labrys Hall.

Through the arched doorway now, darting to the nearest of the huge columns that rose along the length of the six-sided Hall. He waited for any indication it wasn't as empty as it appeared, listened carefully for sounds of someone coming up the grand staircase behind him and off to the right.

He was alone—except, of course, for the statues of Roak and Cassena behind the dais of thrones at the end of the Hall.

He ran ahead, his footfalls loud as drumbeats.

HE DIDN'T KNOW and didn't care what the thing was beside the throne that Vulsa hadn't warmed for very long, though he remembered thinking that it was fawky to put such an ugly, angular stone vat or altar? in a hall of such magnificence; and bound with *rope*, no less. Its height and breadth far exceeded the size of the throne next to it

The Cauldron, now—to the right of the lesser, consort's throne—was another matter. The polished bronze was gouged and scratched, but the Cauldron's value surely exceeded the jewels in both thrones together: it was one of the fabled Six Gifts that Roak himself had given to his children.

Lambrey Tallon laughed, standing before it, wondering what the beggar-seer had bought with the coin Tallon had plunked into his cup to pay for his fortune-told. A thimbleful of scorch-belly? Half a loaf of day-old bread? bought with a single copper coin for a prediction the old beggar probably had used a hundred times.

And soon he'd be leaving here with enough jewels in his pockets to last ten lifetimes, the jewels of Keshkan kings and queens who sat ten paces away in their thrones. How many could he prise from their settings, using the sword point, the flat of the axe as a hammer. Tallon wasn't worried about the clanging. No one would hear. The statues of Roak and Cassena behind the thrones wouldn't come to life, parting hands, stepping forward to stop the theft.

The bronze Cauldron was chest-high, its breadth as wide as he was tall. He ran his hand along the rim that was as thick as his thumb was long.

You are spitting into a kettle beside a throne.

Shide! old man. You can do better than that—am I sitting on the throne?

That is what I see.

Hear that, Falca? I'd say that's worth a coin! Your turn....

Lambrey Tallon worked up a mouthful and spit.

He drew the sword from his belt, tapped the rim of the Cauldron, then leaped up to the dais—and stopped, his grin vanishing.

Someone was coming: echoes of steps on the grand staircase.

Tallon jumped from the dais, hid behind the Cauldron.

Labrys Hall carried sound very well. From where he'd been kneeling before Vulsa that day, he could hear the son sniffing his plaits.

No, sounds like two, no more than that....

First of the Milats? Thinking the same thing he had?

The echoes grew louder.

Let them do the work....

Then surprise and kill them.

He wasn't going to leave this fucking city empty-handed.

Chapter Thirty-Six:

REIVES

ALCA AND VAIENCE walked side-by-side along the dawnstone processional that led through a field of blushed marble to the empty thrones at the end of Labrys Hall, passing through a gantlet of sunlight made possible by the oculi in the ceiling. In front of each massive pillar of the central colonnade, on sculpted oikoe-tail sconces, hung bronze cressets for burning oil in the winter. Below them, garden basins of whinstone—each as big as a trundle cart—contained flowers now browned and wilted.

Rohaise's responsibility probably hadn't included these; otherwise she might have gotten permission to bring her son into Labrys Hall, and Vaience had said he'd never been here. But everyone in Milatum knew what was here.

Beyond the rows of pillars, left and right, triskell-paned windows in the angled wings of the Hall filled it with even more golden light, brightening the friezes on the walls.

They stopped at the edge of the dais, the Hall quiet again except Vaience whispering about Roak and Cassena being not only the father and mother of Colza, but Cazcus too—the founder of Skarria. So perhaps no surprise Vulsa hadn't yet demolished the statues.

Carved from alabaster and naked except for Roak's torc and Cassena's necklace, they loomed high over the backs of the thrones, rising from a plinth of waves, as if coming ashore; Cassena's breasts large as baskets, Roak's phallus thicker than a hawser. Two hands entwined, two hands outstretched like the Wovens, the legendary couple offered a welcome to everyone who came into the Hall—and a reminder that the particular arses sitting on the thrones were not the same as yours.

But they were and always will be, Falca thought.

Still, they were impressive, these statues, the painted eyes so lifelike they seemed to be staring at him. Which was the point. Why else were Roak and Cassena here if not for…presence?

And maybe that was why Falca had the uneasy feeling he and Vaience weren't alone here.

He glanced beyond the statues, to the gilded doors at the corners of the Hall, expecting at any moment for Skarrians to charge out. He looked back at the processional, feeling foolish because he would have heard the sound of footfalls.

Was the emptiness so surprising? There'd been no Skarrians on the walls, no one at the Kelefion's open gate, no one challenged them at the top of the grand staircase. So why would there be any Skarrians here in this Hall that had to be large enough to berth one of the royal barges still smoldering on the Queensmere? That was Vaience's guess, anyway.

And what do you do if you're in such an empty and magnificent place like this?—you a ditchlicker from Draica—standing before the dais and the greater and lesser thrones of Keshkan kings and queens, flanked by the two most revered artifacts of the kingdom Colza had founded a thousand years ago; brought the Cauldron with him, he did—*Thanks for the gift, Father, but it was a pain in the arse to lug it all this way*—and discovered the Labrys when he got here.

What do you do?

Yahh well, you take the three steps up to the big throne and sit your arse down on the gold threads of the blue velvet cushion that the Skarrian Priaptor hadn't sat in for long, thanks to all the Milats who'd died on the Queensmere today and probably were still dying in bloody rucks from Linnisvale to Linnisheer.

You're not smiling and neither is Vaience—who hopefully isn't thinking you have some other idea in mind. *Do* you? *Nahh*. Only a flare of wonder that you'd come so far to Milatum to find the woman that Ossa Vere never stopped loving up to the moment he stepped off an embrasure of Scaldasaig's keep, to join his daughter in death; and wind up sitting on a sky-blue alabaster throne put together with triskell-shaped splines of gold and studded with enough jewels to shame a constellation.

To your right, a few steps away and below the lesser throne rests the huge bronze Cauldron—one of the Six Gifts Roak gave to his children. And to your left, where Vaience is standing, holding the Claw over his shoulder, is the much older and bigger Labrys.

And you're thinking that whatever the problems that might arise with Vaience's plan, the cutting of the cords stretched tautly around the Labrys surely couldn't be one of them. What else could those cords be made of than kraken-skin? Because in a thousand years no one has been able to cut them.

"You're sure about this, Vaience?"

"Only that *someone's* got to keep the chair warm until Cymra returns."

"Then you…em, you give it up when she does, collect your thanks for passing the salt at the table—you're welcome—and she becomes Sanctress of Keshkevar? And after that?"

"I'm thinking of travel. The edificia in Castlecliff is evidently quite remarkable. Who knows what I might find there to help decipher what we found on Angessa."

"Sure, you'll never know till you get there," Falca said, thinking that the edificia in Thetis was much closer, but then a certain Demizell wasn't there. How Vaience must wish it would be *her* coming back and not the sister to reclaim the House of Keshkev's Labrys Throne. But of course a married Cyalla wouldn't be available for the job, would she. *So on to Castlecliff with the hope that you and she can pick up where you two left off at the Widow Yist's—and please, my friend, do a better job with your trysts there, will you?*

"Just so you know," Falca said, "while you're keeping this chair cushion warm for Cymra, I won't be far away—gotta make sure it's still your arse that's doing it and not someone else's." He grinned. "Even Sanctors need a deek—especially Sanctors who're thedrals."

"Yare well, that goes for a Draican burreen, too. Like I said on the way here, it doesn't matter to me which of us it is as long as it's one of us. *You* could cut the Labrys cords as easily as I with the Claw. I wouldn't be here if it wasn't for you. Colza's Bridge was your idea. Cor! you deserve—"

"Ach, I hate that word, Vaience. It's useless. It's rancid meat the Fates love to bait us with. No one *deserves* a fucking thing just because he happens to exist. There was a throne at Scaldasaig too, and I didn't leave it only to sit in this one. So it's all yours until Cymra gets here." Falca got up, and stepped down from the dais.

"What a pair of clacking spoons we are!" Vaience said. "If that throne was a door, we'd never get through it: *'After you…no, please, you first…oh but I couldn't…but you must!'*"

Falca laughed, pointed at the Labrys. "Go on then, cut the cords, Your Exalted Clawness. You gotta be warming the cushion when company arrives, which should be soon."

The Labrys was roughly-hewn of bluestone, six-sided—what else?—and to Falca looked like little more than a common town-square well but without bucket or draw. A *big* well, though. And very much out of place in the Hall named after it. After indeed: Vaience had said the Labrys had been found buried in the ruins of the city that had been here when Colza arrived.

Claw in hand, Vaience stepped up to the ledge surrounding the Labrys. Falca joined him, and they slowly walked around. He skimmed a hand over the cords that seemed as taut though a little thicker than the bridge strings. Three separate lengths of cords were aligned with the corners of the Labrys and stretched over its round cavity, perhaps five feet across. Halfway between the outer edge of the maw and the corners were grooves for the cords which angled down, disappearing into holes.

They leaned over the maw, Vaience careful with the Claw. "There's the Ark of the Mistra. Hard to see but it seems bigger than I thought it would be."

"A lot bigger than the spaces between the cords—no wonder it's still there. But how'd you know it was here?"

"*Everyone* knows it's here," Vaience said, stepping back. "Plays have been written about the mystery of the Labrys and what the Ark might contain, and what happens when the cords *are* cut. Mothers and fathers—the midwife who cuts a baby's cord—gives the same blessing: *'May you live to cut the cords of the Labrys.'*"

Falca, thinking that in Draica it was more like, *may you never be so poor or thirsty you must drink from a canal,* said: "And how long have they been saying that?"

"Well, not as long the legend of Roak's Lottery—you know, that decided which parts of the new world his children would settle. For the Labrys lottery, about 600 years. If one of the winners of the lottery does it—cuts the cords of the Labrys—he or she becomes the first Sanctor or Sanctress of Keshkevar, the claim to the throne to supersede all others."

"Ah, no wonder the tradition's lasted for 600 years."

"Yare, it's the high point of Roak's Week festivities. Or was. Thousands of markers from all of Keshkevar, not just Milatum, were brought here and put in the Cauldron. The king announced the three winners in Scunder Square. Last year, though, all three were from Milatum: a Linnishill fish-monger; a royal marine from the fleet's flagship; and a widower who owned a water-wagon business in Linnisvale."

"The winners are brought here to give it a try, then?"

Vaience nodded. "With anything of their choosing. One year a shepherd from the Vales became famous for a week after he said the cords couldn't be as tough as the meat his wife puts on the table—and tried to gnaw them off and—evidently Rhakotis had a laugh at that."

"He wouldn't have been laughing if the shepherd succeeded; he would've lost his job."

"No worries there since it's never happened in a thousand years—Colza was surely the first to try."

"But if he *had* succeeded, the shepherd, or the widower—any of 'em."

"Who knows? There could have been trouble. People took the tradition seriously, even though most understood it was a game with no eventual winner; a bone thrown to them, an empty promise."

Falca looked over at the throne. "Yahh well, *there's* empty—you ready to do it?"

Vaience nodded, pushed up his spectacles, and held the Claw over a cord…and brought it down.

As with the strings of Colza's Bridge, the cord parted as if melted. He cut the other two just as easily. He lifted the ends of the severed cords from the deep well, and then leaned the Claw against the side of the Labrys, as if he'd finished sweeping with a broom.

"You're a calm one," Falca said, "seeing as how you just ended a 600-year-old tradition."

"The playwrights will just have to find other things to write about, won't they? And there will be other blessings for new-borns." Vaience took off his spectacles to wipe them clean. "What's so amusing?—they're smudged."

"Now that you're the Sanctor of Keshkevar, you'll be able to appoint a royal Polisher-of-Spectacles."

"That's highly disrespectful…though not a bad idea—you have the job."

"What's the pay?"

"It will be an honorary position, but you may keep the used cloths."

"I'll pass."

"In that case, be prepared for severe consequences for your impudent refusal."

"I knew this would happen: scratch a thedral, get a tyrant."

"But still a very curious one—I'm going down there, to see if I can lift it out, the Ark."

Vaience clambered over the top of the Labrys, sat for a moment, then grabbed one of the cut cords—mere rope for his hands now—and slid into the maw.

Falca leaned over—and drew back quickly, coughing from the dust of a thousand years Vaience had disturbed. When he looked again, Vaience stood by the Ark, the crook of an arm covering mouth and nose, his head well below the rim of the Labrys. His back to Falca, he swept an arm across the lid of the Ark.

Suddenly the maw brightened.

"It's gold, all right," Vaience said, his voice muffled. "But...that's not what's giving off the light. It's the corners...they're shaped like trees, some sort of raised inlay, and the branches...they spread over the top, but there's a center space between them—oh my, *of course* there'd be more of it."

"More of what?"

"Sixer writing. The same as what's on the Angessa pages...only a single line of it...Falca?"

"Yahh?"

"I'm going to try and...no...it's too heavy, the Ark. You'll have to come down and help me lift it out. We can raise it to the edge. I'll balance it, hold it there while you get out, then you—"

"Just open it up, take what's there—we'll figure out something later for the Ark itself, you want."

"It...there doesn't seem to *be* any way to open it up. The seam is so tight I couldn't push a needle through."

"Must be some way to raise the lid—a pull or latch."

"If there is I don't see it."

"All right," Falca said, and was over the top, holding onto a cord as Vaience had done.

He sank up to his ankles in dust, waded around Vaience—a tight fit—and plunged his hands through the sediment of ages, feeling for the underside of the rectangular Ark. *Shide, it is heavy...*

Vaience positioned himself on the opposite side. The illuminated tree corners of the Ark, the lid branches, cast his face in a silvery light, reflecting on his spectacles.

"Ready?" Vaience said.

Falca knelt, spread his hands wider for a better lift. "Ready...no, wait..."

"What's the matter?"

Two fingers of Falca's right hand grazed over a raised, square nub. He pushed it one way, then another....

The lid opened slowly.

WHAT ELSE COULD you do but laugh.

Falca leaned back, feeling the weight of the dust at his thighs, Vaience still on the opposite side of the Ark, gripping the thick, solid gold edge, staring at its golden emptiness as if he'd seen a Sixer child with two heads in there. He slumped back into the dust, mustering a disgusted smile. "I think I'd rather the mystery—well, now we know."

"Only that they had a stiting good sense of humor."

"But it makes no sense. Why go to the trouble of protecting this—and put nothing in it." He rapped knuckles on his side of the Ark.

"Em...unless something *was* in there, and someone took it out. One thing hasn't changed—you had your reivers two thousand years ago, too. Maybe they wanted for whoever put that something in here to *think* it *was* still here...and after our Sixer reivers took it out, they replaced the cords they'd cut."

"That makes no sense either," Vaience said. "Back then, using kraken-skin cords to protect something valuable would be like...like Crayfish locking his money-chest with a key everyone has."

"Now *that* makes sense: back then everyone must have known that a kraken's claw cuts kraken-skin."

"Maybe the cords were like sealing wax—doesn't keep your letter safe but you know if it's been opened." Vaience got up, shedding disgust and dust. He coughed. "Whatever happened...empty is empty."

Falca, standing now, leaned over the Ark to close the lid....

"Ahh, not quite."

He reached within, almost to arm's length, thinking this made no sense either, making a box of gold so deep and putting into it something so insignificant, flat on the bottom; something that looked like nothing so much as a *stable blanket*—except that this one was much smaller than Gurrus' kinnet.

Vaience's raised more dust with his eagerness to see, the both of them coughing now as Falca draped the kraken-skin over a hand, brushed fingers over it. "Feel the etching." He gave the single page of kraken-skin to Vaience who held the square piece of skin up to a corner of the Ark lid.

"More writing," he said, and began counting softly, whispers: "Twelve lines of it…more words we have no idea what they mean."

"But we do—*something*, anyway. Roak's balls—you don't write just *any* skein of words and then hide it away inside one box then another. Maybe you write it some kind of code or gliff, but *whatever* it says it's—"

"Something that must be worth much more than a solid gold box."

"And it'll fit a lot better in your pocket," Falca said.

Vaience carefully folded the kraken-skin on the edge of the Ark. "And more words to go with the other pages of their writing, so more of a chance to find repetition; a pattern to help decipher them."

"For a newly-hatched Sanctor you talk just like a thedral—so fuck the Ark, we're leaving it?"

Vaience smiled. "Fuck the Ark—for now. But in the event someone takes a look and wonders where the Sanctor and his deek hid the jewels—you know, the ones we found in there the size of your fist…" He closed the lid to the faintest *click*.

Falca climbed out of the Labrys first, but it was Vaience who noticed the Claw was missing.

LAMBREY TALLON PAUSED on the wide footbridge, glancing back toward the Kelefion, wondering where they were: Breks and the other one who didn't talk like any crouch-alley Breks met on the streets of Milatum. Were they only now coming out of that…Labrys?

He walked quickly on, sure this processional led to the cove where he'd find what he needed—if not before, and looked back again, not stopping this time.

Where *was* Breks?

Anything was possible on this day of all days, but could Breks have been so stupid to waste time frantically searching for the reiver elsewhere in the Hall or adjacent floors? Probably not…but then again something was wrong with him. Whatever the reason why he was *here* and not at *Scaldasaig*—which to Tallon was as astounding as Breks surviving a white rancer bite—he'd become a weakling.

The canny ditchlicker who'd betrayed him, got him sent to the prison hulks, miraculously survived the rancer, and stole Scaldasaig out from under 4,000 Wardens—*that* man would've betrayed the thedral, killed him for this Claw, and be warming the Labrys Throne right now as the…*newly hatched* Sanctor of Keshkevar.

Tallon saw up ahead a huge sundial, the circular plate wider than the processional though a part of it. To his right, another avenue intersected with the sundial, leading to some monument of rising stone spirals.

He thought of what Breks had said to the thedral, in a voice deeper than Tallon remembered—*You gotta be warming the cushion when company arrives—which should be soon*—and decided to wait here.

Let company come to *him*.

Wasn't that what a king, a *Sanctor* did?

Whose claim to the throne to supersede all others'….

The sundial's bronze blade, wide at the bottom and tapering to a point, curved up to a height greater than his own. On a day like today…he wouldn't have been surprised to see shadows suddenly vanish everywhere, but he laughed and stepped into the narrow wedge of shadow cast by the blade, all there was given the hour. The blade pointed directly to the south, from where company would be coming.

Falca Breks was formidable, as Tallon well knew, but against two or three others…five?…a dozen? And this…Vaience hadn't sounded like someone who'd be useful in a fight. A soft thedral who wore spectacles? Then again, there had to be something there or Breks wouldn't be with him.

Maybe there wouldn't be a ruck, Breks and the thedral still looking for the reiver in the citadel, or facing up to the fact that since they didn't have this mazer Claw they had no proof of what they did.

Tallon still couldn't believe he had it in his hand.

The hardest thing he'd ever done was keep quiet, crouching there behind the Cauldron, listening….

Where had they found—stolen—it?

Didn't matter. Tallon didn't much care now—and no one else would, either.

No, not the hardest thing....

The hardest thing was *not* killing Breks in the Hall.

But he had that falcata with him; Tallon saw it, risking a peek, their backs to him. No telling what might have happened, Breks the quickest he'd ever seen with a blade that size and heft. And there *were* the two of them.

Tallon had too much to lose, now and later as Sanctor of Keshkevar, *his* kingdom eventually stretching north through Myrcia to Scaldasaig after he recaptured the fortress.

Let everyone ponder the mystery of where he came from, the man who'd done what not even Colza, no one else in a thousand years could do—*and thank you very much for that gobbet of history, Vaience, whoever the fuck you are....*

There was no one in Milatum—no one anywhere—who could unmask him as a runagate Lucidorian Warden. Except of course Falca Breks and his—

And there they were—not Breks and his deek.

Company.

Tallon grinned.

All he had to do when they approached was give them proof of what he'd done, these first of his slew-dogs. Then loose them for the hunt. But before they killed Breks, he needed answers to a few questions. He wasn't worried Breks and the eddy would escape; there was no way off the island except at the cove and Tallon would make sure they didn't skelter that way.

Tallon counted six men—no, there were eight. *Even better....*

The eight would grow to twenty, then fifty before nightfall, a hundred tomorrow. Within a day at most, Breks and the thedral would be dead, killed for what they were: prisoners the Skarrians hadn't fed to stalkers—any reason would do—who'd somehow escaped and tried to steal the Claw from the savior of Milatum.

Reivers they were.

Tallon had the Claw, Breks and the eddy didn't.

All he had to do was tell the eight men that he'd cut the Labrys cords with it, and bring the men to the Hall. Proof enough there, but more not far away if needed to prove that the new Sanctor of Keshkevar first cut the cables of

Colza's Bridge…and delivered Milatum and Keshkévar from the scourge of Skarrians.

And there they were, the reivers, hurrying toward the footbridge that crossed the gardens' stream—but stopping now, having surely seen the men approaching him.

The nearest of them carried a gaff, others scaling knives, and one man the same kind of sword Tallon took from the priest; he'd tossed the axe into the stream.

It wasn't likely these…fishermen would mistake him for a crazed Skarrian, defending what was no longer his. Still, if he had to kill one or two of them to knuckle the others, so be it.

THEY WERE ON the footbridge when the man stepped away from the sundial blade to greet the Milats. Vaience hoped that what the man raised over his head, stabbing the air, was only another sword and not the Claw—but then he shouted:

"With *this* I have delivered us from the Skarrians! With *this* I brought down Colza's Bridge and cut the cords of the Labrys! Come with me to the Kelefion and bear witness! I am your Sanctor. I am *Scalda Saig!*"

Vaience recognized the name…that place Falca said he'd left…and from the look on his face he'd gone back there in heartbeats.

"It's *him*. It's Tallon," Falca whispered, and began walking ahead, falcata in his left hand.

Vaience caught up quickly. "*Falca…wait—*"

He shook off Vaience's restraining arm as if it was a cut, useless cord of kraken-skin. Vaience tried again, got in front of him, Falca staring past his pleas: "There's nothing for it now…there are too many of them." Falca shoved him aside so hard that Vaience stumbled.

Through it all—from Angessa to Mereshaven—Vaience hadn't felt this kind of fear, seen the smile of someone who didn't care what the odds were.

His friend…*his brother*…was far away with someone else.

The woman? who died because of…*Lambrey Tallon?*

What was her name? All Vaience could think of was…*Larks on the Bough*….

He remembered.

"Falca! It won't bring Amala back if you die! She wouldn't want the waste of it."

He stopped, looked back at Vaience, then at the men, Tallon off to the side, talking to them; now pointing at Falca. Vaience hurried ahead, hurrying his words: "We must go now while we can! They can't be sure of him yet; that it's what he claims. They'll go first to the Hall, then come after. He thinks there's no way we can get—"

"There's always a way."

For a sickening moment—a twist in his gut—Vaience thought he'd failed. Then Falca sheathed his falcata and Vaience knew he'd meant something else. "Someday…but not now. I know where he'll be."

He turned abruptly and bolted over the bridge, Vaience running at his side along the path in the same direction they had before—then, as now—the only possible way.

CHAPTER THIRTY-SEVEN:

A CUP OF FISH OIL

ROHAISE WINCED.

She tried again, piercing the livid edges of the sword cut on her left cheek with the needle, and pulling the thread though tightly. "That one was better. Enough?"

"Nine should do it," Banch Redallion said, thinking that most of his men, if they had to stitch themselves up, would have been fashed more than Roh. Slife, *he* might have, too; as an augeron he'd been gashed and cut aplenty—but someone else had always done the sewing.

Rohaise picked up the scissors from her lap, snipped the thread, tied it off.

Banch slid the mirror he'd been holding for her onto the table where they were sitting, the door open to the gloaming. With the last light of day also came the smell of smoke still drifting off the Queensmere.

She put the scissors, needle and spool of thread on the mirror, then loosened the thick auburn hair she'd tied back for the stitching. "Any more knitting and I'd be tempted to toss the mirror after I pull them out."

"Which I'll only buy you a new one when I get back, so you won't have to take my word for it that you're still beautiful."

"Sweet man, but I think I'm done with mirrors."

It was just as well they'd waited to do the repair. Never mind the needle, Roh couldn't have threaded the open bottle of blige her son—and the man with him—had left unfinished: wherever Vaience was now, he'd been *here*.

Kulu was tugging at Roh, mewling words, standing at the edge of the folded quilt, where the oikoe had been licking at the reddened flesh of her tail. The fur had been seared off.

"I think she's saying she wants to lick your wound, like she did before," Banch said.

"She is, but the honey-girl will have to wait. Your turn now, Ikonos Redallion. Let me see it again."

Banch lifted his right hand. Fire had scorched the hand and arm almost up to the elbow. "Some cold water, maybe. I won't be holding a blade for a while, but it'll be all right. No blisters yet."

"There will be, the looks of it. You need more than cold water."

"If you're going back to that stink-up, Roh, I'm going with you."

After the night of the intruders, they'd taken the first possible refuge they came to on Colza's Way though it hadn't been their last: a looted two-storey shop that sold unguents, perfumes and incense. Broken vials, bottles and finger-jars crackled underfoot, the sweet stench sneezing-awful as they made their way in the dark up to the garret above the shop, Kulu leading the way.

"You don't have to," Rohaise said, and got up. "I've got something here that's as good as anything there. I used it when Vaience once tipped a hot skillet of oil and burned himself."

"When was that?"

"Just before he got accepted at Sulserra's. It only splashed his leg but the fireheart had healed the burn by the time he went."

"Fireheart?"

Rohaise nodded, pointed toward the door. "It's near the top of the steps. There's more than enough blossoms. Cut some up, add water. It's almost as good as oikoe-tongue, which we'll do later but not now—Kulu could lick your hand and wrist but even the gentle rasping would hurt. Soaking's better now."

She went outside with a big mixing bowl, Kulu padding behind her, and Banch thought of what was on Epona's grave, what her son had left—who else would have done that?

She came back with the bowl full of blossoms, sat down, used the scissors to cut them into small pieces, and then poured water into the bowl from the ewer she'd filled after they arrived here in the late afternoon. "They must steep for a while, so we'll have to wait," she said, shifting in the chair so she could put her left hand over Banch's good one yet still face the doorway. She tapped the tips of her right-hand fingers at her lips. She often did that when was in a thoughtful mood, but it was more than that now. She had to be thinking about her son…because the fighting wasn't over out there.

Maybe it was on Mereshaven, where—incredibly—over half of Colza's Bridge lay in the water, they heard. And it was over on the Queensmere. But elsewhere the fighting would be going on through the night. On the way back here they'd heard that the Orphic Gate had been retaken; or at least that's what the graylock had said, the old man carrying a short-shaft glave—maybe he'd once been a royal marine. The boy with him—couldn't have been more than twelve—held a long dagger with a broken quillons. He said, staring at Rohaise's cheek: "That's where we just was, granda'n me."

And somewhere out there was *her* boy.

Banch had never met the young thedral, who'd taken a pair of spectacles from his room, Roh said; gone out there again after hastily burying the two quay-stompers and leaving flowers on the grave. He'd also left his name on the letter she'd written to him, which could only mean he hoped his mother was still alive.

"I almost wish everything here was as we left it," Rohaise said. "Then I could believe Vai was safe in Girvan or somewhere else. He would have had the sense to get out, if that rumor was true about the Skarrians sending troops there. So what does Vai do?"

Despite everything, there it was: a smile, a little headshake.

"Your boy came back to get you out, I believe that."

"Oh, Banch—I hope it wasn't just that, because if something's happened to him…"

"Wait now," he said softly. "You're jumping to *ifs* when it hasn't been that long since he was here. Cor! he got *into* a city full of Skarrians—which by the way I'm looking forward to finding out how he did *that*, he and the other one, probably. So wherever Vaience is now, he can take care of himself."

"Yes he can…but you also need to be lucky."

Nothing he could say to that; it was true. They'd been lucky out there.

"If Vai was only a cutling, I'd be doing more than waiting for him to come home, which is all he has now that Sulserra's is ash and rubble. I'd be searching the streets until I found him. I love him more than my life…but he's a man now."

And he might never return—which was why Banch couldn't wait with Roh for more than the few days it would take to find a ship to take him to Averdenn.

He was going to miss her terribly. He'd fallen in love with Rohaise Loquin the moment he heard her laugh, seen it linger in the gray eyes that held her laughter. He wished he could take her with him, because however dangerous his mission was, things were going to be rough *here*. He wasn't concerned so much about the Skarrians. The gates would be closed for a while, everyone fearful of Skarrians outside the city, to the north and west; most of them making their way back east, marauding along the way. There probably weren't enough of them to pose a new threat to the city, but there were likely enough of them out there between Milatum and Girvan. So a ship would be the best way to get to Averdenn, *especially* with what he'd be taking with him. His men, the last of the Labryssons, would be waiting for him there. And the sooner they set sail for Castlecliff…well, the sooner he and his men could bring back the Demizells.

Still, the mission would take months. And in the meantime it was going to be rackety here, even after the Skarrian threat was completely gone. Someone would see that as opportunity—and probably already had. And then another—this one also with followers. There would more blood in the streets as the packs of dogs fought each other…before he returned with Cyalla and Cymra to reestablish the House of Keshkev. Such was Epona's last command as a dying queen and mother. But—here was an idea—why not still take Roh with him to Averdenn? He'd assumed she'd want to stay in her home now and wait until he got back. And he'd been concerned that the brigands on both sides of the Girvan awe up near Averdenn might have decided to take advantage of the turmoil to the east. But if not, the situation in Averdenn might be better than here. *You should have asked her what—*

"Banch?"

He squeezed her hand. "I was thinking about the ship…and Epona and—"

"That's what I have to talk to you about."

"Shouldn't be a problem getting one. There were seven or eight bluewaters left along the Lazza quay. Finding a master to take me to Averdenn will cost dear, but—" he smiled— "I think there's enough to meet his price; enough to tempt him but not so much to arouse suspicion. A few pearls should do it—the white ones not the black. It's probably best to pick a Gebroanan ship that got trapped here. But any master will be eager to leave as soon as the Cleave is open; Nesky's chains should be lowered soon. The Skarrians won't be coming back in that way, they have no ships. Anyway, it's best if I arrange passage soon, since there are a limited number of ships and doubtless other people wanting to leave the city. So I'll be going down to the Lazza quay tomorrow morning and—"

"I'd like to go with you."

Banch smiled. "I was just going to ask you if you would like go to Averdenn with me."

"Yes—*and* Castlecliff."

"Roh, that's—" He let out a *whoosh* of a breath— "That's not possible. It's…much as I'd want to have you with me, it's not a good idea."

"But it is."

"No, it's not. Never mind the *getting* there. Roak only knows how it will go in Castlecliff. Forty Labryssons won't prevent the worst from happening."

"All the more reason for me to be with you to help *make* things happen the way they *must*. Sometimes a woman can see a path overlooked by men. Anything can indeed happen, oyah—including the Sanctor deciding to keep Epona's jewels *and* Cymra *and* Cyalla in her marriage."

"Roh…."

"In which case…perhaps while *you're* offering him *most* of the jewels as a ransom—whatever we're calling it—*I'm* elsewhere dispensing the rest of them as bribes where needed to walk the Demizells out the gates; in disguise, of course. Or…hmmm, I've heard the Spurrose Gardens in Castlecliff are quite magnificent. So surely the once-royal gardener of Milatum would want to see them in the company of two young women who were last seen in the Spurrose Gardens but seem to have lost their way, didn't return, must be *somewhere* in the city…only we're *not*—oh, I don't know, Banch, but it seems to me we should be—"

"Prepared to use, ah, more thread to stitch the cut?"

"Just so, my love," she said, wincing a little with the smile.

"Cor! You deploy your arguments better than I do my men."

"I'm not done, Ikonos. As for the return, I'm sure the Demizells would welcome the presence of a woman. I've spoken to Cyalla before and I think she enjoyed our meeting as much as I did, regardless of the consequences."

Banch knew what those had been.

"What of your boy?" His tone softer now.

"If Vai…if he doesn't return here before we leave…I'll leave another letter for him, let him know we've gone to Averdenn. Maybe tell him more—such as why. We should talk about that. But first, I understand Epona gave you the command, not me. Whether I go to Castlecliff is up to you. If you decide I'm to stay in Averdenn I'll respect your decision, though I won't like it."

He wondered if she'd give the last of her reasons, which might have been the first all along: the Myrcian mast-lord to whom she'd been married long ago, who never knew she'd been with child; she hadn't either until after he'd left Milatum—for the last time as it turned out. And never arriving in Castlecliff, his ship wrecked on the Flaggy Shore of Gebroan, all hands lost.

This time she wanted to go, regardless of what might befall them.

"All right, then" he said. "It's the *both* of us getting seasick on the voyage to Castlecliff—is this steeped enough?" Banch nudged the bowl, rippling the blood-red water sludgy with fireheart blossoms.

She nodded. "In you go, my man."

He hunched closer to the bowl, curled in his hand and wrist.

"I'm going out to the springhouse," she said. "We haven't checked the pot since we've been back. If it's not there, neither of us will be getting seasick."

She kissed him and left, Kulu following her out the door.

The soaking felt good.

He was so tired he could have fallen asleep right here in the chair. He leaned his head against the high back, closed his eyes to the red water, but all that did was bring him back to a Queensmere clotted with debris and burning boats and the roaring of the fiery tresreme; and all around him in the furnace heat the Skarrians clinging to whatever they could as Milats on boats that weren't afire stabbed and clubbed them as bleating seals; and so many other churgs drowned or drowning, sinking, their plaits like weeds in the water, all of them steeping in the Queensmere. Milats too....

And that Skarrian, his plaits black, not yellow, slashing at Roh, the tip of his sword just missing her neck, her eyes; and the gush of blood in the water before Banch killed him with his sword: this as he swam—helping Roh who couldn't—from the second boat they'd set afire; he and Kulu burned when the Milat—on the way out from the east end of the Lazza he said his name was Jossuk, used to be a Glass Gardens lamplighter—tipped the open butt of oil, igniting it too soon and—

Banch heard Rohaise shriek, got up so fast he sloshed red water over the table, the letter; the spill spinning the spool of thread to the floor. He grabbed his sword, rushed outside...and saw her at the top of the steps, embracing her son; the other man lower but moving up past them to give them their moment—

the one who'd clumsily signed his name on the back of the letter's last page? He didn't have the dark eyes of a Milat. A tall, braw northron. Unkempt black hair and scruffed beard. Smiling now as he sheathed a falcata.

HE PUT THE whetstone and falcata on top of the terrace wall as Rohaise approached, her white night-dress gray in the moonlight. She held a cup in one hand, a cloth in the other.

"I'm sorry I woke you," Falca said.

"You didn't—not a chance of that tonight. We didn't hear a thing until Kulu tugged at me, saying someone was outside—and soon the three of us were wondering where you were, and then we heard it, and Vai said you'd do that in your sleep if you could, the keening." She put the cup and cloth by the falcata. "It's fish oil. Banch said you'd need it, but save a little for him, his own sword."

"One-handed?"

"Oh, he'll work it out, he always does. Anyway, there you go. I always keep a little here for sharpening the garden tools, which aren't crucible steel like what Banch says you probably have with that beauty there, but then my tools weren't salt-soaked in the Queensmere...yare, like all the rest of us, including Kulu—there she is. Go on back in, honey-girl, I'm along soon."

Rohaise had only glanced to her side but still knew the oikoe was standing on her hind legs in the doorway, not making a sound that Falca could hear, anyway.

"I'm glad you're coming with us," Rohaise said.

"I hope it'll be enough: three deeks for Banch and his Labryssons."

"Deeks?"

"Mostly what I was to Vaience on Mereshaven."

"Who's the third?"

"You...what I heard this evening, Rohaise."

"Well, I suppose we all take our turns if we can; mine was swinging a spade and helping Banch bury Queen Epona. And it's Roh...please. By the way, what you *didn't* hear was Banch telling his...deek that when we get back with the Demizells there'd be no finer Labrysson faldings than the two of you. Maybe a bit old for new recruits, but then he was even older."

"Vaience is gonna have other plans." *And so will I....*

"I told Banch the same thing, and that you didn't seem the sort of man who'd like the fit of a uniform. He said that may be so, but didn't it also depends on who he's wearing it for?" She smiled, a weary one: "Of course, you'd both have to learn how to swim, all Labryssons do. If Banch wasn't a good one, I wouldn't be here."

"Yahh, I'm past due for learning—the next time there may not be a table to use as a raft."

"So you reckoned if it could seat four, it'd be big enough to float two in the water?"

"With a lot of kicking."

"That's the best use the table's ever had. I never did much like it. Every King's Own who ever lived in the cottage must have carved his name or made his mark on the top; most of them probably thinking the bigger the carving, the more they'd be remembered."

"Yahh well, there wasn't much left of of the names after we slid it down to the water; yours too—if you carved your own."

"Never did. The table wasn't mine, not really. Still, it got you to that boat and the one-eyed fisherman who pulled you in—half-way to Linnishill was it?"

"At most, but far enough he couldn't hear what they were shouting from the bluff, more of them than were with Tallon when Vaience and I skeltered."

"Was he with them on the bluff?"

"Hard to tell, that distance. But he knew soon enough we got away. And the sooner we're *all* away, the better, Roh."

"And until we are...about Epona's jewels. Vai asked before he went to bed. You should know too...just in case. They're in the big stirrup pot...under a handful of Kulu's dried shit—excuse me, her leavings."

Falca had to smile at that. The House of Keshkev jewels—a lot of them, anyway—under a crown of dried oikoe shit and Roh calling it what it was.

"I'd better get back in," she said. "I'm sorry the quilt's all I have for you to sleep on."

"It's fine but I think I'll stay out here."

They said goodnight, but then, two steps to the door, she turned.

"This mazer krael—what the Timberlimb priest gave you...what saved your life in the Rough Bounds after what Tallon did. I...well, it wasn't the right time to ask you this evening, all of us at the table, and then I forgot. Maybe it still isn't the right time…but I'd like to know."

He knew what she was going to ask. But suddenly, after all this way to tell her about Ossa—after all that had happened—he blinked. "Em, ask what?"

"Why you did it. I got the impression that chunk of krael was the last you had. You didn't know Vaience at that point but you gave it to him anyway."

"I think he has an idea why."

"Well, I suppose that's what matters—that he does, not his mother."

"No, you should know, but…would you mind if we talked about it later?"

"Of course. Time enough on the voyage to Castlecliff. But for now…I just wish there was more in that chipped cup than two fingers of fish oil to thank you for what you did—Cor, even the Queensmere itself wouldn't be big enough."

He almost told her, because you never knew if you'd have the time; there hadn't been enough for Rohaise Loquin and the man she knew as Mott Demoul. But all he did was thank her for the cup of fish oil, and they said goodnight again, the moment passing that likely would have led to the dawn and down through all the years she'd thought he was dead.

He heard her bar the cottage door, thinking of the other common cup that for all too brief a time as a boy in Draica he believed could be filled with dreams. He smashed that cup the day he left home for the streets, an orphan, nowhere else to go.

Now, here was another; fish oil in it, not dreams.

All this way, people sometimes asked him—especially the tillerman on the Lake Tremizene packet he took south from Arzardys—where he was bound for; asking what his business was in Milatum; curious is all, seeing as how he was clearly a northron, hadn't the look or voice of any Keshkan going home, and Falca saying there was a woman there. *A Keshkan wife, then? Some purlie bower you're sweet on? No? Sister or mother? No? Who then?*

Only a woman he'd never met before, all he could say. And that was always the end of it, even for the gattling tillerman. Because someone who travels so far to see someone he's never met has to be loonzie or maybe has a secret stashed in some hard room between his ears, and either way better left alone….

So on the Castlecliff-bound ship—if not before, on the way to Averdenn—he'd tell Rohaise why he gave her son the krael. And probably a lot more.

It was the last piece but I'd used another to save the life of Mott Demoul many years after you thought he'd died in that shipwreck. But his troubles were only beginning, Roh, and it took him more years before he was free to make a choice: return to you in Milatum or to the daughter in Castlecliff he never told about. He chose his daughter, thinking maybe he'd find the courage to see you again and tell you what he should have long before, though he reckoned by this time there was another man in your life. But then he was imprisoned, disfigured, branded on the face—the Sanctor's Trice—because he'd killed the man who did something terrible to his daughter. He took the name of Ossa Vere to begin a new life searching for her. He knew he could never see you again. He didn't say this to me but I think it was because he feared that brand would be all you would ever see. Despite his faults, Ossa was the finest man I've ever known, and fearless, but he feared that. And only moments before he died, he told me his love for you had never waned.

The daughter he searched for and never found? Vaience's half-sister? He did find her, at a place called Scaldasaig. She'd become a shadden who intended to kill me and a young woman named Raleva Barra for the secret of krael, where more could be found. He believed he had to make a choice—and he chose to take his daughter's life—and then his….

No, Falca couldn't have said all that tonight, or earlier. There was only that look from Vaience, a little shake of the head that Roh and Banch didn't see; a gesture that wasn't, *Don't tell her now,* more like, *It's up to you. She's my mother and she's found a good man, but it's your choice; you've come all this way to make it….*

Falca dipped the cloth in the cup, wiped the falcata blade, glancing at her garden tools, the spade she'd used on the third ganger before he fled that night.

All the way back on the fisherman's boat, even after the last of the steps, Roh there at the top, her hand over her mouth after the squeal of joy; and into the evening, before she and Banch Redallion revealed who was buried right over there, Falca had been going over it in his mind: how to get *back* to Mereshaven soon…how to get close enough to Lambrey Tallon to kill him, to do what he probably should have tried to do when he had the chance, because the odds now were much worse than on Kelfion's Way.

Or were they? Sure, the odds were steep against successfully bringing back both Demizells, though much better for Cymra alone. But say the mission was successful, the Myrcian Sanctor deciding that he could always find another wife for his son, and such a boon to the royal treasury was rare indeed. Once back in Keshkevar, it would be a matter of exposing Tallon for the fraud he was, and after an hour out here on the terrace Falca knew how that could be done. And once Blue-gums returned to what he'd always been, *Scalda Saig* no longer, there would just be the two crouch-alleys from Draica facing off against one another—with no other lives at stake.

But there would be until Roh and Vaience and Banch were safely away from Milatum.

By now most of the Skarrians who hadn't escaped would be dead. There was fighting probably still going on elsewhere in the city, but not in this part of Linnisheer, the Lazza below, the quiet night carrying unmistakable sounds of celebration: drunken shouts, the *rump-rump-rump* of drums and a sharper clapping to the quick, skipping slashes of a flinarra's music—no wistful laments tonight.

Nor would there be on Mereshaven.

Lambrey Tallon probably wouldn't be drunk. In the Draica days, Falca had never seen him stumbling drunk or in throes of too much scrape; rife—and blue gums—came later. But even if he was drunk, there would already be men watching over the savior of Milatum; and already he'd have fucked the first of the women eager to make their own history by slaking the new—and first—Sanctor of Keshkevar.

He'd let his ecstatic new subjects believe what they needed to believe about where he came from; or maybe he'd claim he was descended from the Old Ones—*whatever he calls the Sixers*—who'd built the bridges and made the Labrys. How else to account for the fact of what he'd done? By tomorrow, the word spread, there'd be thousands of Milats in Scunder Square, waiting to see Scalda Saig; the channel between Mereshaven and Linnisvale so crammed with boats he'd be able to walk back to his coronation in Labrys Hall.

And if he hadn't done so already, he'd soon release descriptions of the two rapparees who'd tried to steal the Claw from him—the sceptre of his power; who *did* loot the Ark of the Mistra. The new castellans of Milatum's gates would have those descriptions. Would Tallon post guards all along the Lazza quays? Probably not. For one thing he hadn't the manpower—yet. Too many of the Meresguard had been killed in the fighting. And for another, he didn't know Falca and Vaience had entered the city by boat, much less a ship, so it was possible he wouldn't think they'd *escape* the same way. He didn't know they had the means to pay for passage, Banch saying it would be dear, though far less than even a pittance of Epona's jewels. So if a week or more passed and the...criminals had yet to be caught, he'd likely assume they were still hiding out somewhere in Milatum.

But after a day—a few at most—Lambrey Tallon could think what he wanted. They'd be off with the jewels, all the Sixer artifacts, and the blueveil ring Falca had in his safekeep.

And something else you couldn't put in your hand.

He rasped the whetstone down the top outer-edge third of the falcata; he'd already worked the angled inner edge. The habit of almost daily keening the sword had begun when Amala gave him this falcata to replace the common one he'd lost in Gebroan. The jewels of the hilt meant little to him compared to the falcata's balance, the crucible steel.

And now a new habit. Yahh well, not yet; and not really a habit like keening a blade even if it didn't need it. He'd always done that, often when others slept—Amala and Gurrus, Ossa and Raleva. Styada. But always in places to which he'd likely never return. So this was new, because he *would be* returning, or at least he knew he *wanted* to—and not just to make sure Lambrey Tallon paid for what he'd done at the falls in the Rough Bounds, a day that had begun as one of the best in his life.

He'd return not to this cottage, but eventully to a place of his own that was like it…that was more than what it was made of…which was maybe something he'd been seeking all his life and never quite knew it. Call it what you will but it wasn't the place where he'd been born.

Falca hoped they couldn't hear the rasp of the keening, that they'd finally crossed over. They were all so tired, and Roh uncomfortable with her wound, and Banch his burned hand. He was indeed a good man; she'd chosen well. Ossa would be glad.

And Vaience—had he fallen asleep wondering what would happen when he saw Cyalla again?

For now they were all safe in the darkened cottage, but Falca wasn't quite done yet, and so he dipped the cloth into the cup of fish oil again, wiped the blade, and kept on with the keening for a little while longer.

CHAPTER THIRTY-EIGHT:

THE STONE MANGER

T HE RAT WAS the biggest he'd seen so far, size of a vairg's egg, and so it didn't scurry away from the bodies as fast as the others. Vulsa Hork hit it with the blunt, flared end of the warhammer, his Gavilor, but got mostly tail, the rat only stunned. He quickly drew the dagger from the inner sleeve of his left boot and skewered it.

So far he'd killed and eaten four of them, all feeding on Kessoch, Voket and Plevvy whom he'd dragged to the end of the steps and turned face down, wanting their faces to be the last part gnawed away. Nothing else he could do honor the deaths of these loyal Ghosts who'd been with him since Laggunsea, well before the start of the campaign through Keshkevar. He had a pick—the frowning spike of his Priaptor's Gavilor—but it would take a month down here to carve out a grave big enough for all of them, and long before that the rats would be feasting on *him*.

He'd scattered the local rats for the time being, but there were many at the slorries he'd dragged into a walled enclosure so he wouldn't have to look at the feeding while he got water from the nearby pool. But he could hear the rats chittering and squealing as he trudged back toward the hillock with his skewered meal, breathing through his mouth, the stench down here so rank. Maybe there were openings high above in this...Skellig—but he caught no whiff of good air, only the stench of rats and the other slorries—the prisoners who'd been dead here much longer. Probably the criminals had been too diseased or weak to climb the long steps after the guards emptied the prison to provide more men for Vulsa's to kill on the city wall. In Skarria, criminals who weren't quickly executed didn't last long in the wilderness exile of the Cazcus Wilds. There was no need for prisons in Skarria.

Vulsa wasn't supposed to have lasted this long here, coughing at the stink of rats and the dead, and human waste and the cakes of animal dung the prisoners had been given for cooking fuel—the stench of it all making his eyes itch and water. But here he was, stopping now to lean his Gavilor against one of the pillars supporting the vaulting arches of the Skellig's lid, knuckling his eyes.

Maybe he'd wake up from all this and see through the triskell-paned windows of his quarters in the citadel—he'd taken the king's bedchamber—and see the blue and brightness of the day, the dazzling evidence of what *he* had done; what only *he* could have accomplished.

Which was why he was here, opening his eyes to the underground wilderness of the Skellig's perpetual twilight.

It had probably been a dawnstone quarry, abandoned after the bigger, more easily worked veins were taken, leaving only enough illumination for prisoners to cook their food and find the latrine—wherever that was. Didn't matter where. He was the only prisoner here now, the entire Skellig the private latrine of a man who had once been hailed as the *Hammer of the East, the Hammer of Tholos.* The conqueror of Milatum now smashed rats with the magnificent jeweled Gavilor the Tholarsh had given to him to hammer Milatum into submission—and all the while the Tholarsh knowing that if his brilliant though occasionally difficult Priaptor with the unfortunate family history was successful, he'd no longer be needed....

Vulsa took the steps up to the leveled-off hillock. A semi-circular, chest-high wall of loose rocks topped the rise. Clearly this had been the residence—such as it was—of the man who ruled this underground prison kingdom. There was a passageway that opened to a private chamber, but Vulsa hadn't been inside. What was the point?

Someone had ruled here. As above so below: lords held the high ground.

Which was *his* now. All that was missing—what made a lord's life worth living—were subjects to knuckle their brows, kneel before him, and tremble in his presence.

He slid the rat onto his brazier, wiped the dagger on the edge of a mattress that had probably been stitched together by some prisoner from clothes taken from the dead. He slid the dagger back into its boot-sleeve, and added a couple more dung cakes from a sack full of the crumbly shit-bricks he'd found, to rouse the fire from coals. He'd found the means to do so in that enclosure into which he'd dragged the dead Milats.

The brazier, bigger than the others he'd seen elsewhere, was large enough to accommodate an iron pot he used to heat suspect water before drinking— one of the few Tholosian Tenets of Purity that had ever made sense to him.

Foul smoke rose from the revived fire, but Vulsa had discovered there were currents in the fetid air down here and so had moved the mattress accordingly to avoid the worst of the smoke. After the rat had sizzled for a while, he turned it over with a two-pronged fork, then put the fork back in a bowl that contained a few bone toothpicks, a spoon, flint and steel, and shredded pieces of the mattress left over as tinder for his first fire.

He moved aside the vairg-shell cuirass he'd taken off. The Priaptor's blaze on the front was splotched with dried slorrie blood. He flicked away something crawling on the mattress and lay down, draping himself with his black-and-gold cloak. Despite his closeness to the brazier, he still felt chilled.

On Mereshaven and elsewhere in the four Linnises, his men at their postings were seeking what respite they could find from the sun, if in fact it *was* daytime above. The cabal of betrayers—Zyarees foremost—would be more comfortable in the halls and chambers of the citadel Vulsa had intended to rename in honor of the Tholarsh. When he arrived he'd be impressively shocked by the murder of the Priaptor, whose life had been tragically cut short so soon after blessing Skarria with such a magnificent victory. Such would be the laments of the Tholarsh—Purest of the Pure…the Eye of Tholos Everlasting…Keeper of the Nimbus and the *Book of Vate*…Dispenser of Slevaig's Eternal Ashes…the Bane of Threads….

The cock-sack.

Vulsa was determined to stay alive until his betrayers came for him; or rather came for what they expected to find: bones and shreds of rotting flesh.

A Skarrian should die in battle and this would be his last. They would kill him, but better to die killing as many of *them* as he could. And he would. After all, the Hammer of the East had the high ground down here.

It was too much to hope that Zyarees—the leader of the plot—would accompany those he sent down. The Five-eye purisee and probably Lomelax too, would wait above for what they would think was merely a matter of retrieving Vulsa's corpse, Gavilor and cuirass. All that was left of the Priaptor would be brought back to Mereshaven for full honors, along with a story to be told to massed ranks of karlings—Vulsa's fanatically loyal Ghosts in particular—about what had happened. And Zyarees would probably order the public execution of a hundred mongrel Milats at least in retaliation for the murder of the Priaptor by ten treacherous Milat slorries hiding in the Skellig.

Maybe he should have smelled a plot, been suspicious of Zyarees' suggestion to inspect the Skellig. But he'd sensed nothing treacherous in the priest's suggestion to tour the Glass Gardens in Linnisheer....

...After all, Priaptor, the Tholarsh is justly renowned for his love of beauty and architecture. So when he arrives to consecrate your victory, he might want to see this district called the Glass Gardens, renowned throughout the Six Kingdoms for its beauty, so I've heard. And while we're there, surely he will be amused to know that the Milats built part of the Glass Gardens very near an old dawnstone quarry they'd turned into some sort of prison or asylum. Perhaps we could inspect it, the better for you to offer suggestions to the Tholarsh about how you intend to utilize this unique feature of Tholosia; it's called the Skellig, I believe....

Vulsa agreed.

Zyarees said he'd inform Hemarr Lomilax to secure the Skellig prior to the inspection. Which also seemed to make sense as the karl was in charge of that part of Linnisheer, though Vulsa didn't much like Lomilax, considering him ineffectual. The karl, an insufferably devout Tholosian, was a fens-man from Lake Skarba and exceedingly handsome even by Skarrian standards. He was also competent only in the way a shopkeeper prides himself on orderly shelves. Of all the skirranx of karlings, his had performed only adequately, doing more looting than killing slorries—which was fine, but not before the killing was over.

Hindsight again: Lomilax the hoof-polisher was a perfect choice to sit on the Labrys Throne in the betrayal's aftermath, to be manipulated by Zyarees after the oh-so-very-tragic death of the Priaptor—and eliminated as soon as Hezruval was a little older and took his place on the throne. Which was what the Tholarsh must have always wanted for his son, once *Vulsa* did the killing necessary to make that happen.

So Vulsa left with his hand-picked escort of Ghosts, riding his black vairg, surrounded by his men on theirs. Zyarees and Lomelax waited for him inside the Meresguard castlet with their own men; of course they'd have their own, no suspicion there; presumably they'd just come up from securing the Skellig.

Vulsa left two of his Ghosts above, sent three down first through the hatch at the back of the castlet.

Later, he figured they would have pushed him if he'd suddenly suspected a trap.

Ten steps down, Vulsa heard the scuffle above.

He raced back up. Swords met him at the hatch which didn't stay fully open for long, slamming down on the shoulders of Sennsenik, the Ghost already dead. Swords stabbed through the narrow opening, jabbing past his dangling arms, and then withdrew as Zyarees began telling him that...

...*Surely* he would understand why the Tholarsh deemed him no longer necessary and quite possibly untrustworthy, given the magnificence of his victories in the east and especially Milatum; *and* his popularity with many karls, northern and southern-bred alike; *and* of course with the Ghosts he'd so thoroughly rehabilitated after their humiliation at the hands of the Keshkan glaves occupying Laggunsea the year before. Oh it *pained* him! but he, Zyarees, was foremost a servant of the Tholarsh who desired another...*arrangement* now and he was merely following the wishes of the Most Pure to make that happen in a way that would incur no suspicion in the skirranx, *especially* the Ghosts....

"Who would have thought," Zyarees said, "that there were ten Milats down there, eager to cut the throats of any *churgs* who ventured down into the Skellig and how *astounded* they must have been to see the Priaptor himself and a few of his Ghosts."

Vulsa pushed up against the hatch but the weight was too much, Lomilax' men kneeling on it.

"But rest assured," the priest continued, "we shall be back for your body, to bring you to Mereshaven, to give you in death your well-deserved reward. Far be it for me to speak for the Tholarsh, but I'm confident he will order the commissioning of a suitable monument to commemorate Skarria's tragic loss. Upon his arrival I will have personally evaluated a few sites for your monument, perhaps something in glass—the slorries do glass well—and we *are* close to those particular Gardens. I'm sure the Milats will vandalize it, and perhaps we shall execute a few of them for the reminder that one's ambition and fame can be a fragile thing indeed."

Swords poked through again. Sennsenik was quickly pulled out. The hatch slammed shut. The locking bar slid home with a *clack*—probably the signal for the ten Milats below to begin their attack. Whatever Zyarees or Lomilax had promised the ten slorries couldn't have been their freedom, only the prize of killing the Skarrian Priaptor.

By the time Vulsa got to the bottom of the long switch-backed steps, two of his Ghosts were dead and one mortally wounded—but they'd killed seven of the Milats, wounded another who was crawling away toward the hillock. Screaming his rage, Vulsa swung his Gavilor into the knee of one Milat, whirled to smash another in the face, and then finished off both with the Gavilor spike. On the steps leading up to the hillock, he broke the back of the crawling third, and kept on pounding his head with the hammerhead of the Gavilor until he exhausted himself, fell to his knees....

Now, he put another dung-cake on the brazier. Soon enough the rat would be charred; there was no other way he could force himself to eat it. He settled in to get some sleep, puzzled at why *they* hadn't yet come for him. But if they did today—was it daytime?—he'd be ready for them, his Gavilor and the pile of the Milats' swords within easy reach. He trusted himself to wake in time, their coughs rousing him or hearing them coming up the steps to the hillock, if not before.

He felt himself drifting toward sleep with the nagging thought: had Zyarees—and the Tholarsh—*known* what he'd done long ago? Somehow discovered his secret?

No, they couldn't have, the priest would have told him if he knew; that his fate was merely long-overdue punishment for not obeying the will of Tholos, for breaking Skarrian law which strictly forbade mercy for a baby—in this case a son—born impure.

In every Skarrian town and village, the resident purisee designated a place in the closest forest where parents had to abandon corrupted issue: a Stone Manger with a carved Eye of Tholos. The law stipulated that no flenx and snagwolves could be hunted within a mile of the Stone Manger. Abandonment happened often enough for predators to know that in these tiny clearings there would be easy meat to kill and drag off into the surrounding forest.

Vulsa had glimpsed them in the forest verge that afternoon as he took one last look at his squalling son, and began walking away. He did not look back, did not see the boldest of the flenx emerge from the forest, but he heard the faint clicking of claws on its head-horn, that signaled a warning to the other flenx: *this meat is mine, not yours.*

Vulsa was not alone that day.

And in his dream now, he heard a scream and then....

"Father?...*Father?*"

How was that possible?

He woke...and saw someone kneeling by the smoky brazier: a young man holding the Gavilor as if trying to force the shaft into the stone of the hillock floor, one impure six-fingered hand draped over the hammer, the other over the spike....

THEY STOPPED NEAR the outer gate of the Meresguard castlet, in the shadow of the sentry tower, the moons bright enough for shadows. There was little chance of being seen here, shielded by trees that lined the short avenue to the Glass Gardens and the nearest of the Trellises. Vulsa could hear revelry—a woman's trilling laugh, splashes: that fountain at the center of the district. He remembered thinking as he passed through the first of the four so-called Rainbow Trellises—arches of myriad prisms—that *here* was as close as he'd ever get to Purity, passing *through* color like this.

If Vulsa hadn't fully believed what his son had told him below, he did now: the Milats celebrating not far away were proof enough.

And the *reason* for the disaster, he realized, had its roots in the betrayal because the heart of the army had been *his*. Milatum in hand, he could have ordered his men, certainly the Ghosts, to massacre the detested Red Cape warrior priests, perhaps even purisees attached to the other skirritons—and in hindsight throw in a few karls like Lomelar—and he had no doubt his men would have obeyed. He hadn't wanted the Capes—the Tholosian Guard—in his army; hadn't in any case thought the Tholarsh would let them leave Zakros, but he did as a condition for agreeing to Vulsa's ambitious Keshkan campaign.

Much later, Zyarees insisted on keeping the Capes on Mereshaven, which hadn't overly concerned Vulsa because he had his elite troops—the Ghosts—on Mereshaven too, quartered in the Labrysson barracks on the other side of the island from the Capes.

And the rest of the army, spread out elsewhere in the city...seeing the fate of the crack Ghosts on the Queensmere? Some would have fought on, to be sure, screamed at by purisees. But how many? And how many would have deemed it time to go, their Priaptor dead, and kill the priests who tried to stop them?

Koll had brought the answer, saying below that while there seemed to be fighting still going on in parts of Linnismorn and northern Linnisvale, elsewhere it was over. He'd heard a rumor that the Milats had taken the gates. Which probably meant the gates had been abandoned in the wake of a Skarrian retreat from the city; even now a few thousand karlings fleeing east toward home. And with them any hope for Vulsa to salvage the disaster: he had no troops left *in* Milatum to rally.

Koll was smiling now as he had below, their talking done, when Vulsa indicated that his son should lead the way up the long steps and hatch—Koll having come in that way, not via his Mitoll's tunnel; Koll smiling then at his father's caution but saying softly now: "Are you thinking that maybe we should thank the priest, father? Seeing as how you're one of the few Skarrians still alive in the city."

"I'm alive only because of you…you are so much more now than a secret to be kept. I could not be prouder of what you achieved."

"When I wrote that letter, I never expected to hear that from you."

"It's long over-due."

This would have been the moment to banish all the years and distance with the easy meat of a fierce embrace. But Vulsa didn't sense that in his son. And Koll couldn't either because it wasn't there in the father. A price came with the pride in what his own flesh-and-blood had done, but Vulsa didn't want to risk feeling it slide into his belly, ripping up into his heart in the moment of an embrace.

The long-ago cradling of an infant son would be all he'd ever have. Koll was no longer what Vulsa carried to the Stone Manger; he was now the flenx waiting at the forest verge. For whatever reason he hadn't taken the easy meat of a sleeping father who'd given away his son. But he still could try.

They made the exchange, Koll accepting the folded Priaptor's cape and Gavilor, and stuffing both in the sack of his Mitoll's swag he'd come to retrieve from the Skellig; Vulsa taking from his son a handful of coins.

"Do you want more?" Koll said it fast, like they did, the slorries.

"No, any more might be suspicious for the man I'm supposed to be now. The guards at the Orphic Gate will probably take what I have anyway. I'll get what I need outside the city."

"Doesn't seem a fair exchange."

"It's more than fair. My head could be in that sack, delivered along with the cape and Gavilor to this new Sanctor with a story that would make you famous within days—how tempted were you?"

"It was a close thing. Watching you sleeping, and knowing you could have carried me into exile instead of handing me off like a sack of vetch to Cashol and Yola. It would have been so easy to kill you with your own Gavilor. I thought of that yellow-haired youth who'd taken my place—not knowing he wasn't your son.

"But I decided I wanted the pleasure of telling you he was dead, and I wanted to ask questions that couldn't be answered if you were dead. And after all, you could have left me for a snagwolf or flenx to devour. Such a secret for you to keep for so long, father."

"And now yours," Vulsa said, though he had one more he preferred to keep for himself: who the new Sanctor really was. The habit of secrecy was a hard one to break. The Milats could only know he wasn't a Keshkan, and wonder about the blue gums. And such was idolatry, they probably wouldn't care that their savior, Scalda Saig, was a Lucidorian traitor who'd come to Milatum peddling a story about a magnificent fortress almost free for the taking.

"And such a worthless bequest, isn't it?" Koll said. "What can never be spent. Yet still priceless, never to be forgotten; certainly not when I kneel before the Sanctor and offer him your cape and Gavilor."

"What lies shall you also offer him? By now you must know the best are closest to the truth."

"Oh, it seems the six-fingered gullyman's son was one of ten men who were hunting for churgs to kill—and why not see if any were hiding in the Skellig? So down they went and found the Priaptor himself and a few bodyguards— Ghosts you said? And when it was over, the gullyman's son was the only one not killed in the bloody ruck."

"Hmmm…not bad. But why didn't he bring back the Priaptor's head for further proof of the kill?"

"Do you bag offal? The churg—all of them—had cut their plaits to the skin, possibly before they went below, to disguise themselves. The gullyman's son was so enraged he wore himself out smashing the Priaptor's head to a pulp with a Skarrian war-axe, and left what remained for the rats. By now, there will be nothing left but gnawed bone. Tell me, father, if *you* were the Sanctor, how would you reward the son's deed?"

"Women and a pouch of gold."

"Yare, that would do for a start; but I'm hoping for something more from the man who took what was yours by conquest—and you about to sneak out of the city with only the hope of finding enough of your men to return to Skarria and kill the Tholarsh."

"In time…in time. Stalking your prey requires patience." Vulsa drew his dagger from the boot sleeve. He sliced cloth from one of a slorrie's short trews; below, he'd stripped the best and least bloody of the Milats' clothing. He tied the scrap of cloth around his forehead. "There—does it cover the Eye?"

Koll nodded.

Vulsa tapped his boots. "And it's possible the gullyman took these from a dead Skarrian but…they'd better stay."

"Look at you! My father the gullyman."

"You do what you must."

"Above as Below, oyah. Common advice like the other, about patience, but I'm glad you heeded it long ago." Koll shouldered the sack, a tinker's sack—except for the Gavilor shaft sticking out.

"What you said down there, about my mother…killing herself out of shame for delivering an impure baby, and her fear of producing another. She didn't do that, did she."

My son shouldn't smile. He's more handsome when he doesn't….

"She was prepared to do what the law required. She'd given birth to you two days earlier, and on that sweat-soaked and bloody bed she turned her back to you as soon as she saw your hands. I named you after our word for a high hill or overlook, though naming an impure baby was against the law, too, as killing a corrupted infant was deemed harder to do if it had a name. I still don't know why I—"

"You haven't answered my question."

"It wasn't a question; you know the answer: I killed her moments after she put you in the Stone Manger. *She* was the meat the flenx dragged away after I left and brought you to the Prastagis; they were not far away."

"They never told me her name, nor have you."

"Lucetra."

"No one suspected?"

"It was assumed by all that she killed herself, too, at the Manger. She was so devout, everyone said, but her beauty masked a defect within. I may have been the least devout Tholosian in our respective families, Koll, but only in the excusable manner of a soldier with the pulse of youth. I made amends afterwards, or at least a convincing pretense of it."

Vulsa paused, his eyes on his son's hands, but saw nothing in them, Koll nodding with the look of a purisee satisfied with the blood on his flesh-whisk after a session of scourging, or the ashes and bones of the unrepentant in an Iron Wicket.

"And no one would believe I could have killed such a beautiful wife. She would weave silver strands in her black hair, the silver a close match for her eyes—nimbus eyes they're called, and much prized. You have her coloring—the hair and eyes—though you gained your height from me."

"And much else. Maybe even Milatum."

Vulsa smiled. "That would indeed be a reward for a gullyman's son. When the opportunity arises, how will you do it?"

"Father, I'm surprised you even have to ask! What does *any* man do, Below or Above, with his hands on the mount of a raised arse? Can there be much difference between the Labrys Throne and a Mitoll's Mount except better air, a run of steps and the boldness of rats? But first, the gullyman's son will ask only for the reward of further serving this Scalda Saig. Now that Mereshaven's barracks are empty, the Sanctor will be keen to fill them again with his own loyal Labryssons..."

Except he'll be calling them Wardens....

"...And surely there'll be a posting for the man who killed the Skarrian Priaptor. Who will care that he has twelve fingers or nimbus eyes? This is mongrel Milatum, after all. You chose well."

"Perhaps we both did."

"Shall we leave it there, then?"

Perhaps....

Vulsa nodded. "Goodbye, Koll."

"And you, father."

Vulsa waited before following his son...until he was reasonably confident Koll had kept walking east, hadn't stopped somewhere to go back and follow his father west, to the Orphic Gate, the nearest way out of the city, so he'd know where his father would be sleeping for the rest of the night—or however many nights before the gate would be opened—and *this* time kill him.

Delivering to the Sanctor the Skarrian Priaptor—head attached—would fetch a greater reward.

Or greater still—a boon to Koll's ambition—if he brought before the Sanctor the Skarrian Priaptor bound and breathing. Labrys Hall would echo with

Scalda Saig's laughter: Vulsa Hork—the Hammer of the East—caught trying to escape the city he'd conquered, dressed in the clothes of a common gullyman.

Vulsa walked back to where he'd left the bundle of slorrie clothes he'd brought up from below. He began sharpening the dagger on the smooth stone steps leading up to the castlet's sentry tower. The blade had to be much keener to shave his head of yellow hair.

Still, did the Sanctor's namesake even exist? That impregnable fortress from which—so Comitor Lambrey Tallon claimed—his Warden Allarch would have begun the conquest of central Myrcia, creating a Seventh Kingdom…if betrayal had not shattered the dream.

If Scaldasaig was a ruse it was a brilliant one; a way for the Warden traitor to get into Milatum and stay alive long enough to play on the ambition of the Skarrian Priaptor and—correctly—assuming that the conqueror of Milatum would be nothing if not ambitious.

No, Lambrey Tallon had been telling the truth….

Nothing rang as true as vengeance.

But Vulsa couldn't smash the head of the Tholarsh into offal without an army to march on Zakros. He had a pocketful of coins instead of an army. Even if he could gather a thousand—two thousand—of his men out there, it wouldn't be enough. He'd never make it to Zakros. He was the Priaptor who'd lost Milatum, as his grandfather had lost Castlecliff. But he might gather enough of his men—fellow exiles now reeking of failure—to search for Scaldasaig. Making the quick march through Myrcia; what Lambrey Tallon had proposed.

Scaldasaig exists….

Vulsa had seen the man's impatience, his eagerness to pursue his vengeance. Kullerioc had confirmed that. Tallon offered Scaldasaig in return for the woman—what was her name?—Shar Stakeen. And for the opportunity to kill this Falca Breks. Both of them evidently responsible for the betrayal that had made vulnerable an impregnable island castle, and shattered not only the Warden Allarch's ambition but Comitor Lambrey Tallon's as well.

Who knew why the Draican had left Scaldasaig only to wind up in Milatum's Skellig. Different men? How many Falca Breks from Draica could there be? Had to be the same…*crappie* Koll had mentioned in the letter he showed to Vulsa; who killed his boneys, wanted to kill him, too; replace him as Mitoll. Maybe the man would have succeeded—if the Skellig hadn't been emptied of prisoners. As if that would have made a difference on the walls.

Scaldasasig *did* exist, Vulsa was convinced of it. And besides the woman, only Breks and Tallon knew where it was. Vulsa couldn't look for the Draican in Milatum, for obvious reasons. So he'd have to find it himself. And act quickly, before the Myrcians or Lucidorians became aware of its existence—Tallon's impatience. Or others besides the Timberlimbs whom Tallon said were its sole garrison.

But how formidable could these forest-dwelling...animals be? even if Vulsa had only a few hundred men—and no vairgs—to scale the walls of the fortress.

Still, he couldn't see how Scaldasaig and Tallon's seething desire for revenge, *and* what happened while he was eating rats in the Skellig, were connected. How could an imprisoned Tallon, who had only a Warden's axe and the clothes on his back, have done what he claimed: bringing down Colza's Bridge? Accomplices? Where would a Warden from Lucidor, arriving alone at the eastern gate of a city he presumably had never been to before, have gotten accomplices to do what he couldn't while he was under guard?

Was he a mage?...a Thread?

Tholosian purisees were fanatic in their belief that the High Fates plucked threads from the tapestry they wove at their Loom Eternal, and animated them, sending them down from the heavens to reward the impure, tempt those who were not, and otherwise subvert the will of Tholos the Everlasting. The priests believed the Threads walked as mortals—and so did Lucetra: her last words to Vulsa were that *he* was a Thread.

Vulsa believed in them as much as he believed vairgs could spin gold for silk—though he had to concede the High Fates could be clever; how could they *not* be? when they could see both beginnings and endings. But if Lambrey Tallon was a Thread, the Fates were more clever—and playful—than they needed to be, giving the man enough rife in that Lucidorian prison to turn his gums blue.

No, something *else* must have happened, and maybe Koll would someday find out how *Scalda Saig* had done it; the man a mere mortal, who'd come to Milatum bristling with a desire for vengeance by way of peddling the location of a fortress that of course he'd thought could be his again.

Which, now that he was Sanctor of Keshkevar, could *still* be his for the taking.

Which was why Vulsa Hork, once the Priaptor of the Skarrian army—and now dead—had to get to Scaldasaig first.

Vulsa smiled. Now *there* was something a Thread could do—give a dead man a head-start.

And perhaps in time—that Warden Allarch's dream now his—march to Milatum, sweeping all before him, north to south. Perhaps the High Fates would oblige, if only for the amusement of a bloody reunion for father and son: the reconquest of a Milatum ruled no longer by Lambrey Tallon but a gullyman's son; the Fates laughing that he should have killed the father when he had the chance.

And then on to the east with his army, arriving in Zakros hopefully in time to bag a head of Most Pure offal....

He was getting ahead of himself...but if you didn't do that, how could you know where you wanted to go?

The dagger was keen enough now. Vulsa began slicing off his yellow plaits and tossing them away. He skimmed away the remaining stubble, pulled off his boots and replaced his Priaptor's raiments with the foul-smelling slorrie clothing. The low-cut boots were too small but he could endure the discomfort until he found a better-fitting pair outside the city. He made sure the cloth still covered his Eye, the kerchief that gullymen surely wore to keep sweat from their eyes as they worked the streets of Milatum.

He walked through the outer gate of the Meresguard castlet, confident that come the morning, or whenever the Orphic Gate reopened, the guards wouldn't give him a second look as he passed through, on his way to the causeway and mainland beyond, pushing a cart—the idea coming from reading Koll's letter—his face and arms still smeared with the ash from the brazier in which he'd burned the letter.

He'd left the two fingers for the rats.

CHAPTER THIRTY-NINE:

THE BLUEVEIL RING

G ABEEKA LENDREE LEANED against the corner buttress of a Lazza
quayside warehouse, keeping his eyes moving since he didn't know from
which direction Redallion and the woman would come.

But come they would: to the ships. There were six of them—mostly cogs
and galliots, all that were left of any size—berthed at these westernmost docks.
Farther down the quay to the east the docks were empty of bigger ships, which
made sense; they'd been closer to where they were needed on the Queensmere,
the crews no doubt forced to bring them out and set them afire. Lendree saw
a few smaller boats berthed closer by, but he didn't think Redallion would be
leaving in one of them. He'd be for the blue water beyond the Kingsmere.

Lendree adjusted the kerchief covering his nose and mouth. Where the
quay widened to become Customs House Square, smoke from the pyre had
gotten worse since he'd taken up his vigil. The brisk wind also carried smoke
from other fires in Linnismorn and Linnishill, and probably corpses were being
burned there too; more bloated meat washing ashore. It didn't take long for the
warm Queensmere to give up the drowned.

Across the quay over a dozen Lazzans were hauling them from the water,
dragging them to where the wharves met the quay, and stacking them. From
where he stood, Lendree couldn't easily mark the differences between Skarrian
and Milat bodies until they were heaved onto separate piles. A burly woman
had appointed herself overseer of the work, swinging a gaff at the mound of
Skarrian corpses, shouting at new arrivals to the scene, "*Nane but churgs! Nane*

but churgs!", as if she were hawking wares. Which was indeed the case. Before he looked away, Lendree saw swollen fingers hacked off for rings, and wrists for the silver armillas the churgs wore; both Skarrians at the Chase had them.

Some of the smaller boats were heading out from the docks, and what little doubt Lendree had that Redallion had gotten on one of them with the stallion chest soon vanished when the boats kept on to the north; probably to join others out there, to see what could be salvaged from the huge charred wrecks of the royal tresreme and barges.

Lendree had been on the larger of the two barges once, as part of the Labrysson detail for the wedding of a prominent ephor's son. The politician's daughter was more beautiful than the bride though heavy with child—Lendree had always disliked the sight of a plump belly. Such a waste. What possible good was a pregnant woman to him or any man except the husband who'd plunged her.

Epona wore a lacing of pearls in her hair that day, Rhakotis a golden triskell torc; both the royals frowning after the ceremony, whispering *"where is Cyalla?"*— Lendree close enough to hear them despite the hundreds of guests dancing on the midship tessellated floor to the music of flinas, lap-harps and flutes. The king dispatched him to find the Demizell and *"bring her back from wherever she's hiding"*— Lendree, a Labrysson officer, now a chaperon for the occasion.

It took a while but he found her on the third tier of the afterdeck, sitting alone, half-hidden by one of the dozens of flower planters surrounding the pool and fountain. She was reading a book. It crossed his mind—long enough to salvage an irritating day—how easy it would be to clap his hand over her mouth, drag the girl behind a screen of flowers and after a quick finish, toss her body overboard after breaking her neck, and inform the king the Demizell was nowhere to be seen. But he only tossed the book away....

The gulls and spanners were doing their own salvaging this morning, cawing and screeching for quayside spoils; darting and swooping over the dozens of carts, trundles and wagons carrying both Skarrian and Milat corpses down to the pyres in Customs House Square, the smoke rising high above the adjacent Temple of Pelagia.

Every horse in Linnisheer must have been eaten by now, so men were pulling the wagons and carts that rumbled over the quay. The larger, bolder spanners spread themselves as white quilts atop the piles of the dead, pecking and tugging at gray, bloated flesh.

One of the wagons creaked slowly past Lendree, three men grunting at the yoke. All wore a kerchief, too, around nose and mouth. A Skarrian slid off the top of the mound and fell to the bricks. Disturbed from their feeding the spanners lifted—a rush of wings—and wheeled over the wagon as two of the men heaved the body back up. One of these had Skarrian plaits tied to his belt, and glanced at Lendree a few beats too long—wondering where he'd gotten the unmistakable Labrysson sword when he wasn't dressed like a Labrysson? Took it off a dead one? He pulled down his kerchief, whispered to the other, who shook his head, clearly disgusted.

It was a good thing the wagon went on, because if the yapes had said anything to his face he'd have killed them, and he didn't need that distraction, not now. Still, there was no cause for them to spit in his skillet—he'd done his part....

Back in the Chase, Lendree had heard the *thock...thock* off in the woods, which could only mean one thing. He carefully picked his way over, congratulating himself for his patience.

But it wasn't Redallion, hewing a tree to float his woman and the jewels across the Narrows.

One of the two Skarrians was wounded, bloody right arm crooked at his belly, watching the other working the axe, chips flying, plaits swinging with every cut.

Deserters? Not likely.

But *something* must have happened to bring two churgs here.

He waited until the brawny axeman got tired trimming the log and put the axe back in the belt loop, and followed both Skarrians as they walked the just-big-enough tree, end-over-end, through the woods toward the scree-slope, the wounded churg helping as much as he could.

Lendree killed the big one first, the axeman's back turned, both hands on the tree, the churg and tree toppling about the same time.

And before Lendree killed the other one, he found out why two Skarrians needed a middling log to escape from Milatum.

He left the Chase at a run that exhausted him—he wasn't built for pace—and by late afternoon had gotten to Delmarrion's Bridge. There'd been a ruck on the bridge—and a big one. But already young boys were climbing on and through the charred remains of a stalker near the Linnisvale, the stench seemingly not bothering them as they played a grisly game of hide-and-seek

The Milat dead were being hauled off to the shoulders of the bridge, the Skarrians dumped over the sides, presumably to later be burned below. Even so, the path through the carnage was so narrow Lendree had to continually step over the dead, and by the time he reached the Linnisheer end, his boots were smeared with blood.

He figured Redallion wouldn't be leaving by ship so late in the day, but even so he watched the quay for most of the evening and then found an empty second-floor room in a tenement behind a Lazza warehouse. He hadn't been lying on the pallet for long when a woman began crying in a room below; hard to tell whether she was mourning or weeping for joy. Not so the thumping, moaning sounds of rutting coming from a room above.

Lendree had been watching now since the early morning and still no Redallion. He wasn't worried yet. There was no reason for Redallion to keep to the old plan, make the swim from the Chase across the Narrows, the jewels in a sack or the small stallion chest, Epona had called it, tied off on a narrow raft of saplings.

Nor was it likely that Redallion and the Loquin woman would try to walk through the Orphic Gate. There were any number of risks in taking a slow road to your destination with jewels of the House of Keshkev in your possession: not only brigands were out there but also Skarrians, hundreds of them, probably more, who hadn't been in the city when disaster struck.

And not likely either that Redallion would be staying in Milatum now. The man couldn't risk being seen when the Averdenn Labryssons came back— which they surely would. They'd have a lot of question to ask Ikonos Banch Redallion, wouldn't they?

No, he and his quiv would want to be somewhere far away with the jewels when the Labryssons realized they'd been betrayed.

It hadn't taken Gabeeka Lendree long to know—not guess—what Redallion would do and where he'd do it; what any man with wits would do: find a ship in the Lazza to take him out of the city.

Lendree looked off to his left, where the quay narrowed into a street leading up to the windmill that winched heavy wagons down to the quayside and up to Colza's Way. That was the direction he'd taken from Delmarrion's Bridge and it was as much of a possibility as any for Redallion to appear.

So Lendree was looking distantly, when Banch Redallion suddenly appeared on the nearby street, three spits away—with the woman *and* two men.

Lendree quickly turned his back to them.

When he looked again, over his shoulder, the four—an oikoe, too—had stopped to wait out a mob surging past along the quay, some of them—lips and gums smeared with blue dye—chanting "*Scalda Saig!…Scalda Saig!*" Whoever that was.

A half-dozen men were pulling on ropes tied to the forelegs of a dead stalker, dragging the hideous thing over the bricks. Women and youths danced alongside the procession, beating the stalker and screaming that name—*Scalda Saig*—over and over. Others with hangars, long-shank daggers and Skarrian war-axes stabbed at the stalker's abdomen, releasing streams of yellowish blood.

It was a slow-moving mob and people on the blocked street hurried on to the west or east along the quay, a few joining the throng; but Redallion and the others stayed where they were.

Of course they did, had to wait for the mob to pass so they could get to the wharves.

Lendree gauged his chances. Most of his face was covered by the kerchief so he wasn't too concerned about getting sprayed by the oikoe. Or what the woman would do. Or the gangly one with the spectacles. And while Redallion had his Labrysson sword, his right hand was bandaged—which had to be the reason why he'd hired the street-buster for protection. The man had the skin of someone not used to southern sun.

Where had Redallion bought a northron blade, hands like that?

This big quay-stomper could be a problem: shelves for shoulders, the kinked scabbard at his belt—a falcata. Those weren't for spindle-wrists.

The mob passed but the strappy-jack kept staring at its wake as if he wanted to join them, or had seen someone he knew among them, saying something to Glass-eyes as the two caught up to the others. But before Lendree lost sight of them, heading toward the westernmost docks, he realized that he wouldn't have to make his move on the quay and risk the northron.

He should have seen it before, but he'd been distracted by the mob and surprised Redallion had two men with him—one of them sized for trouble.

None were carrying the stallion chest or a sack.

They didn't have the jewels with them.

Yare, maybe Redallion had a pocketful to buy passage to wherever they were going. You don't bring all the beauties, pick out a few from the chest or sack to shine the master's hand—and let him know you have a *lot* more.

What you do after you've bought your passage, you come back with the rest of your belongings, a cloth-covered chest full of jewels among them—and for all anyone knows, you're bringing aboard only what you'll need for the voyage.

They'd been coming from the south through the loins of the Lazza—from the general direction of the steps where he'd waited for *his* hirelings to earn their money subduing Redallion and his woman up at her cottage.

Lendree pulled down the kerchief over his smile. *That's where it'll be hidden....*

Maybe Redallion and the woman had fled after the attack, maybe not. But if they *had* skeltered, why take the jewels from a hiding place and risk encountering a Skarrian curfew patrol before you could stash the stallion chest elsewhere?

The jewels would be up there, all right.

He just had to find where they hidden the chest.

Lendree took off at a run, already knowing how *he* would be leaving the city with the jewels. Redallion would never think to hunt for the rapparee in the one place no longer needed to escape the city—*and thank you very much, Ikonos Redallion....*

Just hole up quick after—they'll be looking for a man with a chest over his shoulder...find some rope and a couple of ordinary sacks to double up, put the jewels in...get to the Chase...

And thanks, too, for the churgs there, and that axe he'd need to cut a short middling log to add to the other; the skinny raft wide enough to float his sword, a sack of supplies—*and* the life of a *very* wealthy man that would be doubly sweet because he'd taken it from Banch Redallion.

GABEEKA LENDREE'S SHORT, bollard legs pounded up the steps.

At the top, hands on knees, chuffing breaths, he looked back down.

Not yet.

He skimmed sweat from his brow

To his right: the weathered door to what had to be a cave carved out the hillside. A springhouse.

Wouldn't be there. You'd keep it closer—well-hidden—but close. A cup on the terrace wall reminded him how thirsty he was—time enough for that later.

He walked ahead, still breathing hard, not concerned about someone inside the cottage seeing his sword: no one was peering out either of the two windows flanking the yellow door; no one coming around the side of the cottage.

The mounds: Epona's had to be the larger; his hirelings the others. And there was the fecking spade leaning against the cottage wall by the cistern spigot—Cor! he was thirsty. *Not now....*

The cottage had to be empty—Redallion wouldn't have hired someone *else* to patrol these wee ramparts while he and the others were gone. There was enough risk in having the northron street-buster suspect the reason for his employment, assuming Glass-eyes wasn't a worry.

No lock-plate on the door: not surprising. The Loquin woman could surely afford one but she'd had this small cottage before she became the royal gardener, was probably never here much.

Lendree shouted: "Anyone here? A thirsty man would like to drink from the spigot."

He didn't wait for a reply, lifted up the latch, pushed the door open— answer enough.

Which also meant the stallion chest would be very well-hidden.

Inside: oikoe smell, scent of that bush near the top of the steps; the usual hearth, brazier within, cupboards, a bathing tub; beyond the dining table a corridor, a room off that. Another to the right. Walls painted a light green. Hanging tapestries, the biggest of a windwhipper inbound from the Cleave. A table crowded with a large bowl filled with red water, a ewer, a hand-mirror— and three sacks that appeared to be recently made from a harlequin quilt, the sheared scraps piled on one of the chairs.

All set to leave and confident about buying passage? Sure they were: only a handful of the jewels could *buy* any of the ships docked at those western-most wharves—*and* a crew.

Lendree didn't immediately see the chest because it was on a chair, far side of the table, a cloth draped over. He put his sword down on the sacks the woman must have made, flung the cloth away.

How fecking *stupid* could you be? leaving it here, for anyone to come in and take. Served them right.

The chest was a little over a foot long, black lacquer finish. Collapsing bronze handles, not that you needed them. The only ornamentation was on the lid: an ivory triskell inlay of three rearing stallions. The chest had to be one of the least exquisite of royal possessions that Lendree had seen as a Labrysson, but must have been the handiest to take in the rush of departure that day.

He pushed out the chained spline from its hasp, lifted that up, opened the lid.

The chest was almost full, the biggest thing a book—*Across the Chasm*—so old the leather was stained and cracked. Maybe it was hollowed out, filled with *some* of the—

Not there.

Nor underneath. Only a few sheets of skensy, small jar of ink, two quills and a paring knife to sharpen them; some kind of thin folded hide; a bone stylus, pages of strange writing. Maybe all of it meant something to Glass-eyes—but worthless to Lendree.

He slammed down the lid—*crack*.

Not so stupid after all.

He emptied out the quilt-sacks anyway, dumping clothing, parcels of food to the floor.

But the *chest* was here, which meant Redallion stashed the jewels *somewhere* in this cottage.

Lendree ripped down the tapestries—no hidden niche in the wall behind any of them. He tapped the big stone flags of the floor for the sound of a hollow beneath, then the facing stone of the hearth for a cache behind. He lifted the grate of the brazier, pulled out the cupboards, sending plates and housewares crashing down. He toppled cases of shelves in both rooms to look behind. He moved the beds to check underneath, tossed the mattresses.

Back in the main room he flung half a plate at a window, fracturing a glass pane.

Where did you put them? you fecking whoreson acrobat....

He forced himself to calm down.

The easiest thing to do also carried the most risk: hide somewhere, maybe around the far corner of the cottage; wait for their return, let them get the jewels, then kill them all, the northron first of course. But much could go wrong with all that. He'd do it if he had to...but right now he was back again to...*where-did-they-hide-the-jewels?*

It didn't make sense that Redallion would have buried the jewels in something other than the chest. Why do that? Even if you're going to transfer them into those half-filled quilt sacks, you'd do that after you dug up the chest. And what were the jewels in *now*? Lendree didn't have time to *dig*. Already they could be on the steps coming up—which he'd better go see now if they were, then check the springhouse and lastly the roof and the cistern; get up there somehow if there wasn't a ladder on the side of the cottage.

At the top of the steps: not yet.

He took the half-dozen steps down to the lower terrace, the garden now mostly weeds. Halfway to the springhouse door he noticed a glint to his left, just off the narrow path.

A ring.

He plucked it from the weeds, turning it over with his sausage thumb and forefinger.

Roak's hanging balls—here's something better than nothing…much better….

Even if Redallion and the others were at the bottom of the steps—they weren't—Lendree would be fleeing with a small fortune in his pocket. Only once before had he ever seen a blueveil gem, when reputedly the wealthiest of the Summer Princes of Trigel came to Mereshaven, the wife he'd brought along wearing a pendant blueveil smaller than the gilded mole on her cheek.

But *this* blueveil—a slender oval—was half the size of his little finger, the setting of gold though the band wasn't. Not silver either. Brighter shine than silver, almost white.

A woman's ring…and not just *any* woman's; certainly not one who must clean her fingernails after working in her terrace garden.

A queen's ring. He'd never noticed Epona wearing it. Then again he hadn't been a household Labrysson, and she probably had dozens of other rings to wear.

Had she taken it off when she changed clothes?—when they all had to do that, before going into hiding in Linnisheer after the aborted escape from Milatum. And put it in the stallion chest?

Where else?

He could think of only one reason how the beauty wound up here: the transfer of jewels from the chest to…something else. And when was a better time to do that than at night? the woman holding the lamp, Redallion scooping out handfuls of Epona's jewels from the chest…all but the blueveil ring that slipped through his fingers. So many jewels, so easy to miss seeing one drop.

Lendree dropped the ring, picked it out from the weeds.

Redallion wouldn't have heard a sound either.

He smiled, pocketed the ring, and walked quickly to the springhouse, the only place where the…*something else* could be.

○

But it wasn't.

Wherever they'd hidden the jewels it wasn't here in this small, cave-like chamber, the floor now littered with shards of the earthenware jars large and small he'd smashed, dumping out their contents—preserved vegetables and fruit, posca, salted fish. All that remained on the three tiers of narrow ledges cut into the hillside opposite the door he left open for the sunlight were glass jars which sure as the chill in here weren't filled with jewels.

Where *were* they if not here? Had Redallion stashed them in smaller containers, prised out rocks in the terrace wall, put them behind, replaced the rocks?

But he might not have time to check the wall. Even now, Redallion and that brick-fist northron might be halfway up the steps.

Still, at least he had the ring.

On his way out he saw what he'd missed coming in, sure that the jewels were somewhere on the stone shelves in front of him: a big stirrup pot half-hidden behind the door.

Lendree flung off the lid...and instantly drew back from the stink. He thrust his hand in anyway, brought out a handful of...dried shit. The woman's fecking garden muck. He threw it away, one of the hard turds *tinking* against a glass jar behind him.

He was in the doorway, squinting for the sunlight—and stopped.

Why keep garden muck in a springhouse?

He went back, tipped the stirrup pot, felt the weight—a pot of dried shit couldn't be *this* heavy—and dug his hand in again, deeper. Something stung his finger. He went in again, other hand.

And lifted out a palmful of rubies, stardonix, black and white pearls and pieces of shit. He dug in again, came up with emeralds, *more* blueveils, a sunstone the size of the wen on his neck and a flarenet brooch.

Lendree laughed: a giddy, hiccuping, braying laugh.

A stung finger was a small price to pay for all these loose jewels that could easily be taken and individually cashed for exile—except for bigger treasures like the stunningly beautiful flarenet brooch on whose pin he'd pricked himself.

He quickly left the springhouse, carrying the stirrup pot with both hands, glanced down the steps.

You're too late, Redallion....

Back in the cottage Lendree decided he wouldn't take the chest to carry the jewels, nor one of the quilt sacks. They could recognize that from a distance; not so much the plain linsey sheet from the bed he'd tossed in the smaller room with the escribore. He doubled it over, emptied the jewels from the stirrup pot in the middle—no time to pick out the shit. He lifted up the corners, twisted them, tied the knot.

Outside again, he crouched behind the upper terrace wall, peered over, having a feeling....

And there they were, far below on the steps; looked to be Redallion in front.

Lendree scuttled away, rising only when he was sure they couldn't see him from below. Not a bad head-start; plenty of time to reward his thirst.

He'd never tasted water as delicious as what he guzzled from the cistern spigot.

He ran to the side of the cottage, the makeshift sack chattering as he hurried up the steps.

Of course they'd know the thief had gone up. But by the time they got to Colza's Way, they wouldn't know which direction he'd taken. They wouldn't split up, not with only one of them—the northron—worth a damn in a ruck, Redallion having the injured sword hand.

And even *if* they chose the right direction, he'd be lost in the crowds of Colza's Way.

CHAPTER FORTY:

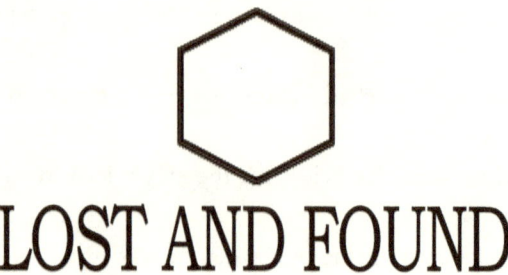

LOST AND FOUND

T HEY WALKED DOWN the steps like they were going up, Vaience carrying the chest, everyone else a quilt-sack, Falca last in line.

He'd been the first into the cottage, falcata in hand, to see it all—the empty stirrup pot on its side in Vaience's room, and felt like he'd taken a cudgel blow to the gut.

He'd been first to bolt out the door to go after.

Kulu lost the scent when they got up to Colza's Way; maybe even a dog would have lost it amidst all the people, the dead stalker that hadn't been burned yet; the two women who were inside an Iron Wicket, kerchiefs tied around noses and mouths, sweeping out ash and bones into a trundle cart, some of the ash swirling away in the wind, the wind brisker up here on the heights of Linnisheer. They'd already piled skulls into the cart. Falca counted five before he walked on, thinking that an Iron Wicket—a cage on wheels—was not so much different than the stockade pen on the shore of Lake Shallan where the Wardens had kept their stock of Timberlimb slave labor, and in the end had set it on fire in an attempt to kill them before they could escape. Not all had.

Would Warden Comitor Lambrey Tallon have another version of an Iron Wicket?

Soon enough Blue-gums would be out among his new subjects, reveling in their adulation and the chants of *Scalda Saig!...Scalda Saig!* They knew nothing of the stockade pen and their Sanctor's role in working hundreds of Timberlimbs—the Kelvoi—to death building Scaldasaig.

Falca and the others had kept on, heading west, seeing people with creels, baskets of salvaged belongings and a baby in one of them; people shouldering yoked jugs of water, a drooping carpet; a weeping man carrying a dead child; another man swinging a Skarrian's severed head by the plaits. They spotted filled or half-filled sacks, sure, but whatever was in them couldn't have been Epona's jewels because the sacks were coarse, not a bedsheet, and the Milats carrying them were too old to have ransacked Roh's cottage.

The man who did could have holed up in any of the dozens of side streets and alleys off Colza's Way.

He could be anywhere.

Banch called a halt to the hunt when the ramparts of the Orphic Gate drum towers loomed in the distance. They couldn't risk getting closer because by now Tallon would have sent Falca's and Vaience's description to guards at the gates of the city.

And they couldn't spend even another hour searching; had to go back to the cottage, then get down to the Lazza and the ship. Its master, Temon Zwig, was eager to leave, having heard the Cleave was open. Banch offered five white pearls for the passage to Averdenn, three upon boarding. Five pearls for each of them, including Kulu.

Done, Zwig had said, smiling like he would have taken two. He was impatient to get underway, had someone in Thetis promise him that for his birthday she'd shave her poose bald as a hetera's. He winked at Banch saying he hadn't seen *her* pearl yet, all this time trapped in Milatum while his birthday came and went, and the fecking Skarrians looting the cargo he'd brung in. But five pearls he could put in his pocket were worth a few extra days getting to Thetis.

Rohaise, who was right beside Banch, winked back: "She'll shave her poose so you could find it?"

Zwig looked at her like he might raise the price—then laughed.

Two hours ago…all smiles.

And then….

The moments after were beyond curses, Banch leaning over the table on the fist of his good hand, head down, staring at one of the quilt sacks as if it was the map of a campaign that had ended in disaster.

Which it had.

Banch took the blame on the way back to the cottage after calling off the hunt: the thief wasn't merely a looter; nothing else had been taken. The man knew what he was looking for. Could only have been a Labrysson. And he may have tried before.

Hold on there, Rohaise had said. *Those three men weren't Labryssons....*

No, but they could have been *sent* by one to go up to the cottage, do rough work short of killing, get paid off, leaving the rest to the Labrysson. Whoever the traitor was, he'd have gotten what he wanted from Banch or Rohaise, one way or the other.

Hold on there, Rohaise said, after Falca told them about the Sixer woman's blueveil ring. *You could have lost it anywhere....*

Vaience thought so, too: *Anywhere, Falca....*

Yes, but...no.

If there was any fashing to be done, he should be the one doing it.

Banch had decided Falca should carry the pearls; no Lazza wharfinger would pick him for a mark. So Falca was with him when he came out of the springhouse, wrapped the pearls in a cloth, which Falca stuffed in his safekeep. And that's when it must have happened: the ring pushed through the hole in the bottom of the safekeep, an opening he hadn't been aware of in the stitched seam. And the ring dropped to the ground, lost in the weeds, two spits from the springhouse door. Falca had a burr halfway up the steps, coming back from Zwig, checked to see if he had the remaining three pearls—this about where they were now going back down. The *pearls* were there in the cloth, but underneath....

He said not a word then, or after he later checked the area around the springhouse. Nothing.

Yahh, he *could* have lost it anywhere. And the Labrysson thief *could also* have found it, thought he was close to finding the rest of the jewels...and that was the reason why he so thoroughly searched the springhouse.

In hindsight—that fucking meatless bone—maybe they *all* should not have gone to the Lazza to buy passage to Averdenn. But who would they have left to guard the jewels that would never have been found unless someone *knew* they were there? Roh and Vaience? Or send *them* down with pearls in a pocket?

No, they'd all agreed: sticking together was best.

Yet terrible as it was, could have been worse if they'd separated—because they didn't know for sure if there wasn't more than just one Labrysson involved in the theft. Leave Roh and Vaience up at the cottage, they could have been killed, the jewels still taken.

Together they'd cleaned up the cottage, Roh saying that even if she might never return, she wasn't going to leave her home asunder.

◯

AT LEAST THE galliot was still there, berthed stern-in at the last, western-most wharf which, like all of the docks, angled toward the northeast. The ship was smaller than the *Lysidia* and without oar loops. A frayed taffrail pennon was missing one of the three sunbursts on a field of red, that marked the vessel as Gebroanan. The last two letters of the name—*Sea Spider*—had faded from the cracked, sun-bleached sternplate.

Seeing them approaching his couty ship, Master Temon Zwig lurched over to the gangway port and stood, slightly canted, as if he was also missing length from his right leg—as well as the hair on his head, half his crew, and all the cargo of Gebroanan salt, spices and wine which the Skarrians had confiscated, Zwig had said earlier, grutching that he had no money to buy his usual consignment of Milatum glassware, mosaic chips, unguents, dyes and bottled incense and fragrances—especially the orchalica and tirrynium that always sold well in Thetis—that now might take weeks to deliver to the Lazza quay.

The plan had been to get to Averdenn on Zwig's coastal trader, and once there take whatever available ship—Banch thought it likely there'd be one large enough to accommodate the Labryssons, however tight the fit—and continue on to Karsor's Bay or Sandsend, where they'd easily find a larger ship for the blue-water sail to Castlecliff. The safety of the jewels would not be a concern with Labryssons to guard the treasure.

The plan now—at least beyond Averdenn—was nothing more than the smoke that soured the quay-side air.

Banch was first up the gangplank, then Rohaise, then Vaience with the chest.

Falca didn't follow, put down the quilt-sack, as if the gangplank—the ship itself—wasn't there.

He'd had plenty of burrs before but nothing like *this* strange feeling that if he didn't stay he'd be abandoning something important. It seemed something else besides a sudden, grippy fear that if he left Milatum he'd never be able to return for the unfinished business with Lambrey Tallon.

They were looking at him now, surprise tightening to concern; Banch ignoring Zwig's nasally harrumph that if the northron didn't come the price remained the same.

Go on now…if it's that important it'll still be here when I get back…and so will Tallon….

He hefted the sack, slung it over his shoulder and walked up the cleated gangplank

EVEN KULU, FRONT paws on the rail, stood along the bulwark, starboard quarter, watching the gig slowly tow the *Sea Spider* away from the wharf—too slowly for Zwig. He was at the bow, Falca closest to him, shouting at the four sailors at the gig's sweeps—his entire crew except for the helmsman Quags at the wheel.

"Ne'er mind the floaters…pull! you slackhoops!"

"This fecking cesspit," he muttered, and plucked the plugs from his hairy, bulbous nose and flicked them overboard. A loitering gull, seeing the movement, dipped and skimmed under the taut towline to get them.

Once clear of the end of the dock, the *Sea Spider* made a lazy turn and Zwig bellowed again at the gig: "Keep on now!—that hinny comer'll wear away."

Vaience shook his head.

"S'gonna be close," Falca said.

Zwig erupted, hands flailing at the oncoming fishing boat. "*Wear away there—yer dead-on mine!*" he screamed, and let loose a skein of curses.

The sailors frantically backed oars, the towline drooping as the fishing boat slowly glided past the gig's prow, angling for the next dock. Zwig's counterpart at the tiller laughed at him and a sailor in the gig stood, gesturing crudely before another pulled him down, benching him before the collision. The *Sea Spider* hadn't yet lost its momentum, was still coming on, Zwig shouting at Quags— "Bear off!"—as the gig-men yanked in the oars just in time.

Rohaise and Banch stepped away from the rail, Kulu dropped to her fours.

Falca felt the shiver of the galliot grating along the port side of the gig, stretching the towline, spinning the gig around before it stopped. He glanced at the others, Roh calmly shaking her head, Banch rolling his eyes, muttering: "At this rate we'll be three weeks to Averdenn."

Vaience gave Falca a look—*Did you sense something before that we didn't?* Then: "Why did you, by the way?—hesitate to board."

Falca shrugged. "I was thinking about Tallon getting away with it."

Close enough.

The towline lifted from the water as the sailors in the gig resumed their clacking sweeps. The *Sea Spider* began moving again, the gig still close enough to the stern of the fishing boat that one of the sailors could have reached out and smacked the rudder with the tip of his oar. Zwig swiped at the knob of his nose, and fingered a gesture Falca hadn't seen since his days as a Catchall dockheave, and bellowed another curse; in response the tillerman tapped his crotch with the same three fingers before hopping off his boat. After he secured mooring lines fore and aft to dock bollards, he offered his hand, in turn, to help two passengers disembark; the third, a tall black-haired young woman with cross-draped panniers, spurned his assistance.

Falca moved quickly past Vaience for a better glimpse, Vaience giving him another look—*What now?*

The fishing boat tillerman had moved too, blocking Falca's view of the woman. He picked her up again as she walked down the dock, her back to Falca, past the stacked bodies of Skarrians and two Lazzans hauling another corpse from the water beyond the fore mooring line. The other passengers had glanced at the bodies, hurrying past but the woman didn't. She walked slowly, either weary or unsure of where she was going. The tillerman pushed up his skiff-cap, staring after her, shaking his head as if she hadn't paid her fare and for some reason he couldn't do anything about it.

Moving aft along the *Sea Spider*'s starboard bulwark, Falca almost tripped over a coil of rope. Maybe if she turned around, for whatever the reason, he could see if….

She didn't, kept on. But at the edge of the quay she stopped two men, one of whom was pushing an empty trundle cart. The other pointed to his left, across the quay toward a side street. Falca saw her nod—thanking him?—and after she walked on, the direction-giver lifted his hands, palm up, weighing the air, the gesture to his companion unmistakable. The men stepped ahead of the cart to catch a last glimpse of her as she disappeared into the crowd, as did Falca moving quickly aft—

Can't be her…not a chance…no way….

Many Milat women had dark hair, and some even this one's lighter complexion—she was simply taller than the average here. So what if she had a traveler's trim unusual for any woman: boots and those panniers. And while her clothes looked to have a northron cut—as his had been—her duvelin and tunic were bright with southron colors, yellow and red.

It's not possible....

Shar Stakeen had short hair then, but even shaddens couldn't grow it longer after they're dead.

She'd plummeted a hundred feet from an embrasure of Scaldasaig's keep into Lake Shallan. Hitting water from that height would've snapped her neck or spine. She'd have died as surely as her father had.

Sure, sometimes you see what you *want* to see, but in this case, Shar Stakeen would have been the *last* person Falca wanted to see, never mind what they'd shared at Scaldasaig before he discovered who she was: a shadden hired by Havaarl Damarr to kill him and bring Amala back to Draica. But after what happened at the waterfall in the Rough Bounds—she had to have been there, seen the miracle on the ledges below the waterfall—she realized that here was a ditchlicker worth *far* more alive than dead. Until she got the secret of that miracle from him.

Krael.

And if Ossa had chosen differently that night on the ramparts of Scaldasaig's keep, she *would* have gotten its secret from either Falca or Raleva. Forcing information from those reluctant to give it was doubtless a part of a shadden's training. And then she planned to kill them both, to ensure the secret of krael was hers alone, and Ossa's—so he said before he took his own life.

All that was after Falca, Amala and Gurrus had left Draica assuming that Amala's father had sent a few slew-dogs to go after them…but Falca had no idea the miserly patroon hired instead an expensive *shadden*. Falca reckoned that taking a canal boat all the way to Bastia—Harro Scapp's corry—would throw off Damarr's men. Looking back, that had gained them time with Shar Stakeen. Still, they were lucky to get out of Bastia before she caught up.

But time ran out that terrible day at the waterfall: Tallon and his Wardens… Amala killed and Falca helpless to prevent her death…and hidden somewhere close by…Shar Stakeen. She must have arrived too late to save Amala, but not so late she didn't see Gurrus' krael bringing back the Draican crouch-alley from the certain death of a white rancer bite….

How different it all would've been if Falca hadn't lightened his load outside of Bastia, on the lake—because Shar Stakeen surely would've caught up to them if he, Amala and Gurrus hadn't taken the Wardens' boat.

Lighten your load, boy....

He'd forgotten why his father said it; maybe one of those problems that to a boy seemed worse than it was. Barla Breks had taken his own advice later, either abandoning his wife and two young sons, or killed in some tavern ruck in Catchall and dumped into the Old Marshfang Canal or in the bay off Swayman's Neck.

On the night Falca took the boat from Wardens on the strand of Lake Meleke and saw what was in the prouty, he'd been more than reluctant to lighten *that* load. But he had to if he and Amala and Gurrus were to escape by water—their only recourse then. So they dumped the six heavy sacks of the hoard the Allarch's son and three other Wardens had stolen from the Shofet, lord of Bastia and governor of the province. Because hauling those sacks of treasure into the Banishlands to the east and then the wilderness of the Round Bounds beyond was not lightening your load—

Which is still there....

A long detour, to be sure, but well worth it, *oyah.*

Would Harro Scapp and his sister still be plying Motessin's Moat, Draica to Bastia? If not, some another canaler, then...to take some of the Labryssons all the way, the others keeping pace with the towpath mule. But hopefully it'd be Scapp...and cut him in for a share and a song, use his corry on the lake, the Labryssons bringing up all the shine.

Naah, not just the Labryssons.

Shide! For this *I'll damn well learn to swim....*

And *two* more swimmers even better to recover the treasure from the bottom of Lake Meleke.

But Vaience, without his spectacles?

Falca laughed. Vaience would probably bring up more than *any* of them, seeing as how the Shofet's gold was gonna be bringing back Cyalla.

Grinning as if the hole in his safekeep never was, Falca glanced back at him and Banch and Roh. They were at the companionway hatch, Zwig at the wheel with Quags, staring at Vaience with the chest, probably wondering what was in it and wishing he had the rest of his crew to find out if there were more pearls than just the five.

Somewhere, between here and Bastia—had to be Averdenn or Motessin's Moat—Falca and Vaience would learn to swim like Labryssons. Banch would teach them, no question there.

Falca looked again for the woman—not that he expected to see her.

Sure, he would have remembered eventually about the Shofet's hoard, by now the sacks rotted away at the bottom of Lake Meleke. But it would still be there, and so would the marker: the outcrop of rock that had reminded Gurrus of a flenx head.

But that black-haired young woman, whoever she was—a traveler from the provinces?—made him remember sooner rather than later; and from the somber looks of Roh, Vaience and Banch as they took their belongings below... why wait to tell his friends they wouldn't be needing Epona's jewels after all?

Lightening *their* load sooner was much, much better.

Falca finger-tipped his forehead and flicked his thanks toward the quay, where he'd last seen the jolie bower.

CHAPTER FORTY-ONE:

SHADDEN'S REST

H E'D ALWAYS COME into Milatum by water and so she'd wanted to do the same, though the fishing boat she'd gotten in a hamlet on the north shore of the Kingsmere was hardly a three-mast windwhipper. She'd been surprised that after all the years since her father had been here, the hillside above the Lazza seemed to be the same as he'd described.

Only when she was on the steps did she fully realize how steep the rocky hillside was, probably the reason why it was still so barren. She had to stop to rest, grateful for the ledge carved into the slope alongside a landing halfway up.

In those few hours at Scaldasaig—before everything changed—her father told her about Milatum; what he never told her when she was a girl. He couldn't know he'd also been giving her directions for the way home.

The steps began behind the biggest of the Flunt Stree tessarias at the base of the hill, the one with the mosaic statue of a small but voluptuous woman, supposedly a lure for business, he'd said with a laugh. She was as naked as the gargantuan Pelagia in the Queensmere, her nipples worn off from many years of passing caresses.

And now rubble, but a marker nonetheless.

He neglected to mention the switchbacks of steps were scarcely more than notches cut into the rock, saying only that they were the quickest way to get to the cottage from the Lazza. But you had to be careful: turn around higher up for the magnificent view and you might lose your balance, and if you fell you might not get back up.

Later, she wondered if when he said that he was aware—consciously or not—of what was to come. Had he already decided? No…he couldn't have. At that point she hadn't even told him—and as it turned out she never would—about what she'd had to do in Draica to survive after she escaped from the Vasper and his Cassenite cult.

So he'd continued with the past, almost as if he was once again going up the steps to the cottage, the manse looming above it, to Colza's Way: Milatum's artery that linked the city's ancient, fabled bridges and its four districts—Linnises they were called—that were once peaks before their summits were leveled. He'd been to them all with Rohaise—except, of course, the royal isle of Mereshaven in the northern reach of the Queensmere. But home for them was in Linnisheer.

There was an open market there called the South Gets, actually a broadening of Colza's Way, he said. A hundred vendors could sell you anything you needed and a hundred more hawking whatever you didn't but wanted anyway. That's where he bought the red ring-tailed kirrie the size of a loaf of bread, a passel of them just in that day from the Forest of Aknanore the vendor told him. Her father chose the one with amber eyes to give to her, his young daughter, upon his return to Castlecliff. It survived the long voyage—and without a name; he was going to let *her* name it—but not the distemper of her mother. Vasia got rid of the kirrie the day after her husband left again for another voyage to Milatum. She ignored her daughter's tears: *You may have bathed and combed its fur, but it was a dirty thing nonetheless, Flury, your Pooka; perhaps useful to catch rats on your father's ship but we have none in this house, so I gave it to one of the servants to let loose in the Carcass where there's plenty….*

At Scaldasaig, Rohaise Loquin no longer a secret, she asked her father who Rohaise thought the gift was for, since he'd never told Rohaise he had a daughter in Castlecliff, much less another wife.

A brother's daughter; a favorite niece….

He admitted it was Rohaise who picked out the kirrie. She had a way with animals—bought, feral or stray—but mostly oikoes. She had two oikoes at the cottage who didn't bother the kirrie as it had her scent on its fur….

She rose from the ledge, shouldering her panniers. She could see part of the manse above, but not the cottage. Her father said it was small, tucked back into the hillside on the bigger of two terraces Rohaise's grandfather had carved and dug out—an extraordinary labor for one man. *There's a fine story to that, but time enough later to tell you about it….*

There wasn't.

She kept on. Soon enough she'd see if the cottage was still there. And if not? Well, she'd just have to find a place to stay for the night, at least; some hostelry along Colza's Way.

If it *was* still there, quite possibly someone else occupied it now. But if the cottage was still Rohaise Loquin's home—with or without a husband or lover—there was a good chance she would suggest it best if her unexpected visitor found someplace else to dwell on the past.

After another dozen steps she saw the cistern atop the flat roof, and then the color of the door: the yellow her father remembered, but a yellow bleached almost white by the sun.

She was almost there now, passing on her right a narrow terrace and the low, open door of what had to be a springhouse excavated from the hillside. She stopped a few paces beyond the last of the steps to rest again—but also to give anyone inside the cottage the time to see her, a stranger. She sensed emptiness but someone *had* been here recently, leaving a common drinking cup on top of the larger terrace wall. Garden tools leaned against the side of the cottage near the cistern pipe and spigot.

And there was also an unnaturally high mound in the middle of a fallow garden plot, which could only be a grave.

The yellow door was closed; one of the two facing windows broken.

She shouted: "Rohaise Loquin?"

And again, louder, when no one opened the door and no face appeared in a window: "*Rohaise Loquin?*"

She waited a little longer—a shadden's caution, the training to see beyond what one cannot. But there was no need to draw the throwing knife in the sleeve of her right boot. At the corner of the cottage stood a shoulder-high screen of mortared stone. Probably the…necessary. She checked it anyway, kept her distance as she peeked around, even looked into the bucket below the hole in the narrow ledge. The usual smell but faint, the bucket empty and dry: no one had used the latrine very recently.

She made a circuit of the cottage, winding up back at the yellow door, the hinges squeaking as she pushed it open. She paused, listening for the breathing of someone in either of the two rooms off the main living area.

Along the wall between the two rooms was a raised bathtub, one end flaring high…stepstool and water bucket by the stoppered drain plug in the middle...stiff brush in the bucket to scrub the tessellated tub, the swirling mosaic of the same light green color as the room, except for the deep blue of the top edge.

A woman's home; few men would need or bother with a stepstool to get into the tub, or keep a cleaning brush so handy. But there had been men recently here; she could smell sweat that wasn't hers.

She checked the other rooms, cautious at the doorways: just the usual furniture in both. The escribore and single, narrow bed in the smaller room seemed evidence that Rohaise Loquin had a son or daughter and a literate one at that—the writing desk. Her having a child wasn't a surprise.

Rohaise was a beautiful woman...auburn hair and gray eyes...I'm sure she married again after I never returned....

She would have heard about the wreck of the *Flury* on Gebroan's Flaggy Shore, all hands lost. All of them had been—except for Mott Demoul and a swale, saved by wreckers; the swale dying later when both of them were swept up in a bloody local war...and Mott Demoul imprisoned and then forced into the Gebroanan king's disastrous campaign against Tarranga Ullmark, an Iron Lord of the Crumples...and captured again and sent to work in one of Ullmark's mines but eventually escaping and...*it was years before I got back to Castlecliff and then I found out what my brother-in-law had done to you....*

Tapestries hung from the cottage walls: one of two sleeping oikoes, long tails entwined; another a wildly colored rendering of a garden's meadowbride, sunsbreath and harlequin roses. But it was the largest tapestry that drew her close, a catch in her throat: the white-hulled windwhipper, Pelagia in the backround, was in-bound, coming home, sails furled, towed by an oared pilot boat. The Myrcian pennon—gold spurrose on a field of azure—fluttered at the mizzen.

Rohaise Loquin must have stitched that herself. All the days—*months*—of fine needlework to complete such a handsome work.

Who else could have done it but her? Anyone else could not have seen, or held in memory what Rohaise Loquin had, only a dozen paces beyond the door.

She brushed fingers over the tapestry, saw no stitched initials or name. Another person would have done that. But not Rohaise; she knew the tapestry was hers, and it was something she'd never sell. She would have known the name of the windwhipper—*Flury*—but she wouldn't have known her mastlord husband had named it after his daughter, who much later took the shadden name of Shar Stakeen; just as she would never know her husband had taken the name of Ossa Vere to begin a new life inwardly branded by the shame of marital duplicity, his face grossly disfigured by the branding of the Myrcian Sanctor's Trice, his punishment for killing his dead wife's brother, who had sold thirteen year-old Flury to the Vasper….

She took off her panniers, put them on the kitchen table along with the leather pouch that contained the stingvine Styada had given her when she left Scaldasaig. Falca Breks' Timberlimb friend had shown her how to use the weapon that could stun a man or beast to immobility for an hour. Which might be good enough anywhere else should a problem arise, but not in a village by Lake Tremizene; not with Lambrey Tallon surely close by. There was nothing for it, her shock at seeing a Warden almost proving lethal. She had to use her throwing knife on the soldier. If she hadn't there would have been *two* Wardens hunting for her.

She wasn't worried that Tallon would find her, but there was another matter: just how private—or public—were the steps out there that linked the Lazza with Colza's Way? If they were the quickest route for her father to get to the cottage, perhaps others knew that too—such as the two men on the quay who'd told her how to get to Flunt Street. She'd sensed their following-eyes; she stopped soon after to make sure that's all they were doing.

So she kept the throwing knife in her boot-sleeve when she went outside to see if she'd overlooked a formal marker for the grave besides the stems of red flowers.

There wasn't one.

Maybe that was the reason why she doubted the grave was Rohaise Loquin's. The husband or child who tucked her in would have left something more than flowers that would decay, the wind blowing them away, leaving nothing.

She'd made sure that wouldn't happen at her father's grave in Scaldasaig's outer ward.

She crafted it herself the day before she left: a circle of tightly interlaced greens fixed to a sturdy post upon which she carved both his names and something else. Styada promised that he would renew the greens as needed, saying he'd made another promise to bury the bodies after they had risen from the depths of Lake Shallan, Falca Breks having left Scaldasaig earlier believing there would be *two*, of course.

Bury her alongside her father, Styada. They should be together. After so many years apart they had but hours here....

Styada swore Falca said that to him.

Would an eternity be enough time to understand what had happened, to find peace and forgiveness?

She didn't need an eternity. She understood the choice her father made at the embrasure.

To become a fledged shadden you had to pass all of the Fifty Tests. The last test the senior cabalistors required was to fulfill a contract by killing someone without using metal, wood or bone; poison, fire, common rope or stone; or flesh-on-flesh. She'd been the youngest—male or female—to pass all Fifty. And years later at the Scaldasaig keep embrasure, she unwittingly passed the last test again—because of who she had become; because of her greed for the wondrous krael which could have made her the wealthiest and most powerful woman in the Six Kingdoms; and because of her stated intention to kill Falca Breks and Raleva Barra after she got its secret from them. And shaddens always do what they say they will do.

She had assumed her father—in the glow of their reunion—would go along with her plan to make them both rich beyond measure. But all she'd done was give her father no choice other than to stop her, and then afterwards—because he couldn't live with the memory of what he'd done—take his own life.

She'd as much as killed him.

He didn't survive his fall but she did hers: the shadden training, the test called Knife-to-Water, making her body a blade to stab the water.

Bury her alongside her father, Styada. They should be together. After so many years apart they had but hours here....

From where did that come? Styada told her Falca had discovered who she was. Falca should have said to Styada, let her bloated body drift to the shore, to be scavenged by snag-wolves. With such sensibilities how had that crouch-alley survived the streets of Slidetown and Catchall in Draica? knowing that...what? That you can indeed kill someone you love? Want to kill him? Try to kill him?

Did he know that you can love someone even more after that person is gone?

She knew that you can also love someone so much after he's gone that you travel far to the south to the place where you knew he'd been so content, so in love with an auburn-haired, gray-eyed woman; his happiness all the more intense because the time he spent with her amounted to months, not years....

Her thoughts had taken her to the terrace wall, the top of it sun warmed. The wind off the Queensmere had picked up since the morning though it still carried smoke from the quayside pyres in the Lazza. She looked off to the west. Was that the place? the hill where kites were lofted over the Queensmere in intricate displays for festivals and royal birthdays?

He'd smiled: *Only in Milatum would there be a guild of* kite-artists....

Kite Hill was a promontory jutting out from Linnisheer, not far from Delmarrion's Bridge. He and Rohaise had been there once for the Queen's birthday celebration. They'd watched the display for hours, beginning after nightfall, the tails of the kites illuminated by lunelings specially bred for very small size.

It was as if the kiters were animating constellations. They were that good, Flury—do you want me to still call you that? Or is it Shar Stakeen now?

Father, I wish you'd told me long ago about the kites, about everything; made that choice. If you had, you never would have had to make the others. Did you think you'd have to take me away from my home in Castlecliff? Wherever you were was my home....

She carved those last six words on his grave post.

Her home was here now, this cottage; a place to think about what she would do to survive. She'd been very good at that for a long time.

So yes, her home—at least until Rohaise Loquin returned with or without a husband, a son or daughter; in an hour, tomorrow morning, the next day... or never.

She had enough money for a few months. Styada's Timberlimbs had found a pouch of silver in what had been the barracks for Scaldasasig's Warden garrison. He'd given the shine to her, saying the Kelvoi had no use for money.

And Falca?

She hoped he never reached Milatum, though he'd told her that's where he intended to go. Besides her disbelief that he'd abandon such a magnificent prize so dearly won—and won together—she'd hated him for another abandonment.

Yet something else had stirred within her at the *shushing* ledges below that waterfall in the Rough Bounds and she didn't know it, so consumed was she by having failed to save Amala Damarr from Lambrey Tallon and his Wardens, then stunned later by the miracle. But had it begun when she saw a dying, crawling Falca Breks trying to reach the side of his dying woman? Or what he did later, before slipping Amala Damarr into the pool at the end of the ledges?

Somewhere between there and Scaldasaig...she'd fallen in love with the Draican crouch-alley.

And Scaldasaig was where she ceased to be a shadden. The cabalistors had been emphatic: a shadden must *never* become prey to the weaknesses of love and hate.

Falca Breks had preyed upon her and he never knew it, turning her into someone other than the person she'd trained so hard *not* to be—though he'd *done* nothing to her all the way through the Rough Bounds; *said* not a word to her until Scaldasasig.

She'd wanted the krael, but she wanted it—and Scaldasaig—with *him*. And when it was clear that wasn't possible....

So easy now to believe she wouldn't have killed him and the Barra girl after she got the secret of the krael. They both knew where more could be found. But at the time, hating Falca for leaving her to go to Milatum—as her father had left her long ago—she must have been very convincing to her father in those moments before he made his choice at the embrasure.

Wherever Falca was now, he was probably dead if he had indeed reached Milatum, one of the many killed by the Skarrians. The fishing boat captain said it had to be in the thousands. But if Falca had stopped short of the city, learning as she had about events farther south, he might be on his way back to Draica. Or maybe he was in Castlecliff even now, somewhere in the Carcass, back on the bricks, plying his old trade in a new city.

Whichever destination—eternity or alleys—he was gone.

She took the cup from the terrace wall and walked past the grave to the cistern pipe spigot near the spade leading against the cottage wall. She rinsed the cup and filled it. The water was warm, of course, and tasted like...fish oil. But she was thirsty and drank a second cup before going into her new home where, in about six months, she would give birth to her son or daughter. And Falca's. She knew without a doubt it was his, not Lambrey Tallon's.

And—a smile now—she realized that Styada had *somehow* known before she did. But she'd thought he was just talking in a Kelvoi mehka's riddles. At Scaldasaig, as a dozen Timberlimbs were opening the outer gate for her, she asked him why he was letting her leave.

"Falca is in no danger from you," he said. "You would be killing part of yourself. And it has been weeks now since he left; we cannot keep you here forever—and could not have anyway if you were still what you once were, which was far less than what you are now."

She had no doubt that giving birth and raising the child by herself might well be more difficult than the Fifty Tests she'd passed to become a shadden. She'd need someone assisting the birth, though she would push the baby out herself if she had to. But one of the vendors in that Colza's Way market— surely to return again sooner or later—would know where she could find a mid-wife. And while she was at it, maybe she'd buy a kirrie, if there were any just in from the Forest of Aknanore.

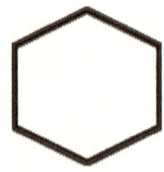

ABOUT THE AUTHOR

BRUCE FERGUSSON is the author of five works of fantasy and three suspense novels, and has received award nominations in both genres: the Crawford Award for best first fantasy novel, and the Pacific Northwest Booksellers' Association Award for best novel.

His Six Kingdoms fantasy series includes *The Shadow of His Wings*, *The Mace of Souls*, *Pass on the Cup of Dreams* and his latest, *Kraken's Claw*. The updated 95-page *Six Kingdoms Codex* is a companion volume for the series, featuring an introductory short story, extensive backround history of the world, a glossary and four maps.

Bruce's other novels are *Morgan's Mill*, which weaves history of the Civil War and Underground Railroad into a contemporary narrative of suspense, *The Piper's Sons* and *Two Graves for Michael Furey*, both literary thrillers.

A graduate of Wesleyan University, Bruce has been a newspaper sportwriter and reporter, advertising copywriter, furniture mover, landscaper, restaurant waiter and an instructor for the Writer's Digest School. He founded and was the inaugural editor of *The Seventh Week*, the still extant newsletter of the annual six-week Clarion West Writers' workshop. Bruce also once worked in an aluminum recycling facility which was only marginally better employment than a previous gig on the graveyard shift at an agricultural feed plant.

He can attest to the fact that building stone walls is easier than writing, having built too many dry-stone walls of varying height and length, most recently at his home in Salem, Oregon where he lives with his family and is working on the next Six Kingdoms novel.

Find out more about Bruce and his books at www.brucefergusson.com.

www.ingramcontent.com/pod-product-compliance
Lightning Source LLC
Chambersburg PA
CBHW021120260626
47169CB00005B/1374

ALSO BY BRUCE FERGUSSON

THE SIX KINGDOMS SERIES
The Shadow of His Wings
The Mace of Souls
Pass on the Cup of Dreams
Six Kingdoms Codex

SUSPENSE
Morgan's Mill
The Piper's Sons
Two Graves for Michael Furey